Starlight

Book 1 of The Dark Elf War

William Stacey

Cover designed by Scarlett Rugers Design www.scarlettrugers.com
Formatting by Polgarus Studio www.polgarusstudio.com

To my mother, Judith Anne,
Entirely by yourself, you raised three unruly children
I like to think we turned out okay.

You are the defining role-model in my life and taught me right
from wrong... even if the lesson needed to be repeated many,
many times. I will always be that little boy you busted the first time
he ever tried to skip school.

You will live forever in my heart and in the face of my child.
Love, complete and eternal.
Love.

Part 1
Gazing into the Abyss

Chapter 1

Maelhrandia, Princess of the Fae Seelie, Mistress of Red Moon Rynde and the Tarloth Delta, hid in the jungle, peering out at the ambush site she had set beside the flowing river. Although the night was overcast and black, she had still cast Shadow-Soul on herself, altering the light around her, making her invisible from all but the most gifted mages. Ten of her best boggart warriors, armed with neck poles and chains, hid farther back in the thick brush in two kill-capture groups, waiting for her instructions. The boggarts controlled her pack of hunting gwyllgi, which had already caught the scent of the approaching prey. One of the beasts, anxious to kill, snarled—too loudly—and Maelhrandia exhaled softly, her nostrils flaring. If released too soon, the animals would bound forward and prematurely set off the ambush. After that, they'd be that much harder to rein in.

Maelhrandia needed prisoners this night, not ripped-apart carcasses. She closed her eyes and flashed a message through the mind-tether she had established with her boggart captain. *Fool! Keep them silent, or you'll be fed to them.*

When she opened her almond-shaped yellow eyes again, she saw the first of the intruders approach the riverbank. Like all fae seelie, her night vision was superb, but it took her some moments to comprehend what she was looking at. She had never seen their kind before. There were four of them, each attempting to move with stealth, clearly trying to be wary of their surroundings. They walked upright, with two arms and two legs, just like her people, but they were tall, broad in the shoulder, and wore strange armor with rounded helmets and four-eyed devices over their faces, giving them a bizarre, bug-like appearance. They held strange objects tightly against their bodies as they moved, pointing them like weapons. They reminded Maelhrandia of crossbows, but she saw no bolts.

Even more bizarre, she sensed no magic. Were they mundane?

She had expected... well, she didn't know what, exactly— perhaps dwarves. After all, the intruders had left behind a mechanical device of some kind hidden in the branches of a tree. That was how she had found them. Redcap children had discovered the device while playing. Their parents, knowing well what could happen to them if they kept this discovery secret, had reported it to Maelhrandia's guards. Then, it had simply been a matter of waiting. For three days, she and her warriors had lain in wait. Now, that patience had paid off. She didn't know what these creatures were, but their hubris was astonishing. No one spied upon the fae seelie. All the lesser races of faerum had already learned that the fae seelie were the rightful rulers of this realm. Even the dwarves—dirty, grubby technocrats—had only been able to hold her people off for so long, and then it had been because they'd hidden away beneath the earth like the worms they were.

Making fists, she dug her fingernails into her palms. These creatures were new, unknown. She could still release the gwyllgi then have her warriors rush behind them and try to take all four at once. Four captives would be best; their testimony could be compared, contrasted. One could even be made an example of, to loosen the tongues of the others. But her intuition warned her against that course of action. *What you don't know could easily kill you.*

And Maelhrandia was, if nothing else, a survivor.

When the four intruders reached the base of the tree that they had hidden their device in, all except one of them dropped down onto a knee and pointed their crossbow-like weapons outward, watching all about themselves. The fourth climbed into the tree.

No, she decided. *Safer is always better.* Her muscles tensed as she filled herself with magic and prepared to cast Drake's-Gift. *I am the knife in the shadows.*

* * *

The first warning Major Wallace "Buck" Buchanan had that something was wrong was when a sheet of flames swept over Saunders, as if he had been doused in gasoline and lit with a match. The flash flared out Buck's Quad-Eye Ground Panoramic Night Vision Goggles—GPNVG—and the optics struggled to compensate. The heat was staggering, and Buck fell away, instinctively putting distance between himself and the burning man. Saunders screamed and started spinning in place like a top, whipping the flames higher in the process.

Still half-blind, Buck activated his MBITR—AN/PRC-148 Multiband Inter/Intra Team Radio. "Contact, contact, contact. Wait out," he screamed into the microphone hanging near his lips.

They had no comms with anyone but the covering team back at the LZ. He could warn them that he was under attack and let them know he was in the shit. But they were too far away to help.

His optics adjusted to the flare-out. Ignoring the screams of Saunders, Buck scanned the jungle around them, aiming down the combat sights of his silenced M4 carbine, seeking the source of the enemy fire. Had they been hit with a flamethrower? A Molotov cocktail? Only feet away, Bolin had tackled the burning Saunders and was now frantically trying to beat out the flames. Someone else opened up with an M4, firing short bursts of suppressed fire. The smell of cordite mixed with the stench of burning flesh.

"Who's firing?" he yelled. "Call the target!"

"Nothing," MacDonald—one of the Canucks— answered, pausing to look over the smoking barrel of his M4. "I got nothing."

"Then stop shooting, jackass."

They needed to move, to get out of there immediately. Somehow, Bolin had managed to put out the flames on Saunders and was now bent over the thrashing man, trying to help him. Saunders had stopped screaming, but the wet noises coming from his throat were far from reassuring. Buck had seen enough men burn to death in Afghanistan and Iraq to know that Saunders wasn't going to make it—there was no need to even check. As if on cue, a long wet gurgle came from Saunders's throat, and then the man lay still.

Bolin looked up at Buck. "I think he's—"

"We're out of here," Buck said. "We're in a kill zone." He keyed the mike on his MBITR again. "Newf, we're Oscar Mike to your location, coming in hot. Danger close."

There was a single chirp in his earpiece as Captain Alex Benoit, the covering team leader, acknowledged. Buck pointed at the dead man. "Pick him up. We need to—"

Bolin flew backwards into the air as if he had been sent flying from a blast—but there had been no explosion, nothing. The man vanished into the thick foliage. Buck stared dumbfounded, his mouth open.

MacDonald jumped to his feet and spun about. "What the hell?"

Buck grabbed his arm and yanked him along, dragging him away from the river, back in the direction they had come. "We're out of here," he yelled, firing his M4 blindly behind them, not giving a damn that he was now doing what he had just admonished MacDonald for.

"But we've got men down," said MacDonald.

"Dead. We exfil now," Buck said as he pulled a smoke grenade from his load-bearing vest, popped it, and then tossed it behind them. In moments, dense clouds of smoke filled the air. Buck began to run, fear and adrenaline giving him speed. In moments, he was far ahead of MacDonald, leaving the other man to keep up as well as he could.

This was bad, real bad. Two men down. Saunders was dead for sure, and Bolin was... well, maybe Bolin was dead. He didn't know, but he sure as hell wasn't hanging around to find out. That had been a hard contact, but who had hit them? His blood pounded in his ears, and his breathing became strained, but he pushed himself on. By now, he must be out of the kill zone. If he kept moving, he should be able to stay ahead of any pursuer. He was going to survive, thank God.

This wasn't his fault, but he knew Colonel McKnight would hold him responsible even though Intelligence was at fault, not him. Someone should have seen this coming. When he got back, he was going to punch the Task Force Devil intelligence officer in the throat. He owed it to his men. He'd—

Something big and heavy crashed through the jungle behind him, and Buck heard MacDonald yelp in surprise then begin screaming, calling out for help. Buck spun about to see MacDonald on his back, a massive creature on top of him—like a dog or wolf but way too large, easily several hundred pounds. Another one of the monsters—flames trailing from its open jaws—was almost on top of Buck himself. Its eyes glowed with an eerie light as it leaped through the air. Instinct, more than anything else, drove Buck's actions as he opened fire with his M4 in a long, wild burst. The monster rammed into him, knocking him down, but Buck scrambled back, still firing, with one hand, point-blank into the thing's snout. His M4 finally stopped when it clicked on an empty chamber, but the wolf creature was dead, its head shredded by 5.56mm fire. He scrambled to his feet as he rushed to reload.

"Buck, help me. Jesus, help me!" screamed MacDonald as he fought to hold the massive wolf's jaws away from him. In the jungle behind them, Buck heard something crashing through the trees, almost on top of them. He only caught a glimpse of them—large man-shaped figures, coming right for him.

He turned and ran. MacDonald's screams chased after him.

* * *

Captain Alex Benoit and his four-man covering team lay prone in the jungle clearing, behind the stone ruins, surveying the terrain around them in every direction. Since Buck's initial contact report, there had been no further communications from the patrol.

He briefly considered calling Buck and asking for a situation report but immediately discarded the idea. Buck was an experienced soldier. When he could, he'd radio in and let Alex know what was going on. If he didn't make it back, Alex's orders were clear: activate the keying device, link back to the Gateway, and get out. But could he do that? Could he leave men behind?

His attention shifted to the sound of something crashing through the jungle—coming right for them from the same direction Buck and his team had gone, making no attempt at stealth. His thumb moved near the firing selector on his M4. Alex flicked his M4 to automatic, peered through his M68 Collimated Combat Optic—his CCO—and let his finger touch the trigger.

And then Buck broke through the screen of bush, staggering toward them. He no longer had his M4 or much of his equipment. Even his armor was gone. Had he stripped it all off? In his hand, he held only his 9mm pistol. Alex rose from behind the stone rubble. "What's going on?" He looked past Buck for the others. There was no one else.

Buck stared at him through his Quad-Eye GPNVGs. He was panting, and spit ran down his chin. He shook his head, bent over at the waist, and gasped for air, coughing as he did.

"Talk to me, sir." Alex stepped closer. "Where are the others?"

"Be... be... behind me," Buck squeaked. He reached out and gripped Alex's shoulder, leaning on him. Buck was a big man, at least six foot three, and he towered over Alex.

"The others are behind you?" Alex asked.

Buck stared at him again as if he couldn't understand him. What the hell had happened?

"No. Enemy," Buck stammered. "We were hit."

"Where are our people?"

Buck shook his head. "Dead."

Alex looked past Buck but saw nothing else moving in the trees. "We should go look. A quick sweep just in case they're only hurt."

Unexpected rage filled Buck's voice. "I said they're dead! We're not going anywhere. Activate the keying device."

Alex paused, speechless. "Sir..." He searched for the words to calm his superior, to make him understand. Combat was frantic, and things were never as they seemed at first. "I can take one man with me, do a quick sweep, real fast. We won't be long, and then—"

Buck ignored him and pointed in the direction he had just

come from. "Concentrate defenses in that direction. Keep an eye out for giant wolves."

Wolves? "Look, sir, if it's just animals we can still—"

Buck rounded on him, jamming the barrel of his pistol into Alex's face, literally smashing it against the lenses of Alex's GPNVGs. "Newf, one more fucking word out of you, and I'll shoot you myself. Got it?"

"Yes, sir." His hopes sank.

"Now, activate the keying device."

Alex nodded then turned away to do as he was ordered. He had done what he could, and it wasn't as if he could fight his superior because he didn't like his orders.

He pointed at the keying device, a flat black cylindrical metal machine the size of a footlocker, with carrying handles on its sides. It sat in the center of the shattered remains of stone columns and bizarre elf-like statues. Once they turned it on, it would recall the Gateway. Then, after they were gone, it would become a lump of burned-out metal and melted electronics. "Turn it on," he said, hearing the defeat in his own voice. "We're going home."

He shook his head then walked away to the edge of the clearing and stared out into the trees. *Who does this? Who leaves men behind?* There was a bright flash behind him as a streak of multicolored light appeared in the air in the center of the clearing. The streak extended and grew then pulsed out, forming a circle five feet in diameter. On the other side of the glowing circle, Alex saw the lights of the Jump Tube, and through it, home. The Magic Kingdom.

"Let's go," Buck said.

Buck was the first man through the Gateway, followed by the other three members of the covering team. Alex paused one last time and stared into the bush behind him, hating himself. In the distance, something howled, and Alex couldn't help but think it sounded like a cry of triumph.

He stepped through the Gateway.

Chapter 2

It was almost six in the evening by the time the Dash-8 stopped in front of the terminal at North Peace Regional Airport, just outside Fort St. John. Cassie Rogan smiled at the flight attendant as she exited the aircraft and began to descend the metal stairs. The cold mountain air was a welcome relief from the too-hot little aircraft. It was May, but unlike coastal Vancouver, the weather this far north would remain cool until the height of summer. Northern British Columbia wasn't exactly the land of the midnight sun, but it was still the North.

She turned and shaded her eyes as she gazed out at the Rocky Mountains to the west. One year ago, those mountains had promised adventure, an escape. Now they mocked her. There would be no getting away for her: tiny Hudson's Hope would be her life now. She'd remain there with all the other losers who couldn't get away, and end up married to some oversized trucker or logger, popping out a herd of children and working at some shit job she couldn't stand until she was too old and fat to care anymore. Flicking a strand of blond hair out of her eyes, she recognized the self-pity for what it was but couldn't help how she felt. She could always join the army, she supposed, like Lee was going to do.

No. No she couldn't. She had been a lousy student; she'd be a worse soldier. Adjusting the strap of her carry-on, she began making her way across the tarmac to the terminal.

The interior of the North Peace Regional Airport hadn't changed at all in her absence, but then, nothing *ever* changed up north. Pillars interspersed throughout the tiny terminal held up a cedar ceiling, glass partitions lined the walls, and a single snack stand with posters advertising Molson Ice beer catered to three customers. In the entire terminal, there might have been a dozen people—a far cry from the urban hustle of Vancouver International Airport. A ten-foot carving of a grizzly bear stood silent vigil beside a glass display case with wood carvings of prospectors and early pioneer life.

Welcome to northern British Columbia, everybody. Contain your excitement.

The other passengers surged forward to greet loved ones, hugging and laughing. Cassie's eyes scanned the terminal. It wasn't like her sister Alice to be late for anything. And then she saw her, standing alone, a look of trepidation in her eyes, her hands clasped in front of her. Alice was shorter and stockier than Cassie and had their mother's auburn hair. At twenty years of age, Cassie was not only fifteen years younger but also taller and more athletic—at least she had been until she'd dropped out of track and took up partying as her new major, living on fast food and beer. She still looked good, though, and still grabbed men's attention—especially when she was dressed as she was now, rocking a tight T-shirt, shorts, and sandals. Alice looked old and worn out. For a long moment, they stood frozen in place, staring at one another. Then Alice smiled, and the years melted away. She rushed forward to embrace Cassie. An unexpected surge of emotions washed over

Cassie. She hugged her big sister back—hard—surprised at how much she had missed her.

"Let's get your bags." Alice's eyes widened when she stepped back and saw Cassie's short blond hair and pink streaks.

Cassie smiled and tossed her head. "You like?"

"Let's go get your bags," Alice repeated.

* * *

Alice drove her pickup truck east along One Hundredth Avenue, cutting through the heart of Fort St. John. They passed the old Lido Theater and other places that brought back memories from Cassie's youth. Growing up in Hudson's Hope, if you wanted to see a new-release movie, you first had to make the hour-and-a-half drive to Fort St. John. A person *really* had to want to see a movie to come all this way.

They drove west with the Rocky Mountains looming before them and turned onto the Alaska Highway, the only real highway in all of the Peace River Valley. In minutes, the friendly little shops and businesses of downtown Fort St. John were gone, replaced by ugly brown pulp and paper plants. Cassie sipped her Tim Horton's coffee and warily contemplated the plumes of dark black smoke rising from the stacks of the mills. How much carbon monoxide did these mills release into the atmosphere each day? The forests of northern British Columbia were among the most beautiful in the world, yet the main focus in the north seemed to be all about destroying them. She sighed.

"What's up?" her sister asked.

"Nothing," Cassie answered. Her sister worked for a logging company. There was no point in bringing up greenhouse gases and the environment again.

Minutes later, on the outskirts of the city, they drove by the provincial park built around Charlie Lake. In the light of the setting sun, the surface of the lake looked as if it was on fire. It was so pretty that just for a moment, Cassie forgot why she was home—but just for a moment. Then she saw the new sign on the side of the highway, advertising the economic benefits of the new Site C Dam and reservoir built along the Peace River.

"They built it already?" She heard the bitterness in her own voice but didn't really care.

"It went up fast—*surprisingly* fast actually," Alice answered. "It's been operating for over a month now."

"The first two dams weren't enough?"

"Guess not."

"One more nail in the planet's coffin." Cassie sipped from her coffee.

"People need electricity, Cassie. Even environmentalists."

"Whatever."

Her sister slowed the truck down and turned left onto Highway 29, a two-lane road that climbed through the twisting foothills of the Peace River Valley. They drove past a Shell station, the last gas station before Hudson's Hope, the last symbol of civilization before Cassie was back in exile.

Cassie had taken this route so many times she could have followed it in her sleep. Once they were out of in the suburbs of Fort St. John, the few residential areas on either side of the Alaska Highway gave way to vast forests of lodgepole pine and spruce— one moment civilization, the next wilderness. They were in the real north now, unforgiving and ancient.

"So," said Alice, hesitation in her voice. "Can we talk about this?"

"Not a whole lot to talk about," said Cassie, not wanting to talk about it at all.

"Cassie, baby, I'm not stupid. I know the semester isn't over yet."

"It is for me." Cassie turned her head and pretended to watch the trees flow past.

"What do you mean? It was *a lot* of money."

"You've told me that before, a thousand times."

"That's not what I meant." Alice glanced at Cassie. "You know what I mean. It's just that, well, there isn't that much money. Are you... pregnant?"

Cassie snorted, shook her head. "God, Alice. Right to that, huh? No. I'm not pregnant."

"Well, why?"

"I kind of got into a fight."

"Oh, Jesus, Cassie. Did you hurt someone?"

"I'm fine, thanks."

"What happened?"

"Look. The fight, the thing with the police... this was just the last straw. Things weren't really working for me at UBC. University wasn't my thing."

"The police?" Her sister's eyes grew large.

"Watch the road!" Cassie snapped.

Alice swerved back to her side of the road just as a large transport truck blared past and then bit her lip. She looked so tired that Cassie felt guilty again, but then her anger forced it back down. Alice might have paid for university, but only because their parents had left her in charge of Cassie's money, money they had left for Cassie. It didn't mean Alice owned Cassie or got to make decisions for her. She wasn't her mother.

"The police?" her sister repeated.

Cassie sat quietly for a few moments. "There was a party in one of the dorms. Actually, there were a lot of parties in the dorms, but this one may have gotten a bit out of hand."

"Drugs, Cassie?"

"No, *not* drugs, Alice. Are you going to let me tell you or not?"

"Sorry, go on."

"So, I was there with a friend, Belinda. I leave her alone to go to the bathroom, and when I come back, this asshole is trying to get her out the door. She's barely conscious, and he's practically carrying her, and no one is saying a word or doing anything. I didn't even know this guy, and he wasn't a student, just some dirtbag who crashed the party. I'm pretty sure he slipped her something. Anyhow, no one else was doing anything, so I did."

"Oh, Cassie. Why?"

"So, I tell him to leave her alone, and he gets all up in my face and starts threatening me and—"

"Really, Cassie? Threatening you? Are you exaggerating a bit?"

"Were you there?"

"Go on." Her sister's expression was strained as though she was sitting on the toilet.

"So, I stopped him."

"Oh, for God's sake, Cassie! You assaulted some poor man, didn't you?"

"Weren't you listening to what I just said? This is how serial rapists operate."

"Don't be so melodramatic. You're not the hero here."

Cassie felt her face flush. She shook her head and looked away. Why did she even bother? Alice lived in an isolated community in the North, a world where bad things didn't happen, where there were no rapists, no drug pushers. And in her naiveté, she insisted the rest of the world was just like her, all evidence to the contrary. Even now, she just couldn't accept what Cassie was telling her. She'd do anything to maintain her delusion that the world wasn't dangerous and that it wasn't full of really bad people who did really bad things.

Cassie *hadn't* been wrong. She couldn't prove it, but that guy *had* been a shitbag who showed up at dorm parties to troll for young women. And he *did* slip something into Belinda's drink—Cassie was sure of that as well. Belinda might have been drunk, but she hadn't been insensible. Had it not been for Cassie, that asshole would have raped her—if he didn't kill her as well and then drop her body into the Pacific Ocean to wash up on English Bay days later, bloated and half eaten by crabs. Bad things might not happen in Hudson's Hope, but they sure as hell did in Vancouver—things that would send her naive sister into a spin wobble if she knew only a tenth of them. She'd never—not ever—get Alice to see that.

"Anyhow," she continued. "The police took him to the hospital and me to jail."

"Oh my God. Is he pressing charges?"

"I don't think so."

"Oh, Christ, Cassie. We can't afford lawyer fees, not with the tuition."

Cassie bit her lip and stared at her hands. "That might not be a problem anymore," she said so softly it was almost a whisper.

"Why? You can still go back and finish the semester, can't you?"

"They kind of asked me not to. I'm not doing so good. In fact, I'm kind of failing."

"Failing what?"

"Everything."

"Cassie, how much were you partying?"

"That's not it. Well... not all of it. The truth is it's just too hard for me. This is not who I am. I'm not cut out for university."

"That's nonsense. You're smart enough, and you know it. You're just not trying."

"I'm trying. You don't know!"

"Yes, I *do* know. It's all about the accident, isn't it? You haven't given a damn about anything since Mom and Dad died."

Cassie rounded on her. "Don't bring that up again! Not this time—not every time!" She knew she shouldn't yell but couldn't stop herself.

Alice slowed the truck down and pulled over to the side of the road, her tires crunching on the gravel. When the vehicle stopped, she turned and faced Cassie, torment in her face. Once again, Cassie felt the weight of guilt. This was all her fault. Everything was always her fault. She screwed up everything she did.

Alice tentatively reached out and put her hand on Cassie's forearm. "Baby, you have to make peace with what happened. It's ruining your life. Can't you see that? It wasn't your fault."

"I know it's not my goddamned fault." She felt the tears welling in her own eyes, but she wasn't going to talk about this. She wasn't *ever* going to talk about this.

"No, baby. I don't think you do know that. I think you blame yourself. I think you've given up trying—given up on everything."

Cassie's world was spinning out of control, and it needed to stop. "Please. Please. Just let it go. I've moved on, and I don't want to keep talking about it."

Her sister's eyes had also filled with tears. "That's just it, baby. You haven't."

Cassie wiped her own eyes and looked away. There was nothing but trees as far as she could see. "Please. I just want to go home, to be alone for a while. I need to catch my breath, to figure things out."

Her sister patted her arm. "We'll work them out together, baby."

Cassie said nothing more, and after a long period of uncomfortable silence, Alice pulled back onto the highway.

Chapter 3

Maelhrandia stalked the clearing where the rest of the strange intruders had simply vanished. She had meant to capture at least two of the spies, but her boggart warriors had been too slow, and one of the gwyllgi had managed to savage its prey so badly that she had decided to just give the sad creature to her boggarts to finish off. They may have been a tad... extreme with their knives, and the strange creature had survived longer than she would have thought possible. But at least now she had a sense of their toughness.

There had been other intruders in these ancient ruins as well, but somehow, they had simply vanished. Now, all around her, boggart guardsmen combed the brush, seeking further evidence of the invaders. Boggarts, huge and muscular, made wonderful warriors but were of little use for anything else. Even now, several of the four-armed, blue-skinned warriors followed behind her gwyllgi hounds as they sniffed for scents in the jungle. The ambush had not gone as well as she had planned, and the invaders had actually managed to kill one of her gwyllgi. Their strange weapons threw fire, but she had sensed no magic in them.

She had underestimated the intruders, and she'd not make that same mistake again. But who were they? *What* were they?

Her sister Horlastia, Princess of Terlingas, the Mistress of Dunnewinder's Shadow, was kneeling at the center of the ruins, examining the bizarre metal cylinder that was all that now remained of the intruders. It was the size of a small trunk but made entirely from metal. Truly, it was a wondrous device with intricate markings and colored glass. Whatever its purpose had been, it was useless now. Flames had burned it from the inside out, scorching its interior, cracking and scarring the glass, leaving it destroyed. Horlastia would take it with her, anyhow—just in case their mother, or her gnome tinkerers, could discover anything from it.

Maelhrandia had an unsettling heaviness in her stomach, and chills ran through her as she let her gaze drift across the ancient stone slabs within the clearing. These were fae-seelie ruins; there could be no doubt. Centuries ago, her ancestors had built these stone obelisks—for a purpose she did not fathom—yet she, the ruler of this holdfast, hadn't even known they existed. Horlastia would underscore that fact with their mother. The message would be subtle yet unmistakable: what kind of princess could not know of the existence of a place of power within her own holdfast? If Maelhrandia were lucky, her mother would simply believe she was stupid and lazy; if she were unlucky, her mother would suspect Maelhrandia had always known yet kept their existence a secret, a betrayal that would see Maelhrandia executed.

These ruins were a place of power. There was a ley line here, an arcane convergence. The place was throbbing with esoteric power; she could feel it in her bones, in her very being. She didn't have her mother's divination talents, but she could still sense a ley line—the cosmic thread that wove together space and time. It could be no accident that the invaders had broken through in such a place, but where had they come from? Where had they gone back to? And when would they return?

Maelhrandia's talents lay with manipulation—using the forces of magic to cloak herself. She was perhaps the finest mage-scout of all her people. Whereas Horlastia, a mage-warden, excelled at destruction spells. Maelhrandia, while capable enough with Drake's-Gift and Storm-Tongue, would never be able to stand in combat against her sister, a fact Horlastia never let her forget. Maelhrandia glanced at her sister's armored back. Like all fae seelie, Horlastia was slight of frame with dark lavender skin the color of night. She wore dragon-scale armor but had removed her winged helmet, so her white hair hung down just above her collar.

"There are ley lines here," Horlastia said.

"I sense it as well. The invaders must have used it to link to us."

Horlastia snorted. "Not *it*, sister. *Them.* There are at least two, maybe three, all converging here."

"That's not—"

"Possible?" Her sister cocked her head, raised an eyebrow, and smiled condescendingly. "I say it *is* possible, sister. The convergence of three ley lines all within the ruins of our own people."

Three ley lines? Now she did feel them. She had been so overwhelmed by the magical energy present that she hadn't noticed there was more than one ley line. This must be one of the old sites, from the time of the *Banishment*. Maelhrandia felt the weight of her neglect upon her shoulders, her ignorance weighing her down. Not one of her sisters would ever accept that Maelhrandia had not known of this place. She would never have believed it, either. But her sisters didn't rot away here the way she did. Her holdfast, the Tarloth Delta, was overgrown jungle for hundreds of leagues. The ruins of an entire city could have been swallowed by the jungle in the span of only a handful of years. This was not Maelhrandia's fault. No one could have known of this place's existence—not without stumbling upon it. Or being led to it. By invaders.

"I shall guard this site," Maelhrandia said. "You must bring word of this attack to the seelie court, to our mother."

"Must I?" Horlastia let the smallest smile creep across her lavender features.

Maelhrandia's face burned. "Sister. The invaders have not attacked my holdfast. They have attacked the Fae Seelie Empire. They have spied upon us and have brought violence to our servants. Mother *will* wish to know."

"Oh, of that I have no doubt... dear sister."

A boggart captain approached and stood not ten paces away, his fishlike head bowed. She smelled him before she saw him. Behind him, his warriors still moved through the thick bushes, still searching. Yet all they had found so far had been boot prints and broken ground. The intruders had left almost nothing else behind except this burnt metal device.

Horlastia rose, brushed the dirt and twigs from her dragon-scale armor, and adjusted her curved saber so its hilt was close at hand. Maelhrandia considered her sister, feeling somewhat insulted. Did she really believe that Maelhrandia would attack her head-on? Idiot warriors.

"I shall leave immediately," Horlastia said. "Our mother was most insistent that I bring back the prisoner."

"Of course. I shall have it brought to you."

Horlastia, looking uninterested, turned away and headed toward her mount at the edge of the clearing.

Maelhrandia glanced at the waiting captain and nodded. "Report."

"Mistress, we've found nothing but these strange metal pieces— talismans perhaps."

The captain, still holding his shield and sword in his outer arms, held out one of his thin, short inner arms, palm up. In it, he held the odd metal tubes that they had found scattered elsewhere after the invaders had used their fire-weapons. Maelhrandia reached out her hand but refrained from touching them.

"They are not iron, Mistress."

Frowning, she took one, forcing herself not to flinch as she did. One end of the tube was open, exposing its hollow interior. She held it to her nostril and sniffed, immediately wishing she hadn't. It stunk worse than a dwarven forge. She dropped the object onto the ground and wiped her palm against the captain's dark-green cloak.

"String up the carcass of the one your warriors played with. If these spies return, make the carcass the first thing they see but also leave enough warriors to deal with them if they don't turn and flee." She turned away as the boggart captain bowed deeply.

Her sister was already at her wyvern near the outer edge of the clearing, where it had just enough space to land. The boggart warriors wisely avoided the creature, giving it all the space it wanted. The beasts were stupid but had foul tempers and were prone to lash out at anything that came within reach—with the exception of their riders. Now, her sister mounted the wyvern and sat upon its ornate black-leather saddle. Behind her saddle, tied like a corpse, was the sole surviving invader, a black hood over his head. He struggled in his bonds, but it did him no good. He was larger than Maelhrandia and her sister but shorter and less muscular than a boggart. And his skin was pale and revolting, the color of maggots, not at all the beautiful lavender hue of the fae seelie. The large saddlebags on the side of the wyvern held the weapons and equipment the invaders had been carrying. Her mother would want to see everything.

Maelhrandia, hiding her hatred behind a smile, stepped up next to her sister's leg. "Bring our mother my love."

"I'll bring her your prisoner, dear sister, and news of this place."

And news of my failure. That's what you truly mean.

Maelhrandia stepped back as the wyvern began to beat its massive bat-like wings, buffeting her with air. In moments, the Dragonling was in the air and rising above the jungle, her sister nothing more than a speck upon its mighty back.

On the opposite side of the clearing, as far away from the wyvern as it could get, Gazekiller lifted his huge horned head and brayed loudly. Maelhrandia smirked, hearing just a hint of residual anger in the beast's roar. Gazekiller disliked wyverns. Actually, Gazekiller disliked most creatures, but he really hated wyverns and would have gleefully killed and devoured the creature had he not been under Maelhrandia's control. Maelhrandia glared at the diminishing figure of her sister atop the wyvern as it flew away. She understood Gazekiller's urge to kill.

Chapter 4

Mary Elizabeth Chambers lay on her bed in her dorm room and used her highlighter to mark a long passage in her textbook on the principles of business law. It was a brand-new highlighter, and Elizabeth loved the sharp chemical smell, the bright contrast of yellow on white. It was such a silly little thing to be so pleased about, but she was. When she turned the page and saw that the textbook's previous owner had highlighted another passage, her good mood took a dip. One of the many problems with used books was that you had to live with what the last owner had thought was important—which, in this case, wasn't. All the extra highlights would make it harder for Elizabeth to focus. She sighed and flicked a lock of dark hair out of her eyes. Brand-new textbooks would be so cool, but that wasn't going to happen anytime soon.

A quick glance at the digital clock beside her bed told her it was just after two in the afternoon. She had been hitting the books for almost four hours—a long time even for her. It was a very efficient way to spend a Saturday afternoon. Proper time management was so important.

Now, though, she needed a study break and maybe a cup of

green tea. She slid the heavy textbook away and sat up, extending both arms over her head and stretching. Her roommate, Sandra, was still out with her boyfriend, Neil, doing whatever it was the two of them did on a Saturday afternoon in a small town like Dawson Creek. Most likely, they had gone to a movie in Fort St. John. Sandra's absence was kind of a relief. She always insisted on talking—even when Elizabeth had her face in a textbook. For whatever reason, Sandra couldn't stand silence nor did she seem terribly concerned with her grades.

Elizabeth walked out of her bedroom, past Sandra's bedroom, and into the suite the two women shared at the Dawson Creek Campus for the Northern Lights College. The suite was small but still larger than the others. The walls were painted a somber white, although Sandra had plastered gaudy posters over most of them. The common area held a round wooden table with two rickety chairs, an old green sofa that had clearly seen better years, and a computer desk, upon which sat Sandra's Mac. Elizabeth walked into the tiny kitchenette and plugged the kettle in.

Someone knocked on the suite's door. When Elizabeth opened it, she saw Sarah, another first-year student. Sarah pushed her glasses up her nose. "You got another phone call. I think it's your mother... again."

Elizabeth chose to ignore the tone of annoyance in Sarah's voice. She brushed past her. "Thanks."

Sandra had a cell phone and had told Elizabeth many times before that she was welcome to use it, but Elizabeth preferred using the communal telephone in the hallway. The truth, as terrible as it sounded, was that she didn't want to make it that easy for her mother to call her. In the hallway, the telephone's handset was hanging against the wall where Sarah had left it. Elizabeth stared at it for a moment, took a deep breath, and then snatched it up.

"Hello, Mom."

She heard her mother's voice in the receiver. "Mary Elizabeth, dear, why are you still there? We need you here today with everything that's going on. I told you that this morning."

Her mother had been drinking again; Elizabeth could hear it. This early in the afternoon, and her mother was already half in the bag. She closed her eyes and said a quick prayer, asking for strength. "Mom, we've already discussed this. I'm a student. I can't just drop everything and come back to Fort St. John."

"I need you here, dear." The desperation in her mother's voice came through crystal clear. "Your father needs you, and so do your brothers. Just come for a while. Come and help me with the baby."

"Mom, Steven is seven years old. He's not a baby anymore."

"Why won't you help? You're my daughter, my only girl. I need you."

Her mother was crying again. After twenty years of marriage to Elizabeth's father, her mother could turn the tears on and off at a moment's notice. Elizabeth felt her anger spiking.

"Mom, you don't need me. You need to stop drinking and get away from him."

"You ungrateful little bitch!" her mother snapped, her voice rising to a shrill yell that Elizabeth was certain anyone walking past her in the hallway could hear. "You think you're so special because you're in college. It's not even a real college. You're not special. You're no better than us. So what if I have a drink now and then. I've wasted my life looking after my children. They don't care. No one cares. Do you know how much that stupid college is costing us? We can't afford it. No one can afford your shit."

Elizabeth sighed, aware her own eyes were watering. "Mom, I have a scholarship. You're not paying for anything."

"You're a whore. God knows it, too!"

"I have to go, Mom. I have to study."

"It won't work, you know. You won't graduate. Your scholarship runs out this year, and you don't have a job. And we're not paying for you. You belong here, helping us, not spreading your legs for everyone with a prick at that school for sluts."

"Good-bye, Mom."

Elizabeth's hand trembled as she hung up. She leaned against the wall, her heart hammering in her chest. It was always like this with her mother, always. When she sobered up, tomorrow, she wouldn't even remember the hateful things she had said—or she would just pretend this conversation had never happened. Her mother was an expert at avoiding problems. Elizabeth, aware she was drawing the attention of other students walking down the hallway, wiped her eyes, put on her best stone face, and then returned to her suite. She closed the door quickly and leaned against the back of it as if she could hold the world out.

For most of her life, Elizabeth had felt like she had raised herself. She was amazed at how well she had turned out although she lay awake at night and worried about her brothers: they stood no chance as long as they were in that home. Elizabeth went back into her bedroom with her tea, closed the door, and stared at her open schoolbook. If she could get a full scholarship, rather than a partial one, her future would truly be golden. *If wishes were wings,* she thought, *then we'd all fly. God helps those who help themselves.* She'd succeed; she'd escape her family, their poverty, and she'd make something of herself. God had a plan for her; she knew He did. He had to.

Returning to her textbook, she focused on school, finding relief in the principles of business. Soon, thoughts of her mother were replaced by economics and best management practices. When she heard Sandra and Neil return, she glanced again at her clock and was surprised to see it was already 5:00 p.m. She had been completely lost in her work.

There was a knock on her bedroom door, and Sandra called out to her. "Lizzie, you there?"

Elizabeth frowned. She hated when people called her Lizzie. She opened her door to see Sandra sitting in her wheelchair. Sandra was blond, thin, and pretty but suffered from slight acne. Neil, holding an open beer can, waved from the couch. Neil was overweight, had gross neck hair, and had far worse acne than Sandra.

"Hey," Elizabeth said. "You're back."

"You been in there all day, honey?" Sandra asked.

"You know me. Study, study, study."

Sandra smiled. "Yeah, I know you. So, how many times did your mom call today?"

Elizabeth felt her face warm. "Just the one time, but it was a doozy."

"Come here, honey." Sandra opened her arms, and Elizabeth, stepping in closer to Sandra's wheelchair, let the other woman hug her. She even wrapped her own arms around Sandra's thin back. When they released one another, Sandra shook her head. "You never should have given her the number to the dorm."

"I didn't. She found it herself."

"Just hope she doesn't get my number," said Sandra. "Then she'll call nonstop."

Elizabeth shook her head. "Only when she's drinking and feeling sorry for herself."

Sandra backed up and then spun about and rolled over to sit next to Neil. Neil placed a pudgy hand on her knee. Elizabeth frowned.

"Hey, Lizzie," he said with a bucktoothed grin as he held up a

Ziploc bag filled with marijuana and several already rolled joints. "Wanna get baked?"

For some unfathomable reason, Neil saw himself as a big man, the campus drug dealer. "I don't do drugs, Neil. You know that. I've told you that. *Repeatedly.*"

Neil laughed although Elizabeth wasn't smiling. "I know, I know. It's a sin and all that shit, but there's always hope for you."

"You know you could try it," said Sandra. "It might relax you."

"We gonna par-tay." Neil inelegantly pushed himself off the couch and turned on the small stereo. Music blared out of the speakers.

"Actually, Neil, if you don't mind, I want to keep studying." Elizabeth forced the anger out of her voice, but it wasn't easy.

Neil swayed to the music as he lit the joint. Instantly, the stench of marijuana wafted through the room.

"I'd really prefer you didn't do that in here. It's illegal, and it stinks."

Neil plopped down again at the end of the couch near Sandra, casually dismissing Elizabeth with a wave of his hand. "Mellow out, Miss Mormon. It's just a thing. Jesus can't see you."

Sandra looked uneasy, but she giggled and took the joint from Neil before taking a hit. Shaking her head, Elizabeth walked over to the window and opened it. The cool spring air that blew in didn't make much of a difference. She crossed her arms and turned back to face the two of them, tapping her foot against the tiles of the floor. "Actually, Neil, He *can*. That's kind of the whole point."

"Whatevers," answered Neil just before he took another hit.

Someone banged on their dorm-room door and then, a moment later, opened it. Once again, Sandra hadn't locked the door behind her. Three of Neil's loser buddies poured into the suite, carrying six-packs of beer which they proceeded to place inside the fridge in the kitchen. They grinned, said "What's up?" and exchanged high fives with Neil, each one giving Sandra a kiss on the forehead.

"Really? Again?" Elizabeth glared at them. "Come on, guys. This is my dorm room, too."

Rupert, one of Neil's buddies, sidled up next to Elizabeth— stinking of BO—and slipped his hand around the small of her back. "What up, Mary Magdalene? Want to have a religious experience with me?"

She shuddered and pulled away, her face burning with embarrassment. Within moments, the suite was filled with people, noise, and smoke. Someone cranked up the music even more.

"Come on, Lizzie," urged Neil. "Party with us just this one time. You're in college, for God's sake."

"Yeah, Lizzie," said Rupert. "You need to loosen up."

"And get laid," giggled Sandra, apparently already stoned.

They all burst out laughing. Red faced, Elizabeth turned and stormed into her room, slamming the door behind her. She clenched her fists, wanting to scream. The walls vibrated from the noise. They weren't going to stop, and they weren't going to go somewhere else. She knew damned well that each one of Neil's buddies figured if he hung out here often enough, he could get into her pants.

As if she would ever—ever—be that desperate.

She could go for a run, calm down. When she came back, she'd take her book and go study somewhere else, somewhere quiet. Her mind made up, she quickly changed into shorts and a T-shirt, keeping a wary eye on the door. It wouldn't be the first time Neil or one of his buddies *accidentally* opened it without asking. She double tied the laces on her running shoes and walked back out into the common area, where Sandra and Neil were making out,

Neil awkwardly leaning over the side of the couch to get around Sandra's wheelchair. Rupert and the other two were engaged in a lively debate, gesticulating wildly with their hands. All three stopped talking when they saw Elizabeth and leered at her instead. One of them actually whistled. Rupert offered to help wash her back after her run. The sound of their stupid laughter chased her out into the hallway.

Jerks. She stormed down the hall, her face hot. She didn't deserve to be treated like this. It was her dorm suite, too. She paused beside the wall-mounted telephone in the hallway and stared at it.

* * *

Forty minutes into her run, Elizabeth was feeling much better. No matter how difficult her life happened to be at any particular moment, once the endorphins started flushing through her bloodstream, she felt as though she could take on anything. The euphoria that came with running, with pushing her body, washed away all doubts and fears… all feelings of guilt. She felt alive when she ran.

She left the main campus, ran down 116th Avenue, then turned right onto Seventeenth. Along the way, she passed both the Bethel Pentecostal Tabernacle and Grace Lutheran Church. She ran through a residential area with pretty little homes on either side of the cracked pavement. Small children ran and played, and grown-ups smiled and chatted with their neighbors. It all seemed so friendly, so surreal, like something out of a Hallmark television movie. What would it have been like to grow up in a home where the parents weren't drunk most of the time—where families laughed instead of yelled?

She cut across the road onto a hiking trail that wound its way through several small parks in the center of town, passing people walking their dogs. She ran along the trail for several kilometers before it came out onto the Dawson Creek-Tupper Highway, a busy four-lane road that led back to the campus. By now, she was well into her fitness zone and had run almost five kilometers. Most days, she ran this route twice, but it was getting late.

The run had helped. She wasn't angry anymore, and she felt as if she could deal with Neil and his friends. With God's help, she could deal with anyone and anything—including her mother.

Cars and trucks breezed by her, trailing exhaust. She passed the Dawson's Creek Mall on her right with its Shoppers Drug Mart, Dollarama, and Safeway. Across the highway sat a White Spot restaurant, its parking lot already full. She had gone on a date there once, but it had been a complete disaster. Her date, supposedly a good Christian boy, had expected her to sleep with him because he had bought her dinner. It wasn't even much of a dinner. She increased her pace, hurrying past the restaurant. God had a plan for her, and nobody was going to treat her like an object.

Up ahead, she saw the well-manicured lawn of the campus, and she veered toward it and onto the grass. A half hour ago, the campus's students had been spread out over the lawn, throwing Frisbees, sitting, talking, hanging out—now, they were all clustered near the parking lot of the residential dorms, standing around flashing red-and-blue lights.

She slowed to a walk and put her hands on the small of her back, letting her heart rate return to normal. The students clustered near two Royal Canadian Mounted Police—RCMP—cars. As she approached, she put her fingers against her throat and counted her pulse. One of the Mounties stood beside his open driver's-side door, talking into a radio. A third RCMP vehicle—a blue-and-white van—now pulled into the parking lot, its lights flashing and siren blaring. Two more Mounties got out of the van and opened the back doors.

The Dawson's Creek RCMP detachment was there in force, it seemed.

Elizabeth slipped through the crowd and watched as another officer came out of the dorm, pushing a handcuffed Neil in front of him. The young man was wild-eyed and white faced, looking as if he were about to start crying. The Mountie led him to the back of the van and pushed him into it. Elizabeth knew she shouldn't take comfort in others' misfortune, but she couldn't help it—after all, she was only human—and she smiled. Moments later, Rupert and his other two buddies, also in handcuffs, were led out of the dorm building, joining Neil in the van. The crowd had grown, and the buzz of excited conversation spread among them. Elizabeth couldn't imagine anyone was all that surprised. Just about everyone on campus knew they could score weed from Neil. The only real surprise should be why it had taken so long for him to be caught.

The crowd went silent when another Mountie, a young woman, came out of the dorm building, pushing Sandra in her wheelchair. Sandra was in tears, and her head swung about in disbelief. When she spotted Elizabeth in the crowd, she raised her arms out to her. "Elizabeth, please," she pleaded, her voice breaking. "They're going to arrest me. You have to tell them this is a mistake. I can't be arrested."

Several of the other Mounties gathered about Sandra's wheelchair at the rear of the van, and together, they lifted her up into the back. Then they strapped the wheelchair, with Sandra still in it, in place so it wouldn't move, right next to Neil and the others. Elizabeth edged closer, stopping about ten feet away.

"Elizabeth, do something. Please." Tears ran down Sandra's cheeks.

Elizabeth cocked her head and placed her fingers against her throat, taking her pulse once more. Already, it was back to normal. Just before they closed the back door of the van, Elizabeth met Sandra's gaze and shook her head, giving her the only response she ever would. Leaving the crowd and all the excitement, she entered her dorm building. At her suite, another Mountie stood waiting, writing in his notebook. He looked up at Elizabeth.

"I'm sorry, but this is a crime scene," he said, watching Elizabeth with a bored expression.

"This is my dorm room," Elizabeth answered.

"*You're* Elizabeth Chambers?"

"That's right."

He pushed the door open and motioned inside with his hand. "Come on in, Miss Chambers."

"Thank you." She brushed past him.

The little living room was a mess. Her and Sandra's things had been scattered about in their search.

"You found the drugs?" Elizabeth asked.

"Yes we did, thank you," the officer answered.

"Good."

"I'm going to have to take your statement."

The officer motioned to the couch, and Elizabeth sat down and placed her hands in her lap. "Whatever I can do to help."

The Mountie sat down on a chair across from her. He paused, holding his notebook in his lap and watching her face intently. "Your friend is in a great deal of trouble, you know. There was a considerable amount of marijuana."

"You'll have to call her parents," Elizabeth said. "I can give you their phone number. They'll want to know about this. They'll be worried."

The officer nodded. "You understand Northern Lights will

probably expel her. Some people, maybe *a lot* of people, are going to be very angry with you."

Elizabeth met his gaze and held it. "People can be whatever they want, but a sinner is still a sinner."

The officer's eyes tightened just for a moment, but then he flipped his notebook open. As she began making her statement, Elizabeth wondered how long all this would take. After all, she still had to study.

Chapter 5

Just after six in the evening, Cassie watched her best friend, Ginny, pull up in her old green pickup truck. Even inside, Cassie could hear country music from the truck's radio. She opened the front door and waited. Ginny squealed as she jumped out of the cab, her brown eyes shining with excitement as she rushed to embrace Cassie.

There was a chill in the air this evening, so Cassie wore blue jeans and a hoodie, as did Ginny, but their outfits were about all they had in common. Ginny was pretty but in a wholesome girl-next-door kind of way, not at all the flamboyant punk rocker Cassie had become. Ginny rarely wore much makeup, never dressed provocatively, and was in dire need of a fashion makeover. Where Cassie had short hair with pink highlights, Ginny's hair was long and brown with the bangs perpetually hovering over her eyes. Boys noticed Cassie first but approached Ginny more often; after all, she was the less threatening one. Tonight, her face looked freshly scrubbed with just a touch of makeup—way less than Cassie was wearing.

Hearing Ginny's arrival, Alice and her husband, Rupert, Hudson Hope's fire marshal, came out to say hello. While Cassie was certain Rupert was just being friendly, Alice was being nosy.

"So, who else is going to be at this party?" Alice asked.

Ginny opened her mouth to answer, but Cassie cut her off. "Not Mom."

Alice frowned, her face flushing. "Seriously. What time do you expect to be back?"

Cassie climbed into the passenger's seat of Ginny's cab and pulled the door shut. She rolled down the window. "Not Mom," she repeated.

Ginny, looking embarrassed, climbed back behind the driver's seat and leaned past Cassie. "We'll be back before midnight. It's just a bunch of our friends—the usual suspects."

Cassie shook her head and looked away.

Rupert, standing next to Alice, slipped his arm around his wife's waist. "Don't let the fire get too large."

Ginny backed up onto the street, and Cassie flashed her sister the most fake smile she could before looking away quickly. In minutes, they were out of town and driving west along Highway 29, approaching the suspension bridge that crossed the Peace River. She noticed Ginny glancing at her, a look of expectation on her face.

"What?"

"I said, Lee's going to be there."

Cassie fidgeted in her seat. "How's he been?"

"You guys don't talk?"

"Couple of emails. It's... awkward."

"You should jump his bones, you know? Before he joins the army and goes away forever."

Cassie cocked her head and grimaced at Ginny, who started giggling. Ginny giggled a lot. It was one of those things Cassie loved about her.

"The town virgin is giving me sex advice?"

"Hey, girl." Ginny turned her attention back to the highway. "You've been gone a long time. Things change."

"Really? So, you're no longer a virgin. Who?"

Ginny looked uncomfortable. "There's way more to sex than just... intercourse."

Cassie turned in her seat and considered Ginny's profile. "There is, is there? Tell me all about it, then."

Ginny's face turned a darker shade of red. "Me and Darryl have been hanging out a lot. He's gonna be there tonight."

"Darryl? Darryl Higgins?"

"He's changed. Started lifting weights, doing that P90X stuff. He lost a lot of weight."

"Didn't Darryl spend prom night playing World of Warcraft?"

"Don't be such a bitch."

Cassie laughed. "Okay, okay, honey; maybe he has changed. So, what have you two kids been doing? Freaky Kama Sutra stuff?"

"You know, hanging out, couple of dates. He's really sweet."

"And you're getting all hot and bothered together."

"We've been... you know... doing *stuff.*"

"*Naked* stuff, Ginny Shevchuk? Does your mother know?"

Ginny glanced at her and raised an eyebrow. "You should talk." She fiddled with the radio, picking another station. "I hate this song."

"Don't change the subject, you little Ukrainian skank."

"Hello, pot," Ginny said with a smirk.

Cassie shrugged. "True enough, I suppose. Of course, I'm not a good girl, like you."

"You know, Darryl wants to work for Rupert. He wants to become a volunteer."

"Not much of a career as a volunteer firefighter in a town that rarely has any fires."

"I didn't say he *only* wants to do that."

"Hey," said Cassie as she glanced out the passenger window. "Who am I to make fun of other people's life choices?"

The silence in the cab was long and pronounced, impossible to ignore. Up ahead, Cassie saw the huge gray pillars of the Peace River Suspension Bridge and heard the rushing waters. The road narrowed as they drove across the bridge. On the opposite bank, the ground rose in a series of thickly forested hills. To their right, less than a kilometer away, sat the Peace Canyon Dam. On either side of the dam, the banks rose up—brown, rocky, and steep. A waterfall, only ten feet wide, poured out of one of the banks, cascading into the river below. Ginny's father worked at the dam, and so had Cassie's.

"You going back to Vancouver?" Ginny asked, finally breaking the silence.

The dam and the river disappeared behind them, swallowed by woodland. "I don't think I can. The university was pretty mad at me."

"You really break a beer bottle against some dude's head?"

"Somebody had to. Nobody else was going to stop him."

"Why?"

Cassie shrugged. "Probably too frightened to get involved. Dude was scary looking. Tattoos, muscles, big gut."

"And?"

"And when I told him to put my friend down, he called me a cunt and told me to mind my own business."

"And?"

Cassie raised her eyebrows. "And *cunt* is a really mean thing to call somebody, you know. Hurt my feelings."

Ginny snorted.

"So, I took my beer bottle and broke it against his head. He fell and dropped my friend. There was a little blood. Next thing I know, the cops show up and put *me* in handcuffs. Hardly seems fair."

"That's some messed-up shit." Ginny shook her head. "They should have given you a medal."

"Well... there might have been more than just a little blood. Maybe a *lot*. Dude needed something like ten stitches. With luck, the next girl will think twice before accepting a beer from Scarface."

"Your sister went apeshit, didn't she?"

"It hasn't been fun."

The two girls were silent. The only sound was the radio.

"What now? You don't belong here. Not in Hudson's Hope. It's just not you. It's never been you. This place is just... it's just too..."

"I know. But maybe *something*—maybe fate—doesn't want me to leave. Maybe I should set my sights lower, expect less."

Ginny's eyebrows scrunched together, and she glared at Cassie. "Maybe you should stop being such a stupid cunt, grow up, and get the hell out of here for good this time."

Cassie barked in laughter and punched Ginny in the shoulder, hard. "Maybe I should. Maybe *I'll* join the army, too, and follow Lee around. What's the term—*camp follower?* That wouldn't be too sad, now, would it?"

"It's always an option, at least the army part. I don't know about following Lee around. I think you should just ball the shit out of him and get over him already."

Cassie grinned. "I *am* over Lee already. He's good people, but him and me? It just wasn't meant to be."

"If you say so." At that moment, Ginny squealed and cranked

up the music. "Ooh! I love this song."

Cassie stared at the forests on either side of the highway as they drove. The truck's crappy speakers vibrated. *Is the army an option?*

"So," said Cassie. "Have you given Darryl a blowjob yet?"

The two of them sent peals of laughter pouring out of the truck's cab.

Chapter 6

"Mistress, wyverns approach."

Maelhrandia glanced up from where she lounged on cushions in her study, an Illthori tome open before her. The boggart was panting, spit drooling from his wide jaws. Clearly, he had been running. Boggarts were good soldiers, but running within her keep was difficult for them with their cloven hooves—especially on stairs.

"A wyvern? Why? There should be no visitors."

"*Dozens* of wyverns, Mistress," panted the guard.

Was her keep under attack? Which of her sisters would dare come against her with wyverns—Horlastia? But a moment later, realization dropped over her like a death shroud. There was only one person who could possibly be arriving unannounced with dozens of wyverns: her mother, the queen of the fae seelie.

She leapt to her feet, ran past the guard, and headed for the stairs to the top of her tower. Never before had her mother deigned to visit Maelhrandia. In truth, her mother rarely left her fortress; she had too many enemies—as well as conniving daughters—each scheming for the crown. But Maelhrandia was no ambitious fool. She restricted her plots to her sisters. Her mother had sat upon the

Bane Throne for hundreds of cycles—her power amongst the fae seelie was legendary. There was no good reason for her mother to come to the Tarloth Delta. Maelhrandia was twelfth in line and, sadly, of no great importance within the fae seelie court. She oversaw a minor holdfast filled with sad, miserable Redcap subjects rotting away in an overgrown jungle.

The spies! Her mother's visit must be because of the intrusion. What had the prisoner confessed to?

Did her mother blame her? The intrusion wasn't Maelhrandia's fault. Besides, she'd discovered their pathetic attempts to spy upon her and had ambushed them, teaching them the price to be paid for spying upon the fae seelie. What more could she have done?

She ran out onto the circular stone summit of her keep's tower, high above her covered garden, her pulse racing. To the east, the sun had yet to fully set, and its dying light burned along the horizon. Squinting, she searched the sky.

There. The boggart guard hadn't been exaggerating: to the west were dozens of wyverns, flying in formation, a magnificent flotilla of the prodigiously expensive Dragonlings. She had been right. This could only be her mother.

One of the wyverns descended toward her tower. It was the largest, most magnificent creature she had ever seen, even larger than Gazekiller. On the massive back of this glorious winged beast sat a diminutive, white-haired rider dressed entirely in crimson-and-black dragon-scale armor, a blood-red cloak flapping in the wind behind her. On her brow, she wore the Spider Crown, set with the multicolored Cavern Stones of the four destroyed dwarven realms. Her mother: Tuatha De Taelinor, Queen of the Fae Seelie Court, Mistress of Spiders, Ruler of all faerum.

The wyvern's giant wings beat the air, creating a storm that whipped Maelhrandia's gown about her legs, threatening to push her back off the edge of her tower. She gripped her gown tightly closed with one hand and dropped to her knee, lowering her head and averting her eyes. The wyvern shrieked, its cry echoing across the sky. Her mother made no attempt to dismount.

"Daughter. I would see the ruins of our past, the intersection of the ley lines, this... invasion point. You will follow and meet me there. Prepare yourself for battle."

Her heart pounded wildly in her chest. Did her mother blame her? "Yes, Mother. At once."

"Do you keep gwyllgi here?"

"Yes, Mother. I breed a modest pack... for hunting."

"Good. Have your servants bring them as well."

"I live to obey, Mother."

The wyvern shrieked once more as its wings pounded at the air, creating another storm that battered Maelhrandia as it rose once more. Only now did Maelhrandia dare raise her eyes. In a moment, her mother was gone, winging south toward the place of power. All the other wyverns—ridden by her mother's legendary stormguards—followed her. Down below, in the covered garden, she felt Gazekiller's rage through the mind-tether and tasted his bloodlust. Her mount barely tolerated wyverns at the best of times and would have perceived the giant wyvern's cries as a direct challenge. She'd have to make sure she maintained an iron grip on the mind-tether; otherwise, Gazekiller might attack and kill her mother's mount. Basilisks and wyverns did not mix well, and Gazekiller—that majestic beast—would be unimpressed by the size of the alpha Dragonling.

Two of her boggart guardsmen waited near the stairs, literally shaking with terror, their huge fish eyes wide. "Prepare my mount," Maelhrandia ordered, brushing past them. "And have the gwyllgi brought to the ruins."

Maelhrandia stared in the direction of the ruins, where the wyverns could just be made out, circling over the jungle. She walked along the edge of a sword right now. The slightest mistake would be her last.

* * *

Gazekiller navigated the thick jungle terrain, not impeded at all by the grasping brush. Upon his back, in a hollow between two of the spikes that ran down his dorsal spine, sat Maelhrandia, leaning forward against his scaled neck, perfectly at ease with his odd eight-legged gait. They rode together so well that both basilisk and fae-seelie rider could have been a single entity. The basilisk wore no saddle; he would never have tolerated such an insult. Gazekiller was no mere wyvern or Heart-stag, no domesticated beast of burden. He was unbridled raw majesty and power, teeth and claw—prideful, the ultimate apex predator. He was controllable only through the mind-tether Maelhrandia had cast at the moment of his hatching—but the power of magic only went so far. Gazekiller would obey her, carry her, and hunt with her, but ever he remained his own master. She never pushed the limits of her bond or forgot that her mount was king in the jungle, master of his own realm—as she was master of the shadows.

She had prepared for battle. Her armor was tanned Bunyip hide, thick enough to turn most blades while still remaining sufficiently supple to allow unbridled movement. Over the priceless armor, she wore her favorite campaign cloak, Transerradina cloth trimmed with the golden fur of a griffin she had slain herself. She had armed herself with her dwarven-forged fighting knife and nothing else. She carried no sword, wore no bow. Such base tools were beneath her. Maelhrandia was a mage-scout, perhaps the finest among her people. She was the knife in the shadows.

She could smell the wyverns before she saw them; so could Gazekiller. The basilisk, angered by the presence of so many of the flying Dragonlings, pawed long deep tracks in the earth, glaring in hatred at them. She drew in magic, reinforcing the mind-tether. If Gazekiller went rogue and attacked her mother's stormguards, Maelhrandia would suffer an agonizing death, princess of the fae seelie or not. Through the brush ahead, she saw the clearing and the ancient stone ruins—as well as a handful of wyverns. Overhead, the majority of her mother's stormguards still remained airborne, flying circles over the jungle on the backs of their wyverns. The boggart guardsmen she had left at the ruins stood back in the trees, far from the dismounted stormguards that protected her mother. At the sight of Gazekiller, they dropped to their knees and placed their heads against the ground.

Maelhrandia dismounted, landing lithely. She placed a small hand against the scaled head of the agitated basilisk, sensing his anger building, his indignation at the presence of these flying creatures in his realm. Gazekiller burned with the need to teach them a lesson—teach them why they should fear the jungle. She smiled, her heart filling with love.

Peace, mighty one, she communicated through the mind-tether. *You shall kill this day, I promise you, but not these Dragonlings. We shall tolerate their presence just this once.*

In reply, Gazekiller snapped his jaws in anger in the direction of the closest wyvern, startling the Dragonling as well as the nearby stormguards, who fingered the hilts of their swords while keeping a wary eye on the basilisk.

She left her mount near the edge of the clearing, opposite the wyverns, and approached the congregation of fae seelie among the stone obelisks. The stormguards eyed her, always ready for a surprise attack on the Queen—as well they should be. Killing one's mother was a time-honored way to ascend to the throne—perhaps the only true way to demonstrate the strength to rule the fae seelie. She ignored the stormguards, walking past them as if they did not exist. Ahead, she saw that several of her sisters, including Horlastia, had accompanied their mother. Even now, they whispered among one another as Maelhrandia approached.

Sitting atop a broken slab of stone, far away from the females, was the only male fae seelie present: Ulfir, the legendary mage-hunter. Taller than most fae seelie and broad in the shoulder, handsome Ulfir wore an expression of complete boredom as he juggled stones in the air, one-handed. But every single fae seelie here knew that, with the exception of her mother, Ulfir was the most dangerous individual present.

Maelhrandia wondered why he had come and what the prisoner had told her mother. Why all this excitement? What was so important that it could impel her mother to actually step away from the safety of her fortress?

Her mother, the greatest mage of the Fae Seelie Empire, knelt alone at the center of the ruins, her head down and her eyes closed. Maelhrandia approached her sisters, nodded briefly at them, and waited. Time passed slowly and without conversation. Maelhrandia, although no sage, understood what was occurring. Their mother was using her remarkable magical powers to divine the ley lines, silently following their trail through the cosmos. The minutes became an hour, and then two. Not one of the fae-seelie princesses spoke a word. Even the jungle around them was silent as if it held its breath in expectation.

When her mother rose again, dusk was at hand, and shadows grew around them. The Queen approached her daughters, who fell to their knees, their heads bowed. She stopped in front of

Maelhrandia and placed a diminutive hand upon her brow. This was perhaps the first time her mother had touched her since giving birth to her scores of cycles before.

"Daughter. You have done well. For uncovering this assault upon us, capturing a prisoner, but most of all, for discovering this place, long forgotten by our people—we are so pleased, so proud."

Warmth flushed through Maelhrandia, but she remained careful to keep the smile from her features. Arrogance could be deadly in the fae-seelie court. Best to be contrite, dutiful, modest, and above all, careful.

"Thank you, Mother. I live to serve."

"As do all my children," her mother said almost in a whisper.

Maelhrandia waited on her knees, still staring at the ground before her. And then, something unprecedented happened: her mother gestured for her to rise, to approach her, and to actually stand beside her. Feeling foolishly happy at this amazing display of affection, Maelhrandia basked in the praise, silently noting—with considerable satisfaction—the look of envy upon Horlastia's otherwise stoic features.

"There are places of power where ley lines intersect," her mother said. "In such places, the forces of magic cascade and grow in intensity. Can you feel this power?"

"Yes, Mother."

The air throbbed with arcane energy, causing the ends of her long white hair to rise and waver. Never had she felt such potency. If she were to fill herself with magic now, she was certain she could blaze like a star—and burn herself out, as well: too much magic would destroy.

"The prisoner you have captured is a manling."

A manling? That wasn't possible. Manlings were only a legend.

"But Mother. That would mean—"

50

"The Old World, daughter, from before the Banishment."

She gasped, forgetting her place and actually looking upon her mother's face. She felt a lightness in her chest, a sense of breathlessness. *Does the Old World really exist?*

Then her mother actually touched Maelhrandia's cheek, letting her fingers caress her daughter's skin. She smiled—she really smiled—and nodded. "In this very place, my child—right here— manlings have pierced the Cosmic Veil and traveled to us from the Old World. I can still sense the rupture they made. Their travel was clumsy, amateurish, but it still resonates through space and time."

"But what does that mean, Mother?"

"It means, daughter, that the manlings have foolishly shown us the path back to the Old World. They have opened a door that they do not have the skills to close behind them, at least not fully."

Despite the heat, a chill ran through Maelhrandia. "But what of the Ancient Foe?"

Her mother shook her head, her smile now replaced by an expression of hatred. "The prisoner knew nothing of the monstrous ones. Ever were the demons few in number, even before the Banishment. Now, they may all be dead. The time may be right for a return."

The jungle around Maelhrandia seemed to spin.

"Unfortunately," her mother continued, "the manling prisoner died after only a short questioning. We know so little of their physiology—only what is in the old texts, and that was insufficient. What I was able to ascertain is that they now believe the masters of the Old World to be themselves, not the Ancient Ones—and certainly not *us*." Her mother shook her head, smiling at the absurdity of the notion. "Yet somehow, these manlings have managed to do what we could not. They have opened the path between faerum and the Old World. What were they thinking, I wonder? Did they really believe they could spy upon us and invade us? Such hubris cannot be permitted to go unchallenged."

No, it can't. Anger for this insult coursed through Maelhrandia, burning within her like a forge. There was nothing that lived that could challenge the fae seelie—certainly not pale, flabby manlings. Even with their strange fire-weapons, when put to the test by Maelhrandia, they had failed and run. As did all lesser species.

Maelhrandia heard the howling of her gwyllgi, arriving from her keep.

"Prepare yourself, mage-scout of the fae-seelie court. The manlings have shown us the path home."

* * *

Maelhrandia stood next to Gazekiller, her hand on the scales of his flank, watching her mother manipulate the invisible ley lines. Her mother's skill as a mage was legendary, but even Maelhrandia was amazed at the sheer amount of magic her mother could hold. The Queen stood in the center of the fae-seelie ruins, linked with a score of other mage-elders who had been flown in from the capital to help her. Together, they had formed a fae circle, lending their magical will to her mother, vastly increasing the power she could wield. For hours, she had sent waves of magical energy coursing into the ley lines, seeking the path back to the Old World.

The Old World. Maelhrandia still found it hard to accept. The fae seelie had been banished from their ancient home so long ago that there were none living who could remember it firsthand. It had become legend, a tale passed down only by scholars through yellowed tomes. But if her mother were to be believed—and Maelhrandia could think of no reason why she would lie—then the manlings now believed themselves masters of a realm that truly belonged to Maelhrandia and her people. The Ancient Foe—not the sad pathetic manlings—had brought about the Banishment. Manlings were, at best, fodder for long life, not rulers of worlds—certainly not invaders of fae-seelie lands. They needed to learn their place. And this lesson would begin with Maelhrandia. The honor was staggering. She would be the first to return to the Old World since the Banishment. But not the last.

She removed a small globe from a pocket within her cloak and gazed into it. The size of her fist and made entirely of Shatkur glass, it throbbed with magical energy. It was black and flawlessly smooth and so beautiful that her breath caught in her throat as she stared at it. Small pulses of gold lightning forked within it, pulsing across its surface. Similar to a Seeing Stone and ten times as valuable, the Shatkur Orb would be key to her mission. With tremendous willpower, she tore her eyes from its flawless radiance and returned it to its pouch. As she did, her fingers brushed the other pouch in her cloak's pocket, the one that writhed and moved on its own. The creature was angry—but grimworms always were.

Overhead, bolts of red lightning lit up the sky, crackling in a near-continuous stream. All wildlife within the Tarloth Delta, sensing the unnatural flows of magic, had become mad with fear, running away as if the jungle were burning—and in a sense, it was. The wyverns had become so agitated they had to be grounded, bound, and blindfolded back at her keep, else they would have taken to the air and fled. Her hunting gwyllgi—poor simple creatures, now crazed with fear—were held in place with magical bonds of air. Five of the beasts stood like statues on the edge of the clearing, their eyes mad with terror but unable to flee.

Only Gazekiller had the courage to remain in place. Only the magnificent basilisk, king among his kind. Gazekiller wished to act—to kill and rend. *Soon, mighty one, soon.*

Her pulse raced, her mouth was dry, and all her senses seemed heightened. *Very soon.*

Horlastia looked from their mother to Maelhrandia, glaring at her, clearly hating her for the honor their mother had bestowed upon her. Maelhrandia smiled. Her mother's instructions had been clear, and she understood exactly what was needed. This mission was delicate. It called for a mage-scout, someone with the skill to remain hidden, not a clumsy mage-warden, blundering about stupidly with her sword. This was *her* time, her moment. And when she succeeded, her standing in the seelie court—and perhaps even her place in the royal succession—was going to grow considerably.

Beside her, Gazekiller raised his mighty horned head and brayed in irritation and anger. And then it happened: her mother and the linked mage-elders opened a Rift-Ring.

One moment, nothing. Then a ring of fire, blazing like a star, grew from the cosmic nether in the center of the ancient ruins where the ley lines intersected. Maelhrandia shielded her eyes, and Gazekiller shrieked in rage. The Rift-Ring pulsed and grew again, now widening to at least a dozen paces across. Through it, she saw a strange alien landscape, a forest filled with trees the likes of which she had never seen.

The Old World!

Her mother turned, her normally stoic features now showing the strain of such tremendous effort.

"Now, daughter, now!"

Maelhrandia cast magic into the consciousness of the five hunting gwyllgi at the same time as she released the bonds of air that held them in place. The hounds bounded forward, compelled by Maelhrandia—straight into the Rift-Ring and the Old World. The moment they crossed through, she lost control over them, the magic severed. No matter. On their own, the gwyllgi would do what gwyllgi did best: kill.

Maelhrandia leapt up onto Gazekiller's back and gripped one of his dorsal spines with both hands. The landscape through the Rift-Ring changed. Now, she looked out upon a hilltop devoid of trees, high above the surrounding terrain.

Now, mighty one. Now!

There was no need for her to compel the basilisk to move. Gazekiller did not hesitate to follow where mere gwyllgi had already gone. The basilisk rushed forward, straight into the Rift-Ring.

And Maelhrandia, anticipation rushing through her, rode to glory.

Chapter 7

Cassie and Ginny followed Highway 29 as it skirted Moberly Lake. Near the southern shore of the lake, they pulled off the highway and onto a small gravel road. The road was bumpy, but they were only on it for a few kilometers before arriving at Moberly Lake Provincial Park. Ginny stopped the truck in a large gravel parking lot, already filling up with other vehicles. Dense stands of white spruce, aspen, and poplar trees grew all around them.

Moberly Park was as remote and secluded as one could get: the closest town was Chetwynd, about twenty-five kilometers to the south, far enough away for Cassie and her friends to let loose. As long as things didn't get too wild, the park officials generally left them alone. Drinking was tolerated if people were discreet and didn't bother the other campers. Sometimes, the boys would get a little stupid and there might be a fight, but usually, these parties were pretty tame. There wasn't much chance Cassie would have to break a beer bottle over anyone's head here.

Cassie and Ginny climbed out of the truck, and Cassie stretched her arms over her head. To the west, the Rocky Mountains rose above the tree line. To the east lay the Peace Plateau. Moberly Lake filled a broad shallow valley between the foothills of the mountains and the plateau—a perfect camping area. A wonderful breeze blew in off the surface of the lake, caressing her skin. A loon cried out, its call echoing across the park, and Cassie smiled, finding herself relaxing for the first time since coming home. Maybe everything would be all right after all.

Ginny walked around to the bed of the truck and, reaching over the tailgate, pulled out two folding canvas chairs and a small cooler with wine spritzers. Neither woman planned on getting drunk. Ginny was too responsible to drink and drive, and Alice would go apeshit if Cassie got wasted after everything that had happened in Vancouver.

Cassie took the cooler while Ginny lugged the chairs and a backpack with their bathing suits and towels. Feeling pretty good, Cassie followed Ginny into the park.

Cassie walked right into her friend, who had stopped abruptly.

"Holy shit," Ginny said, a tremor of fear in her voice.

Cassie followed Ginny's gaze. Her breath caught in her throat when she saw the moose standing in the trees, not fifteen feet away. She froze, her pulse throbbing in her throat. Any wild animal was dangerous, but moose were particularly frightening because of their size, and this one was no exception: clearly a bull, it had to be close to seven feet high at the shoulders. Its long legs were thin and spindly, but its upper body was massive, well over a thousand pounds of muscle. Its antlers were still covered with spring velvet. In the summer, those antlers would be wide and majestic; now, they looked small on that giant head—a head that was fixed in place, eyes staring at the two women.

"Cassie," Ginny whispered, her voice cracking.

"Don't move, baby," Cassie said.

The moose lowered its head, and Cassie could see the shiny brown hackles rising on its back.

Oh, God; it's going to charge.

She tensed, preparing to step in front of Ginny, when another vehicle pulled into the parking lot, its tires crunching loudly on the pebbles, music blaring from its cab. The moose stared in the direction of the noise. It glanced back at the two women and then turned and trotted off into the trees, disappearing within moments.

Cassie sighed in relief, and Ginny hugged her. That had been weird, really weird. Usually moose avoided people. Why had this one been so aggressive?

She heard a car door slam, and when she glanced over to see who had just arrived, her heart seemed to skip a beat. Lee Costner, standing beside his truck, froze when he saw Cassie. Then he smiled and waved. "Hey." He ambled over. "I heard you were back."

Wow, he looks good.

Eric Towler, one of Lee's buddies, pulled a case of Molson beer from the truck bed and carried it toward them.

"Holy crap," blurted Ginny. "Did you just see that?"

Lee, staring at Cassie, didn't answer.

Eric staggered up next to them and lowered the beer to the ground. "See what?"

"How you been?" Cassie said to Lee, her heart still beating too fast.

"The giant freaking moose." Ginny turned and pointed into the woods.

"What?" said Eric, the disbelief clear in his voice as he stared past Ginny.

"I'm not kidding." Ginny grabbed Eric's shoulder and forcefully turned him in the direction the moose had disappeared. "It ran away when you drove up."

"I was going to call." Lee ran his fingers through his short brown hair, looking sheepish as if he had done something wrong.

"I… uh. I wasn't sure if it was cool."

"It's cool," said Cassie. "I was going to call you, too, but… well, you know how it is with my sister."

Lee smiled, exposing his perfect white teeth. "So, how long you gonna be—"

"Are you freaking kidding me?" Ginny put herself between Cassie and Lee, glaring at the young man. "Have you heard nothing I just said?"

"What?" asked Lee as if seeing the young woman for the first time.

Ginny sighed, picked the cooler up, and shoved it into his arms. "Oh, for God's sake. Never mind."

* * *

Elizabeth pulled a textbook off the shelf in the campus library and thumbed through its table of contents. It wasn't the book she was looking for, so she growled to herself and slipped it back. Moving over to the next shelf, she scanned the titles on the spines of the textbooks. *Aha! There it is.*

She snatched up the economics book and added it to the growing pile on the cart she pulled along beside her. Only one more book to find, and then she could start going through all of them, performing her own form of triage, deciding which ones to tackle first as she organized her thesis. Dragging the cart to another long row of bookshelves, she noted that—other than the single librarian, who kept casting annoyed looks at Elizabeth—she was the only person in here. Through the large windows along one wall of the library, she saw that it was already beginning to get darker outside. Any minute now, the librarian would stop being polite and remind her it was time to close up. Elizabeth picked up the pace, hurrying to find her last book.

* * *

Duncan Walton Hocking closed the back door of the fast-food restaurant behind him, slid between two garbage dumpsters, and lit a cigarette. His hairnet itched, as it always did, but if he pulled it off while on break and forgot to put it back on when he went back in, as he had a habit of doing, Clarence would jump all over his shit again and lecture him about health standards.

What a bat hole!

Duncan inhaled deeply, relishing the hit of nicotine. He rammed his cold fingers into his jean pockets as he watched the sunset over the trees. The rear of the A&W always reeked of garbage, grease, and piss, but he was used to it after four years. He could hear the traffic on the street out front as the city started to come alive. He sighed, knowing that once he got off his shift, in an hour, he'd spend another Saturday night alone playing video games. His drunken father would stagger by his room, sneer at Duncan, and berate him for not having any real friends. *Fuck him!* Duncan had plenty of real friends; they were all just virtual.

Trailing his fingers over his long, drooping mustache, he sighed. The rear door of the A&W slammed open. Chris, hugely obese and suffering from a nightmare case of acne, stuck his head out, quickly looking in both directions. When he saw Duncan, he grinned then glanced over his shoulder, no doubt making sure no one was watching.

Duncan snorted. *Like anyone gives a shit.*

When he was sure the coast was clear, Chris ambled over to Duncan, pulling crumpled twenties from his jeans pocket. "We cool, man?"

Duncan nodded. "We cool."

Chris thrust the money at Duncan, his eyes darting all around them as if he expected a major drug bust. Duncan forced himself not to roll his eyes as he took the money, counted it, and then pulled out a small plastic baggy containing more crumpled money and a half dozen small pills. He pulled four pills out and handed them to Chris. Chris's large fingers were sweaty as he grasped at them, hid them in his shirt pocket, and immediately spun about and headed for the door.

Duncan took another drag and exhaled. "Have fun tonight." The door slammed shut behind Chris. "I know I will."

* * *

As Cassie and her friends approached the campsite, they heard music blaring. A score of their friends were already there, sitting at the wooden picnic table, drinking beer. A couple of guys were on their knees in front of the stone-ringed fire pit, blowing into the fire, and the aroma of wood smoke cut through the air. Several brightly colored tents were set up around the site for those planning on spending the night. White spruce, aspen, and poplar trees surrounded the campsite, intermingled with wild sarsaparilla and rose bushes. A stone's throw away, Cassie could see the still, smooth surface of Moberly Lake through the trees.

Cassie picked up the pace and rushed forward to greet her friends. Ginny handed her a wine spritzer, and she popped it open as she chatted with her friends, telling them about Vancouver and UBC.

Squirrels darted about the roots of the trees and bushes, surprising her with their boldness. A loon cried out once again, its distinctive call echoing across the lake. Cassie sat on the edge of the picnic table and sighed contentedly. *Being back home isn't all bad.*

She jumped when something touched her leg. Looking down, she saw a small, adorable pug, obviously a puppy, rubbing itself against her. Squatting down beside it, she began to rub its neck and belly and make cooing noises. The excited pug peed on her hand.

"Sorry, sorry," said a young red-haired man with glasses as he ran up to pull the puppy away.

"It's okay." Cassie stood back up, shaking her hand then rubbing it against her jeans. "Nice to see you again, Everett. Who's that?"

"This," he said, now holding the pug in his arms, "is Caspar. And he doesn't normally go around peeing on pretty girls. He's been acting all screwy for hours. Something has him all worked up."

"Maybe it's all the squirrels," said Cassie.

"Maybe," he said as he walked away, still holding the delinquent Caspar in his arms.

As the sun began to go down, more of their friends arrived, and soon a large group had gathered, laughing and horsing around. She didn't know why, but she felt uneasy. She knew she totally shouldn't; she was surrounded by friends. Not far away, Ginny was telling everyone about the moose, exaggerating how close it had been—although, to be fair, it had been pretty close. Someone passed around a joint, but Cassie shook her head when it was offered to her. A song she liked was playing on the stereo, and she rocked in time to it, feeling no need to get drunk or stoned.

Out of the corner of her eye, she caught Lee watching her. He looked away. She saw with some irritation that he was talking to that redheaded skank, Vicky Dodds. True to form, Vicky was standing way too close to Lee. There had always been an underlying tension between them, caused by Vicky's all-too-obvious crush on Lee. It was clear she was still hot for him. She kept finding excuses to touch his arm and tittered at everything he said. Vicky would no doubt be more than happy to pull her skirt up right there and ball the shit out of Lee. *What a troll.*

At that moment, Vicky locked glances with Cassie and smiled, her lips parting as she moved in even closer and placed her hand on Lee's chest, once again giggling at something he had said.

"You wanna break a beer bottle against *her* head?" Ginny plopped down on the picnic table next to Cassie.

Cassie snorted, smiling. "It's a thought."

"You know," said Ginny, pausing for a moment as she looked from Lee to Vicky. "He's not into her. He's still hung up on you. There's still smoke there."

"Whatever smoke was there is gone now. And he's going away. He deserves to escape from this place."

"You know, not everyone feels that way about Hudson's Hope. Some of us love it here."

Cassie reached an arm around Ginny's shoulders and pulled her in close. "Sorry, girlfriend. I didn't mean anything. I'm just bummed about Vancouver."

"Shit happens. But it's not the end of the world. You can still get away if you want."

"I don't know. It's all so hard now. Since..." Cassie's voice trailed off, and this time it was Ginny who hugged her, giving her a big kiss on the cheek.

"I know, baby, I know. They love you, *wherever* they are now. They still love you, and they're watching over you, especially your mom."

Cassie had to look away before she lost all control. When she felt she could speak again, she said, "What do I do now?"

"Go to another college. Hell, go to Northern Lights. Get a degree and move on. You know you want to."

Cassie sighed and shook her head. "It wasn't just the fight. I was failing all my courses as well." Cassie stared at the bottle she was holding between her knees. "Turns out I can't really do anything right."

Ginny's eyes narrowed, and she watched Cassie's face for several moments before speaking again. "Honey, how hard were you really trying? You were getting all A's before your parents—"

"That's not it! University is harder—too hard."

"I don't want to fight with you. I love you. But someday soon you're going to have to start coping with what happened and stop blaming yourself. If you don't—"

"I have to go to the bathroom." Cassie jumped up and stormed away.

Ginny was trying to help, and she really did mean well, but she was wrong. She was so wrong. Cassie wiped her eyes with the back of her hand as she made her way to the park washroom, a log cabin.

Cassie *had* killed her parents. Everybody knew that, even if they didn't come out and say it. She could see the judgment in their eyes, condemning her.

Okay, maybe she had partied way too much in Vancouver, and maybe she had missed a lot of her classes out of sheer lethargy. But what was the point in even trying if she was just going to fail anyway—the way she had failed her parents?

Overhead, dark clouds gathered in the dwindling light. A storm was brewing. There wasn't supposed to be a storm.

* * *

As the night progressed, the dark clouds continued to gather over Moberly Lake, roiling and churning. On occasion, spectacular bolts of red lightning lit up the sky, and thunder boomed in the distance. But there was no rain.

Despite the cold—and the threat of lightning—Cassie and

most of the others put on their bathing suits and ran screaming into the ice-cold waters of Moberly Lake, laughing and splashing one another. Hundreds of years ago, Deane-za tribesmen had believed this lake to be bottomless and home to an ancient creature that would occasionally come to the surface. For countless generations, locals believed the lake held sea monsters—Fort St. John's very own Loch Ness. Every now and then, someone would claim to have seen one of the creatures.

Cassie had put her earlier somber thoughts behind her and now tried to enjoy herself. Ginny and her new boyfriend, Darryl, were splashing in the water nearby with Ginny sitting on his shoulders. Lee, standing only about ten feet away, met Cassie's eye and raised an eyebrow as if to ask her if she wanted to meet their challenge. Cassie was about to oblige him when Vicky splashed through the water behind Lee and jumped onto his shoulders. Just for a moment, Cassie saw annoyance flit across Lee's face, but he turned and pushed through the water toward Ginny and Darryl. A battle ensued as Ginny and Vicky tried to pull each other off. Cassie smirked when Vicky fell backward into the water.

Afterwards, they left the beach, wrapped towels around themselves, and jostled for position around the blazing campfire. Goose bumps pricked Cassie's skin, and she rubbed her upper arms, wondering again what had possessed her to go swimming in May.

"Would you look at that," Darryl said, pointing into the sky.

The northern lights were ablaze that evening, more powerful and vibrant than Cassie had ever seen them. They shimmered and shifted in the most spectacular curtains of green, red, and purple.

"I have never, *not ever*, seen them that clearly before," Darryl said.

Cassie had to agree. Growing up in the North, they had all

grown accustomed to seeing the northern lights, but tonight was something special indeed. Caspar began barking—short little high-pitched bursts—as he ran in circles in front of the picnic table. At first, everyone laughed at his antics, but then Caspar paused, looked once at his master, and darted off into the trees as if he were being chased. Everett yelled at the dog to come back and stood up to chase after him.

And then, as if by magic, a hush descended over everyone. Standing not twenty feet away was a grizzly bear. Vicky stood frozen between the bear and the others. She moaned in terror, swaying in place, her hands opening and closing. Someone turned off the radio. Everyone else seemed to lump closer together. Cassie's heart pounded against her chest. Like moose, bears usually didn't come this close to people. Lightning flashed, illuminating the world in a brilliant shade of red.

Someone warned everyone to be still.

No shit.

As if energized by the lightning, the bear began moving, approaching them on all fours and then stopping again about ten feet from Vicky.

"Don't move, Vicky," Lee said softly.

Out of the corner of her eye, Cassie saw Lee sliding up beside her. The bear must have also seen him because it suddenly raised its snout, exposing its teeth, and growled in warning. Lee froze.

The bear rose up on its hind legs, towering over Vicky. It stood over ten feet tall, easily a thousand pounds of raw power. Its reddish-blond fur was silver tipped at the ends and matted with twigs and dirt. The prominent hump over its shoulders clearly identified it as a grizzly and not its cousin, the smaller brown bear. Its face was shaped like a dish, its head enormous. The long curved claws on the ends of its massive paws could tear bark from trees—

or skin from bones. Given the time of year, this bear must have just woken up from hibernation.

It would be hungry.

"Vicky, stand taller," said Lee. "Raise your hands over your head."

Vicky whimpered but tentatively did as Lee said.

No. That's wrong. Cassie knew that doing that, trying to make herself appear larger, would only piss off a grizzly. These monsters weren't intimidated that easily. Lee, meaning well, was going to get Vicky killed. Cassie took a step forward. "Vicky, listen carefully. Don't do that."

Lee said, "But—"

"Lee, baby, shut it," said Cassie without taking her eyes off Vicky and the bear. "Vicky, get down—very, very slowly—and curl up into a ball."

Vicky trembled, like a leaf. "Somebody help me, please. I'm so scared."

"Vicky, honey, just get down and close your eyes," said Cassie. "I promise you everything will be fine." She was lying, and she knew it. Everything was *not* going to be fine. She exhaled and took another step closer. "Whatever you do, don't look into its eyes, it'll think you're challenging it. In fact, everyone, that goes for you all. Look down at the ground. Do it now!"

Red lightning flashed once again, and when the thunder boomed, Cassie almost jumped out of her skin. The grizzly dropped back onto all fours.

"Vicky," Cassie said, keeping her voice low but willing steel into it. "Get down right goddamned now!"

For a moment, Cassie was afraid Vicky was too terrified to move, but then, oh so slowly, the other girl dropped down onto her hands and knees and curled up into a sobbing ball. The grizzly stared at her then puffed out an exhalation of cold vapor before stepping closer. It was now right beside her. It sniffed at the girl's red hair, and Vicky whimpered in terror, her eyes tightly shut.

"Vicky, honey," said Cassie softly. "Everything will be all right, I promise." She risked a quick glance behind her, at the others. "Does anybody have bear spray?"

"I do," Everett said, his voice breaking. "But it's in the tent, in my backpack."

"Which tent?" asked Cassie.

"The red one."

The grizzly continued to sniff at Vicky's hair, occasionally looking up at the young people near the fire, who still averted their gaze.

"Go away," whispered Cassie. "There's nothing to be frightened of here—just go away."

It might go away, she knew. Sometimes, if they didn't feel threatened, bears would just sniff about for a bit and then move off to forage elsewhere. Maybe, just maybe, the animal was only curious. When the grizzly licked Vicky's hair and face, Cassie knew it wasn't going away, wasn't curious. It was going to eat her.

Bizarrely, knowing the worst was about to happen was liberating. Cassie surprised herself when she stepped forward and walked past both Vicky and the grizzly, coming within feet of them. She kept walking, aware now that the grizzly had stopped licking Vicky's face and was watching her instead. It growled, but she just kept going toward Everett's tent. At any moment, she expected the bear to rush her, knock her down, and bite into the back of her neck.

At the tent's entrance, she bent down and crawled into its open interior, her back exposed. Her heartbeat pounded in her ears like a drum as she grabbed at Everett's backpack and started patting it down, feeling for the container of bear spray. If it were hidden away at the very bottom, underneath his underwear and socks, she was probably going to die before she ever found it. But it wasn't. It was in one of the side pockets.

She yanked the pocket open and pulled the can free. Backing up on all fours, she came back out of the tent and turned toward the animal. The grizzly was still watching her, its head swinging back and forth, saliva dripping from its muzzle.

Cassie stood up and fumbled for the release tab. The container was about the size of a water bottle, all black with a bright-yellow sticker wrapped around it. She didn't need to read the instructions. She had carried a can of bear spray every summer that she had worked for the forestry service. Still keeping her gaze averted, she yanked the safety tab free and shook the can vigorously. Not liking the sudden movement, the bear growled and stepped away from Vicky, now approaching Cassie. Its ears sloped back dangerously. The hair rose on its back and neck, standing up like needles.

It was going to charge.

"Cassie," Lee called out, stepping closer.

"Don't move," said Cassie.

Lightning flashed, but now it was like nothing she had ever seen before, coming so fast it resembled a strobe light, again and again and again, turning the world red.

The grizzly glanced back at Lee, pawed the ground once, and then charged.

One chance. All she was going to get was one chance. She sprayed the air in front of and above the charging bear, but it was so close already she didn't know whether the pepper spray would even have time to register in the creature's senses before it reached her. The bear ran right through the spray without slowing. It had been too close after all.

And then *something* flowed into her—filling her instantly with the most amazing feeling. Almost indescribable, the energy that rushed through her was like nothing she had ever experienced before yet somehow completely natural at the same time, as though it should have always been a part of her. She was aware of an odd metallic taste in the back of her throat.

Time slowed down, becoming a series of snapshots.

The bear charged, almost upon her, its eyes feral, primal, and unstoppable.

Lee, poor stupid Lee, was running after it as though he was going to tackle it.

The others all stood frozen around the blazing bonfire, the flames two feet high.

No! She raised her hands toward the bear, and the flames from the bonfire roared up as though a gasoline bomb had just gone off within its coals. The others fell away as the flames jetted out, twisting and turning, wrapping around the grizzly.

The ground in front of her exploded, and she flew back through the air, unable to breathe. Her world was all white light as though she was staring at the sun. And then it went dark.

* * *

Both Elizabeth and the librarian had run to the window as the lightning struck in the wilderness, turning the sky red again and again in a nonstop display of God's majesty. Her mouth open, Elizabeth turned in wonder to the woman beside her—and then something flowed into her, something wonderful, filling her with a brilliant glow.

Oh, God—it's the Rapture! Elizabeth dropped.

* * *

Duncan yanked the fries from the pressure cooker, the oil splattering on his hand. "Jesus, crap, shit, fuck!" He danced about, rubbing his hand.

Chris, the fat bastard, was laughing at him, his face all shiny with sweat.

Duncan gave him a dirty look. "It isn't—"

At that moment, Duncan felt the greatest high he'd ever had in his short life. It was so amazing—it felt as though he was sent to a world that he had never known could even exist, a world of lights and colors all popping in his head like carbonated soda.

He was only vaguely aware of Chris standing over him, staring down at him. Then the lights and colors took him away.

* * *

On a hilltop clearing, surrounded by dense forest, red forks of lightning sizzled and flared, hitting the ground again and again. Nearby aspen trees erupted in flames, jumping from one tree to another and spreading outward in a ring. Then, from out of nothing, a glowing red circle of translucent energy appeared in the air above the smoking, charred surface of the hilltop. The circle of fire throbbed and grew, spreading to the size of a small house. Air blew outward from the fiery sphere with a tremendous hissing as a giant form hurtled out of its center.

Maelhrandia and Gazekiller landed on the hilltop. The basilisk, more than thirty feet long from his head to the end of his spiked tail, reared up on his back legs. His horned head whipped back and forth as he searched for threats. Sitting on his back, Maelhrandia stroked his scaly hide, her gaze also sweeping the terrain.

Nothing. Where were the gwyllgi? They had gone through first.

She had half expected to need to fight the moment she arrived, but she was alone. Her mother must have sent the gwyllgi to a different location as a distraction. This was the Old World, though; she was sure of that. She had studied the ancient texts describing their ancient home. This looked... right. Behind her, the Rift-Ring collapsed back in upon itself, disappearing in a moment. Maelhrandia dropped from her mount and gasped. *So cold!*

Goose bumps pebbled her arms beneath her armor, which was even now changing color, becoming lighter. Now, terror gripped her. There was so little magic in the air.

She opened herself to the magic, feeling the instant comfort of it coursing through her body. There was magic here, just not as much as she was used to. She felt giddy with relief. Without magic, she would be defenseless.

Despite their fire-weapons, none of the manling spies had been mages. It seemed impossible that they would send a war party to spy upon the fae seelie and yet not bring a mage with them. Perhaps they had no gift for magic. Some creatures were entirely mundane.

The mundane ones are the easiest to drain.

Gazekiller hissed, steam hurtling from his nostrils, as his blue eyes scanned the trees in the forest below the hilltop. She sensed the basilisk's unease; he wanted to move on, to leave this exposed hilltop and hide amongst the trees. Filling herself with what little magic there was, she bent the light around her, casting Shadow-Soul, disappearing from sight atop her mount. Gazekiller trotted down the still-smoking hilltop and into the dense cover of trees. Gazekiller was fast and far more agile than a creature his size had any right to be. Maelhrandia leaned over his back as they ran through the forest.

Her nose wrinkled in distaste. Something stank—a foul, sulfur-like odor similar to a dwarven forge. She directed Gazekiller in the direction of the stench. After some minutes, she heard a bizarre sound, one she had never heard before: a dull thrumming. Was she moving too quickly, too recklessly? Her sisters would rejoice if she were to die within moments of beginning her mission. Her eyes scanned the alien trees, so different from the jungles of her holdfast.

The basilisk burst out of the woods and onto a road—but what a road! Far wider than any she had ever seen before, this one was constructed from stone but seemingly all of one piece and as black as the Spider Mother's heart. Her head whipped back and forth. The road ran as far as she could see in either direction. *This is the source of the stench.*

Then, behind her, she saw bright lights and heard an ear-piercing screech of torment coming from the same direction. With reflexes superior to that of a manticore, she leapt from the back of Gazekiller and away, hitting the ground in a roll and coming upright again in the trees along the side of the road. The basilisk, nowhere near as agile, spun about on his eight legs and hissed in challenge.

About twenty paces away from her mount was the most wondrous thing: a steel carriage, one with no mounts pulling it. It was bright yellow with four black wheels that still smoked from the friction of its sudden stop. The brightest lights she had ever seen, glowing eyes almost blinding in their intensity, lit up the carriage. Gazekiller shrieked in rage. At the front of the carriage was a single piece of curved glass, and Maelhrandia saw a female manling sitting within the carriage behind the glass. The eyes of the female were wide with terror and disbelief.

Now, she ordered.

Gazekiller lowered his head and glared at the female, and then the glow in his blue eyes pulsed with arcane energy, becoming bright. The female's mouth opened in horror and then stayed open. Her skin hardened and cracked.

Maelhrandia always wondered if a basilisk's victims could still be alive at this point. Could they see the fate that was about to befall them although helpless to do anything to stop it?

No matter. That was a question for sages, not mage-scouts.

Gazekiller's head darted forward. In a moment, his powerful jaws ripped into the steel carriage, tearing it open and exposing the petrified female. A moment later, his teeth ripped into her torso, biting it completely in half. Blood splattered the interior of the carriage as it dripped off Gazekiller's mouth. The war had begun.

Chapter 8

Once again, as she had so often before, Cassie dreamed of that night.

Rain had pelted the windshield of her parents' Honda Civic, obscuring the dark highway that climbed through the forested cliffs of the Peace River Valley. Her father had set the wipers to the fastest setting, but they barely kept up with the constant deluge of rain. Cassie sat in the back seat, still a little drunk, still angry about how the night had turned out. She didn't like calling her parents for help, but when she did, they were supposed to just help, not beat her up over having needed them. *This is bullshit,* she thought. *Maybe I should have just taken my chances with Allister.* No, she knew she couldn't have done that. She was tipsy, but Allister was hammered.

"It's not that we're angry, Cassie." The tone in her father's voice underscored the fact that he *was* angry. "It's just that… well, you're too smart to be pulling a stunt like this. And you dragged Ginny into it as well."

"Sure, you're not angry." Cassie looked out the rain-covered passenger window of the car although she couldn't see anything but dark trees and the never-ending deluge.

"Don't, young lady. Just don't," her father said.

Her mother placed a hand on his arm. "We've been telling her for years to call us in an emergency. That's what she did. No guilt, remember?"

"I know but—"

"We told her to call us."

"I know. It's just…"

"It's two a.m., and you're not in bed. How awful for you," Cassie said.

"Cassie. You're not helping," said her mother with exasperation. She turned in her seat and faced Cassie. "It's hard for us, okay? We're not used to getting frantic phone calls waking us up, asking us to come and get you from some bar in Fort St. John. Especially when you're supposed to be at Ginny's. You lied to us."

Cassie looked away. "I just wanted to have some fun… for once in my life."

"Oh, please," said her father, shaking his head. "Your life is so hard, isn't it, Cassie? You have things so rough, a roof over your head, plenty of food and activities, friends, clean air, and beautiful forests."

"You really think I want to spend all my time in the middle of nowhere? Butthole, British Columbia? With nothing to do? Nothing to see?" Cassie leaned forward against her seat belt. "I'm sorry, all right? I didn't ask for those guys to start causing trouble. Allister said he was okay to drive, and he wasn't going to drink very much. But then he starts doing shooters, and the next thing I know, he's wasted and picking fights."

"And that's another thing," said her father. "What the hell are you doing with *him*? Where's Lee? He'd never pull a stunt like this."

"Like you care," said Cassie.

"Honey," said her mother, "not tonight, okay?"

Her father sighed. "Let's have this discussion after some sleep. Maybe we'll all be less irritable."

"Whatever," said Cassie.

An uncomfortable silence settled over them, broken only by the sheets of rain gusting against the windshield. This was a crappy night to be out on the highway, but Cassie wasn't that concerned. Her father knew every inch of this route, had driven it hundreds of times in the past. After all, it was the only way to get to the civilization of Fort St. John.

"Oh, my," said her mother. "Have you ever seen this much rain?"

"It'll blow over," answered her father. "Besides, we're not that far from—"

"What's that noise?" her mother asked.

Cassie looked out her window, staring into the mass of trees and steeply rising terrain on their right. On their left, the road cut off abruptly into a deep embankment. She frowned, now clearly hearing what her mother had. Her father turned off the radio. There was definitely a rumbling sound outside, gaining quickly in intensity.

"Stop the car," said her mother. "Something's wrong."

"I don't—"

"Stop the car!"

Her father began to slow the vehicle down. There were no other cars on the twisting mountain road and hadn't been for at least the last fifteen minutes. They pretty much had the road to themselves. Cassie cracked her window open to listen better. Instantly, her face was pelted with cold wind and raindrops. Now, she could hear loud cracking noises interspersed with the growing rumbling. Terror spiked through her, and she jabbed at the window's button as if the glass could protect her.

The cracking noises were trees above them—snapping and breaking!

"Dad! It's a—"

Cassie's words were lost in the roar of the mudslide. The ground shook as a flowing river of mud, rock, shattered trees, and debris fell upon them. The trunk of a massive tree smashed into the road just in front of them, barely missing the car. A moment later, the slurry of mud did hit their car, sweeping it off the road and down the embankment. Cassie was jerked about, violently thrown against her seat belt. The car flipped, then flipped again, before stopping with a bone-shattering jolt against a tree trunk near the bottom of the ravine. The Honda Civic was almost standing on its hood; only her seat belt kept her from falling forward into the front seat and windshield.

Cassie screamed—and bolted upright in bed, her skin drenched in sweat, her breathing wild. *A nightmare. It was only another nightmare. Goddamn it—when is it ever going to stop?*

And where am I? She was in a spacious, well-lit room with cream-colored walls. Bright sunlight poured through the open curtains of a large window. Through the room's open door, she saw hospital beds. There was another bed in the room with a vaguely familiar-looking young woman with long raven-dark hair sitting up in it. Beautiful, in an entirely too wholesome sort of way, she looked to be about the same age as Cassie. On her lap, she held a hardcover Bible.

A Bible?

Their eyes met, and once again, Cassie felt certain she knew her from somewhere. But then memories of the campsite and the bear attack rushed back upon her, overwhelming all other thoughts. *A hospital! Oh my God! Have I been mauled?*

Her hands flew to her face. The skin felt normal—clammy and sweaty, maybe, but intact. She ripped away the bedsheets, exposing both legs, feeling immense relief. She didn't seem to be hurt, at least as far as she could tell, but something felt... *different*. It was hard to describe the feeling, but it was as though something that had been missing all her life was now there, filling her. She felt... *energized*, like a battery. It was the most amazing feeling.

I have to be stoned. They must have me on something.

"Hey, you're awake finally," the young woman said. "I'm Elizabeth. Your family is here. Your sister just stepped out."

Cassie stared at her in confusion. "What?"

"Everyone was wondering when you'd wake up. *If* you'd wake up. Thank the Lord."

What was she talking about?

The dark-haired woman—Elizabeth—picked up what looked like a small television remote control attached to a long cord. There was a prominent red button on the end of the device, and she pushed it with her thumb.

"Your sister's been here pretty much since I've been here, off and on."

"What happened to me? There was a bear, but... I don't think I'm hurt. Am I okay?"

"Yeah, I guess. A bear? Really?"

Cassie looked about, bewildered. The panic from her dream began to subside, but now a new fear built within her. What the hell was going on?

She saw trees outside and cars moving along a busy road. This had to be Fort St. John. A thin, middle-aged redheaded nurse came through the room's doorway and smiled when she saw Cassie sitting up in bed. Bending over to examine Cassie's eyes, she said, "Morning, hon."

"What's going on?"

"Everything's fine, hon." The nurse placed a warm hand against Cassie's cheek. "You're in the hospital in Fort St. John. You've been here for almost three days now."

"Three days?" Cassie's stomach lurched.

There was a cry from the doorway, and Cassie looked over just in time to see Alice rushing toward her. Her sister nearly knocked down the nurse as she leaped onto the bed and embraced Cassie, hugging her so hard she had trouble breathing. Relief rushed through Cassie, and she hugged her sister back.

"How's Vicky? Did the bear hurt anyone?"

"No, baby," her sister gushed, still hugging her. "It ran away. The lightning strike chased it off." Her sister let go of her, pulled back, and held her shoulders as she stared into her face.

"Lightning strike?" Once again, just for a moment, Cassie saw the grizzly's enraged face, the massive teeth and paws. She remembered the fire, twisting and turning on its own as it wrapped about the bear. Had it been lightning? Had a bolt somehow struck the bonfire, throwing the flames? That made no sense. "I'm okay, right? I don't feel any injuries."

"You're fine. But you've been in a coma... or something." Alice's voice broke, and tears appeared in her eyes. "I've been so scared, baby. Most of the others didn't wake up."

Others? Cassie's eyes tightened in confusion. "I don't—"

"You've been chosen," Elizabeth said, her eyes filled with an intensity that could only be born of religion. "It's the Rapture, or maybe just the beginning of the Rapture."

Cassie stared at her in bewilderment. Alice's expression darkened for just a moment as she glanced at the other woman.

"How do you feel, Cassie?" the nurse asked, putting her hand on Cassie's forehead. "Are you in any pain?"

"I feel... different," Cassie mumbled. "Like something's wrong. No, not wrong. New."

Another woman walked through the doorway, this one wearing a doctor's white tunic and a stethoscope around her neck. She was about the same age as Alice and looked to be of Asian descent or maybe native. A small woman, she wore glasses, and her hair was cut short, just above her ears, giving her an elf-like appearance. "Hello, sleepyhead," she said as she shook Cassie's hand. "I'm Dr.Ireland. We've all been waiting to meet you. We thought your sister was going to move in and start living here."

"Doctor," Cassie said, "what the hell's going on? What is this Rapture shit?"

Dr. Ireland's eyebrows rose in surprise, and her smile faltered only for a moment. "Can everyone step back and give Cassie some room, please?"

Wordlessly, the redheaded nurse backed off and exited the room. Alice gave Cassie one last quick squeeze and then moved back away from the bed, clasping her hands in front of her as she stood only feet away, waiting.

Dr. Ireland sat down on the edge of the bed. "Cassie, I need to check your pupils. Is that okay?"

Cassie nodded, and the other woman removed a penlight from her tunic pocket and very softly opened Cassie's eyelid a fraction more before shining the light into her eye. "Here's the thing, Cassie," she said as she moved the penlight back and forth. "You're going to hear about this soon enough anyhow, so you might as well know what we know—and don't know—right away. Three days ago, during a bizarre storm, you and Elizabeth lost consciousness."

"What do you mean? I was attacked by a bear. At least, that's the last thing I remember."

"And that, young lady, is a small miracle just by itself.

Whatever else that storm did, it also scared off that bear. Very lucky for you."

"I'm not following you," Cassie said. "We *both* passed out during the storm?"

"I was in the Campus Library," Elizabeth said. "The Lord was watching over me because I would have been alone otherwise. No one would have seen."

"Seen what? What campus?" Cassie asked.

"At first we thought you had been hit by the lightning bolt that chased off the bear, but that wasn't the case," Dr. Ireland continued. "There would have been burns. There are *always* burns with lightning strikes."

Cassie blinked rapidly, before looking away from the light. It was becoming uncomfortable.

"You both passed out at exactly the same time," Alice blurted.

Cassie turned and stared at her sister. "What?"

Dr. Ireland sat back and lowered her penlight. "Here's where it gets really weird, Cassie. It wasn't just you and Elizabeth."

Cassie ran her fingers through her hair as she looked from face to face, trying to make sense of what the doctor was saying. "I... I don't really... understand."

Dr. Ireland reached out and took both of Cassie's hands in hers and squeezed them until Cassie met her gaze once more. "Listen very carefully, Cassie. I don't want you to stress, but I'm going to tell you the truth as I know it, and there's still a great deal we don't understand yet."

"Doctor." Cassie heard the panic in her own voice. "You're starting to scare the shit out of me."

The doctor nodded and tried to smile reassuringly, but Cassie could see the discomfort in her eyes. "At 20:25 on Saturday night, during a really, *really* strange lightning storm—so strange the provincial weather office still can't describe what happened—you and Elizabeth passed out at, as far as we can tell, the exact same moment."

Cassie's eyebrows bunched together.

"There's more," Alice whispered from behind Dr. Ireland.

"There were other cases within a span of about two hundred kilometers—Grande Prairie, Dawson Creek, just outside of Prince George—other people also passed out. In total, there were seven of you… but there may still be others, especially in the more isolated native communities."

Cassie shook her head. "What?"

"All at the exact same moment," Dr. Ireland said.

"The others didn't wake up again," Elizabeth said. "The Lord took them."

"What?" Cassie's head whipped toward the other woman.

Dr. Ireland raised her hand to motion to Elizabeth to be silent. "This is true. We don't know what happened, but not long after they passed out, the five others slipped into comas and passed away."

"People died?" Cassie whispered.

"It seems the stress of this… *incident*, whatever it was, was too much. They went into cardiac arrest and couldn't be resuscitated. Most of them were elderly, not young like you and Elizabeth. One was a baby."

"Oh my God." Cassie's hand flew to cover her mouth.

"This is why we're *real* happy to see you awake again. That's a great sign. You were the last one."

"You've been chosen," said Elizabeth. "Just like me."

Cassie stared at Elizabeth and then back at Dr. Ireland. "What are you talking about?" She gripped the doctor's wrists suddenly, perhaps too tightly. "All of us just *passed out*, all at the same time?

That's not possible. You know that's not possible."

"We don't know yet what happened," said the doctor. "But clearly *something* has happened."

"Tell her the rest," Elizabeth blurted. "She's been chosen. She deserves to know about all the miracles."

"Will you shut the hell up?" Alice snapped at her. "Mind your own goddamned business."

The young woman looked away but not before mumbling something under her breath about sinners.

"Miracles?" asked Cassie. "What's she talking about?"

"Don't worry about that now," said Dr. Ireland. "We can talk about that later."

"We're gonna figure this out, Cassie," said Alice. "We will. The hospital staff are all working really hard. The government will—"

"The government will do nothing," said Elizabeth. "The End of Days is upon us."

The back of Cassie's neck became hot, and a strange sensation coursed through her. Somehow, it reminded her of the bear attack, the electrical storm. The weirdest thing of all, though, was that she was certain the source of the sensation was Elizabeth. She stared wide-eyed at the other woman. Once again, she felt that odd metallic taste in the back of her throat.

And then the pages of the Bible on Elizabeth's lap began to turn on their own, flipping back and forth as if invisible fingers moved them. Elizabeth's gaze met Cassie's, filled with fierce triumph.

* * *

Colonel Oscar Redford McKnight placed the handset for the secure telephone back in its cradle, removed his reading glasses, and rubbed the bridge of his nose. As a soldier of African American descent, he had overcome more challenges during his long career in US Special Operations Command—SOCOM—than he could easily count, but today was turning out to be a real bitch. He was used to difficulties and the occasional ass chewing, but the conversation he had just had with the Canadian project director in Ottawa had been something special. It made a lie of the myth that Canadians were overly polite. And it wasn't just Ottawa—his own political masters in Washington were already making veiled threats about sending someone else down to take command of Task Force Devil and Operation Rubicon if he didn't get a grip on the recent series of shitshows that his command was turning into. He was only forty-six years old, but at the moment, he felt more like sixty.

What he needed was a vacation or maybe a visit with Louise and the girls. Neither would be a possibility anytime soon. Leaning back in his chair, he absentmindedly ran his thumb over his tie—he was accustomed to combat uniforms, not suits. The only people wearing combat uniforms here were the security forces and the operators despite the fact that many of the two hundred people working at the Site C Dam complex—jokingly referred to by the operators of Task Force Devil as the "Magic Kingdom"—were military. The others, all civilians—engineers, construction workers, and scientists—were employees of the Canadian and US Government, carefully vetted and sworn to secrecy. There were no defense contractors here—no shortcuts on security. Everyone employed within the task force was subject to constant monitoring, impromptu lie-detector testing, and the unspoken promise of government retribution if they stepped an inch out of line. Some secrets had to be kept even at the cost to civil liberties.

He picked up the red file with the reports he had been sent from Ottawa on the recent bizarre occurrences, got up from his mahogany desk, and crossed the floor of his office to stare out the window, his hands jammed into his pants pockets. The pristine beauty of northern British Columbia always took his breath away, and today was no exception. He had the best office view on the planet, overlooking a bend in the Peace River where the Site C Dam had been built. Sprawling before him was the earth-filled dam and reservoir, its calm surface sparkling in the midday sun. Someone knocked on his office door, ruining his only calm moment of the day. He exhaled, set his shoulders, and faced the door. "In," he called out.

The door swung open, exposing the three people McKnight was expecting: Major Wallace Buchanan, Captain Alex Benoit, and Dr. Helena Simmons. The three of them couldn't have been more different. Buchanan—Buck—was a longtime veteran of Delta Force and the senior tactical operator for the US contingent of Task Force Devil. They knew each other well, having served together in El Salvador. Not all of their history was good, however. Buck had a nasty temper and a tendency to resort to violence. On the other hand, he was damned good at being violent, which came in very handy when you absolutely, positively needed to kill someone.

Benoit—Alex—was very different. In truth, he was exactly the type of fine young man that McKnight liked to command in covert operations. Unremarkable in appearance, thoroughly professional in his duties, he consistently achieved superb results. A native of the province of Newfoundland, he still spoke with a trace of a maritime accent that McKnight had always found charming. Alex was the senior Canadian Special Forces officer assigned to Task Force Devil and a member of Canada's elite Joint Task Force 2.

The last person to enter the office, Dr. Helena Simmons, was middle-aged and slightly overweight. She always wore a somewhat stunned look on her face, giving the impression that she was overwhelmed by life. In fact, she possessed a razor-sharp mind and was, without a doubt, the most intelligent and capable person McKnight had ever worked with—she had a doctorate in experimental physics. He had no doubt that she was the smartest person standing in his office. He needed that intellect today more than ever.

Buck plopped himself down on the plush leather visitor's couch in the center of the office. Alex waited for Helena to seat herself then also sat down, his hands resting on his knees. McKnight settled into the lounge chair and observed the three visitors from across the glass coffee table. He tapped the red file against his lap. "So here's the problem. Somehow, and unless one of you have already figured it out..." He paused while he waited for one of them to speak up. When none did, he continued. "Somehow, we've had a breach."

Buck leaned forward. "Sir, the Jump Tube is secure."

Helena shook her head and glanced quickly at Buck. "I don't think the colonel is referring to the Gateway Machine, are you, Colonel?"

McKnight shook his head. "This isn't us."

Alex's eyes narrowed, but he said nothing. Helena looked as if she were about to throw up, and Buck looked confused.

"Sir. How is that possible?" Buck asked.

McKnight opened the file on his lap and picked up the first page. There was a RCMP logo on it. "Three days ago, during the massive gamma-radiation spike we were tracking and the unusual weather patterns, several huge..." McKnight paused. His eyes drifted to the page in his hand, and he read, "Demonic, wolflike creatures trailing fire from their mouths were seen running away from a bushfire on the outskirts of Fort St. John."

"I..." Buck paused.

"Demonic wolf dogs that breathe fire, Major. Sound familiar?"

Buck sighed. "Those are the creatures that hit us on Rubicon, sir. This can't be a coincidence."

"No. No it can't, can it? We have a problem—one that our handlers in Ottawa and Washington are now aware of. Helena, can you help? Do we have any theories?"

Helena raised her hands, inhaled deeply, then lowered them again, wiping her palms on her knees. "A working theory only, Colonel. I think you're right. Somehow, we have had a breach. But I have no idea how. Maybe—and I'm entirely speculating now— maybe there was some kind of... unintentional resonating event."

"An unintentional resonating event?" McKnight heard the skepticism in his own voice.

"I just don't know, Colonel," said Helena. "It shouldn't be possible, but the gamma radiation we recorded was identical to what we see during an entry mission."

"I was hoping for more, Helena. Even the politicians in Ottawa and Washington have come to the same conclusion, and they're looking for solutions."

Buck scowled, his eyes turning into slits. "Useless-ass politicians," he muttered.

McKnight closed his eyes, seeking calm. "Our political leaders have a right to be concerned, Major. We have dead soldiers. And now we have what looks like an unintended transdimensional breach, alien infestation, and worst of all, civilians passing out and dying. *Civilians,* gentlemen. The very people we're sworn to defend. This is really, really bad."

"We don't know if the civilian thing has anything to do with us," Buck said. "It could have been a gas leak... or something."

McKnight leaned forward. "A gas leak, Major? A gas leak that occurred over a two-hundred-kilometer area and affected less than a dozen people out of how many thousands? And of those that were affected, only three have survived?" McKnight paused and inhaled deeply. "And all this just happened to take place at the exact same time we had our *unintentional resonating event?*"

"No," said Buck. "I... I see your point, sir."

"This is getting out of hand," said McKnight. "You see that, right?"

"Sir," said Alex, contributing for the first time. "I agree with Helena. There's been a breach, and we need to determine where it was and if it's still open."

"I don't think it is," said Helena. "The gamma spiking was only elevated for a brief time. Whatever caused the breach, I'm fairly certain it's no longer open. We'd know."

"Fairly certain?" Alex asked.

Helena sighed. "Reasonably certain."

Reasonably? Jesus Christ. What are we going to do? McKnight looked from one to the other, then he turned his attention back to the file on his lap and flipped through the papers. "Of the three people that we know survived this... event, two have demonstrated... *unusual* abilities."

"Yes, Colonel," answered Helena. "I'd call them *psychic* abilities—if there were such a thing—which there isn't... or rather *shouldn't* be."

"Seems like there is now, doesn't it?" Alex said. "We've all seen what he can do."

"Any explanations for what Mr. Hocking is able to do, Helena?" asked McKnight.

She sighed and shook her head. "No. I have no scientific explanation, Colonel. Psychic abilities is about as... *alternative* as I'm willing to go. But testing is ongoing with Mr. Hocking as we speak. The preliminary results have been very interesting so far, but it's too soon to make a definitive judgment."

McKnight sighed. "Well, thank God he's agreed to help us, because we need to understand what's happened, and we need to understand it fast."

"There's another possibility," said Helena.

McKnight paused, glancing at the doctor. "Let's hear it, then."

"We've crossed over numerous times now, but we don't know what the long-term effects are, nor do we really understand why it's easier to open a Gateway here in Northern BC than at the original testing site in Arizona."

"I thought the Earth's gravitational fields were more malleable here," said McKnight.

"In truth, Colonel..." Helena paused, looking very uncomfortable. "That's just a hypothesis that's been thrown about without any real scientific proof. It's been repeated so many times that people who really should know better just accept it as fact. But it has never been anything more than a guess. The truth is we just don't know why it's easier to open Gateways here. There is something unique about this particular region of North America. The point I'm trying to get to is this: we just don't know enough yet, and without more testing, without more clinical trials, we run the risk of inadvertently changing the dynamics of Rubicon."

"Please be clear, Helena," said McKnight.

"My concern, Colonel, is that we've somehow weakened the interdimensional veil, made it possible for travel from Rubicon to Earth."

"You're saying we may have left... interdimensional holes," said Alex.

"Or somehow left a trail back to us," said Helena.

"But that would mean..." Alex's voice trailed off.

"That something on Rubicon was capable of creating a

Gateway," said Helena.

McKnight leaned forward. "Nothing we've seen so far would even hint at that level of technological development. Is that even possible?"

As all three men stared at her, uncertainty flitted across Helena's features. "We don't know. We've never done anything like this before. No one has. Although there were whispers that the Soviet Union was experimenting on transdimensional physics in the seventies, those were almost certainly just urban legends."

"*Something* has changed," said McKnight. "If Operation Rubicon has somehow created unintended breaches for animals to wander through..." He sighed again, feeling older than ever. "Okay, here's what we're going to do. We need to determine what happened three days ago. Was there a breach? If so, where? We need to find it."

"We're on it, Colonel," Alex said. "But..."

"But what, Captain?"

"Colonel, this is some pretty remote country. We're talking about an area of old-growth boreal forests that's twice the size of Arizona. Some of it—hell, most of it—is inaccessible other than on foot. It's not going to be easy."

"That's the job, Captain."

"Yes, sir."

"What about UAVs, sir?" asked Buck. "They'd make it a hell of a lot easier to search."

Alex shook his head. "No way my government is going to authorize that. They're unhappy enough with the Osprey."

Buck's face turned red. "Well, goddamn—"

"Enough, Major," said McKnight, raising his voice just enough to silence the other man. "Not our country, not our call. Got it?"

"Yes, sir," said Buck, glaring at Alex.

McKnight turned his attention back to Helena. "And let's see what Mr. Hocking can do for us. Maybe there's something to be gained from this disaster."

"Yes, Colonel," she said. "So far, the results are… exciting."

"The other two—the two women in the hospital—we need to… deal with them as well."

"Sir, I'll look into them," Alex said.

McKnight nodded. "Good, but focus on these goddamned wolf animals first. Find them and put them down before they kill someone."

"Yes, sir," both men answered.

McKnight met Alex's eye. "The Canadian government is flying in a Royal Canadian Mounted Police official who's been brought up to date on Operation Rubicon. Once he gets on the ground, he'll facilitate your interactions with the local police force, but until then, you and Major Buchanan need to stay ahead of the local constabulary. You already know your cover. We've been over this before. We can't have creatures from Rubicon showing up on the evening news. It'll draw too much attention. Operational security trumps everything else."

"Understood, sir," said Alex. "We'll run them down."

"Damn right *I* will, sir," said Buck.

McKnight nodded. "Do it fast."

Chapter 9

Cassie lay on her back on a gurney, a rubberized net of sensors wrapped around her head. Standing just beside her, Dr. Ireland watched a monitor highlighting Cassie's brain activity. "This is really strange," Dr. Ireland said. "Fascinating, really."

"That's exactly the sort of thing I like to hear at moments like this, Doc. You're the best."

Dr. Ireland smiled and squeezed Cassie's shoulder. "Sorry. Not much fun for you, is it?"

Cassie stared down at her slipper-enclosed feet. "Not really. So, tell me about these *strange* things in my head."

"Maybe *strange* wasn't the best word. *Interesting* would be more appropriate."

"Interesting like I should be really concerned, or interesting like you're starting to figure out what's wrong with me?"

Dr. Ireland pushed her horn-rimmed glasses up higher on her nose and stared intently at the screen. It was several seconds before she answered. "I'm not entirely sure there's anything *wrong* with you. Or Elizabeth either."

"Trust me, Doc. There's a lot wrong with my roommate."

"Not getting along, are we?"

"I don't think she approves of me."

"Well, just remember she's trying to cope with this as well. And she's doing it all by herself."

Cassie's face felt warm, and she bit her lip and looked away. Every day she had been in the hospital, Alice had made the drive from Hudson's Hope. So had Ginny and Lee. Even Vicky had visited once to cry profusely and thank her over and over for saving her life. Elizabeth had not had a single visitor, and Fort St. John was her home. Where were her family and friends?

"So, tell me again about this EEG test," Cassie said.

"Electroencephalography. It measures electrical activity, brain waves, along the scalp. The nodes on the skull cap you're wearing record the brain's spontaneous electrical activity over a short period of time."

"And again, Doc, how is this interesting?"

"Usually, an EEG helps recognize and diagnose epileptic activity or confirm a coma, which is what we originally thought was going on with you."

"I'm not in a coma, Doc."

Dr. Ireland raised an eyebrow and cocked her pixie-like head. "Yes, Cassie. We figured that much out when you started talking to us." She turned her attention back to the monitor and then jotted something down in her notebook. "At any rate, an EEG can be a useful tool, particularly if you don't have access to an MRI or a CT scanner, which we don't. For that, we'll have to get you to Vancouver."

"Vancouver? I just came from Vancouver. I'm in no hurry to go back. Not just yet."

Dr. Ireland's face showed her puzzlement, but she continued her explanation. "Anyway, the brain's electrical charge is caused by billions of neurons exchanging ions across their membranes. Once enough of these neurons are pushing on each other, it creates a wave—a *brain wave*—of activity that the EEG can pick up on and measure."

"And this is useful and interesting how exactly? I know I'm not in a coma or having an epileptic episode."

"Actually, we don't really know that at all."

"Wouldn't I be like shaking and convulsing and shit if I was epileptic?"

"Not necessarily, but I don't think this is epilepsy. That just doesn't seem to make sense."

"Make sense? Are you kidding me? How much of this makes any kind of sense?"

Dr. Ireland shook her head. "Trust me, we'll figure this all out and get the answers. There's always an answer. There are some very clever people working really hard to help you—not just here in Fort St. John but in Vancouver as well. We've asked the province for help."

Cassie bit her lower lip. "Could it have been a terrorist attack of some kind? A biological or chemical thing."

"No, Cassie. That's not it. There weren't any symptoms of that."

"So why aren't I normal?"

"It's not that your brain activity isn't normal. It's just that your rhythmic activity is way beyond what it should be."

"You're not making me feel any better," Cassie said.

"The brain's rhythmic activity is normally divided into bands of frequency—delta, theta, alpha, mu, and gamma. The highest frequency we should be able to measure is the gamma band, which measures your somatosensory cortex."

"I don't have a clue what you're talking about."

"The EEG will pick up on gamma activity in your brain and

many other types as well, but the gamma band is activated when your brain uses cross-modal sensory processing—that is, when your brain tries to combine two different senses, like sound and sight. When that happens, we get a measurement that should top out at about one hundred hertz. If it shows a decrease, however, it may indicate an association with cognitive decline."

"Does it?" Alarmed, Cassie started to sit up.

Dr. Ireland reached out. Placing her hand on Cassie's shoulder, she guided her back onto the mattress. "No, of course not, honey."

"So, what is it, then?"

"The problem is—and it's the same with Elizabeth—your gamma measurements are off the charts. They're so high we can't even measure them. It's like your brain is processing far more than just differences between sight and sound. *Something* is really firing up those neurons. And it's not just the gamma band. The mu band is also way too high, as is the delta and beta. I think that you and Elizabeth have become… *sensitive* to something that the rest of us aren't."

"Something like what?"

Dr. Ireland sighed and shook her head. "This is new, but we're doing the best we can."

"Can it be ESP?"

Dr. Ireland opened her mouth but didn't say anything. Cassie was about to repeat her question when the other woman finally answered. "I don't know what happened up there with that Bible. I've never seen anything like that, ever. But from a medical point of view, there's just no such thing as psychic powers."

Cassie closed her eyes and imagined the electrical energy coursing through her brain. So, what was she sensitive to?

"What does all that mean?" Cassie asked, her eyes still closed.

"I don't know yet, honey, but we're not going to give up on you."

* * *

Two days later, Cassie sat alone in the hospital's cafeteria, sipping her tea. It was early afternoon, and she had a break scheduled before the hospital ran its next test. Not wanting to be around Elizabeth anymore, Cassie had grabbed a paperback novel and headed down to the cafeteria. She was tired of being a patient; she was tired of the tests; she was tired of just about everything. There had been some talk of releasing her and Elizabeth and having them come back as outpatients for more testing. That would be nice, Cassie had to admit.

Mostly, Cassie felt the same as she always had, although—and she refused to admit this to anyone—something *was* different. It was impossible to describe, but the bizarre sensation she had first felt the night of the lightning storm was still present, almost as if there was a new quality to the air around her. It was like swimming in water that evaporated the moment she touched it yet still retained that essence of… heaviness, of invisible mass.

Dr. Ireland thought she was sensitive to something, but what? Elizabeth thought it was the power of God, believing she had been *chosen,* a new twenty-first-century saint. But Cassie didn't believe in God, not since her parents had died. Whatever had changed the night of the electrical storm, it wasn't because of God; it was something else—something that could be explained… maybe.

Unable to focus, she placed her paperback down. She had read the same paragraph eight times in a row.

Elizabeth had moved the pages of her Bible without touching it. Was it ESP? Why wasn't the hospital testing them for that? Dr. Ireland said ESP didn't exist, but Cassie couldn't think of another way to explain what she had seen. Weren't the Americans, the CIA, always working to develop those sorts of psychic abilities?

What was to stop her from trying it herself? Cassie held her cup of tea in both hands, felt the warmth of the liquid through the porcelain, and stared at it. *Use your mind,* she told herself, *and push the liquid.*

A ripple of movement disturbed the surface of the tea. She almost dropped the cup, putting it back down on the table, reacting as if it had burned her.

Okay, that was all in my head. I scared myself—that's all.

She grasped her hands together beneath the table and glared at the tea in front of her.

I did not make that tea move. I do not have telekinesis.

The back of her neck became warm. The conversations of others around her in the cafeteria had become muted as if she were hearing them from underwater. Again, the air around her seemed to have some new quality she could almost reach out and touch... if only she willed it. Her skin felt energized. The little hairs on her forearm were standing up as if she were standing near an electrical current, yet even that didn't fully describe what she was feeling. Without thinking about it any further, without consciously meaning to, she *opened* herself up and drew the unseen energy into the very core of her being. Instantly, a nebulous vitality filled her. It was cold and hot, insubstantial yet somehow malleable—and all at the same time. It felt wondrous!

The porcelain teacup flew off the table, sailed across the cafeteria, and smashed against a wall. Her tea ran down the cement wall in rivulets.

Cassie gasped for air, as if she had been holding her breath for minutes. She jumped to her feet, knocking her chair onto the floor. Everyone was staring at her. She staggered away from the table, turned, and bolted from the cafeteria, almost running into her sister, who had just come in.

"Cassie, what—"

She kept running.

Chapter 10

When Buck drove the van around a bend in the road, Alex, sitting beside him in the enclosed cab, saw the farmhouse and the RCMP cruiser parked in front of it. "Shit," Alex muttered.

Buck stepped on the brakes and pulled to a stop next to the police car. He leaned forward and held his hand up, silently telling Alex to wait. Then he bobbed his large head and grimaced. "All right. This isn't that big a deal. We cope. This is what we get paid for."

A middle-aged man in coveralls walked out from behind the rear of the farmhouse, accompanied by a uniformed RCMP officer. Alex noted a woman watching them from the window of the farmhouse. It was ten thirty in the morning on a weekday, so there probably wouldn't be any school-age children present. When the RCMP officer saw the van, he paused, staring at them. The van was a blue, windowless medical-transport vehicle. The paneling on the side simply read Government of Canada Medical Transport.

Buck sat back in his seat for a moment, staring at the police officer. Then he reached over and picked up a secure cell phone sitting on the dashboard. "All right, Newf. This is why you're here. Go talk to him. Be friendly. I'll call it in."

Alex frowned at the other man before opening the door and climbing out. He forced a smile onto his face as he walked over. Alex wore blue jeans, a long-sleeved buttoned shirt, and a vest. He carried a clipboard in one hand, knowing from experience it set people's mind at ease. He extended his hand in greeting. "Hey, how you doing, officer?"

The police officer shook Alex's hand, but his face still showed his suspicion. "What can I do for you?"

Alex reached into his vest pocket and pulled out a plastic ID card that identified him as Alex Bennett, an Environment Canada Enforcement officer. The police officer examined it carefully then jotted Alex's name in his notebook before handing it back.

"I don't know you," he said. "Where's Miller? Where's your uniform?"

Alex shrugged. "I don't know Miller. Is he provincial?"

The officer's eyes narrowed. "You're a Fed?"

Alex nodded. "Sure am."

"Why are you here? What's the federal angle in a dead cow?" The plastic name tag on the officer's bulletproof vest identified him as Constable Groulx. He spoke with a very pronounced French-Canadian accent.

"Thing is, officer, we've had an incident at a holding pen up at the airport in Fort St. John. We were moving some animals and… somebody screwed up. An animal got loose."

"No kidding. Have you seen that thing back there? What the hell is it? It looks like the biggest damned dog I ever saw."

"It's still here?" Alex asked in alarm, looking past the man.

"Dead," said the farmer, speaking for the first time. "Goddamned thing burned one of my cows, so I shot it."

Constable Groulx frowned at the farmer. "I don't really know what's going on, exactly, but Mr. Granger here did shoot a large predator. The carcass is in the field behind the house. Exactly what were you people moving?"

Alex smiled sheepishly. "Wasn't us. We were called in to help clean up the mess, but it's an Armenian wolfhound. Big bastards, or so I'm told. I've never actually seen one alive before."

"You're not gonna see one alive now neither," said the farmer.

Alex glanced at the field behind the man's shoulder. "Mind if I take a look?"

"Sure," Constable Groulx said.

Together, the three men walked out into the field. A wooden fence had been built around a large pasture where a small herd of dairy cows were all clustered in the far corner, clearly staying as far away as they could from the still-smoking carcass of a cow and the remains of a massive doglike creature. The stench of burnt meat and blood was thick in the air. Flies buzzed angrily over the remains.

"Killed my cow," the farmer said. "Set her on fire. Who's paying for that?"

"We'll pay for your animal," Alex said. "I'll write you a government check before we leave."

"Really?" Constable Groulx asked. "That fast?"

"We want to help." Alex stood over the smoking remains of the cow. "This is clearly our animal, clearly our fault."

The farmer sniffed, nodding his head.

Constable Groulx frowned. "How is it *your* fault a cow got hit by lightning?"

"Wasn't lightning," Granger snapped. "That damned dog did it. I saw it."

Alex raised his hand, hoping to stop the conversation from going any further. "Can I ask you two to keep back a bit?"

The farmer and constable stopped where they were, and Alex

moved closer and squatted in place, examining the carcasses. The dairy cow was partially charred as though someone had aimed a flamethrower at it. Long tendrils of smoke rose from its steaming remains. It had also been disemboweled, and something had clearly been at the entrails; they were partially devoured. The grass around the cow's carcass was stamped down and covered in blood. The stench was unimaginable—a mingling of barbecued beef, blood, and feces. Alex wished he had thought to bring a mask. A real Environment Canada officer would have brought a mask.

The real problem here, though, wasn't the dead cow but the huge carcass lying beside it. There was no doubt this... *thing* was from Rubicon. Alex had never seen one himself, but Buck had done a pretty good job describing them. Roughly the size of a small pony, it looked like a cross between a wolf and a hyena. Its dead mouth was open, exposing long rows of wicked-sharp teeth—some still had pieces of raw cow stuck between them. A long black tongue hung from its open jaws. Alex pulled a pen from his shirt pocket and poked at its tongue. Steam puffed from the tongue when the pen touched it, actually melting the plastic.

Alex stood up and backed away.

"That your Balkan wolf dog?" the RCMP officer asked.

"Hound," Alex replied. "Armenian wolfhound, and yeah, that's it. How about we move back to the front of the house. This thing really stinks."

The two men quickly agreed and followed Alex.

"Mr. Granger, right?" Alex asked the farmer.

The farmer nodded.

"So, what happened?"

"Last night, around nine o'clock, I hear howling like a pack of dogs."

"A pack?" asked Constable Groulx, turning to stare at Alex.

"How many of these things you guys lose?"

"Just the one," he said. "But at night, it probably sounded like more, especially with the echo." Both constable and farmer looked skeptical, and Alex didn't blame them. He quickly moved on. "Course, we don't always get told everything, so I'll leave you my number." Alex handed the farmer a scrap of paper with a cell phone number on it. "Just in case, you know what I mean? So, Mr. Granger, what happened next?"

"Well, the dogs start barking, going nuts, then running and hiding. So, I take my shotgun and a flashlight and go out to see what's up. Then, I see the flames out back, lighting up the night like a bonfire, and the cows screaming."

"A fire?" Constable Groulx looked skeptical. "You got any neighborhood kids who might be playing with homemade bombs?"

"Hey, you saw the carcass. Something lit it up," said the farmer.

"Not our animal," Alex said. He inclined his head toward the constable. "I'd say you're probably right. Maybe some kids were screwing around with firebombs and killed the cow. The animal probably just took advantage of a dead carcass."

"No, no, no! That's bullshit," said the farmer. "When I came up on this thing feeding on my cow, it looked up at me. Its freaking eyes were glowing red, and there were still flames coming out the side of its mouth."

"Could it have just been chewing on burning meat, maybe with some gas or something on it still giving off flames?" the constable asked.

"Possible," said Alex. "These things are scavengers and are known to pretty much eat anything."

"But burning meat?" asked the constable.

Alex raised his eyebrows as if to say, *Who knows?* "So you saw this thing chewing on your cow, and then what?"

"Then what? Then I shot the goddamned ugly thing." The farmer glared at Alex. "There ain't no kids around here that'd throw a firebomb at my animals. It just doesn't happen. They're good kids hereabouts."

"He's right about that," said the constable. "We don't really get arson around here."

"This mean you're not paying for the cow?" the farmer asked.

"No, no, we're happy to pay for damages that you incurred as a result of the incident."

The farmer seemed to settle down, and the constable was opening his mouth to say something else when Buck appeared from around the side of the farmhouse, pushing a squeaking cart up the dirt road.

"This is my partner," Alex said, indicating Buck with a toss of his head. "Buck, this is Mr. Granger and Constable Groulx."

"Hey, how ya doin'?" Buck asked, nodding at the two men, before turning back to Alex. "What we got?"

"It's our Armenian wolfhound, all right," Alex said. "Mr. Granger here killed it."

"Oh yeah?" asked Buck, now squinting at the farmer, as if he were sizing him up. "Good on ya. These things are mean."

"You don't care that your escaped animal is dead?" Constable Groulx asked.

Alex glanced quickly at Buck. Buck, towering over the constable, looked down his nose at him and scowled. "Course I care. But dangerous is dangerous." The constable looked away first, and Buck glanced toward the back of the house. "We gotta take it back with us." He turned away and started pushing the cart toward the back of the house.

Alex held his hand out to the RCMP officer. "Constable

Groulx, it was a pleasure."

The RCMP officer paused, watching Alex's face for a few moments, then reached out and took his hand. "That a Newfoundland accent I hear?"

"Cornerbrook," Alex replied.

"Long way from home," the officer said.

"Sounds like you're a long way from Quebec, as well," Alex replied.

"True enough." The officer turned to the farmer. "I'll write a report, ask around about the local kids, but I think we're probably done here."

"Weren't kids," the farmer insisted.

The RCMP officer nodded, pocketed his notebook, and walked away toward his patrol car. Alex helped Buck push the cart around the back of the house, while keeping an eye on the police officer. A minute or two later, the patrol car drove off down the dirt road toward the highway. The two men stood in front of the doglike animal's carcass, staring at it. Buck handed Alex a pair of surgical gloves and kept a pair for himself.

"Fuggly things," Buck said, nudging it with his toe. "Still smoking from the mouth."

"This one of the things that hit you?" Alex asked.

"Oh, shit, yeah. Nothing like this on planet Earth."

"These things take out a patrol of Tier One operators, but a farmer takes it down with a shotgun?"

Buck stared at Alex, his eyes cold and hard, and Alex tensed, certain the other man was on the verge of becoming violent. Instead, Buck sighed and looked away. "Wasn't just these fucking hellhounds. There were other... things that were controlling them. And maybe Farmer Brown here is just the luckiest man in Canada."

The moment had passed, and Alex forced himself to breathe, to act normal and pretend he wasn't hanging out with an insecure psychopath. "He said he heard howling, like a pack."

"They run in packs like wolves."

"If there's more, we're gonna have to run the rest of them down." Alex bent over and, with a gloved hand, grabbed the creature's hind legs and waited for Buck.

"Gonna need a tracker," Buck said as he took the creature's front quarters.

The damned thing must have weighed two hundred pounds, but the two men hoisted the carcass onto the metal gurney. It shuddered under the weight, and its wheels sunk into the soft ground, but they were wide, designed to move across rough terrain.

"Man, this thing stinks," Alex said.

"They're way worse when they're alive and breathing fire at you," Buck said.

"I can imagine."

Buck snorted. "Trust me, Newf—you can't. Let's get back to the Magic Kingdom. McKnight is gonna want to see this thing, and Simmons and her lab dorks will want to take it apart."

The two men pushed the cart back to the van. Mr. Granger stood near his front door, watching, as they shoved the cart up the ramp at the back of the van and rolled it into the vehicle. Once inside, they strapped it into place.

Buck glanced over at the farmer. "Just give him cash, and let's get the hell outta here."

Alex nodded and, walking over to the farmer, pulled hundred-dollar bills from a large roll he had stuffed in his shirt pocket. He ended up giving the man way more than a single cow was worth, but the money didn't matter.

Soon, they were back on the dirt road, heading for the highway.

As always, Buck drove too aggressively. When the van hit a bump in the road, it jumped into the air, landing hard and jarring Alex's teeth. Buck grinned.

Dickhead.

Wham! Something smashed against the side of the van, jarring it. But both men turned and stared wide-eyed at one another. The thumping was coming from the enclosed body of the van. A moment later, they heard the creature howling.

Buck slammed on the brakes, and the van screeched to a halt. Without a word, both men jumped out of the cab, each stopping only long enough to reach under the bench seat and pull out a P90 submachine gun. They ran to the rear of the van.

Alex glanced about. There were trees all around them and no one else in sight. He grabbed the rear-door handle, still holding the submachine gun in his firing hand. Buck positioned himself about ten feet away, at a firing angle but not directly facing the rear door, his weapon in the ready position. Both guns were equipped with sound suppressors that extended the length of the short weapon, and the fifty-round plastic magazines that were fitted flush against the top of the weapon's frames were loaded with 5.7x28mm SB193 subsonic ammunition. Buck braced himself then nodded at Alex.

Alex yanked the door open and jumped out of the way. A jet of flames ten feet long shot out of the back of the van. At almost the exact same moment, Buck let loose with a long stream of submachine gun fire; he paused for a moment and then fired another, shorter burst. There was a brief, cut-off screech of pain from inside the van. Alex moved beside Buck, making sure he stayed out of his line of fire. He aimed into the smoking rear of the van and then also began firing short bursts of subsonic fire.

"Wait," Buck called out.

Alex kept his finger on the trigger and his weapon pressed into his shoulder. As the smoke cleared, he saw the carcass of the creature now lying on the van's floor. A large pool of blood was spreading out around it. Both men stepped closer. The back of the van was shot to shit with the monitors shattered and shards of broken glass and pieces of metal strewn about. The inside of the rear doors was charred, and a small fire was still burning where the damned thing had tried to burn its way out. From about three feet away, Buck put two shots into the hellhound's skull, making sure it was dead this time. Alex rushed to the cab to get the fire extinguisher, and a moment later he was back, aiming the hose at the flames and putting them out with a burst of compressed CO_2.

Buck, gritting his teeth, nudged the creature with his boot. He looked over his shoulder at Alex and then grinned like a fiend. Alex couldn't help himself, and both men began laughing. They slammed the door shut again, got back in the cab, and drove away.

Chapter 11

Corporal Jean Alexis Groulx was driving down One Hundredth Avenue in downtown Fort St. John when the call came in. Up until that point, it had been a typical slow afternoon with the only excitement being the burned cow and escaped animal at the Granger farm earlier that morning. "Dispatch," said a female voice, clearly excited. "This is Car 7, 10-33 at the corner of Juniper and Hemlock. Code 5, I say again Code 5."

Jean's eyes darted to his VHF radio. The officer putting out the call was Corinna Trotter, a new constable in the Fort St. John detachment, transferred only a month earlier. She was a good officer, cool and professional, but there had been panic in her voice. Code 10-33 meant officer in trouble; Code 5 was high-risk danger—guns drawn.

That almost never happened in Fort St. John. Jean reached for the handset. He had felt a sense of unease hovering over him all day; now, that apprehension was intensified. He keyed the mike, pausing only a moment before speaking. "Dispatch, this is Car 4, responding."

He turned on his patrol car's lights and siren and accelerated toward the scene of the call. As he maneuvered around traffic, he pressed the switch on the microphone once. "Car 7, this is Car 4. What is the nature of the emergency?"

When she didn't answer, his unease grew.

"Car 4, this is Dispatch. We're getting numerous calls describing a... wild animal threatening a school bus at the corner of Juniper and Hemlock."

That was just outside of town, in a small subcommunity called Clairmont, only about four kilometers from his current location. "Roger," Jean acknowledged. "Bear or moose?" Just for a moment, he wondered if another one of those weird wolf things had escaped the feds. Jean's eyebrows knitted together as he waited—too long—for the dispatcher's response.

"Car 4, neither. The calls are claiming there's some sort of... dragon."

Jean swung out around a dump truck and then ran through a red light where the traffic had stopped. He keyed the mike again. "Dispatch, say again what type of animal."

"A dragon. The callers are describing a giant lizard of some type."

Five days ago, they had found the wrecked remains of a car on the highway. It had caught on fire and burned, and the driver, a thirty-six-year-old woman, was missing. He remembered thinking that the roof of the car had looked as though it had been peeled back but, at the time, had discarded that idea as crazy. Now, Jean wasn't so sure. Maybe some idiot had brought a wild animal—a tiger or a komodo dragon or something like that—up north. Could an animal even do that to a car? Jean stepped on the gas.

Corinna's voice came over the radio again, clearly desperate this time. "Please, Dispatch; I need help. Send everyone. Send SWAT. It's going to kill a bunch of kids."

The tires of his patrol car screeched as he pulled off the Alaska

Highway and onto a side road. He was almost there. Moments later, he was into a residential area, roaring past stop signs and praying he wouldn't run into some kid playing in the street. His pulse raced; his heart pounded beneath his vest. Just ahead, he saw a fire truck stopped at an intersection, its lights flashing. Corinna's patrol car was there as well. Black clouds of smoke rose from a burning car, obscuring the scene. A yellow school bus had driven off the road, right into the side of a house. He saw the terrified faces of children inside it. A man was slumped over the wheel.

His tires skidded as he screeched to a halt beside Corinna's car. As he was stepping out of his patrol car, he saw it.

"*Osti de Criss,*" he whispered. His palm rested against the handle of his service automatic in its holster. It wasn't a komodo dragon—it was a real dragon.

Twice the size of an elephant, it stalked about on eight legs. Foot-long spikes ran down its back, giving it an otherworldly appearance. It was covered in overlapping scales of dark green, each the size of his hand. Its long, thick tail whipped back and forth as it paced alongside the crashed school bus. Without warning, it shrieked in fury—a stuttering, alien cry—and smashed its massive horned head, the size of a fridge, against the school bus's frame, shattering windows and rocking the bus. The children screamed.

This isn't possible.

Then he heard the distinctive popping of handgun fire and saw Corinna standing beside the red fire truck. Two volunteer firefighters stood next to her, wide-eyed. She held her service pistol in both hands as she fired again and again at the dragon. The creature ignored her completely as if the pistol fire were nonexistent. How thick were its scales? He ran to her side, only then realizing he had drawn his own handgun. Aiming down his weapon's sights, his vision seemed to tunnel in on the monster.

"Aim for its head," he said, amazed he could even speak coherently.

He began to rapidly squeeze the trigger. The pistol jerked with each shot, but Jean let its barrel fall back onto target before squeezing it again. In seconds, he had emptied his entire ten-round magazine, and his slide was locked back.

He had hit the monster, he knew he had hit it, but it kept smashing its head against the school bus, oblivious to their fire.

His empty magazine fell from his weapon, clattering against the pavement as he loaded another and released the action of his weapon, chambering another round. In moments, the second magazine was empty as well.

"It's not doing anything," Corinna said, desperation in her voice. "It's gonna kill those kids!"

She was right. Its hide had to be too thick for pistol fire, or maybe the 9mm rounds were just too small to do more than sting it. He was breathing too fast. If he didn't get a grip, he might hyperventilate. Once again, the dragon smashed its head against the metal frame of the school bus, shattering windows. It tried to bite the side of the bus but couldn't get its teeth into the metal. Jean's thoughts returned to the wrecked car on the highway, its roof literally ripped clear. If that thing managed to get a grip on the metal of the school bus, it was going to rip it open—and then it'd start eating the children. He wasn't going to let that happen.

Looking about himself, he saw the hose of the fire truck, coiled against the side of the vehicle. An idea came to him. He grabbed the shoulder of the nearest firefighter. "Get that hose loose," he yelled. "When I give you the order, I want you to hit that thing with a blast of water."

The firefighter, an older guy, maybe forty pounds overweight with panic in his expression, stared at Jean for a moment.

Jean shook his shoulder. "You hear me?"

The man's eyes snapped toward Jean's, and he nodded, his face still ashen. "Yeah," he muttered. Then, as if released from a spell, he turned and yelled at the other firefighter, a young guy with bright-red hair and a goatee. "Help me, Ed!"

Both men ran to unroll the hose.

Jean turned to Corinna. "Can you drive that school bus?"

She stared at him in confusion. "What?"

"Corinna, damn it. Focus! Can you drive that school bus?"

Her head darted to the bus, and she nodded. "I guess."

"You're sure?"

"I'm sure, but how will I get in? That thing is in the way."

"Just be ready to move. We're gonna distract it. When we do, you get that bus out of here as fast as you can go. Don't stop; don't wait for me. Just go, and keep going."

She nodded quickly, staring again at the dragon.

Jean turned back to the firefighters. They had already unrolled the hose and were attaching it to a fire hydrant.

"You ready?" Jean called out.

When they didn't answer him right away, he repeated his question, yelling this time. The older firefighter glanced up and nodded. The younger guy ran to the hydrant to turn it on. The cords in the older guy's neck bulged as he yanked the hose into place, his face now bright red.

"*Tabernac!*" Jean swore under his breath. *He's gonna have a heart attack.* He ran over to help drag the hose into position. He stood behind the older man, each of them holding the hose. Then, he glanced over at Corinna. "You ready?"

She nodded, her face white.

"Crank it," Jean yelled. *Please, God; please work.*

A moment later, the hose jerked to life, almost flying out of their grip. Jean set his feet and manhandled the hose back into position.

"Brace yourself," the firefighter yelled as he opened the nozzle.

A blast of water as wide as a man's fist jetted from the nozzle. Jean and the firefighter adjusted their aim, striking the dragon square in the face and knocking it onto its side. It screeched in anger and frustration, whipping its body about. As it did, its massive tail smashed into the side of the bus, rocking it. The dragon spun to face them, but it took the stream of water right between its open jaws and was knocked down again, this time farther away from the bus, creating the opening Jean had hoped for—although the dragon was pissed at *them* now.

"Go!" yelled Jean to Corinna.

She bolted for the bus, but Jean's focus was on the dragon, which was trying to get back up. They readjusted their aim, keeping it off balance. Each time it tried to get up, they knocked it down again. It shrieked and howled in rage, sending shivers down his spine. Sooner or later, it'd get at them. This couldn't last.

He heard tires screeching and risked a glance to see the bus flying backwards, away from the house it had hit, and onto the street. Corinna was seated where the driver had been slumped over. Her face was a mask of determination as she yanked on the bus's wheel, turning it away from the dragon. Seconds later, the bus sped away from the intersection, toward the highway.

Merci, Jesus. Way to go, Corinna. Way to go!

He turned his attention back to the monster trying to get at them. Jean yelled at the younger man next to the fire hydrant to come take his place. In the trunk of his patrol car was an Arma-Lite C8 carbine. The young man grabbed the hose, and Jean ran for his rifle. He needed to kill this thing, and he needed to do it now! Out of breath at the trunk of his car, he fumbled like an idiot for the code that released the latch.

Too long, he thought. *This is taking too long.*

The dragon was still shrieking, still trying to close the distance between itself and the men with the hose, but they kept sweeping it off its legs with the powerful spray.

Yes! He finally got the code right, and the trunk popped open.

Jean unzipped the bag holding the rifle and drew the weapon out. The carbine was a heavily modified version of the famous US Army M-16. Its barrel was shorter, but it took the same 5.56 ammunition in a thirty-round magazine. He inserted a magazine into the weapon then drew back on the cocking mechanism, inserting a round into the firing chamber. There were another ten fully loaded magazines in the trunk—more than enough to put this damned thing down!

He turned toward the monster, his weapon pressed up into his shoulder, ready to fire. And then, in horror, he saw the dragon leap over the stream of water the firemen were aiming at its head. The damned thing was unbelievably agile, and it had jumped about twenty feet, landing just in front of the two men. They tried to readjust their aim to knock it back again, but at that moment, its eyes glowed with a blue fire. The two men stood frozen in place, their skin turning gray, cracking, and flaking—like stone.

The barrel of the carbine dropped as Jean stood transfixed. The dragon rushed the two men, bowling them over. It dropped its wide jaws over the older man, biting his body in half. Blood sprayed as the dragon raised its head, chomping as it swallowed. His lower body remained standing upright, exactly as it had been. The hose whipped through the air, spraying water everywhere.

Jean shook his head, forcing himself to move. He raised the weapon once again, aiming down the barrel. "Let's see you shrug off this, you ugly eight-legged bastard." Strangely, he felt very calm. He even managed to aim for one of the creature's glowing blue eyes the size of a dinner plate. His finger tightened on the trigger—

And then a diminutive, thin woman stepped in front of him. She gripped the barrel of his weapon in one hand and yanked it aside. *Where had she come from?*

She was beautiful beyond words, with wide almond-shaped yellow eyes and long white hair. Her skin was painted purple, contributing to her savage, otherworldly air. Jean stared at her as she stepped in close to him, only then realizing her skin wasn't painted. That was its real color.

Sharp, biting pain ran through his midsection. She leaned in closer, almost breathing into his mouth. There seemed to be sadness in her eyes, and her beautiful wide lips were parted and wet. She jerked her hand across his body, and he realized she had stabbed him beneath his bulletproof vest, cutting his stomach open.

Jean collapsed to his knees and fell over just as his vision faded.

* * *

Maelhrandia watched the manling, a soldier of some type, die. Nearby, Gazekiller devoured the remains of the other two, noisily crunching their bones. It ate them clothes and all and would later vomit up the stone exterior. Maelhrandia looked about, but the manlings had all fled.

No matter. She wasn't interested in battle; she had merely wanted to test them. And the manlings had been surprisingly effective, arriving much faster and in a more coordinated fashion than she would have thought them capable of. Threatening their younglings had indeed stirred them up; it always did. Lesser species became so emotional, so irrational. Of course, she didn't enjoy killing younglings. She was no monster—in fact, she rather enjoyed little ones, especially Redcap babes—but she had a mission, a duty, and there was no place now for softness or weakness.

Manlings, including their younglings, were a lesser species—of no real importance other than her mother's plans for them. They were clever, though, far cleverer than she had at first realized. She had no idea how they had managed to make that stream of water appear. It wasn't magic, but it had been impressive—for a time. Even now, the strange hose they had been holding danced about wildly on its own, like a snake, spewing a seemingly unstoppable amount of water. But effective as it had been, nothing could stop Gazekiller. The water stream could only momentarily frustrate the noble beast.

She squatted down and ran her fingers over the dead manling's weapon. It was cold and smooth, so very alien, far beyond what even a dwarven smith could fashion. She stood up, holding the weapon by its end, the long tube. The other manlings had carried such fire-weapons as well. They were far more dangerous than they appeared, throwing metal darts that could rip and tear from a great distance, akin to crossbows but much faster. But they were entirely mundane, so they were beneath one such as her, a daughter of magic. She dropped the weapon onto the street and approached Gazekiller just as he slurped up the last of his foes.

For five days, Maelhrandia had remained hidden in the woods, silently observing the manlings. Today, she had decided it was time to take a risk and stir them up. Even now, she heard their alarms. If she remained, she'd be overwhelmed, and perhaps even Gazekiller would be unable to fight them all off. No doubt, they'd arrive better prepared for battle, with larger and more forceful weapons. Their little fire-weapons had no effect on Gazekiller, but then, basilisk scales were so very, very strong. She could heal him if he were hurt, but she didn't want to take the chance.

And then, for the very first time since her arrival, she felt someone else using magic. She spun in place, seeking an enemy mage. Was she ambushed? No. No threat, not here. The mage was far away, to the east—near the great town she had been watching from the woods.

So, the manlings weren't entirely mundane. They did have mages, after all. *Interesting.* Her mother would want to know more. Maelhrandia would have to test them.

She leapt atop Gazekiller. He raised his great horned head and shrieked once in challenge before turning about and loping away toward the tree line.

Chapter 12

Alex rapped his knuckles once against the door to McKnight's office then waited.

"Come in," McKnight's voice called out from inside the room.

Alex opened the door and waited in the doorway.

The colonel was at his desk, his jacket off, his sleeves rolled up, papers laid out before him. When he saw Alex's face, he pushed the papers away and leaned back. "Okay, Captain. Go ahead."

"There's been another attack. A police officer has been killed… among others."

McKnight's face didn't change, but his posture became more erect. "Where?"

"About six k from the farm site."

"The dogs… the hellhounds?"

Alex shook his head. "This is something new, something big, some sort of… dragon."

McKnight rubbed his palm against his face aggressively. "Okay," he mumbled, perhaps to himself. "Do we have eyes on?"

Again, Alex shook his head. "Gone."

"A dragon? Gone?"

"That's how the eyewitnesses described it—a giant eight-legged lizard creature the size of a truck."

"Eyewitnesses?"

"At least a dozen, maybe more. It's in the press now, going huge on all the major channels, the Internet. Someone recorded it with a cell phone. This is no longer containable. It... it attacked a school bus full of children."

"Oh my God. Any—"

Alex shook his head quickly. "No. They're all fine."

"Why a school bus?"

Once again, Alex shook his head.

"And now it's just... gone?"

"Yes, sir."

"Where's Major Buchanan?"

"Already out with a team, looking for it."

McKnight pushed himself up, turned away, and walked to his window, where he leaned against it, looking out over the river and dam infrastructure and the vast tracts of woodland.

Alex waited silently.

"There's more I assume, Captain," McKnight said without turning around.

Alex bit his lower lip, uncertain how to broach this. "Sir... two of the dead, the victims... witnesses said the monster... turned them to stone with its gaze."

McKnight stared at him. "A giant eight-legged lizard that turns people to stone?"

Alex nodded.

"God help us," McKnight whispered, almost too softly for Alex to hear. "I fear we're going to need help. All the help we can get."

"The civilians?"

The phone on McKnight's desk began ringing, an incessant two-toned discord. Washington or Ottawa? Whichever government it was, the other would be calling as well.

McKnight rested a hand on the phone. "If you don't mind, Captain."

"Yes, sir." Alex closed the door, thankful this time that he wasn't the one in charge of Task Force Devil and Operation Rubicon.

Chapter 13

Cassie sat propped up on her bed, absentmindedly flicking through the channels of the crappy little television that hung from the ceiling. All the channels were talking nonsense anyhow about some big dinosaur thing—clearly a big network joke. Alice sat on the bed with her, reading. Elizabeth sat in a chair by the window, reading a Bible.

Seriously. Who actually sat around reading the Bible? That was just about all Elizabeth ever seemed to do. She had no interest in anything else. And she clearly wanted nothing to do with Cassie. In fact, Cassie couldn't remember the last time someone had had such scathing contempt for her.

Cassie had been there for five days, and she'd had more than enough. So far, the series of tests had revealed nothing. Zip. Nada. And although the doctors, including Ireland, wouldn't admit it, Cassie knew they didn't have a clue as to what was wrong with Cassie and Elizabeth.

Someone knocked on the door, and all three women glanced toward it at the same moment. The hospital staff didn't knock. Alice got up from the bed and opened it. Standing in the doorway was a middle-aged black man. Just behind him, peering over his shoulder, was a much younger—and very good-looking—young man with short dark hair and intense eyes. Beside him stood a young woman with red hair tied up into a tight bun. All three wore dark business suits. The middle-aged man smiled at Alice and held his hand out. "Hello. You must be Mrs. Heller. My name is Oscar McKnight. I'm with the government. Do you have a few minutes to talk?"

His hair was short and gray, not much more than a crew cut, really. His bearing was erect and proud, giving him the appearance of being much taller than he actually was. And he radiated confidence, reminding Cassie—she realized, with a momentary throb of loss—of her father.

"The government?" Alice asked, confusion in her voice. She looked over her shoulder at her sister. Cassie nodded then glanced quickly toward Elizabeth who was staring at the man, her eyes narrowed. "Please come in," Alice said, stepping out of the way.

McKnight entered, but the other two remained outside. Even in business attire, Cassie could tell they both had athletic builds. They radiated the same aura of confidence and professionalism that McKnight did. They looked, Cassie decided, like police officers or bodyguards.

"Are your friends coming in?" Cassie asked.

"No, let's just talk amongst ourselves for a bit first," McKnight said. The young man pulled the door closed while the woman stood staring down the corridor—exactly like bodyguards.

McKnight approached Elizabeth, his hand out. "You must be Elizabeth. How do you do?"

She stood up and shook his hand. "Who are you again?"

"My name is Oscar McKnight, and it's truly a pleasure to make your acquaintance." He turned from Elizabeth and approached Cassie and her sister, still holding his hand out. His grip was firm and strong, and despite her trepidation, Cassie found herself liking him. He made an excellent first impression. He smoothed out his pants and sat down in one of the chairs, facing all three women. The two sisters sat down on the edge of Cassie's hospital bed. Elizabeth pulled her chair over as well.

McKnight placed his hands in his lap. "This must be very challenging for you."

"Are you with the province, Mr.... McKnight?" Alice asked.

"No, I'm with the federal government, ma'am. I run a research facility in the area."

"There's no federal research facility around here," Elizabeth said, crossing her arms as she regarded him.

His smile only faltered a moment. "Actually, Miss Chambers, there *is*. We're just very discreet."

"What research facility?" asked Cassie. "Why are you here?"

"I'm here, Miss Rogan, because your country needs your help."

Cassie stared at him. "Excuse me?"

McKnight grimaced. "I just heard how that sounds. Let's start over. Five days ago, on the third of May, at exactly 8:25 p.m., a number of people around the Peace River Valley collapsed into comas at the exact same moment. Most of those people died. You two haven't."

"We know all that," said Cassie. "What happened to us?"

"We're not entirely sure," said McKnight, "but the fact that you're still alive is very interesting to us."

"It's pretty goddamned interesting to me as well," said Cassie. "But what's this got to do with the government? What's going on?"

"We don't know," said McKnight. "And that's the simple truth. What we do know is that five days ago, unprecedented weather patterns developed over the Peace River Valley area and nowhere else."

"What are you saying, Mr. McKnight?" Alice asked.

"I'm saying you just don't get electrical storms localized like that. It should be impossible. Something we don't understand took place five days ago. Understanding what happened, and how it affected the two of you, has become a matter of national security."

"Bullshit," said Cassie.

"Have you considered that there is a very simple answer to all of this?" Elizabeth asked, "and that all this is God's design for us?"

McKnight turned to face her. "Perhaps it is God's design, Elizabeth, but we need to find out, and quickly."

"Why?" asked Alice. "What does it matter to the government?"

"People have died," said McKnight.

"Oh, I get that," said Alice, waving her hand at McKnight. "I understand why the province would be concerned. This could be the beginning of an epidemic or something. What I don't understand is why the federal government cares. Fort St. John is a long way from anywhere important."

"*Everywhere* is important," said McKnight.

"It's the Lord's will," Elizabeth said.

Cassie frowned at Elizabeth then turned back to McKnight. "What does this have to do with me?"

"*Both* of you, actually," McKnight said. "You two survived. Whatever affected you may have left some trace elements, something that can be measured and examined. If we can determine what's affecting you, we might be able to help others if this phenomenon resurfaces."

"So far," Elizabeth said, "the hospital hasn't been able to determine anything."

"We have resources this hospital doesn't." McKnight steepled the fingers of his hands and rested his chin on them. "Plus, not to insult this facility, but we don't think they are... best equipped to help you."

"Where are your resources?" Cassie asked. "And help us how, exactly?"

"I'd like the two of you to come with me to our research facility. We'll run tests and maybe discover what's going on. You'll be our guests, and I can guarantee you'll be better taken care of than here. At the same time, you'll be doing a community service, helping others who may become afflicted." He paused and let his gaze travel from Elizabeth to Cassie. "I understand, Elizabeth, that you have already demonstrated some... telepathic abilities."

"Not telepathy, miracles," Elizabeth said. "I've been chosen."

"Indeed," replied McKnight. "Could you show me something now?"

"Excuse me," said Alice. "How do you know that? Isn't this confidential information from hospital records and that sort of thing?"

"Normally, yes, Mrs. Heller, but these are special times. Trust me; I have clearance for everything."

"Well, Mr. McKnight," said Alice. "This is all happening very fast. Where exactly is your facility?"

"I'm sorry. That's confidential. But trust me—we will take excellent care of your sister."

"Confidential?" Cassie asked. "You want me to go off with you to some secret lab somewhere so you can probe me?"

"It won't be like that," McKnight said. "We're not going to probe anyone. We're not talking Area 51 nonsense. We're going to help you."

Cassie shook her head. "No. You're not. I have no intention of going anywhere with you."

"Cassie..." Alice reached out a hand and placed it on her knee. "This is the government. Maybe you should think about—"

"I'm not thinking about anything," snapped Cassie. "I'm not going anywhere. I'm perfectly happy here. The answer is *Hell no,* Mr. McKnight."

"Cassie?" Her sister was staring at her.

"No." Cassie crossed her arms over her chest. "No way."

"I'll go," said Elizabeth. "*I'll* help you, Mr. McKnight. The Lord has chosen me for a reason. It would be a sin not to help others." At that, Elizabeth glared at Cassie.

Cassie was really tempted to flip her the bird. Instead, she snorted and shook her head. "Well you two have fun. I haven't been *chosen* for anything, and I'm not going off to some secret research lab." She turned to Alice. "I want to go home. Besides, I don't have any telepathic powers. I blacked out—that's all."

McKnight was watching her very closely. "Miss Rogan, we really are your best—"

Cassie raised her palm up to his face, cutting him off. "Thank you, Mr. McKnight. Have a nice day."

At that moment, there was a commotion just outside the door. Cassie turned and stared. She could hear Dr. Ireland's irate voice on the other side of the closed door, demanding to be let in. McKnight got up and opened the door.

Dr. Ireland, her face red, was poking her finger into the chest of the young man who had accompanied McKnight and was now blocking her entrance into the hospital room.

"… can get the hell out of my way before I have you removed."

"Alex, please let the doctor in," McKnight said.

The young man stepped aside, and Dr. Ireland stormed into the room.

"What is going on here? Who are you people? If you're with the press—"

"My apologies, Dr. Ireland. My colleague can be a bit

overzealous. My name is McKnight, and we're with the government." He pulled an identity card from his jacket and handed it to her.

He knows her name. Why does he know the name of one of my doctors? She could understand McKnight knowing her and Elizabeth's names, maybe—and it was a big maybe—her sister's name as well, but the name of a patient's doctor? Who the hell was that well informed? No one, Cassie realized with a burst of revelation. The only people that well informed were spies. McKnight was a spook of some kind. This *was* some Area 51 bullshit.

Dr. Ireland snatched the card from his hand and stared at it. "Health Canada? *You're* from Health Canada?" Cassie saw the doubt clearly in the doctor's face as she stared at McKnight.

McKnight took his card back. "A special advisory task force, Doctor. Please contact your hospital administrator. You'll find she's already aware of me. We're here to help."

"What are you doing here?"

"He's here for me," answered Elizabeth. "I've been chosen, and I'm going with him."

"Chosen for what?" Dr. Ireland turned and stared at Elizabeth. "Nobody's going anywhere until I know what's going on."

"Dr. Ireland, we'll wait here until you've spoken to your administrator, but Elizabeth has volunteered to serve her country, and she'll be leaving with us."

"The hell she will! I'm contacting security." The small woman shoved past McKnight, forcing him to jump back, as she stormed out the door.

McKnight frowned. "Trying times. People can be very emotional at times like this, but you've made the right choice, Elizabeth." He turned to face Cassie. "If you change your mind, young lady, you can reach me at this number." He handed her a business card with a phone number written on it. "We really can help you. Perhaps we're the only ones who can."

* * *

Alex carried Elizabeth's suitcase from the hospital room out to the parking lot. Elizabeth silently followed behind McKnight. As they reached the first of the two vans they had arrived in, Sgt. Clara Anderson, another Canadian operator, took the suitcase from Alex. McKnight had insisted on a female soldier accompanying them, saying that a soft, attractive face would help put the young women at ease. It seemed to work. Elizabeth smiled at Clara as she climbed into the van. Out of sight, Alex shook his head and glanced at Clara. Soft? Nobody who had ever seen Clara Anderson in a bar fight would ever believe she was soft.

Just before getting into the van, McKnight paused and looked over his shoulder. McKnight said nothing, only nodding slightly while meeting Alex's eye. The door slammed shut, and the engine started up. Alex stood in the parking lot. It was cool that night, reminding him of home. It was always cold on the Rock, Newfoundland, this time of the year. The van's tires crunched on loose gravel as it pulled away. Within moments, it was out of the parking lot and onto the main road. They'd be back at the Magic Kingdom within the hour. Before Alex had made his move.

He walked over to the second van, opened the passenger door, and climbed inside, joining the two other men waiting within. Pearson drummed his fingers on the steering wheel. Anders was in the back. Both men wore hospital-orderly uniforms.

Anders reached forward, handing Alex another orderly uniform. "When?"

"We'll wait until they call in from the main perimeter," Alex answered.

"The sister still with her?" Pearson asked.

Alex nodded, chewing his lower lip.

"You want to wait until she leaves?"

Alex hesitated while he thought about it. "I'm not sure she's going anywhere anytime soon. I think we'll need to take her as well."

"There'll be less people if we wait until later, say three or four in the morning," Anders said.

Alex shook his head. "Less people means more likely we'd stand out and be challenged. We'll go in shortly while it's still busy then take them out on stretchers like they're patients." He paused and turned in his seat, looking the two men—first Anders and then Pearson—in the eye. "I want to be really, really clear about this, though. We don't hurt anyone."

Anders sighed heavily. "But Buck said—"

Alex reached over the seat and jabbed him in the chest with his finger, cutting him off. "I don't give a red rat's ass what Buck said. These are *my* people—civilians—and we're not going to hurt anyone. This is all our goddamned fault anyhow."

Anders opened his mouth but then thought better of it and said nothing.

Pearson nodded solemnly. "Hey, man, chill. I don't like this any more than you do. I didn't sign on to kidnap women."

Alex turned back and stared out the windshield. He was in a bad mood and needed to get his act together—to be more professional. Emotions got people killed. "There's a lot of things we're doing these days that we didn't sign on for."

Chapter 14

Cassie stood at the window in her room, staring out at the hospital parking lot as Elizabeth climbed into a van with McKnight and the redhead. The other bodyguard didn't leave with Elizabeth and McKnight; instead, he climbed into another vehicle and just sat there. *What's he waiting for?*

"Cassie," Alice said from behind her. "We really need to talk about this."

Alice sat on the end of her hospital bed, her hands clasped between her knees.

"We don't," Cassie said. "We really don't."

"He's from the government. If anyone knows what's going on, it's the government. He might be able to help."

"The *government* might help me? Really? You remember what Dad used to say about the government?"

"Dad used to say lots of things. But that was just talk. He'd want you to get better."

"There's nothing wrong with me. I passed out. That's all."

"That's bullshit, and you know it. Something *is* happening to you—the same thing that's happening to Elizabeth. Something amazing. A miracle."

Cassie rolled her eyes. She crossed her arms over her chest and leaned back against the window ledge. "A miracle? Now you sound just like Elizabeth."

Alice's gaze was direct, challenging. "Honey, I saw you yesterday in the cafeteria. You threw your cup across the room without touching it. You have ESP."

Cassie shook her head. Her mouth went dry, and she felt as if she were standing outside herself, watching. "I... it wasn't like..."

Alice stood up quickly and grabbed Cassie's upper arms, staring into her eyes. "I saw you. I saw you. You can't just do nothing and pretend it hasn't happened. This isn't like with Mom and Dad. You can't just run from—"

Cassie jerked back, pulling away from her sister. Her heart hammered against her chest. "It's the same old song with you, isn't it? Whenever you want to pick a fight, you jump to Mom and Dad. You turn everything I do around and twist it so it's about what I did."

Alice reached out for her, but Cassie stepped back, swatting her hand away. "It isn't about the things you *do*, Cassie. It's about the things you *don't* do. Ever since the accident, you've given up on doing anything at all. You're coasting through life without even trying."

"Right, so everything is my fault again, isn't it?"

"That's not what—"

"It's my fault I got into trouble at UBC."

"Yes," Alice said.

"It's my fault I was failing my classes."

"Were you even trying?"

"It's my fault *this* happened, too, I guess." Cassie's gaze swept the hospital room. "I caused that electrical storm?"

"No, of course it isn't your—"

"It's *my* fault Mom and Dad are dead. That's what you really mean?"

Alice's eyes opened wide, and her head jerked back. "No, no—"

Cassie made fists with her hands and stepped closer to her sister. She knew she was out of control, but she didn't care. This train wasn't stopping before it went off the rails. "I get it. I goddamned get it. Everything is my fault. And my poor, long-suffering big sister has to bear the weight of my constant fuckups, because I am a world-class fuckup!"

"Baby, no." Once again, Alice reached out, but Cassie backpedaled out of the way.

"I'm so sick of this, and I'm so sick of you and your constant attempts to run my life. You're not Mom. You wasted your life, staying in Hudson's Hope and marrying the first guy you ever fucked. Now you're trying to live your sad—"

Cassie's head snapped back under the impact of Alice's slap. Her ears rang. For a moment, the two women stared at one another in shock. Cassie's fingers reached up to her cheek, trailing over the burning skin. Shock registered in Alice's eyes, and her face turned white.

Cassie shook her head and stepped back a pace. "Go to hell, Alice. Just go to hell."

Alice reached out for her sister. "Baby, I'm sorry, I didn't—"

Cassie retreated even farther, stepping into the doorway. "I didn't ask for this, for any of it. I'm sorry I killed Mom and Dad, and I'm sorry I'm such a useless screwup, and I'm sorry this is happening to me."

Alice reached for her again, trying to embrace her, but Cassie did... something like she had done with the teacup in the cafeteria. She didn't mean to; it just happened. Invisible energy cascaded from her like a wave. It smashed into her sister, sending her flying back as though she had been pushed. Alice hit the hospital bed and fell across it.

Cassie squeaked in horror, not believing what she had just done. She turned and bolted down the hospital corridor. Behind her, she heard her sister cry out her name.

* * *

Maelhrandia shifted in place, leaning over Gazekiller's great horned head and peering through the trees at the large complex across the open field before her. She had no idea what this place was, but it was the source of the magic use—the mage—she was certain of that. When she had first seen the structure, she had thought it some sort of fortress, but after examining it more closely, she knew it wasn't built for defense: there were far too many entrances, and all of them were unguarded. The land around the complex had been cleared and covered in the same smooth, dark stone the manlings used to build their roads. Even now, scores of their marvelous vehicles sat in long, orderly rows. She had been watching for hours. Occasionally, a new vehicle would arrive, belching foul vapors, and its occupants would get out and go inside the complex. Often, entire families came and went, seemingly without a care in the world. They acted as though they were the undisputed masters of the Old World.

But where were the true masters, the Ancient Ones? There had been no trace of them in the days since her arrival. Were they all dead? If so, then perhaps the manlings truly had forgotten her people. Soon, though, they would remember the fae seelie and why they used to hide in caves, fearing the dark. Those who survived, if any, would become slaves. No doubt, they'd be happier without all the pretense. The lesser species were secretly always more content with the fae seelie ruling them.

Gazekiller shifted in place, pawing at the trunk of a tree, ripping loose a large chunk of bark. The basilisk didn't like being this close to the manlings and recognized the danger. But Maelhrandia saw nothing to fear. There were no soldiers here, no guards—although they were capable of a responding quickly, as she had noted after attacking their children. Their vehicles moved so rapidly, and the manlings seemed capable of almost instantaneous communication, as if with a mind-tether. As soon as she moved toward the complex, they'd call for reinforcements, and this time they'd likely arrive with the more powerful fire-weapons.

Gazekiller's armor was strong, but she didn't want to test it— her skills at healing were adequate at best. No. She needed to move with determination and ruthlessness, and finish before help could come.

She pulled the Shatkur Orb from a pouch and held it in her palm, staring into its depths. Even here, it throbbed with energy. She'd need to be ready to use it once Gazekiller was done. Replacing the orb within her pouch, she slid from her mount's mighty back, drifting among the trees, keeping her gaze locked on the bizarre manling complex as night fell upon it.

Centuries ago, the Ancient Ones had tricked her people, sending them back to faerum in humiliation and then somehow hiding the cosmic link between the two realms. If she were lucky, the demons would all have died by this point. But maybe… maybe they had passed on their magic to the manlings first. She needed to know. She needed to take the measure of their mages. Her mother would expect it from her daughter, the mage-scout. Then she sensed someone within the complex casting magic again. Her eyes darted to a glass window near the top of one of the wings of the complex. There—the mage was there.

Maelhrandia closed her eyes and focused her will through the mind-tether, seeing through Gazekiller's eyes, feeling the mighty beast's need to rend and kill.

Attack, she commanded. The basilisk raised its horned head and barked out a shrill challenge as it pawed at the soft ground with its front legs. Without any further warning, it charged out into the open, covering the ground at great speed.

* * *

Alex was watching the entrance of the hospital through the windshield of the van when the VHF/UHF radio mounted under the dashboard chirped once, then a female voice came over the radio, announcing the arrival of McKnight's vehicle at the Magic Kingdom. He felt the gaze of Anders and Pearson, glanced at his watch, and noted that it was 6:17 p.m.

He nodded. All three men, dressed in white hospital orderly uniforms, climbed out of the van and began making their way toward the hospital's main entrance. Alex ran his fingers over the pistol hidden in the small of his back. Anders carried a small black sports bag, inside of which was a bottle of chloroform and a cloth, and each man also carried a Taser—more than enough gear to kidnap one young woman. How had it come to this? He had joined the army to serve Canadians not hurt them. Overhead, gray clouds blanketed the early evening sky, matching his mood. He increased his pace, and Anders and Pearson hurried to catch up.

* * *

From the cover of the woods outside the complex, Maelhrandia, her eyes shut, once again probed for magic use. The mage was still there; she could feel the residual effects of the casting. It had been very small—barely a spell at all—but for one such as her, an expert in sensing the flows of magical energy, the residual wisps of arcane power were a beacon.

On faerum, magic was everywhere, a part of all living things, so abundant it was hard to sort through the overlapping waves of power. Even the beasts and insects drew upon the ever-present forces of magic. Here, though, it seemed magic was almost nonexistent.

Could magic go dormant when not used? Maelhrandia could not imagine a world without magic. She could barely go an hour without casting. For her, it was like breathing air. In another thousand years of such neglect, would magic disappear entirely from the Old World?

Maelhrandia didn't know. She wasn't some gnome scholar but a mage-scout. Besides, she sensed that the forces of magic on this world *were* reawakening. The magic around her seemed more powerful than it had when she'd first arrived. The hole her mother had ripped through the Cosmic Veil between realms had altered the status quo.

Change was coming. The fae seelie were returning.

* * *

Lee Costner gunned his motorcycle on a straight stretch of road leading to the hospital. Seated behind him, Ginny tightened her grip around his waist, pushing her helmeted head against his back. They were late for their daily visit to see Cassie. Lee had had matters to see to before he left home for basic training in only a few days' time. Up ahead, he saw the sign for the hospital entrance.

* * *

Maelhrandia watched through Gazekiller's eyes as the basilisk bounded across the field toward the complex. She could have cast Shadow-Soul, cloaking herself in magic, and accompanied the beast, but there might be hidden wards that she might unknowingly trigger, as there were in her own keep. Gazekiller leapt into the air, landing atop one of their vehicles, crushing it beneath his bulk. The basilisk's long tail whipped back and forth, and his eyes began to glow with a blue light as he drew upon the weak arcane energy.

Move, she commanded him. *Attack. Kill!*

The manlings ran screaming, scurrying for safety. One, a huge fat man carrying flowers, stood frozen in terror—just before Gazekiller bowled him over, crushing him and leaving a red smear in his wake. Gazekiller charged for the wall of the complex, killing any manlings too slow to get out of his way. Maelhrandia noted the terrified expression in their faces. Had they forgotten basilisks as well as the fae seelie? *Wait until they see my mother's vanguards. Wait until they see a Great Dragon.*

At the base of the complex, Gazekiller leapt into the air, landing on the side of the building. He began to climb the wall. Broken bricks and crushed materials rained down beneath the basilisk.

* * *

Cassie hadn't run far, only down the hall and into a public washroom. Inside, she leaned against the sink, staring at her face in the mirror. She had totally lost it with Alice, not meaning the terrible things she had said. When she lost her temper, she was like another person, one she didn't like very much. "You are a complete fuckup, Cassie Rogan." Her voice cracked with emotion. "That's all you've ever been. That's all you'll ever be."

She grasped at the taps, fumbling with them before finally turning them on and splashing cold water onto her face, washing away the tears. She needed to—

Cassie bolted upright. She had just felt... something *amazing*.

Somebody else was using the same energy she had discovered. She could actually sense them and feel where they were. It was just like when Elizabeth had moved the pages of her Bible without touching them except this person was farther away. And so strong.

Cassie jumped as the hospital's fire alarm went off. She left the washroom, stepping out into the corridor. That was when she heard the screams. Was the hospital on fire? Orderlies bolted past her, almost knocking her over. Cassie grabbed at one of them, spinning him to face her. "What's wrong? What's going on?"

She saw the confusion and fear in his eyes. "I don't know, but that's the lock-down alarm. Go back to your room and stay inside."

"But—"

He tore away from her grip and ran down the corridor.

Why was the hospital on lock-down? Was this a terrorist attack?

Alice! Cassie started running back to her room. Alice would be terrified, and Cassie had done enough harm to her sister for one day.

When she heard the monstrous roaring, she staggered to a stop right in the hallway. It was an unearthly shrieking like nothing she had ever heard before. Wood splintered; glass shattered. It sounded as if someone was tearing the side of the building away. And the noise was coming from just ahead—from her room!

She stood paralyzed with fear, like an animal caught in the open by a predator's attack. When Alice screamed, Cassie bolted forward.

Chapter 15

At the sound of screaming, Alice had run to the large windows in the hospital room to see what was going on. Horror gripped her at the sight of a giant eight-legged lizard, easily thirty feet long, climbing up the wall of the hospital—coming straight for her. Alice staggered backward, her mind reeling. *I'm dreaming.*

The entire room shook as if struck by a wrecking ball. Alice screamed, falling to the floor, as the giant lizard's head smashed through the window, taking large pieces of the wall with it. Its eyes, the size of garbage-can lids, glowed with a blue fire. The monster had pulled back its head and then rammed it forward again, coming straight at her.

* * *

Alex and the other two men burst out of the stairwell onto the fifth floor. When the alarm went off, they'd been waiting for the elevator, but they knew it would stay locked on the ground floor during an emergency. Only slightly winded from sprinting up five flights, Alex began moving down the corridor toward Cassie Rogan's room. Terrified patients and hospital staff ran straight into him, blocking him.

Then, he heard the staccato roaring of what could only be a giant animal. The walls literally shook with its rage. This was no fire.

"There!" Anders yelled, pointing down the hallway.

Alex saw the back of Cassie Rogan's blond head as it disappeared in the crowd, moving the other way.

"What's going on?" Pearson asked.

"I think maybe this is our dragon," Alex said.

"Shit!" said Pearson. "So, what do we do now?"

"We grab the target then get the hell out of here," Alex said. "Move!" Alex ran down the hallway, pushing his way past the terrified crowd.

McKnight was going to be really, really pissed.

* * *

Through Gazekiller's blue-tinted vision, Maelhrandia saw the terrified mage before her. Paralyzed by fear, the woman had remained in her room. No sadist, Maelhrandia received no gratification in the slaughter of lesser beings—unlike some of her sisters—but she did feel the heady sense of satisfaction course through her as Gazekiller rammed his massive head into the room. The wall shattered, and the woman screamed.

Feast, she ordered. And then, another woman—younger with hideous golden hair—ran into the room just as Gazekiller's jaws bit into the mage. Through the mind-tether, Maelhrandia tasted the blood of her victim, felt the basilisk's satisfaction. Blood splattered the other woman's face as Gazekiller bit the mage in half.

All too easy. *She didn't even try to cast—*

A wall of air smashed into Gazekiller's head—so hard the basilisk was knocked back outside of the building. He lost his grip on the wall and fell several feet before managing to hang on again.

Gazekiller had killed the wrong woman. The golden-haired one was the mage. The basilisk roared in rage, tearing loose pieces of the wall as he climbed back up.

* * *

Alex dashed down the corridor. The roaring of the beast, whatever the hell it was, reverberated through the hallways. He came up behind Cassie Rogan, still standing in front of her hospital room, her hands clenched into fists at her side. When he saw the carnage inside her room, he staggered to a stop: A giant horned lizard head reared up on the other side of a twisted, smashed hole in the wall. The monster was literally hanging onto the outside of the wall. Its teeth were the size of his forearm and wickedly pointed. Its bulbous eyes blazed with a blue radiance. On the floor of the hospital room, just in front of Cassie Rogan's feet, was the severed lower torso of a human being. Through the hole in the wall, the wind whipped and blew the scent of fresh blood and rot into Alex's face.

Someone ran into him from behind, snapping him out of his shock. The monster roared. He grabbed Cassie around the waist and wrenched her back, away from the doorway.

"Kill it!" he screamed at Anders and Pearson, who were standing just outside the room.

Dragging Cassie along with him, he ran back down the corridor. She put up no resistance—likely, she was in shock. He glanced at her blood-splattered face. Was she hurt? He didn't have time to stop and find out. Behind him, he heard the distinctive *pop-pop* of small arms as his colleagues fired at the beast. His mission was the woman, but he was pretty sure he had just killed Anders and Pearson.

He dragged Cassie to the stairwell and held the door open as he shoved her through. Risking a quick glance down the corridor, he saw that Pearson and Anders had stopped firing and were standing like statues. The lizard's head burst through the wall of the hospital room, smashing into the two men.

Their bodies shattered into chunks of red meat. *What the hell?*

The lizard struggled as it pulled itself farther into the hospital corridor, but the space was too enclosed. Plaster and debris rained down from the ceiling, and the entire hospital shook. Its giant eyes, filled with hatred and rage, still glowed with that eerie blue light. Alex reached for the pistol in the small of his back, but Cassie chose that moment to yank free of his grip and flee down the stairwell. He cast one quick glance back at the lizard, now smashing its way toward them, before turning and darting after Cassie, taking the steps three at a time.

He caught up to her before she reached the bottom floor, grabbed her arm again, and dragged her with him through the main floor, past terrified patients and frantic staff. As they reached the main entrance, two RCMP officers ran past, their service automatics drawn. "Don't!" he yelled at their backs. "Pistols won't—"

They were gone. He wouldn't have stopped either, he knew, but it didn't make it any easier. He turned away. Saving Cassie was his only goal at that moment. Whatever that thing was, it seemed to be after her. He shoved his way past terrified people, still gripping her upper arm in a viselike grip. Outside, a large crowd swelled near the entrance, pointing and staring at the hospital. They could hear the beast's screaming, hear it thrashing about on the upper level, but obviously, they had yet to actually see it. If they had, Alex was pretty sure they'd be running for their lives.

When that thing gets loose, it's going to kill indiscriminately. "Everyone get the hell out of here!" Alex yelled, waving his free arm. A few onlookers glanced at him in confusion, but nobody moved.

Once again, he heard the beast roar, metal twisting, glass breaking. He drew his pistol free, released the safety catch, and pointing it in the air, fired four quick shots. Now, the crowd screamed and broke, running in all directions. Cassie also seemed to come awake. She stared at his face in confusion then started pulling away, trying to get free of him.

The lizard's head burst out of the wall above them, showering everyone in broken glass. Alex forced Cassie's head down, covering it with his own body. The monster screamed its staccato challenge and ripped more of its body free of the opening it had just created. Had it known where they were, or had it just found them by chance?

The lizard's rear legs seemed stuck. Its giant horned head spun about, clearly looking for something—or someone. Its gaze locked on Alex and Cassie. "Oh shit!" Alex muttered.

The thing's blue eyes lit up like a searchlight, and Alex turned and bolted, dragging Cassie with him. They needed a vehicle—immediately. Alex glanced about. Pearson had had the keys to the van, not him.

They hit the parking lot, running past terrified people hiding behind parked cars. A second RCMP car roared up to the hospital behind them. Its tires screeched as it halted in front of the hospital. Risking a glance over his shoulder, he saw the lizard was almost free of the hospital wall. He dragged Cassie farther away.

She jerked to a stop. "Lee!" she yelled.

Following her gaze, he saw a young man and woman standing beside a motorcycle, still wearing helmets. Like everyone else, they were staring in shock at the giant lizard. Alex let Cassie drag him to them. The young man yanked his helmet loose and dropped it on the ground. His eyes went wide when he saw the pistol in Alex's grip.

"What the hell are you doing? Let her go!"

"Give me the bike," Alex ordered.

"What?"

"Lee," Cassie said. "Alice is dead."

"What's happening? What is that thing?" asked the other woman.

The lizard was free of the hospital now and had bounded to the ground, swiveling its massive head about, no doubt still looking for Cassie.

"We need your bike," Alex said, letting go of Cassie and gripping the shoulder of the young man.

"What?"

Pistol fire rang out from behind them. The police were still trying to stop the creature.

"Lee," Alex said, putting steel into his voice. "Your name is Lee, right?"

He nodded.

"Lee, if you don't help us, that thing is going to kill Cassie. We need your bike."

The young woman turned from Cassie to Alex then to the giant lizard. "Do it, Lee—just do it."

The young man rammed his fingers into the pocket of his leather jacket and thrust his keys into Alex's hands. Alex climbed aboard the bike, dragging Cassie with him. This time she yanked free of his grip, remaining with her friends. Alex locked eyes with her. "Cassie, you have to trust me."

"I won't leave my friends," she said, shaking her head.

"Cassie, if you don't get on this bike, that thing is going to kill you, me, and your friends."

"Cassie, do it—just go," pleaded the other woman.

"Go, Cassie," said Lee.

The pistol fire had stopped. They were out of time. She hesitated only a moment longer and then climbed onto the bike behind him, locking her arms around his waist. The engine roared as it came to life.

"Run!" Alex screamed to the young man and woman.

As they turned and fled among the parked cars, Alex put the bike in gear, gunning the engine. Its tires spun as they fought for purchase. Alex changed gears again and sped out of the parking lot, hitting the street and accelerating. As they roared away, they passed a fire truck heading for the hospital, red lights flashing and siren thunderous.

Alex felt like a coward, but he had no other choice.

"Where are we going?" she yelled into his ear.

"As far away from here as we can get."

Part 2
The Magic Kingdom

Chapter 16

Cassie clung to Alex's back as he drove Lee's motorcycle south, away from the hospital, away from the city. Nothing made any sense, and it was difficult to think clearly, but she was aware that they drove southeast along the Alaskan Highway, through the community of Taylor, and then across the bridge that spanned the roaring Peace River. Unlike Alex, she wore no helmet, so the wind assaulted her face. With no other choice, she placed her cheek up tight against his back.

Alice is dead. How is that possible? It isn't. I'm dreaming, having a nightmare.

But her nightmares were almost always of the night her parents died.

Across the river, Alex slowed down and turned off the highway, heading west along Big Bam Road in the direction of the Big Bam Ski Hill. She had been there many times before, but not in years. Her heartbeat was racing, and coldness began to spread out from her core. She turned her head, looking back the way they had come and seeing nothing but trees. They passed the ski lodge but kept going.

Is there anything else this far out?

Alex slowed down when the paved road ended then pulled onto a dirt road. A large sign warned they were now on private government property and that all trespassers would be prosecuted. Where was he going?

"There's nothing here," she yelled into his helmeted head.

"It's all right," he yelled back. "You're safe now."

Well, of course I'm safe. None of this is real.

She heard rushing water and realized they must be close to the Pine River, a tributary of the Peace River. A moment later, she saw the river and the bridge that spanned it—a new bridge, one that shouldn't be there, all metal and strong looking albeit narrow. Alex slowed down as he drove across it. On the opposite bank, the dirt road continued into the woods.

She closed her eyes again and lost track of time. She needed to sleep—she was so exhausted. But how could she go to sleep if she were already dreaming? And who was tired in a dream? Nothing made sense.

Her eyes flashed open just as she realized she was starting to slip off the bike. She gripped Alex even tighter. He yelled something to her, but she couldn't make it out. It was becoming increasingly hard for her to focus. The chill that had begun in her stomach had spread throughout her entire body, and she couldn't stop shivering.

Now she knew she was dreaming, because up ahead a tank blocked the road. Alex slowed down and came to a stop in front of it. He lifted his visor and started talking to a soldier standing up in a hatch on the top of the tank. She recognized her name but couldn't focus on what they were saying. The soldier waved them on, and Alex drove past. Up close, she realized it probably wasn't a tank after all because it had big, high wheels, and she was pretty sure tanks were supposed to be tracked. Surprised, she also now saw that the soldier Alex had been speaking to was a young woman. Cassie smiled and waved, holding on to Alex with only one hand. She may have been dreaming, but there was no need to be rude.

The female soldier looked confused, but she raised her hand and waved back.

Cassie's vision began to turn gray around the edges, and she could no longer feel her fingertips. Perhaps she should just let go and fall off. She could curl up on the ground and close her eyes, be alone in silence. That might be nice.

They drove out of the woods and into a vast open area that had been cleared of trees and covered in gravel. Ahead of them, she saw a large fence topped with razor wire, surrounding a massive complex of buildings and trailers. Alex drove toward a gated guard building. The motorcycle's tires crunched on loose stones as he came to a stop. Several young men in dark-blue security uniforms and bulletproof vests, carrying machine guns, came out and surrounded them. She found herself staring into the face of a large dog that stood on a leash next to one of the guards. The dog, its ears standing up high, locked its eyes on Cassie and then cocked its head as if confused. Alex was explaining something to the guards—no, that wasn't right: he was giving them orders. She watched them for a moment but then lost interest. Once again, she stared into the dog's eyes, smiled, and fell off the bike.

She heard the dog barking, but it seemed far off and quickly grew fainter as she slipped away.

Chapter 17

Cassie screamed as the avalanche of mud, water, and debris smashed into her parents' car, knocking it off the highway and down the embankment. The car flipped again and again, yanking her against her seat belt. With a crunch of metal, it came to an abrupt halt—right side up but almost standing on its hood, its rear end in the air. She hung forward against her seatbelt, gasping for air. The car's headlights shone against the trunk of the tree that it had smashed into. All around them, the mudslide continued to roar as the slurry sped past. Then, it poured over the hood of the car. She heard screaming and then realized it came from her.

Her mother kept calling her father's name, but he didn't answer. The dark muddy waters reached the front windshield and then began to rise over it. The light from the headlights went dark, and all she could make out was the silhouette of her parents' heads. She frantically jabbed at the release button for her seatbelt, but it wouldn't give. She was trapped.

The waters reached the side windows. Something salty dripped down the side of her head and into her mouth. The waters continued to rise, now reaching the rear windows. Soon, the entire car would be submerged.

"Cassie!" her mother yelled, cutting through her lethargy. "Pay attention. Can you get out?"

"What?"

"Baby, can you get out?" Her mother's voice trembled, but there was determination in it as well as fear.

"I... the seatbelt is stuck. Get me out. Dad, help!"

Her father didn't answer.

"What's wrong with Dad? Make him answer."

"Baby, listen to me." Cassie could just make out the shine of her mother's eyes in the darkness where she had turned around in her seat. "You're hanging against your seatbelt, pulling against it. You need to brace yourself against something first."

"Mom, I'm scared."

"It'll be fine, baby, but you need to move, now!"

The windshield cracked, the sound too loud within the car. The furor of the mudslide was growing dimmer as the car became submerged.

"Hurry, baby. Push with your feet against the front seat."

"But—"

"Now!"

Cassie shoved her feet against the seat in front of her and pushed. Then she jabbed at the seatbelt release button again, certain it wouldn't work.

It did. As the seatbelt snaked loose, Cassie fell forward against the front seat, closer to her parents. Gasping, she wrapped her arms around her mother's neck. Her mother gripped Cassie's arm and sobbed.

"Mom, help Dad."

Her mother pried her arms loose. "Baby, you have to go."

"I'm not going anywhere."

Once again, she tried to wrap her arms around her mother's

neck, but her mother held her wrists away. "Cassie! Listen to me. You need to get out of here now. We'll follow. If you stay, you'll drown."

"But—"

"Do it!"

Cassie grasped at her handle and tried to push the car door open, but it didn't budge. She groaned, gritting her teeth and slamming her shoulder against the door as she pulled on the handle. Nothing.

"Not working." She was nearly breathless with effort and terror.

The slurry lapped over the top of the rear window.

"Here, try this." Her mother reached over and shoved a heavy metal object into Cassie's hands. It was the rod her father used to lock his steering wheel whenever he parked in Fort St. John. It was at least a foot-long piece of solid steel, weighing about five pounds. Her mother had always teased her father about it, making fun of his paranoia. He, in turn, had insisted they needed it, that car thieves were always prowling the city, waiting to steal their six-year-old family car.

The rod was smooth, hard, and cold in her grip. "What should I do?"

"Smash out the rear window. Swim free. Don't stop for anything."

"But Dad…"

"I'll bring Dad. You just swim up. Just go up."

"But—"

"Baby, do it now!" Her mother was shrieking. The panic in her voice was unmistakable, terrifying in itself, and it galvanized Cassie into action.

Turning, she squared off against the rear window and gripped the rod in both hands like a bat. As hard as she could, she smashed the rear window, creating a spider's web of cracks across it, but it held. Frantic, she hit it again, and again, and then again. With each hit, the cracks widened. Water sprayed in her face, cold and terrifying.

"It's not working," she gasped, looking over her shoulder at her mother, but now it was too dark to see anything.

Her mother reached forward, ran her palm against Cassie's cheek. "One more time, baby, as hard as you can."

Cassie paused, panting. "You and Dad will be right behind me, okay?"

"Of course we will. We love you, baby."

This time, Cassie hit the window with every ounce of strength she possessed. She had expected it to stay in place, so when the window suddenly came loose, and an onslaught of cold water and mud rushed into the car, Cassie was taken completely by surprise. The slurry, the consistency of thick soup, filled her open mouth and choked her.

The air, now suddenly released, was sucked out in one huge bubble, carrying Cassie along with it. Panicking, she swallowed even more water. With no idea which way was up, she was certain she was about to drown. But then her head broke free of the water. She hacked, coughing and wheezing, but she was breathing. Air had never been so amazing.

The current grabbed her, carrying her away from her parents' submerged car. *No,* her subconscious told her. *This isn't happening; it's just that damned nightmare again.* With that knowledge, her dreams shifted and went to a better place.

* * *

Eventually, Cassie began to wake. She didn't know why, but her subconscious warned her against waking up. *There's safety in sleep,* an inner voice whispered. It was a way to avoid something horrible that she couldn't face. Inevitably, though, she had no choice. Groaning, she opened her eyes.

At first, she thought she was back in her hospital room, but then she realized she was in another hospital room, which made no sense at all. This one was smaller than the room she had shared with Elizabeth and shrouded in shadow. The blinds on the windows were closed, but there was bright sunlight coming in around the edges and she was covered by warm blankets. It was nice here—pleasant. She heard soft footsteps as someone approached the side of the bed. Gentle fingers took her hand and then brushed a strand of hair out of her eyes. "How are you feeling?" a female voice asked.

How was she feeling?

"Fine," she mumbled then closed her eyes again.

Giant blue eyes flashed in her memory. Once again, she saw rows of jagged teeth dripping blood—Alice's blood! Cassie bolted upright, gasping for air. Heat and power flushed through her body, bringing with it that odd metallic taste in her throat once again. The drape-covered windows exploded outward in an eruption of glass and shattered blinds, instantly filling the room with bright sunlight. Beside her, Cassie saw the terror on the face of a young woman wearing a medical uniform. The woman, a nurse or a doctor, covered her face with her arms.

Alice! Oh, God, no—Alice!

Cassie screamed and was only dimly aware as more people rushed into the room. They gripped her, holding her down on the bed, where she continued to thrash and yell. She felt pressure running through her arm and realized someone must have given her a shot. The power that she had filled her body with was replaced by a wave of numbness. Nausea rippled through her core, and she closed her eyes, trying to breathe through huge heaving sobs. *Alice is dead.*

When Cassie passed out again, it was a blessing.

* * *

When Cassie finally woke up again, Alice was still dead. A moan escaped her lips as she brought her hand up to cover her eyes. There was an intravenous tube attached to the back of her hand, running to a drip bag hanging from a hook on the wall. This time, the lights in the room were on, and McKnight sat in a chair beside her bed, a report in his hand, reading glasses on his face. When he saw Cassie was awake, he closed the file, removed his glasses, and smiled.

"Good morning. Or rather, good evening. It's almost seven p.m.," he said softly.

"How long have I been out?" Her mouth felt as if she had been chewing on an old sock.

"Since yesterday. You woke up once, but there were some... issues. We had to sedate you, move you to another room. The medical staff will want to examine you and make sure you're okay."

"I'm okay. Where am I? What medical staff? Health Canada staff?"

McKnight sat back, regarding her with a piercing look. Long moments passed before he spoke again. "No, Cassie. *Army* medical staff. You never really believed I was with Health Canada, did you?"

Cassie pushed herself up on her elbows then winced as a wave of vertigo rushed through her. "Army? What's the Canadian Army doing this far north?"

"US Army, actually." He climbed out of his chair and approached Cassie's side. "Although we're working jointly with your military. Captain Benoit—Alex, the man who brought you here—is with the Canadian Army." He picked up a remote control attached to the hospital bed by a thick, rubberized cable. Holding one of the buttons down, he automatically adjusted the angle of Cassie's bed, raising it so that she could sit up and see him more comfortably. "That good?"

Cassie nodded, still feeling ill.

McKnight stepped away, disappearing into a bathroom. Cassie heard water running. When he reappeared, he handed her a glass of water, which she took in two shaky hands and drank from, spilling some of it down her chin. He waited by her bedside and took the empty glass back when she was done. "More?"

Cassie shook her head. "Who are you really?"

He sat back down again. "My name really is Oscar Redford McKnight. It's just that the full title is *Colonel* Oscar Redford McKnight."

She nodded. "You look like a soldier, not a government official. You're too... serious looking."

McKnight smiled. "I'll take that as a compliment."

"It isn't a compliment."

He winced.

Despite all the deception, Cassie found herself liking him. She shoved that impulse down, concentrating on her situation. She knew nothing of this man. For all she knew, she could be in grave danger. "So, what do I call you—sir?"

"Colonel is fine."

"Okay, what the fuck is going on, *Colonel*? My sister is..." Cassie swallowed back a sob. She wasn't going to cry in front of this guy. He knew what was going on. He sure as hell knew more than he had admitted to when they had first met. Closing her eyes, she put her head back against her headboard, fighting to control her emotions.

"I'm so very sorry about your sister. If we had known it was going to attack the hospital, we would have been there."

"What was that monster?"

McKnight sighed. His eyebrows rose. "We're not sure. It escaped after the attack."

"It *escaped*? How does a giant dragon escape?"

His face looked pained. "It *disappeared*."

She stared at him. "Disappeared?"

He nodded.

"You're the army. You're the 9-1-1 for the police. Do something!"

"We're trying. That's why we asked you and Elizabeth for help."

"Why us?"

McKnight looked down, unable or unwilling to meet her eyes. "Because we don't understand what's going on." Silence, heavy and unwelcome, settled over them. "Something changed the night of the electrical storm, and we're still struggling to understand what. This creature, the giant lizard, it isn't the first bizarre animal we've come across although it's by far the largest and most dangerous. You and Elizabeth, as well as at least one other individual, are somehow connected to these events—and to that monster."

"That's bullshit. I don't have a goddamned clue what's going on. That thing murdered my sister."

"We think it was after *you*."

Her mouth hung open, and her vision seemed to tunnel in on her. "What?"

"I'm sorry. I can't imagine how this makes you feel, but that creature went straight for your room. Out of all the rooms in that hospital, it somehow zeroed in on yours, the only one containing a sensitive."

She shivered. "A what?"

"A sensitive. A mag-sens. That's how my staff have taken to describing you and the other two affected by the electrical storm—or rather, by the changes that occurred during the storm."

Her eyes narrowed. "Sensitive to what?"

McKnight, looking utterly uncomfortable, ran a hand over his crew cut. "For lack of a better word... *magic.*"

"Magic?" she repeated in a barely audible whisper.

McKnight grimaced and sighed. "I do know exactly how this sounds, and believe me, there's a scientific explanation we just don't understand yet, but you and the other two are somehow able to tap into something—a kind of energy form that's never existed here before."

"*Here* being Fort St. John?"

"*Here* being planet Earth."

She slowly shook her head. "Do you understand how crazy this sounds?"

"You can move objects, can't you, Cassie? So can Elizabeth, and so can Duncan, although Elizabeth is much better at it. That's how you destroyed the windows in your room."

She felt her face go red.

"I... who is Duncan?"

"The third mag-sens. He was the first to join us. You'll meet him later."

"What if I don't want to join you?"

"That creature was after *you*, Cassie, not the other patients. You. If we don't stop it..."

Me. Alice is dead because of me. How many others died at the hospital? She was afraid to ask.

"There's more. You were told that some people affected by the electrical storm went into a coma and didn't wake up?"

She nodded, feeling a fluttery sensation in her stomach.

"That wasn't entirely true. Mostly, it was the very elderly who didn't wake up again, and we think their hearts simply couldn't cope with the stress. But at least one other person, a middle-aged woman, *did* wake up. Unfortunately, she spontaneously caught on fire... and died."

Beneath her covers, Cassie sat up straighter, pulling her knees up against her chest and wrapping her arms around them. "She *what?*"

"Died. She burned to death. And when you woke up earlier today, you somehow blew the windows out of the room we had you in."

"I... I don't remember." Cassie looked away.

"There's more. That monster at the hospital, it also demonstrated an... *ability.*"

Her body tensed, and once again, she saw its glowing blue eyes.

"It turned two of my men to stone. At least... part of them... their skin."

"That's... that's impossible."

"So is moving objects with your mind and spontaneously catching on fire."

"I... don't..."

"The creature that attacked you, that killed your sister—we think it's a basilisk, a creature straight out of our myths. Apparently, it really exists. Or at least, it existed somewhere else, and now it's here."

"What the fuck are you saying?" She heard the panic in her own voice and felt the tremors run through her body.

"This is just a theory, but maybe we know what a basilisk is because humanity has been exposed to them before, just so long ago that we thought they were only a myth. Maybe the myths are based on reality… and so is magic… or at least a force that we just can't adequately explain yet."

She shook her head, almost violently, her lips set to a tight line, and she hugged her knees tighter and began to rock back and forth. "This is impossible."

McKnight inclined his head. "Maybe, but it's all happening just the same, and we need to cope with it right now. People are dying. That thing, the basilisk, is still out there, and there are *other* creatures as well."

She glared at him. "Such as?"

"Giant wolves that breathe fire. My staff call them 'hellhounds.'"

Hellhounds, basilisks, and now wizards. Cassie closed her eyes, feeling the room spin about her.

McKnight got up and sat on the edge of her bed. He took her hand and held it in both of his. "Cassie, I promise you, we are going to get to the bottom of this. Figuring this out is my job. And we're going after these creatures—the hellhounds, the basilisk. We're going to hunt them down, and we're going to stop them before they hurt anyone else. But we need your help."

"I can't—"

"Cassie, somehow, you're all connected. You, Elizabeth, Duncan, the basilisk, and all of the other mag-sens who died, maybe even some who've survived that we don't know about yet. We're going to track this thing down, and we're going to stop it, but if you don't help us, more innocent people might die."

"Who are you people? What is this place? This is the Site C Dam, isn't it? What are you doing here?"

"We've taken over the Dam infrastructure to use as a base of operations. It's private and out of the way. We've put together a very special group of young men and women to go after these creatures."

"What aren't you telling me?"

McKnight let go of her hand and stood up. "I'm telling you the truth, Cassie. I just don't know the answers to your questions—not yet. But maybe we can figure this out together."

It's my fault Alice is dead. It was after me.

When she answered, her voice was small, almost a whisper. "All right. I'll help you... if I can."

He patted her hand and smiled. "You've made the right choice, Ms. Rogan. Cassie."

He got up and walked to the doorway then paused. "Eat. Get some rest. Our scientific staff will want to run some tests." The door closed behind him, and she was alone again.

Chapter 18

Alex sat back in the plush leather armchair in Colonel McKnight's office, watching the colonel, who stood in front of the window, his back to his guests. Buck sat on the couch, his ankle resting on his knee, the same pissed-off look on his face that he always had. At the opposite end of the couch, Helena Simmons sat with her notepad open, scribbling into it. Outside, it was almost dark. In the regular army, a meeting at eight in the evening would be very unusual; in the Special Forces, though, these were normal business hours. Things got done at any hour of the day or night.

Alex's eyes flicked to the large plasma screen mounted on the wall of the colonel's office. It was muted, but the twenty-four-hour news channels were still covering the basilisk attack at the Fort St. John hospital, still speculating on the origins of that impossible creature. The person being interviewed was a paleontologist who claimed that the creature could only be a dinosaur that had somehow survived extinction and was now living in some "Lost World" in the far north.

Alex shook his head. The colonel leaned against his windowsill, gazing out at the dam in the river. When Alex and the others had arrived a few minutes earlier, the colonel had been on the phone.

Alex didn't know if it had been with Ottawa or Washington, but either way, it had definitely been another ass chewing for the task-force commander. The attack on the hospital was all over the news. Giant dragons with glowing blue eyes tended to have that effect. The basilisk had killed twelve people in the attack—including Pearson and Anders. Fort St. John had become an international media circus with animal experts, zoologists, and paleontologists flying in to stand in front of the damaged hospital and give their bullshit opinions about what had happened. Not one of them had a clue. How could they? *The basilisk and the hellhounds came from Rubicon. Somehow, they've followed us back.*

McKnight sighed and turned to face the others. "Ms. Rogan will work with us. So there's that at least—we have all three mag-sens."

Mag-sens—magic-sensitive—was the new term the Task Force Devil scientists were using for those people in the Fort St. John area who were able to draw upon this new energy source. The label made Alex uneasy. Scientists always had to categorize things, fit them into neat boxes for better understanding. But these were people, and they were going through a terrible ordeal. Helena nodded in satisfaction at the colonel's announcement, but Buck's scowl deepened, and Alex had to force himself not to smile. There was no point in antagonizing Buck; he'd only take it out on Alex at a later point.

"She can join the other two later. Just watch her carefully. The basilisk killed her sister right in front of her. That has to mess you up."

"She'll be monitored twenty-four, seven," said Dr. Simmons. "Perhaps a heart-rate monitor and some other electronics for blood and urine testing—wireless devices."

McKnight's lips tightened. "Wasn't exactly what I had in mind,

Doctor." His gaze swiveled to Alex. "Captain, she's closer to your age, and you already have a connection after saving her life. Take care of this yourself."

Buck smiled, and Alex fought back a flash of annoyance. "Yes, sir. Done."

McKnight still stared at Alex as if he were unsure of what to say next, an unusual moment for such a decisive leader. "Captain, I've lost men before. I do understand what you must be feeling, and we're going to honor Specialists Pearson and Anders. Take comfort in the knowledge that you saved Ms. Rogan. You achieved your mission."

Alex looked down at his hands, feeling a thickness in his throat. "Those men died while I—"

"Those soldiers died doing their duty. They chose to serve their country. Cassandra Rogan and the other mag-sens are going to make a contribution to Task Force Devil and Operation Rubicon; I know it. Through them, and their manipulation of this new energy source, we will gain a better understanding of what's happened and how we can fix things and get the mission back on track."

"*If* it can be fixed, Colonel," Helena said.

"Sir," said Buck, leaning forward. "These civilians might not be able to do anything for us other than distract us from what needs to be done. Who cares if they can telepathically make an empty milk container slide an inch across a table in a laboratory? This isn't going to help us. We need to apply basic soldiering skills to this problem set, not scientific mumbo jumbo. We hunt these monsters down, and we kill them. Simple."

Helena's face went scarlet. "That's a vast oversimplification of the control demonstrated by the test subjects. Ms. Chambers, for example, can manipulate much heavier—"

McKnight raised his hand, cutting her off. "Doctor, please. No one means any disrespect to you or your staff's efforts." He frowned at Buck. "Major, you may have the best hammer in the world, but not every problem is a nail."

Buck sat rigid, his eyes narrowed in anger, but he nodded. "Yes, sir."

McKnight sighed and shook his head. Alex glanced at the television screen showing out-of-focus camera footage of the basilisk climbing out of the wall of the hospital.

"People," said McKnight, "we have nothing. Nothing. We were on top of this, and overnight, everything turned upside down on us. People in Washington and Ottawa are asking questions. They've made the connection between the monster and us. If we don't fix this, and right goddamned now, the people in power are going to step in and fix it for us. And that means they're going to fix it *to* us. I guarantee none of you want to see that happen. You will not be happy."

"Yes, sir," both men answered. Helena nodded her head like a bird.

"There are monsters out there," McKnight continued. "Somehow, they've followed us back from Rubicon, and they've brought magic with them, or at least a power source we can't see or measure. We need to find these things, stop them, and make sure they don't manage to come across again. And we need to figure out this energy source, find a way to tap into it ourselves."

Alex leaned forward. "We're going to need bigger weapons, sir. High-caliber weapons. Pistol fire was ineffective against the basilisk."

McKnight paused. "I have plans for the basilisk, Captain. Something other than destroying it, something that may yet save our collective asses with the people in power. But first we need to find it." He turned to face Buck. "Major, any success with finding a local tracker?"

"Done, sir," said Buck. "I got an Indian. He's supposed to be shit hot."

"I think they prefer First Nations citizen," said McKnight.

"Yes, sir, a First Nations citizen—one of the Beaver people." Buck grinned, exposing his two front teeth in what he must have imagined passed for a beaver's face.

Alex stared in disbelief. How did this guy become a major?

When no one laughed, the smile disappeared from Buck's face. "He's in the barracks now. He's ready to go when we are. Says he can track anything around here."

"We're not tracking anything from around here," said Alex.

Buck glared at him, but McKnight raised a hand to forestall any further comment. "Good work, Major, but watch him closely as well. Make sure he doesn't see anything from Operation Rubicon."

"Yes, sir," answered Buck. "I have one of the men keeping an eye on him."

McKnight nodded. "Make sure we have at least two assault teams ready to move. When the mag-sens are ready, I want at least one with each team."

Alex opened his mouth but then closed it again. McKnight stared at him. "What, Captain? Speak up."

"Sir," said Alex. "Shouldn't we wait? They might get killed."

"They might get *us* killed," said Buck.

"Helena's people will work with them," McKnight said. "If they can tap into this... magic... mana... whatever, then maybe they can act as a form of proximity alarm whenever we're near these creatures."

Helena leaned forward. "It's possible. They are sensitive to mana and can usually ascertain whenever another subject is using this energy. So far, Ms. Chambers has consistently been able to demonstrate knowledge of whenever Mr. Hocking has... channeled. They use that term amongst themselves: *channeling*. At any rate, not only has she been able to sense when he's channeling, she's also been surprisingly accurate estimating where he is, often within two or three meters."

McKnight locked eyes with Buck, then Alex. "Might be useful having a human Geiger counter—don't you think, gentlemen?"

Geiger counter or mine canary?

"They could provide a tactical advantage," said Helena.

Buck snorted. "*If* they stay the hell out of the way once the shooting starts."

"Keep them out of the way, Major. These people are unique, the very first humans who have demonstrated the ability to draw upon and manipulate a previously unknown power source."

"Unless we have had earlier interaction with the inhabitants of Rubicon," Dr. Simmons interjected. "Perhaps it has happened before during the early history of humanity, maybe hundreds—if not thousands—of years ago. Think about it. All the legends of wizards, witches, tribal sorcerers, magical creatures. There may be an element of truth to these legends if humanity has been exposed to mana before."

"Lot of 'ifs' flying around this room," Buck said.

"Indeed, Major," said McKnight, "but that's all we have right now: theories."

The room was silent. Outside, in the wilderness surrounding the Site C Dam Complex, a loon cried out, its haunting call echoing across the forest. McKnight was right: overnight, everything they had known had changed. An ambush in Rubicon had somehow resulted in creatures of myth and legend running loose on Earth. Somewhere out there, perhaps very close, a giant lizard that could turn people to stone and a pack of fire-breathing wolves prowled the wilderness. Innocent people had died and were going to keep dying until Task Force Devil found them. The world had truly taken a bizarre turn.

And apparently, magic was now a real thing.

Chapter 19

Cassie was sitting in a chair by the window in her wardroom when someone knocked on the door. The army medical staff would have knocked and then come right in, but whoever was out there was still waiting. She stared at the door, knowing she should say something but just not having the energy to move or speak. It wasn't as if she were doing anything. She was just sitting and thinking with the sunlight on her face.

She didn't want to sleep anymore. Sleep brought nightmares.

"What?" she finally called out, aware her voice sounded strained.

The door opened. It was Alex, Captain Benoit of the Canadian Army. When he looked at her, she recognized a flash of something in his eyes, pity perhaps. "Sorry to bother you," he said. "Colonel McKnight thought you might want to get out of this room."

"And do what?" she asked, not really caring.

He held a battered old army duffel bag in one hand, which he placed on the floor beside him. "We put together some clothing for you. It's not much, but it's more than a hospital gown. Uniforms and gym gear mostly."

Her eyes dropped to the duffel bag, and she stared at it for several moments.

"Cassie…" He watched her, clearly not certain what else to say.

"What?" she said, still staring at the dark-green duffel bag.

"You can't stay in this room forever. I'll wait outside in the hallway while you get dressed, and then I'll show you around."

"Show me around? What's around?"

"Well… for the next little while, home. At least, our home."

She choked back a laugh. "Home?"

"I'll be outside the door while you get dressed." He closed the door, leaving the duffel bag on the floor.

She watched it for several moments and then pushed herself off the chair. *Why not? It's not like I'm doing anything else.*

She rifled through the bag, finding gray sweatpants, a T-shirt, and a blue hoodie. There was a pair of used gym shoes, as well, which she was surprised to find were her size. Had they guessed correctly or measured her when she was passed out? She wasn't sure she really wanted to know.

Dressed, she stood in front of the door. *I can't stay here, hiding in a hospital room. Alice would want me to keep rolling.* Cassie reached for the door handle.

* * *

Cassie hadn't intended to be impressed by the Site C Dam; in fact, she wouldn't have thought it possible, but the complex was something to see after all. Her father would have loved this place, but he had been an engineer. The dam itself was a massive earth-filled concrete structure spanning the Peace River. God only knew what kind of long-term environmental damage it was doing, but it was impressive as hell. Alex led her along the south bank of the river, past the Spillway. From there, he pointed out the huge generating station. The reservoir spread out on the other side of the dam, looking more like a lake than a river. She couldn't help but think about the lands they had flooded when the dam went up, all the wildlife killed or displaced in the name of electricity. All of the site's buildings were located on the south bank of the Peace River. The north bank was dominated by a large cliff, which met the concrete wall of the dam. A single access road ran parallel along the cliff, crisscrossing its way up to the top. Another of those bizarre-looking tanklike vehicles moved along the access road. Most of the land around the south bank had been cleared of brush and was now covered with loose gravel. Alex told her most of it would eventually be paved. As they walked, he pointed out the perimeter fence, a ten-foot-high, razor-wire-topped barrier surrounding the site.

He took her around to some of the site buildings: the large cafeteria—which must have seated a hundred or more people—an impressive-looking gymnasium, numerous warehouses, and a massive hangar, which Alex claimed housed the site's vehicles and aircraft. They also passed several dormitory buildings. One of them Alex pointed out as the barracks she would be moving into later that day. Finally, he brought her by a small redbrick building that Alex said was an all-ranks bar. A paper taped to the glass of the door displayed a cartoon demon with a pitchfork chasing a dragon. It would have been much funnier had that dragon not killed her sister. As they stood in front of the glass door, another one of the ugly boat-shaped armored vehicles drove past, blowing up a small cloud of loose gravel and dirt. Up close, the machine gun on the automated turret looked lethal and high-tech. Something like that would no doubt shred the basilisk.

"So anyhow," said Alex, "this is our home. We call it the Magic Kingdom."

"Why?"

He paused in thought for a moment before answering. "Operators have a weird sense of humor. Someone thought it sounded funny, you know, like Disneyland. Kind of lame now that I stop and think about it."

She stared at his face. She was certain there was more to it than someone thinking it sounded funny but let it go. "Operators?"

"Special Forces operators. That's how we identify ourselves."

"You're Special Forces?"

"Task Force Devil."

He must have seen the frown on her face, because he elaborated. "So, whenever armies put together a special team for a mission—or an operation, which is a bunch of missions—we form what's called a task force, an organization of people, gear, and support facilities to help get the job done."

"So, why that name?"

"Well, remember I said operators have a weird sense of humor?"

She nodded.

"We also have a highly developed appreciation for history and tradition. This is a joint American-Canadian task force. That's actually very unusual, but it's not unheard of. In 1942, during the Second World War, there was another joint unit, the 1st Special Service Force. It was kind of the first-ever Special Forces unit in North America, an American-Canadian version of the British commandos. It was a highly decorated fighting force that did combat in Italy and France."

"So, why *Devil*?"

"The 1st Special Service Force was also known as the Devil's Brigade. German officers referred to them as 'Black Devils.'"

"That's it?"

"I said we had a highly developed appreciation for history. I didn't say it was always super clever."

She smiled, patted his forearm, then grabbed his shoulders and turned him to face the all-ranks-mess entrance. "Is this bar open now?"

He smiled, raising his eyebrows. "Come on. I'll buy you a beer. Then I have to get back to work, and you need to move into the barracks. Tonight, you start training with the other lab rats."

"Nice. You know how to flatter a girl."

He held the door for her.

* * *

Cassie was bored out of her mind. She sat on the edge of her bed in her new room in the barracks and contemplated her surroundings. The barracks was kind of like a university dorm only way less interesting and much cleaner. Her small room came with an uncomfortable little bed with hard white sheets and a scratchy gray wool blanket that had a black racing stripe running down its center. There was no television and only a small radio alarm clock on a bedside table. A flimsy wooden chair sat in front of a small desk near the open window.

It was all very orderly, very functional, and very sad. No Internet, no Wi-Fi—not that she had her phone anyhow. The Hotel Del Spartan, she mused. *And Lee wants to join up and live like this all the time?*

Since her brief walkabout with Alex, she had been left to herself. Testing with Dr. Simmons and her staff was to commence later that evening, but for the moment, there was nothing much to do but sit around, stare at her hands, and contemplate her life.

She was all alone in the world. Her entire family was dead. She was a twenty-year-old orphan. It was like a bad joke, only it wasn't a joke at all. Every time she closed her eyes, she saw the monster again, saw it kill her sister.

She jumped to her feet, deciding she couldn't stay there anymore. It was almost supper time anyhow. She'd make her way over to the cafeteria. Flinging her door open, she stormed out into the hallway—and ran into Elizabeth.

Elizabeth wore dark-green army clothing. The two women stared at each other for a long, awkward moment. "I heard you were here," Elizabeth finally said.

"Hello to you, too."

Elizabeth, clearly uncomfortable, squared her shoulders and looked Cassie in the eye. "I'm... I'm so sorry for your loss. I've been praying for your sister... and for you."

Cassie fought back the tears and nodded, not trusting herself to speak. Down the hallway, one of the female soldiers was coming out of the showers, her skin rosy. The young woman wore a pink bathrobe and fluffy slippers, looking nothing like a trained killer. Elizabeth and Cassie waited silently as she walked past them.

"Thank you," Cassie finally said, watching the young woman's back as she walked away.

She didn't want to think of Alice any more that day. It just hurt too much.

"I was on my way to dinner," Elizabeth said. "Would you like to join me?"

"Sure."

Together, they walked out of the barracks, passing another young soldier on his way out, who nodded in greeting but watched them suspiciously just the same.

"They don't trust us, do they?"

Elizabeth shook her head. "I'm not sure they really want us here. We make them uncomfortable."

"I can't imagine why."

"It's because we can work miracles," Elizabeth stated simply, as if she were talking about the weather.

Cassie watched her out of the corner of her eye. *She really believes that nonsense—that God has chosen us.* Outside, the stench of diesel fuel mingled with the scent of pine trees. The two women walked across a mostly empty parking lot to get to the cafeteria. Cassie stared at the military vehicles parked in front of the cafeteria: large, multiwheeled transport trucks sat beside small, jeep-like off-road vehicles.

A steady stream of soldiers and technicians was gathering near the glass double doors of the cafeteria, forming a line. As they joined the queue, the conversations of those around them died down. It was pretty obvious everyone there knew who they were— the mag-sens, the freaks who could work magic. Cassie pretended not to notice. Any uneasiness these people had was their problem, not hers.

The cafeteria doors opened, and the line began to move. Once inside, Elizabeth handed Cassie a still-wet plastic tray from a rack and they edged forward, their trays held in front of them. Elizabeth glanced at her out of the corner of her eye. "The... creature at the hospital, what do you think—"

"I really don't want to talk about it."

Elizabeth nodded. "It's still out there, isn't it?"

Cassie bit her lip and quickly nodded then looked away.

Elizabeth reached over and patted Cassie's wrist. Then, fortunately, the line moved again, and Cassie quickly found herself standing in front of the food. She ordered barbecued chicken and rice from the menu listed on a whiteboard. With their trays full, the two young women looked about the crowded cafeteria for a table. The other diners made a point of staring down at their plates, pointedly ignoring them.

Cassie sighed. Not that long ago, young men would have been

shoving each other aside to make room for her.

"There," Elizabeth said, nudging Cassie with her elbow.

At a table near a window, a young man sat alone. He was a civilian like them but clearly out of place among the soldiers, technicians, and base staff. Cassie followed Elizabeth. As they stood in front of him, the young man glanced up, startled.

"Cassie, this is Duncan." Elizabeth set her tray down and pulled out her chair, seating herself.

"Hey," said Cassie, sitting down as well. "Cassie Rogan."

Duncan was in his early twenties, maybe just a little older than her. Tall and thin, he was kind of awkward looking—a bit nerdy really. He had a long, drooping mustache, the ends of which ran all the way down to his chin, and long sideburns. His wavy brown hair had been carefully combed across his forehead, but the overall effect was that of a guy trying way too hard to be hip. That impression was reinforced when he smiled timidly at Cassie and hesitated before holding his hand out to shake hers.

"Duncan Walton Hocking," he mumbled through a mouth filled with food. "Nice to meet you."

His grip was weak, but Cassie's eyes widened when she felt a slight tingling in the back of her throat.

Elizabeth reached across the table for the salt and pepper. "Duncan's from Fort St. John as well."

"Born and bred," Duncan said.

Cassie stared at the hairs on the back of her hand, which were standing up. Goose bumps pebbled the skin of her forearm. "You're like us. A mag-sens."

Duncan grinned, and his gray eyes twinkled. "One of the new wizards, a master at the occult manipulation of mana."

Cassie returned his smile.

"You're not a wizard," said Elizabeth. "This isn't magic or

witchcraft, and that isn't funny. You've been *chosen*." Her gaze swept from Duncan to Cassie. "You've both been chosen. We've all been chosen. God wants something very special from us."

Cassie sat back in her chair and carefully considered her words—something she rarely ever did. "Elizabeth, I realize you have strong beliefs, but… I don't share them. I don't believe in God."

Elizabeth's eyes narrowed. She shook her head. "It doesn't matter. He believes in you."

Duncan's glance went from Cassie to Elizabeth. "Maybe we should just agree not to talk about religion."

When Elizabeth glared at him, he shut his mouth and stared at his plate.

"So, Duncan," said Cassie, breaking the uncomfortable silence. "What's this *mana* you mentioned?"

Duncan grinned. "It's a video-game term. I coined it to describe the energy that we're able to tap into. The scientists don't have a better word, so everyone is kind of adopting it."

"Duncan likes his video games." Elizabeth shook her head. "And not *everyone* is using that silly word. Mostly, it's just you."

"How long have you been here?" Cassie asked him.

"Couple of days longer than Elizabeth. Just long enough for Dr. Simmons and her staff to run way too many tests on me." He snorted. "I've never been prodded or poked so much in my life."

"They find anything?" Cassie asked.

Duncan shook his head. "They don't have a fucking clue what's going on."

"Language," Elizabeth said as she cut into her food without looking up.

Duncan's face turned red. "Sorry," he mumbled. "But they don't know anything more than anyone else does, which near as I can tell is nothing."

Cassie nodded. "They ran a bunch of tests on us at the hospital, as well. Brain scans, X-rays, blood samples. I don't think they found anything, either."

Duncan lifted his coffee cup and took a sip. "I'm not so sure they're going to figure any of this out. They need to bring in a psychic, test us for ESP."

"There's no such thing as ESP," Elizabeth said. "That's all nonsense."

Was it? She looked from Elizabeth to Duncan.

"Don't be so sure," Duncan said. "You ever hear of the Stargate Project, the CIA-funded attempt to use psychics to spy on other countries through remote sensing?"

Elizabeth's eyebrows rose, and she smiled condescendingly at Duncan. "Come on, Duncan. Really? The Stargate Project? The ultimate case of misplaced government funding? Is this really the argument you want to make?"

Cassie stared at her plate. *The Stargate Project?*

"Thing is," said Duncan, clearly becoming defensive, "just because the project was canceled doesn't mean there wasn't anything to it."

"Actually, it means exactly that," said Elizabeth. "Trust me; if the US government had seriously believed for one second that they could weaponize psychic powers, they would have kept funding their little science project. There's no way the CIA would have abandoned something like remote viewing if there had been a shred of truth to it."

"Who says they did abandon it?"

"Oh, come on, please. Just drop the conspiracy-theory nonsense and apply some common sense. What's next—the men in black? Alien probing?"

Duncan's face went scarlet. "Jesus, Elizabeth, take a look about you. You're sitting within a secret army base hidden within the infrastructure of a dam, and you're making fun of me for conspiracy theories?"

Elizabeth glared at Duncan. "Watch your language."

Duncan glanced away, flustered. "Sorry, but you have to see what I mean."

"Wait a minute," said Cassie. "I thought the army just moved in here, a temporary setup while they hunt down the creatures. That's what McKnight told me."

Elizabeth and Duncan both paused and glanced about themselves. The dull roar of conversation within the cafeteria continued unabated. "That's just not true," whispered Elizabeth. "Look around for yourself. This place is way more developed than a dam should be. The security is insane, and I don't care what kind of rent-a-cop uniform the guards are wearing—everything about these people screams military."

"I saw an Osprey aircraft the other day," said Duncan very softly.

"A what?" asked Cassie.

"It's a VTOL aircraft," said Elizabeth. "A vertical takeoff and landing aircraft, like a helicopter that turns into an airplane."

"How do you know that?" asked Cassie.

"Because I read things."

Just for a moment, Cassie felt like punching her in the face. Then, she suddenly remembered where she knew Elizabeth from: there had been a track-and-field meet in Fort St. John two years earlier. It had pulled together all the best athletes from the towns in the North and had been a huge deal at the time. Cassie, by far the fastest runner in Hudson's Hope, had been competing in the 100-, 200-, and 400-meter dash—as had Elizabeth. She had lost every single event to Elizabeth. When Cassie had tried to congratulate her, the other woman had completely blown her off, acting as though she were too important to be a good sport.

One of the other competitors from Fort St. John had told her that no one liked Elizabeth, that she was a holier-than-thou pain in the ass. Apparently, not much had changed.

Duncan leaned forward. "The thing is," he whispered, "we don't have those things in Canada—they're American." He grinned. "Hell, our military aircraft are older than my parents."

"You know," Cassie said, "Alex told me that this was a joint American-Canadian operation. He never said why."

Cassie sat back and looked around the crowded cafeteria at the faces of those eating. Everyone was young and fit looking, and there were an awful lot of short haircuts. The occupants of a nearby table glanced in her direction before looking away, too quickly. "Maybe we should lower our voices," she softly said.

Both Duncan and Elizabeth nodded, taking discreet glances at the room.

"So, maybe we are psychic, maybe it's magic, and maybe it's something else," Cassie said.

"It's *not* magic," said Elizabeth, "and there is no such thing as psychic powers."

Cassie sighed then turned to Duncan. "So, what can you do?"

Duncan scratched the back of his neck, leaned forward, and whispered as if it were a secret. "Telekinesis mostly. Move small objects."

He stared down at the table in front of him, focusing on his used napkin. It curled up into a ball. Cassie felt her throat tingle again. The napkin trembled in place, as though a soft wind were blowing it. Then it moved several inches to the side before stopping. Duncan looked up at Cassie and winked.

Cassie smiled, sat back, and without taking her eyes off of Duncan's, opened herself up to the invisible energy around her and focused it back out again. The napkin lifted into the air in front of Duncan's face and began to spin, then stopped suddenly and spun in the opposite direction. Duncan's eyes widened as he snatched the napkin out of the air. The occupants of the nearby table got up abruptly, picked up their trays, and left.

"You probably shouldn't have done that," Duncan said. "Everybody here is already kind of freaked out."

"Vanity," said Elizabeth, shaking her head.

"What else can you do?" Duncan asked.

Cassie cocked her head to the side. "Like what? Can you do more?"

"Elizabeth can. Pyrokinesis. It's pretty cool, actually."

"What?" Cassie asked.

"Pyrokinesis. It's another form of ESP."

Elizabeth rolled her eyes. "It's not ESP."

Cassie flicked a lock of blond hair away from her eyes. "Well, it sounds like magic."

Elizabeth leaned forward, glaring at her. "No, you're wrong. Any attempt at an occult practice is a violation of the First Commandment, a betrayal of faith. What's happening here is that God is working miracles through us. I just don't understand why He's working them through you."

Cassie snorted, exposing her teeth. "You're too kind, Elizabeth." She returned her attention to Duncan. "Thing is, I'm not really following you on the whole pryokin… whatever."

"Pyrokinesis. She can set things on fire," Duncan said.

Cassie glanced at Elizabeth. "Really?"

Elizabeth nodded, cut into her chicken, and took another bite.

"Small stuff," Duncan said. "Pieces of paper, easily inflammable stuff. But she's getting stronger."

"You couldn't do that at the hospital," Cassie said.

"And you couldn't make a napkin spin in the air," Elizabeth said. "Things change."

Cassie began to eat her own lunch. "I guess they do." *Pyrokinesis.* Cassie would remember that word. "Anything else?"

"What do you mean?" Duncan asked. "Isn't setting things on fire enough?"

"What about changing things, changing the properties of things?" Once again, Cassie saw the basilisk's glowing blue eyes.

"I'm not following you," Duncan said.

"It doesn't matter," Cassie answered.

"You're talking about the attack at the hospital, aren't you?" Elizabeth asked. "That giant dragon thing. I heard it turned people to stone."

Cassie nodded.

"Well, whatever that thing was," said Duncan, "I'm pretty sure we're safe here."

Cassie opened her mouth to say something but then closed it again.

Elizabeth's eyes narrowed as she watched Cassie. "What did McKnight tell you?"

"Why do you think we're here?" Cassie asked her.

Realization dawned on Elizabeth's face, and she sat back in her chair. "Okay, that makes more sense. They want to do something about the dragon."

"Basilisk. They're calling it a basilisk."

"Well, that makes sense, too," said Elizabeth. "In mythology, basilisks could turn things to stone with their gaze. Dragons breathe fire."

"What are you talking about?" asked Duncan, looking from

Cassie to Elizabeth.

"The army wants our help going after the basilisk," answered Elizabeth.

"Bullshit," Duncan said.

"Language," Elizabeth said.

"Somebody needs to," Cassie said.

"Not us—not our problem," Duncan said.

Cassie leaned forward. "It's our problem because they need our help. It uses magic. They need a mag-sens to help find it."

Duncan's eyes widened. "No fucking way!"

Elizabeth glared at Duncan. "God has given us gifts for a reason. It wouldn't be very Christian of us to ignore our duty."

"I don't know anything about being a good Christian," Cassie said. "But I am going to help kill that monster if it's the last thing I do."

Chapter 20

When Colonel McKnight had told Cassie that the army wanted to test her and the other two mag-sens' ability to manipulate this new energy source, she had expected… well, more. So when, later that evening, she found herself sitting on a stool with Elizabeth and Duncan in a small classroom, she was underwhelmed. The three of them wore wired nets over their heads, heart-rate monitors, and a series of wires taped to their skin. Cassie had expected a team of scientists in lab coats like she'd seen in the movies. Instead, she got two tired-looking technicians who took notes while the three mag-sens levitated colored rubber balls. It didn't look like the government had any more idea what had happened to them than the doctors at the hospital had.

The wires and heart-rate monitors were connected to a series of electronic sensors measuring their blood pressure and brain activity, much like the EEG equipment had done with Dr. Ireland. Cassie wondered what had happened to Dr. Ireland and hoped she hadn't been one of those killed.

One of the two technicians, a woman in her early thirties, had set up a video camera on a tripod near the front of the classroom. Occasionally, she would put her notebook down long enough to peer through the camera's video screen and ensure everything was still being recorded.

At that moment, a brightly colored green ball came hurtling toward Cassie's head. Resisting the urge to flinch, she instead channeled a trickle of mana, stopping the ball about six inches from her forehead.

She stared at the spinning ball then adjusted the flow of mana, first slowing down and then stopping the ball's spin before forcing it to spin in the opposite direction as she took control of it from whichever of the other two mag-sens had sent it at her. Duncan had an intense but puzzled look on his face, reminding her of a baby trying to poo. She couldn't help but smile as she whipped the ball back at him. He ducked out of the way as it darted past, bouncing off the wall behind him. Cassie snorted happily. Elizabeth, who sat by herself near a large window while spinning four balls—each a different color and each moving in a different direction and arc, inches from her upraised palm—shook her head.

Cassie sighed and turned toward the female scientist. "So, what exactly are we doing here? What have you figured out?"

The woman glanced up, a startled look in her eyes. "What?"

"I said, what have you discovered? What is this mana stuff? How are we doing this? Is it ESP?"

"Well," the woman said, looking uncertain as she glanced at her colleague, a heavyset guy with glasses and a ponytail. "There's a lot we don't really fully understand yet. It's hard to say exactly."

"Well, I'm not looking for an exact answer, just more than I know right now, which is pretty much nothing."

"I'm... I'm sorry. I'm not supposed to..." The woman looked down at her notebook. "We don't really—"

"They don't know any more than we do," Duncan said. "They don't know how we're channeling the mana. They can't see it, measure it, or even tell if it's there. Only we can. They don't even know where it comes from."

Just for a moment, the two technicians shared a quick look, and something unsaid passed between them. Duncan was wrong: these two *did* know something about where the magical energy came from. What were they hiding?

"They can't answer that," said Elizabeth, "because the source is the Lord, and His glory is beyond their machines, beyond their tests. It just is."

"Yeah, okay, Elizabeth," said Cassie. "Thanks for contributing."

Anger flared in Elizabeth's eyes. The four balls she had been spinning fell to the floor, bouncing across the room in different directions. "You know, I do recognize sarcasm when I hear it, and I don't particularly care for it."

Against her own better judgment, Cassie rose to the challenge. "Well, maybe you should dial down the religious bullshit, especially when no one else is asking to hear it."

"I can say what I want to say. My beliefs are my business, and you have no right to—"

"Nobody gives a shit if you're religious or not. We just don't want to hear it all the time."

The electronic beeping of the monitors, which up to that point had been fairly regular, increased in intensity.

"Hey, guys," said Duncan warily as he looked from one woman to the other. "Maybe we should just—"

Cassie cocked her head to the side and glared at him. Duncan, no fool, immediately shut up.

"You never even wanted to be here," said Elizabeth. "You were offered the chance to help out before and you said no. You had absolutely no interest in being a good person until your—"

"Until my sister was murdered. You're absolutely right. So

what? What business is it of yours?"

"So, you don't belong here. You're not a team player. You're not going to help anyone; you're just here for yourself."

"No, that's not true. I'm here to help track down the monster that killed my sister."

"Revenge is not a Christian value."

"Really? Are you sure? *An eye for an eye*, Elizabeth—ever hear that one?"

"You're going to get someone killed. Maybe one of us."

Deep down, Cassie heard the small voice of reason within herself that begged her to shut up. She'd never listened to that voice before, so why start now? She crossed her arms over her chest. "Maybe *you*."

Elizabeth's eyes tightened. "What kind of a person are you?"

"The kind of person who believes in science and reason. I thought you were supposed to be intelligent."

"Belief in the Lord has nothing to do with intellect. It's about faith. Something you don't have."

"No kidding. Yet here I am with the same abilities as you. What does that say about your faith, when an atheist can work the same miracles? 'Cause, from my perspective, I think it means you're full of shit." Cassie lifted her palm and began to levitate a spinning ball inches above her hand. "This isn't a miracle, Elizabeth. It may be ESP, it may be magic, but it's not a miracle. It's not God's power. I know that because I don't believe in your stupid God, but I can still do these things. What does that tell you?"

The ball that spun above Cassie's hand burst into flames, and Cassie fell back off her stool and onto the floor as she scrambled back. The burning rubber ball still floated in the air, and drops of flaming rubber sizzled and dripped onto the floor in front of her.

"It tells me, Cassandra Rogan," said Elizabeth, fury in her eyes as she stood up and advanced on Cassie, "that you need to shut your goddamned lying mouth."

Cassie pushed herself up on her elbows, tensing, getting ready to pounce on the other woman and beat her senseless. "Language, Elizabeth."

At that moment, the sprinklers activated, dousing Cassie and the others in freezing cold water. The fire alarm activated a moment later, and Duncan ran over and helped her to her feet, and the three mag-sens and two technicians fled from the room.

* * *

Over the course of the next few days, Cassie, Elizabeth, and Duncan trained themselves in their new abilities. Two scientists, not always the same ones, watched and recorded and took notes, but they were of no practical help. One of them did offer a theory that the three mag-sens were somehow drawing mana into their central nervous systems and then releasing it in an altered state. Perhaps.

Cassie didn't have any idea; none of them did. They could barely explain to themselves how they manipulated this energy let alone inform nonsensitives about it. Nor could they explain what mana was. As they practiced together, though, their abilities grew. Levitating and manipulating small objects became almost second nature in the days that followed, but each of them had different limits. At best, Cassie could lift objects that weighed about five pounds, but to do that, she had to draw in as much mana as she could, and it always left her mentally drained, sometimes with a pounding headache. Even so, it was still far more than Duncan could manipulate. Elizabeth, however, could fairly easily lift objects that weighed about twenty pounds.

Each was different in aptitude, with Elizabeth clearly the frontrunner. Not only could she levitate much heavier objects, but she could also deflect objects thrown at her, like a shield. And then there was her pyrokinesis, her ability to set small objects on fire. After a day of watching her manipulate fire, Cassie managed to do the same, albeit only with a small tissue. Still, it had been pretty cool when it had suddenly burst into fire. So far, Duncan had been unable to do even that.

Each of them could also sense when another was channeling mana. And in that regard, Cassie was far better than Elizabeth. Not only could she sense when Elizabeth or Duncan was channeling but also where they were, even with her eyes closed.

Unfortunately, after three days of training and testing and developing their abilities, they were still no closer to understanding any of it. It was as if mana had never existed until the night of the electrical storm and then had been suddenly released into the world in a single earth-changing moment.

Did it have a limit? Could it run out?

Chapter 21

"Stronger," Elizabeth said to Alex and Dr. Simmons, both sitting across from her in the back of the Osprey VTOL aircraft. "The mana is definitely growing stronger again."

Dr. Simmons jotted something down in a notebook while Alex keyed his headset radio, speaking to the crew of the aircraft, telling them to level out and fly in the direction Elizabeth had just indicated.

This was her first flight in such a sophisticated aircraft. The way it transformed in flight from a helicopter to an airplane was beyond cool. It was also nice to get away from the Magic Kingdom. She felt a small surge of pride in the knowledge that she was there because she was so much stronger at manipulating mana than Cassie and Duncan were. *Well, not me, exactly,* she admonished herself. *It's God working his wonders through me. I'm just the vessel of his glory.* Still, she was the best. That was why she was the one riding in an Osprey, mapping the ebbs and flows of mana in the vicinity of Fort St. John.

They had been in the air now for about an hour. They'd fly in one direction while she called out whether the mana was intensifying or diminishing. When it disappeared entirely, she would report this, and the aircraft would turn and go in a different direction until the mana became stronger again. The aircrew was responding to Alex's instructions, led by Elizabeth.

So far, the mana in the atmosphere was tied down to a certain area, mostly centered somewhere in the wilderness south of Fort St. John. She wasn't sure, but it seemed after about twenty minutes of flying—in every direction—the mana would begin to fade, to disappear, until finally, there was no mana at all. Whatever was responsible for releasing mana onto the Earth, it was localized in northern British Columbia.

"Oh my God," said Elizabeth, feeling the strongest surge of mana she had ever felt, as though her skin was tingling with energy.

"What is it?" Dr. Simmons asked, looking up from her notebook.

"Here." Elizabeth rose from the cargo-netting seats along the sides of the Osprey then stood and peered out the circular window in the side of the aircraft. There was a large hill below with a bare top surrounded by trees. Alex moved beside her, also gazing below.

She turned to look at him, knowing her eyes were wide with astonishment. "Can we land there?"

He glanced at Dr. Simmons, who nodded eagerly. Then Alex spoke into his headset microphone, once again talking to the aircrew. Almost immediately, the Osprey slowed down and began to circle the hilltop. Elizabeth's stomach lurched into her throat.

But the mana—oh Lord, so much power, so much energy. *I feel your glory, Lord. I feel you. It's like you're here with me now.*

The aircraft shuddered, and the engine whine changed pitch abruptly as the Osprey slowed to a hover, its massive propellers now facing up. The aircraft descended quickly, a testament to the impressive skill of its pilots. Within moments, they settled upon the hilltop. The rear ramp lowered, and Alex went out first, holding some sort of submachine gun in his hand.

When had he picked up a weapon? And from where? Were these people always armed?

Dr. Simmons put a hand on her forearm to stop her, but Elizabeth pushed past the other woman and stepped off the ramp and onto the hilltop. The power here… it was amazing. The air seemed to throb with mana.

Alex looked over his shoulder and frowned at her but only told her not to get too close to the engines, which even now beat at the ground, sending currents of air so strong it was hard to walk upright. Dirt and dust flew through the air, and her long hair whipped about her face.

She channeled. She had to, just to see. Mana surged into her, and she felt as though she could do anything. She felt a huge grin spread across her face. She felt euphoric. *Is this God's love?*

"Ground's burnt," Alex yelled over the noise of the rotors.

He pointed with the barrel of his weapon, and she saw the charring around them—like a perfect circle. The closest of the trees had been burned as well. Now, they were only charred shells.

"We need to go." Alex grabbed her arm and pulled her back aboard the Osprey.

In moments, she was seated again, and the aircraft lifted up. Alex was talking into his radio once more. She recognized the word *breach*. As they flew away from the hilltop, the mana began to lessen, to become more normal.

The hilltop was the source of mana. What had happened there? And why were they calling it a breach?

* * *

"You're certain?" Colonel McKnight sat in his office, across from Helena, Alex, and Buck. On the coffee table between them was placed a 1:50,000 topographical map of the Fort St. John region. Circled in red was the hilltop, surrounded by forest and other foothills.

"It makes sense," Helena said, practically beaming with excitement. "It's the epicenter of the mana the mag-sens report. From there, it extends about 240 kilometers or so in all directions—a circle. This must be the breach."

"Something set a fire there, Colonel," said Alex. "I'd have to agree with the good doctor. I think this needs to be the center of our search efforts."

"Maybe, but why there?" McKnight asked.

Helena shook her head, as did Alex and Buck.

Buck leaned forward and placed a finger on the map, on the highway. "There was an accident here, right around the time of the breach. A burned car was found on the road. The woman who was driving it was listed as missing."

McKnight chewed his cheek as he examined the map. "Only about... how far away?"

"Less than five hundred meters, sir," said Buck. "I think we've found the breach."

"This must be where the creatures came through," McKnight said. "The basilisk and the... what do you call them—hellhounds?"

Buck inclined his head. "Yes, sir."

"It's where the hellhounds came through," McKnight finished. "But why? How?"

"I don't know," said Helena. "Not yet. But we're getting closer to answers."

"Have we learned anything from the carcass we recovered that could aid us in tracking the basilisk?" McKnight asked.

Helena shook her head. "We're trying, but so far, we only have its basic physiology. It'll take time."

Alex leaned forward. "Sir. Elizabeth reported a great deal of mana on the hilltop. If this is the site where the breach occurred… what if we brought her down below to the Jump Tube? She might—"

"No, Captain. I don't think so. They have no need to know about Operation Rubicon."

"Yes, sir."

McKnight made a steeple with his fingers and rested his chin on them as he considered what to do next.

It's a start at least.

"All right," he said. "Use the hilltop. Bring the tracker there. Let's see what we can see. Keep testing the mag-sens. We'll need them yet—I'm sure of it. And if nothing else, both governments have been impressed by their potential. The Project Managers want us to keep developing them. In the meantime, though, we need to find those damned creatures, and quickly, before more people die."

They acknowledged his orders, rose, and filed out one by one, leaving him alone.

The burdens of command.

Chapter 22

It was just after six in the evening, and Cassie lay on her bed in her borrowed gym clothing, procrastinating. She had promised herself that she'd go to the gym after dinner and start back into an exercise routine. Instead, she lay in her room, channeling just enough mana to float a hairbrush and a paperback novel in front of her, the items slowly revolving around each other.

Day after day for an entire week, Cassie had sat in a classroom, channeling mana. The more she used the mysterious energy source, the better she became at it. Her ability quickly outshone Duncan's but still remained behind Elizabeth's.

No matter what she did, Elizabeth always did better. She had even started jogging around the inside perimeter of the base. Clearly, Elizabeth was one of those overachievers who just had to do everything better than everyone else—and let them know it.

Cassie still had trouble sleeping. She had nightmares about Alice. She knew she was run-down, mentally exhausted from channeling mana as well as feeling the pressure of losing her last family member. If she didn't get up and start doing something physical, she was going to fall apart. If nothing else, she figured that working out might help her sleep.

God, she needed some real sleep. Every single time she closed her eyes, she saw the basilisk—its glowing blue eyes, its dripping teeth… she jumped up from her bed, letting the hairbrush and paperback fall to the mattress. *The hell with this; I'm going to the gym.*

Without pausing to talk herself out of it again, she rushed out of her room, down the stairs, and outside. Everything in the Magic Kingdom was close, and within minutes, she was walking into the base's air-conditioned and spacious gymnasium. Racks of rubber-coated dumbbells sat in front of the mirrored walls, an assortment of expensive-looking exercise machines were interspersed around the gym floor, and a row of treadmills were set up across from large ceiling-mounted plasma screens. It might have been the nicest gym she had ever been in, way too nice for a remote provincial dam.

The place was packed. There must have been two dozen people working out, mostly soldier-types but some civilian technicians as well. She walked about for a bit, checking the place out, before deciding to use one of the treadmills. She stepped on it and fiddled with the controls, setting it for a light jog.

After several minutes, she knew she had really let herself go. Before college, before her parents had died, she had always been physically active, competing in track and field and hiking. Now, she was struggling with a light run. She was still thin, but she certainly wasn't fit.

She kept going for another twenty minutes before stopping the machine and getting off. Her skin was flushed and her breathing too fast, but at least it had been a start. She approached the free weights stacked in front of the mirrors and began to do some light weight lifting. Just beside her, a group of young men were taking turns bench-pressing really heavy weights. Cassie watched them out of the corner of her eye as she began to do arm curls. These guys were fit, seriously fit, but not huge like club bouncers or bodybuilders—more like Olympic athletes: strong and fast.

She fooled around with the light weights for another fifteen minutes or so, in truth, not doing much more than waking up long-dormant muscles. Deciding that was enough for the first day back, she stopped by the water fountain for a drink. There were even more people in the gym than before. There wasn't much else to do way out here in the middle of nowhere. The gym was probably its own little community in the evening.

She opened the glass door to leave and jerked to a stop. Lying across the entrance, completely blocking it, was a large German shepherd. Gold-and-black colored, the animal looked as though it weighed at least a hundred pounds, all muscle. It lifted its large head and regarded her with clever brown eyes, its big ears standing straight up. It wore no collar and was, quite frankly, a bit scruffy. She felt a slight bit of trepidation as she stepped over the animal, but it didn't budge; it just kept watching her. This was where it had decided to lie down, and everybody else could just go around it.

She smiled. When she had been a little girl, her family had had a German shepherd named Augy. She had died when Cassie was only nine. Cassie squatted down and put her hand near the dog's nose, letting it sniff her. "What are you doing here?"

In reply, the shepherd snorted, smelling her hand in a somewhat disinterested manner before getting up and moving closer. It nuzzled her hand and then rested its large head against her thigh. Cassie scratched behind the dog's ears. The animal may have been ungroomed, but it clearly wasn't a stray. It looked healthy and strong—actually, it looked very strong. It was probably about three or four years old, a mature working dog.

Behind her, the gym door opened again, and she felt the

presence of someone standing there. "You know, girlie," a man's voice said, "approaching strange dogs is not so smart."

Still scratching behind the dog's large ears, Cassie turned her head and regarded the speaker. Just like the dog, he was out of place here. With dark skin, he was clearly a native and probably in his early forties. He had huge sideburns and a braided goatee. He wore a sleeveless T-shirt and sweat pants. He wasn't a big guy, but he looked powerful. His skin was weathered, and his was the face of a man who spent most of his time outdoors. There was a clever sparkle in his eyes as if the world was endlessly amusing.

"No, probably not," Cassie said, "but he reminded me of an old friend. He yours?"

The man snorted. "Ha! Most likely the other way around." He dropped down on one knee and ruffled the dog's head. "At any rate, Clyde seems to like you well enough. And he doesn't often like white folk."

"Really? That's his name—*Clyde?*"

"You don't like Clyde. Hey, Clyde, girlie don't like your name."

The dog nuzzled Cassie's hand then licked her fingers.

The man chuckled. "I guess he don't care, but then again, he always did dig the chicks. Bit of a suck-up that way."

"Oh, he's just a big old softie." Cassie put her hands around the dog's head and kissed him on the nose.

The man sighed. "No. He's really not. Anyhow, he's Clyde, and I'm Paco. If Clyde likes you, you must be okay... maybe." He offered his hand to Cassie, and she took it. His grip was firm, but he didn't try to impress her with his strength like some other men did.

"You work here?" She stood back up again, and Clyde dropped his large head onto the dirt and gazed up at her with his big brown eyes.

"You sound surprised, girlie."

"Cassie, not girlie. And you don't seem like the army or scientist type."

His face lit up in a huge gap-toothed smile. "As a matter of fact, I *was* in the army... a long time ago. So, what type do I seem like?"

At that moment, a couple of young men walked out of the gym. They paused and then stepped around Cassie and Paco, giving Clyde plenty of space. The dog didn't growl, didn't react, but she could feel the signal he gave off: *keep your distance.*

"I spent some summers working with park rangers around Moberly Lake. You remind me of them."

Paco laughed a deep, throaty chuckle. "Local girl, huh? I knew there was somethin' about you that was all right, and not just your choice of hair color."

"What's wrong with my hair?" Cassie's hand rose up to touch her short haircut, running her fingers through it.

"Nothin'. It's just you don't normally see army girls with pink streaks in their hair."

He was right. She was as much out of place as Paco and Clyde. Clyde stood up again and nuzzled Cassie's hand with his snout. She dropped back down on one knee and started scratching behind his ears again.

"You're First Nations, aren't you?"

Paco nodded, pulling a pack of cigarettes out of a pocket in his sweat pants and lighting one with a shiny silver zippo lighter. "Doig River First Nations. It's my ravishing good looks, isn't it? Gives me away every time."

Cassie grinned, flashing her teeth. "Yes, Paco, it's your ravishing good looks. Where are you from?"

"Same as you—these parts. Just my people been living here a

lot longer than yours."

"Dene-Zaa?" Cassie asked.

Paco nodded again. "Beaver People. You?"

"Hudson's Hope."

"You're not that far from home, are you? Unlike everybody else here."

"I'm not the only one. There're two others. Both from Fort St. John."

Paco nodded. "You're one of these special people, aren't you? The ones they're calling Magic Sensitives. You can do... *things*."

"That bother you?" Cassie stood and watched Paco's face carefully, her hands on her hips.

Paco shook his head. "Relax. You want to play with unknown and dangerous forces, you go right ahead."

"It's not about what I want. If I had what I wanted, I'd have my sister back and none of this bullshit would have happened."

The smile disappeared from Paco's face. "You're the one from the hospital. I heard about you. I wasn't making fun of your loss. Family is everything. I'm so sorry for you."

She looked away, and Clyde nuzzled his head against her leg. She scratched the top of his head. "Thank you," she mumbled, not sure if she were talking to Paco or Clyde.

Paco nodded, smoke drifting from his nostrils. "Still, you might be a good friend to have. You, me, and Clyde should become best buds. A little magic protection can be a good thing."

"Why would you need protection?"

"Army's hired me to hunt this dragon thing down for them."

"The basilisk?"

Paco nodded, exhaling a cloud of smoke.

"You're a tracker?"

"Yes, but mostly Clyde does all the work. I just back him up, keep him supplied with Slim Jims."

"The army doesn't have its own trackers?"

Paco snorted. "Not one that knows this area—not even close."

Cassie nodded. "That makes sense, actually."

Paco smiled widely. "I know, eh? What's up with the government making sense?"

"So when you goin' after it?"

"Don't know, but it's more than just the basilisk. They're keeping it hush-hush, but there's also a pack of wild dogs they need to find."

"I heard. Ones that breathe fire."

His eyes widened. "No shit?"

"No shit."

Paco shook his head. "Wonder when they were gonna tell me that part."

At that moment, a large green aircraft suddenly flew over their heads, appearing from out of nowhere, its engines screaming. It must have been flying just above the forest and been hidden by the treetops. In moments, its propellers pivoted from pointing to the front of its two wings to pointing straight up, kicking up dust and dirt, transforming from a plane to a helicopter. Then it dropped out of sight behind a large hangar. Moments later, the roar of its engines died out.

That was fast, Cassie thought.

"Lot of weird things goin' on around here," Paco said softly.

"What do you mean?"

"That was an Osprey, and I'm pretty sure they aren't normally that quiet. Canadian Army doesn't have Ospreys and sure as shit doesn't have stealth ones."

"American?"

Paco nodded. "Special Forces."

"I heard. Alex told me."

"Alex?"

"I think he's a captain. Last name is Benoit."

"The Newfy guy?"

"Yes. He said that this was a joint American-Canadian operation, hunting down the basilisk. Task Force Devil."

Paco shook his head.

"What's going on? Is something wrong?"

"Joint operations are a *big* deal, not ad-hoc. This is sovereign Canadian territory."

"And?"

"Countries take sovereignty very seriously. Pretty uptight about foreign soldiers carrying weapons on their turf."

"I'm sure Alex is Canadian. You can't fake a Newfoundland accent."

"No. You can't. And a few of the others are French-Canadian for sure, but the rest..." He shook his head. "You seen the big dude, Buck, the one that gives most of the orders?"

Cassie shook her head.

"Well, you *will*. And you'll remember him when you do."

"What about him?"

"I saw him in the gym yesterday working out. Dude had a Ranger tattoo on his shoulder. He's American for sure."

"So?" she asked.

"So Buck's American, this Colonel McKnight is American. The two key positions are American. Why? This is still Canada, right?"

"What are you saying? Canada and America have been allies forever."

He bit his lower lip and shook his head. "This isn't some emergency mission to hunt down monsters. This op is too slick, and these guys are too well equipped... too settled in."

"Maybe they just want the basilisk bad."

"Maybe."

To Cassie's ear, he didn't sound certain at all.

"When do you think we'll do it—go after it, I mean?"

Paco shook his head. "I don't know. Soon, I'd guess. Question is, when will you guys be ready?"

"Can't say as I'll ever be ready, but I need to get that thing."

"Train hard," Paco said. "These kind of people, Special Forces types, they don't like putting things off."

* * *

Maelhrandia slipped through the foliage surrounding the encampment the manling mage had fled to. As usual, she had cast Shadow-Soul around her. If there had been anyone watching, the most they might have seen of her would have been a slight blur in the air, a momentary discoloring as she swept through the trees.

Far back in the woods, she could sense Gazekiller through the mind-tether, waiting for her. There was just no way an animal that large could be as stealthy as she needed to be. This was a military camp, and she needed to be careful when spying upon it. Arrogance could get her killed. A metal fence surrounded the camp, extending all the way to the river's edge. A single road ran through the fence, with a guard detachment controlling access. One of their massive armored war chariots was always nearby. Hidden, she had observed the guards for some minutes. They were well armed and alert and had an animal with them, like a gwyllgi only much smaller. Had she wanted to, she could have killed all of them in a moment, but doing so would have alerted the camp to her presence, and she wasn't ready for that yet.

It hadn't been easy tracking the golden-haired mage. In fact, it had taken her some days of meditation to rediscover the magic-use, but now she was certain she had found her again. In addition, she believed there were other manling mages within the camp. If this place had multiple mages, it must be important to the manlings. Perhaps one of their warlords was here, as well.

Without warning, she heard a horrific screech as something flew toward her. Certain they had discovered her, she filled herself with magical power. She'd die fighting!

One of their wondrous flying machines appeared above the treetops and flew over the camp. Within moments, it disappeared from sight. Then it was silent again.

Such amazing machines they built. Even dwarves couldn't match their skill. It was almost a pity what her mother had planned for them.

* * *

The colored balls Cassie had been levitating dropped to the floor, bouncing away in different directions. She turned and stared, wide-eyed, at Elizabeth and Duncan. Duncan seemed oblivious to the forces she had just felt, but Elizabeth met her gaze.

"What?" Elizabeth asked.

"Was that you?" Cassie asked. "It sure as hell wasn't me."

Elizabeth's eyes registered her confusion. "Was what me?"

Duncan glanced over in their direction. "What's going on?"

"It wasn't either of you?"

"I don't know what you're talking about," Elizabeth answered. "What wasn't us?"

"Someone was channeling mana," said Cassie. "A *lot* of mana."

Duncan said, "No, couldn't be."

"Another mag-sens?" Elizabeth asked.

"Maybe," Cassie answered. "It was only for a moment, and now it's gone."

Elizabeth shook her head. "I didn't sense anything, and I would have. It's probably just your imagination."

Cassie frowned at her then looked away. "Whatever."

Chapter 23

Cassie, Elizabeth, and Duncan were sitting in the lab, chatting, when Alex came in. Cassie had barely seen him since the day he had shown her around the base, a week earlier. He looked apprehensive.

"Guys, I'm going to need you to return to your rooms, throw a change of clothes and some socks into an overnight bag, and meet back at the parking lot in front of the cafeteria in about fifteen minutes. We have an op, and Colonel McKnight wants you on it. Welcome to Task Force Devil."

The three mag-sens glanced quickly at one another. Duncan opened his mouth and then closed it again. Elizabeth flicked a strand of dark hair away from her eyes and inclined her head, but Cassie noticed that her lower lip trembled slightly.

"Is it the... the basilisk?" Cassie asked.

"No," said Alex. "No one's seen that thing since the attack on the hospital. But there's been a hellhound attack—a pack of feral dogs. Something we should be able to deal with easily."

"Dogs?" Duncan's eyes narrowed. "Why do you need us for wild dogs?"

"These ones breathe fire," Cassie said.

"Jesus," whispered Duncan so quietly Cassie almost didn't hear him.

Alex turned to leave then paused at the doorway. "Fifteen minutes," he repeated. "Just use the small pack we gave you, the one that looks like a little backpack. Toothbrush, change of underwear, more socks. You can never have enough socks. And a hat, the bush cap… it'll be hot out there, and we'll probably be out for a few days."

No one said anything.

"Don't be late." Alex slipped out the door.

* * *

It took Cassie longer than fifteen minutes to get to the parking lot with her overnight bag, and by the time she arrived, there was already a large group of soldiers scurrying about next to a pair of the ugly armored vehicles she had originally mistaken for tanks. She had expected someone to be angry with her for being late, but no one seemed to notice—or care.

Each truck was big and high with a boat-shaped hull atop four oversized tires, the tops of which reached her waist when she stood beside them. The windows were tinted dark green and had what looked like a gun port smack-dab in the center. *That,* she thought, *must be bulletproof glass.* At the top of each vehicle was an automated turret to which was mounted a large machine gun. She stood in place, her small pack in her hand, staring at the huge, dangerous-looking barrel on the weapon. If someone had had a weapon like that when the basilisk had attacked the hospital, they would have killed the damned thing on the spot. Her confidence began to grow.

One of the soldiers, the powerfully built redhead who had accompanied McKnight and Alex to the hospital that first time, jostled her then quickly muttered apologies before darting past to toss supplies into one of the open cargo hatches on the outside of the vehicle. *Clara*, she remembered. *Sergeant Clara something or other*. Unlike Cassie, Clara clearly belonged there despite being one of the few women amongst a pack of alpha males.

Just then, a dog barked, and Cassie saw Paco and Clyde standing near the front bumper of the first vehicle. Clyde stood beside his master, his gaze directed toward Cassie, his tongue hanging out. Despite her nerves, Cassie smiled and joined them. Paco, a huge grin on his face, gripped her shoulder and squeezed it. "Hey, little sister, you ready for this?"

Cassie watched the soldiers prepare the vehicles. "Not even a little bit."

"It'll be all right... probably. These guys aren't messing around. This is some pretty serious shit they're going out the gate with. Should be more than enough for a pack of wild dogs."

Cassie snorted. "Not so sure about that."

Paco pulled a cigarette out of his packet and lit it. The smell of smoke mingled with exhaust from the running vehicles. "These are MRAPs—pretty tough; definitely fireproof."

"M-whats?"

"Mine Resistant Ambush Protected. MRAP. South African. We bought 'em for Afghanistan. Designed to survive a mine blast." He exhaled smoke and raised a single eyebrow. "Should be able to deal with a little bit of fire breathing, don't you think? And those are 7.62 millimeter machine guns on the automated turrets. A single round from those bad boys will shred any animal it hits. I'd say you're pretty safe inside the vehicles, which is where you and the other two shamans need to stay."

"But not you." Cassie put her hand on his forearm and watched his face. "You and Clyde will be outside tracking them, won't you?"

Paco scratched his goatee and nodded. "That's the job, at least until we run them down. But don't worry. Once we get close enough to put eyes on these doggies, Clyde and me'll jump in there with you guys, so save some room for us."

Cassie frowned then dropped down on one knee beside Clyde and wrapped her arms around the shepherd's head. "Make sure that you do."

One of the soldiers took Cassie's day pack from her and stowed it in the second MRAP. "You're in here," the young man said, and Cassie nodded.

Duncan's head popped out from the open back hatch of the MRAP. "Looks like we're traveling together." He swung his legs out the back of the vehicle and jumped down on the ground.

Like Cassie, Duncan was dressed in army pants, boots, a dark-green T-shirt, and a floppy bush hat. Cassie had hung her bush hat off a strap on the back of her neck. She was pretty sure she looked out of place in army clothes, but she couldn't possibly be as ridiculous in them as Duncan, who looked like a kid wearing adult clothes. Paco, on the other hand, in worn blue jeans and a dark hoodie, appeared perfectly at ease.

"You two know each other?" she asked, looking from Duncan to Paco.

Duncan shook his head and held out his hand. "Duncan Hocking."

Paco shook his hand. "Yancy Nelson, but my buds call me Paco. This is Clyde."

Duncan eyed the dog nervously. Clyde ignored him and nuzzled his nose against Cassie's hand, wanting more attention. At that moment, two soldiers swept past them, struggling with large metal boxes filled with linked belts of ammunition. Cassie, Paco,

Duncan, and Clyde darted out of the way. Were they really going to need that much ammunition?

"Where's Elizabeth?" Cassie asked.

Duncan indicated the lead MRAP with his head. "They've got her in there with the big tall dude in charge."

"Buck?" Cassie asked.

"Yeah, that's his name," Duncan replied, looking down at his feet.

His real name, Cassie knew, was Buchanan. She had overheard one of the soldiers calling him Major Buchanan. She had no idea what a major was, but in the past few days, it had become clear that the tall, muscular soldier was in charge around the base or, at the very least, was just behind Colonel McKnight in authority. It was also clear that he didn't care much for the presence of Cassie, Elizabeth, and Duncan. Obviously, he didn't expect much from the mag-sens. She could tell Duncan was afraid of him, and it wasn't hard to see why. She had seen his kind before all too often: the type-A—for asshole—personality, overly impressed with himself and his ability to push others around.

"So," said Paco, "what exactly is it they expect you guys to do out there?"

Cassie bit her lower lip then shook her head. "I'm not sure what we can do. We can... move small objects, start small fires, but that's about it."

"You can burn stuff?"

"Little things, like pieces of paper," Duncan replied.

"We can also sense when we're channeling mana," Cassie replied.

"Mana?" Paco asked.

"That's what we're calling the magic," Cassie said.

Paco nodded thoughtfully. "It's as good a name as any other, I guess. So… you think maybe that's what these animals are doing when they breathe fire—*channeling mana?*"

Cassie shrugged, and Duncan stared at his feet.

"There's just so much we don't know or understand," Cassie said. "McKnight promised the government would help us better understand what was happening, but so far, nobody seems to have a clue. The help we're getting here is just some lab technicians watching us practice while they take notes."

Paco snorted. "Don't take it personally. I don't think anyone anywhere knows what's going on with you guys. At least they're trying to—"

"Something's happening," Cassie said.

Near the front of the first MRAP, Alex stood up in the driver's door, looking over the soldiers who were working around the vehicles. Buck stood just beside him, waiting. A uniformed RCMP officer stood beside Buck. Cassie had never seen him before and had no idea the police were working with the army. "Listen up," Alex yelled out in a commanding voice. All talk and activity ceased as everyone turned to watch the young man. "Gather around for a packet briefing. We're rolling in five."

Everyone drew in closer to Alex and Buck, jostling for a place to stand. Elizabeth climbed out the back of the lead MRAP and moved to stand beside Alex, which Cassie found mildly annoying for some reason.

Once everyone was gathered around, Alex nodded at Buck. Buck's gaze swept across the assembled troops. "All right; let's get this going."

Alex unrolled a paper map the size of a bulletin board and used gun tape to hold it in place against the side of the MRAP where everyone could see it. Cassie recognized the Peace River Valley.

She looked around the assembled group, quickly counting.

Including Buck and Alex, there were twelve soldiers present, all of them men except for two young women—Clara and one Cassie didn't know. They looked confident and capable, and Cassie was pretty sure all of them were with Special Forces. She drew some comfort from their presence, but her nerves were still on edge, and she felt queasy as though she was going to throw up.

"The situation, ladies and gentlemen," Buck said, "is that earlier this morning, around oh-four-hundred, the local police received reports of an animal attack on a farmhouse." Buck turned around and used his pen to point to a spot on the map. He then turned back and nodded at the RCMP officer standing nearby. "Special Constable Fitzroy, here, will act as liaison with the local constabulary, letting them know we have jurisdiction on this matter."

Paco placed his mouth near her ear. "I know that farm. The Coogans. Good folk."

"By the time the local police arrived, the house was on fire... and the residents were all dead, at least six bodies—men, women, children."

"Goddamn it," said Paco.

Buck scowled at Paco and then continued. "The police witnessed four animals they described as giant wolves savaging the bodies. When they fired on the creatures, instead of running away, the animals attacked, breathing flames on the squad car, catching it on fire. Luckily, the two police officers weren't injured. The animals ran off." Buck paused and let his gaze drift over the assembled crowd. "I've seen these things before. These *are* the hellhounds, the same creatures that have been stirring shit up for almost two weeks. Only now they've moved from attacking cattle to killing people. They're not afraid of us anymore—*if* they ever were. Trust me on this: these things are dangerous. Do not underestimate them. If you let them get close, you will catch on fire and die horribly. They are four-legged flamethrowers with big fucking teeth."

Once again, Buck paused for effect. Cassie looked at the soldiers. Each looked serious, attentive. She saw no fear in any of their faces. Buck said he had seen these before. When? Had they known about the basilisk, as well? Could they have prevented the attack at the hospital?

"Okay," continued Buck. "Here's the mission. We're going to arrive on scene, where Special Constable Fitzroy will make sure the locals give over to us. I will then take charge. We investigate the site, and then our trusty Injun scout and his doggy sidekick start doin' what they do best—tracking the animals." Buck nodded at Paco with a grin that looked anything but friendly. "So, you all know me. You know I like simple. Here's the plan. We find 'em; we kill 'em—fast, with no bullshit. Let the snipers take 'em from a distance. We've got a chopper on call. Once we secure the carcasses, we get back to the Magic Kingdom."

The soldiers all nodded.

"I'm in charge," Buck said. "If anything happens to me, Captain Benoit takes over." Buck indicated Alex with his chin. "After that, if we both go down, you guys can fight over who gets to be boss." Buck flashed a huge, self-appreciating smile.

"Lead vehicle is call sign Romeo-1; second is Romeo-2. All comms are encrypted. Zero is control, but I don't want anyone but me talking to the boss. We clear? You sure as hell don't say anything to the locals."

Cassie had no idea what he was talking about, but she found herself nodding just like the others.

"Questions?" Buck looked around.

Elizabeth, separated from Cassie by a small knot of soldiers, raised her hand.

Buck glanced over at her, a frown on his face. "Yeah, what?"

"What do you want us to do?"

Buck chewed his lower lip for a moment as he considered her question. "Stay out of the way," he finally answered. "The three of you stay in the MRAPs until you're told otherwise. You don't do nothing. We need you, we'll come get you. We clear?"

Elizabeth stared brazenly back at him. "We might be able to help."

Despite the fact that Elizabeth could be a religious pain in the ass, Cassie felt a momentary surge of pride in the other woman. Clearly, she wasn't intimidated easily.

Buck snorted and shook his big head. "Miss Chambers. If I need someone to float paper airplanes around my head, you'll be the first one I ask. Until then, you stay in the vehicle and stay out of the way. Got it?"

Although her face looked as if she had just sucked on a lemon, Elizabeth nodded.

"Good," said Buck. "Let's mount up and go hunting."

* * *

The diesel engine of the MRAP whined as the vehicle coasted down the woodlands surrounding the Pine River Valley. In the air-conditioned passenger space in the rear of the vehicle, Cassie sat with Duncan and five other soldiers. Alex sat up front in the co-driver's seat, wearing a headset with a microphone extended over his mouth. On his lap, he held a large folded map, which he would turn in order to follow the road. Every now and then, he would press a button on a wire clipped to his shirt and reply to a radio conversation only he could hear.

They had been on the road for about a half hour. The passenger seats in the back were built against the boat-like sides of the MRAP so that Cassie had to sit with her back to the window port, facing the other passengers. In order to look out the wire-mesh-reinforced windows, Cassie had to turn in her seat and look over her shoulder, which was awkward as hell, but staring at the other passengers was boring. Besides, whenever they passed another vehicle, there was always a look of surprise on the faces of those inside. People didn't often see the army in northern British Columbia, especially driving around in large, tanklike vehicles. Did they think the army was here on maneuvers, or were they worried that something had gone wrong?

Something had gone very wrong, beginning with the night of the electrical storm and getting progressively weirder. Despite what McKnight and his soldiers were saying, Cassie was certain they were hiding secrets. She could see it in their faces when they spoke about the attack at the hospital and the farmhouse. They didn't act like people who had shown up to help in an emergency; they acted as though it was their fault and they needed to do something before more people died.

She rubbed her sweaty palms against her combat pants, closed her eyes, and tried to take long, calming breaths. It didn't help; she still felt butterflies in her stomach. Duncan sat directly across from her, looking just as out of place as she felt. He stared at his hands in his lap, his face pale. In stark comparison, the five soldiers she sat among seemed confident as hell, bored even. Each held a rifle loosely between his or her legs and wore a tactical vest stuffed with spare magazines of ammunition and other gear. Like her, they wore floppy bush hats and ballistic glasses with yellow-orange lenses that gave everything a yellow tint but also somehow made everything look clearer. She watched their faces, wondering if they were American or Canadian. Each wore a Canadian uniform with a maple leaf on the shoulder—including Buck—but none of them wore a name tag or rank insignia. One of them was definitely French Canadian, but several others had accents she couldn't place. *If Task Force Devil is this official joint American-Canadian team, why are they hiding their nationalities?* The answer was obvious. *Because it's a covert op—a black op.*

The whine of the engine changed as the vehicle slowed down and took an abrupt turn off the main road. The MRAP began to vibrate as it pulled onto a dirt road and picked up speed again. The forested land that had been on either side opened up into farmland, areas of the Pine River Valley suitable for growing crops.

Paco had known the Coogans. Everyone on that farm had died, even the children. She hoped the bodies wouldn't still be there. The hospital attack had been horrible enough for one lifetime.

The MRAP began to slow. Through the windshield up front, just past the first MRAP, Cassie saw the remains of smoldering farm buildings. Even inside the air-conditioned vehicle, she could smell the stench of burnt wood. Red-and-blue lights pulsed from the police and emergency vehicles on the scene. They coasted to a stop, only feet behind the rear of the first MRAP. Nobody within her vehicle moved. If the soldiers felt any excitement, they were hiding it well.

Cassie leaned forward in her bench seat and stared out the front windshield just as Buck and the RCMP liaison officer dismounted and approached one of the on-scene RCMP vehicles.

Well, I am here to help. Closing her eyes, she opened herself up to the ambient mana, letting the energy rush through her. As it did, her skin tingled, and her senses felt as though they had become supercharged. Her eyes snapped open, and she saw Duncan staring at her, concern in his face.

"What?" Duncan asked.

"There's something weird here. Can you feel it?"

"What do you mean, weird?"

Up front, Alex turned and watched them.

"Channel," Cassie told Duncan. "You'll see what I mean."

Duncan did, and a moment later, a look of puzzlement came across his features. "What?"

"You feel it too?"

He nodded. "Someone was using mana here."

"Or some *thing*," Cassie released her seatbelt and leaned forward, putting her hand on Duncan's knee. "I think it's the animals, the hellhounds. I feel them. I think I can sense their presence or at least where they were using mana."

Duncan's puzzled look gave way to one of fear. "Shhh." He raised his hand and glanced about the interior of the vehicle at the soldiers who were now all watching Cassie and him.

"Duncan, don't you see what this means?"

Alex climbed out of his seat up front and maneuvered himself into the rear between the rows of passengers, kneeling between Cassie and Duncan, watching their faces. Duncan looked like a bird caught by a cat. His eyes darted from Cassie to Alex. "No, I don't see what this means, and you're making assumptions. It may mean nothing at all."

"It means," Cassie continued, hearing the excitement in her own voice, "we *can* help. We might be able to track these things or at least know if they're still about."

Duncan's face went pale, and he swallowed nervously. "I... I don't—"

Alex met Cassie's gaze. He raised his eyebrows. She nodded, and he keyed the microphone attached to his shirt. "Romeo-1, this is Romeo-2. We're coming out." He grinned at Cassie. "There's been a new development."

Chapter 24

Getting out of the MRAP had been a bad idea. Even from a hundred feet away, Cassie could feel the heat from the still-smoldering farmhouse and barn. And the smell... the stench was overpowering, so bad that Cassie had literally gagged, coming very close to throwing up. How did firefighters cope with this? Even now, hours later, the fire department was still spraying water over the remains of the farmhouse. Laid out in a neat row behind the fire truck were six corpses, fortunately all encased in white coroner bags. She had overheard one of the first responders telling Buck that the corpses had been roasted and then torn apart, their internal organs consumed. It seemed the hellhounds liked to cook their meat before eating it. She shook her head as she stared at the row of bags.

The hellhounds used mana when they breathed fire; that was now obvious. She had no idea if they channeled the mana the way she, Duncan, and Elizabeth did—or manipulated it in some other way—but it didn't really matter. She could sense them or, at least, feel that they had been here recently. When she concentrated, she could still feel them far away to the north. How much longer would she be able to track them? She really didn't want to get any closer to those things, but at the same time, she knew that if they didn't go after them soon, they might lose the beasts. Exhaling deeply, she felt queasy suddenly and leaned against one of the police cruisers. A moment later, a hand came to rest on her shoulder, and she looked up. Alex was watching her closely. "You all right?"

"I've never…"

He leaned back against the hood of the vehicle beside her and crossed his arms over his weapon, which hung from a sling so that it dangled down near his hands. "This is a bad one."

"You ever seen… this sort of thing before?"

His nod was barely perceptible. "In Afghanistan—usually whenever something went really bad, which was surprisingly often."

"Creatures like this?"

"No. I'm talking about combat."

"You get used to it?"

He shook his head. "Some guys become numb to it, but I never have. I'm not sure that's best anyhow. Focus on what you need to do for now. That might help."

She watched his face carefully. "You guys did this, didn't you? You didn't come up north to fix this problem. You were here *before* it started."

He wouldn't meet her gaze. Instead, he stared at the long row of bagged corpses. Two clearly belonged to children. "Maybe," he finally whispered. Then, he did meet her gaze, and his eyes held the most profound sadness she had ever seen. "But at this point, does it really matter whose fault it is? Someone has to stop those things. And like it or not, it's our job."

"Can we stop them?"

"Hell yes." He pushed himself away from the police cruiser and walked off.

* * *

While the three mag-sens stood beside the hood of one of the MRAPs, watching, Paco and Clyde went to work. The tracker and his dog began searching the ground, starting from nearby the smoking cinders that had been the farmhouse. In ever-widening arcs, Paco and Clyde circled the ruins. Clyde moved slowly, sniffing the ground, his nose only inches from the grass. Paco, a magnifying glass in his hand—reminding Cassie of Sherlock Holmes—walked beside his dog, stopping every now and again to drop down to one knee and examine the ground through the lens. In his other hand, he held a stick about three feet long with several rubber bands wrapped around its length.

"They're getting farther away," Elizabeth said.

She was right. Cassie could now only barely sense the presence of the hellhounds far to the north.

"What's up north?" Duncan asked, a slight tremor in his voice.

Cassie could tell the young man had been terrified since getting out of the vehicle. Both Cassie and Elizabeth had been sickened by the stench of the burned corpses, but only Duncan had actually vomited. He shouldn't be there, she knew. He was out of his league. Hell, all three of them were out of their league, but Duncan was clearly too sensitive for this. The kind of guy who was always picked on at school, he just didn't fit in among the Special Forces soldiers, all of whom were definitely alpha males—even the two women. Not one of them ever treated Duncan with anything more than complete indifference. Had Duncan not been a mag-sens, he would have been completely useless to these people. Only Cassie and Elizabeth talked to him at all.

Still… frightened or not, he needed to stop acting like such a little bitch.

"Mostly forest and hills. There are some small lakes, then you hit the Moberly River." Cassie paused, shading the setting sun with her hand. "Unless these animals can swim the river, they'll still be on this side. So, at most, they're only about ten to fifteen kilometers away over some pretty rough ground. Wild animals could run around out there forever."

"How do you know all this?" Elizabeth asked.

Unlike Cassie and Duncan, Elizabeth didn't look so out of place in her army clothing. Maybe it was because she had copied the soldiers' manner of dressing, tucking her pant legs into her boots the same way they did. Maybe it was just because she carried herself with an aura of responsibility—something that Cassie, with her hands in her pockets, most of her buttons undone, and sleeves rolled up to her elbows—didn't.

Duncan pulled a cigarette out of a packet from his pocket, his third in less than an hour, and lit up. Cassie reached over, snatched it from his mouth, and took a drag before handing it back. The instant hit of nicotine felt pretty awesome. She only smoked when she was drunk or stressed. "I spent a couple of summers working at Moberly Park as a volunteer ranger. Hudson's Hope is only about an hour's drive to the northeast."

Elizabeth nodded then glanced at the body bags in their neat little line. She chewed her lip. "Did you know these people?"

Duncan sighed. "We should go wait in the vehicles. They don't need us out here."

Neither woman moved or even acknowledged he had spoken.

"No." Cassie shook her head. "This place is pretty isolated. Never really had a reason to come out this way before. Paco says they were good people."

"Goddamn it," said Duncan. "We're *all* good people, but we need to leave this hunting-monsters bullshit to the soldiers. We're just in the way out here. Let's go back inside."

Cassie fought back her anger and frowned at him. "We're not in anybody's way, Duncan. Besides, Paco's the one doing all the work, not the soldiers." Which was true enough. Buck, Alex, and the rest of the soldiers all stood near the hood of the second MRAP—as far from the three mag-sens as they could get—talking amongst themselves.

"It isn't right," said Elizabeth, still staring at the corpses. "They deserve better than to be abandoned like that."

That wasn't exactly true, Cassie knew. No one had abandoned the bodies. In fact, RCMP officers and forensics specialists were still present, photographing them and documenting what had occurred. The fire department was still on site, as well, although there was little they could do other than make sure the fires stayed out. Everybody was waiting, not really doing anything but watching Paco and Clyde. Cassie felt worse than useless, and every minute, the hellhounds moved farther away. Hadn't she come here to help?

"They'll move the bodies when they're ready to," Cassie said.

"Someone should say a prayer for their souls," Elizabeth said, abruptly walking off toward the corpses.

Cassie sighed. Elizabeth would do as she wanted; that was pretty clear. Besides, who was Cassie to argue that saying a prayer for the dead wasn't helpful? It was more than she was doing.

"Let's go back inside," whined Duncan. "I hate this shit!"

"This isn't about you, Duncan. We came here to help, remember?" Cassie turned away, not wanting to see the hurt look on Duncan's face. She felt bad but only for a moment. She approached Paco and Clyde, now about a hundred meters away, kneeling in front of a broken section of wooden fencing.

"Hey!" yelled Buck. "Where are you going?"

Cassie stopped and turned to face him. All the soldiers were now staring at her, including Alex.

"It's okay," she yelled back. "There's no danger anymore. They've gone."

Buck scowled but waved her off then turned back to say something to the soldiers around him. They all laughed—all except Alex. Cassie's face flushed with heat, but she turned away and kept going.

Out in the fields surrounding the farm, the stench from the burned cows was revolting. Most of the carcasses were littered around the edges of the fence. When the hellhounds had attacked the farm, the cattle had run as far away as they could before getting trapped against the fence. Not a single cow had survived. The hellhounds had killed everything and everyone, even though they obviously couldn't consume all the dead. What kind of animal killed just for the pure savagery of it?

As she approached Paco, he remained squatting on the ground, watching her over his shoulder. "Hey, little sister. What up?"

Clyde bounded over and jumped up against her thigh, his tongue hanging out. The animal was so large he almost knocked her over. It took several moments before Clyde calmed down.

Paco cocked his head to the side and examined the dog. "You all done with the pretty girl now, Clyde? Ready to get back to work?"

Clyde locked his gaze on Paco and barked, just once. To Cassie's ear it sounded just a tad defiant, maybe grouchy.

Paco stared into Clyde's eyes, a look of complete seriousness on his features. "*Kaanetaah*, Clyde. *Kaanetaah*."

Immediately, Clyde spun about in a circle and began sniffing the ground again. Paco motioned Cassie over. She knelt down beside him, looking at the terrain he had been examining before she interrupted. There was an opening in the fence about four feet wide. Dozens of large, canine-like prints overlapped one another, creating a muddy mess.

"That was cool," Cassie said. "Dene-Zaa?"

"Yup."

"*Ka-an-etaa-ah.*" Cassie sounded the word out slowly. She had always loved languages, and Dene-Zaa was about as exotic as you could get.

Paco grimaced. "Close enough. You see what happened here?" He let his fingers trail over one of the less-trampled prints.

"There was a break in the fence, so they all funneled in here."

Paco shook his head. "*They* broke the fence—at least, the alpha did. Didn't even burn it first; just ran right through it. The others followed him in."

Really? How big are these things? "Him?"

"Most likely a him. I'm applying wolf behavior to these things, but I don't really know if they're like wolves or not. I just got nothing else to go on."

"So, what now?"

"Look at this." He placed the stick he was holding onto the ground, using it to measure the space between two of the large paw prints. "This is the alpha's track. Look at this bad boy's stride. This fella is a big one, real big. Probably more than three hundred pounds."

"What does that mean?"

"Means his head comes up to your chest. Big, big fire doggy."

Cassie's hand reached her chest, and she stared at it. "Really? That big?"

Clyde whined and flopped down on the ground beside Paco.

"Clyde don't like these things. Can't say I blame him."

"Will he track them?"

Paco snorted, reached over, and scratched behind the shepherd's ears. "He'll track 'em if I ask him to. For now. When we get closer... I don't know. A good dog'll do just about anything you want it to, but you push them too far..."

"Can I help?"

Paco watched her, a grin on his face. There was a large gap between his front teeth. "I don't know, little sister. Can you?"

"I spent some summers working with the park rangers. I'm not useless. I've done a lot of hiking around here."

"No. You've done a lot of hiking in Moberly Park. These things have gone north. Wildlands up north."

"I know. I can sense them. They're getting farther away."

Paco's grin disappeared, and he watched her face closely. "That true—you can *sense* them?"

She nodded. "We all can. But I think I'm better at it than the others."

Paco stood up and leaned back against an unbroken section of the fence. He pulled a small notepad out of his pocket and began writing in it. Cassie heard footsteps and turned to see Buck and Alex approaching. Alex smiled, but Buck looked pissed off, which, near as she could tell, was how he always looked.

"What's going on, Chief?" Buck asked. "When we moving?"

Without looking up, Paco kept scribbling notes. "Whenever you and your boys are ready. You got a map of the area?"

"Course we do, Chief." Buck nodded at Alex.

On cue, Alex pulled a large map from his trouser pocket. It was folded like an accordion, so it could open up as much or as little as needed. Alex handed the map to Paco, who, now down on one knee, unfolded it. Buck and Alex dropped down beside him while Cassie looked over his shoulder. The map displayed the local area, including all of Moberly Lake Park and the Pine River Valley running north to the Moberly River.

"They've headed up this way," Paco said, indicating the area on the map with his finger. "We've got about twenty K of some pretty savage wilderness between here and the Moberly River."

"Can they cross the river?" Buck asked.

Paco hesitated. "Maybe. Wolves might if they thought they had to. But the real question is do they need to? There's lots of terrain to move about in up there and lots of game, including all the farms in the valley."

"Okay, so what then?" Buck asked.

"Well, they've eaten, full bellies, so they're probably gonna go to ground, but if they're like wolves, they may be nocturnal—they may not go to sleep until early morning."

"You think they got a lair up north?" Alex asked.

"Don't know." With hooded eyes, Paco watched Buck carefully. "How long these things been here?"

Buck scowled. "Just track the fucking things, Chief. That's what we're paying you for."

"I need good intel to do my job," Paco said. "Just cut the secret shit and tell me unless you want these things getting the drop on us."

Buck's eyes tightened with anger, but Alex spoke first. "We think they showed up the night of the bizarre electrical storm."

Buck glared at Alex, who simply shrugged. "What does it matter?"

"Two weeks. Probably not long enough to find a lair, then," Paco said. "Also, they won't know the ground well. We got that going for us."

"Okay, what now?" Buck asked

"Clyde and me follow their trail. He follows the blood scent. I follow the sign."

Alex leaned in to examine the map. "We got some trails, maybe big enough for the MRAPs, maybe not." He looked up from the map. "We're gonna have to go on foot."

Paco looked at Buck. "I'm gonna need help."

Buck exposed his teeth, looking like a grinning death's head. "Don't worry, Chief. We've done this sort of shit before. We're pros. You'll have a cover team out watching your ass for you. They'll keep in touch with the MRAPs." Buck glanced at Alex. "You're up, Newf. Take four guys with you."

"We're gonna have to go light." If Alex was worried about stalking through the bush after a pack of fire-breathing dogs, he was hiding it well.

"Go any way you have to," Buck said. "Once we run these things down, you call me in. We'll get ahead then light 'em up good. They may be tough, but they're not bulletproof. And I got a score to settle with 'em."

"There's more," said Paco.

"What?" said Buck.

"I want Cassie with me. She can help track these things."

"No way," said Alex.

"Ain't gonna happen, Chief," Buck joined in. "McKnight'll have my head if anything happened to one of his precious mag-sens."

"Look," said Paco. "It's getting dark. I'm gonna have to track by flashlight."

"So, we wait for morning, then," Buck said.

Paco shook his head. "Can't. Look at the sky."

All of them turned toward the horizon, where dark clouds gathered near the setting sun.

"This trail isn't going to last if it rains," Paco said. "When it does, we'll be out on foot, in the weeds, hunting animals that probably feel pretty comfortable hunting us."

Alex shook his head again. "You got the dog. It can follow their scent."

"Maybe, maybe not," said Paco. "Clyde's a pretty awesome dog. But there's only so much you can ask of any animal, and he doesn't like these things. If he loses his shit out there, we'll be alone and in the dark."

"I can do this," Cassie jumped in. "It's cool. I've done this sort of thing before."

Alex frowned. Buck laughed unkindly. "You've hunted fire-breathing dogs in the wilderness before?"

"That's not what I meant. I've been in this area before. I know my way—"

"You don't," said Alex. "It's cool you're offering to help, but you have no idea what's out there."

"Neither do you, Newf," said Buck. He looked from Alex to Cassie and then to Paco. "Okay, Chief. Here's what we're gonna do. Blondie here goes with the cover team." Alex opened his mouth to protest, but Buck jammed a finger into his chest. "I'm in fucking charge here. Not you. Jesus, I'm tired of telling you that. The girl goes. You keep her alive. If she gets her ass eaten out there, you can explain it to McKnight. She might as well start earning her pay."

Alex stared at the ground, his face red.

"I'm getting paid?" Cassie forced a smile onto her features and tried her best to sound as though she wasn't terrified.

"Service to your country, Blondie," said Buck. "That's all the pay you need."

Chapter 25

"You all set?" Alex asked Cassie.

"Yeah, I'm good."

In truth, she didn't feel good; she felt as though she was way out of her element. This was all happening too fast. It was still surreal. Was she really about to go hunt fire-breathing dogs in the wilderness—on foot?

She had left her small pack in the vehicle. Alex had told her it was best to only carry what she'd need. He had, however, given her a Camelbak water hydration system, which was a small, water-filled backpack with a tube for sipping. If she wanted to drink, all she had to do was stick the tube in her mouth. She also wore a sleeveless equipment vest covered in pockets—a "load-bearing vest," Alex had called it. He had pulled most of the equipment out of it, just leaving some rations, a first-aid kit, and a compass. Dangling over her chest from a strap was a set of night-vision glasses, a heavy and bulky device with four lenses.

"All right." Alex strapped a flashlight to the front of her load-bearing vest. Then he stood back a pace and critically examined her. "So, we're going to be moving quickly, at least as quickly as we can, but I don't want any problems out there. If you're having difficulty keeping up, say something. Tell me, tell Clara, tell Paco. Shit, tell Clyde if you want. Just don't keep problems to yourself out there. You can become a heat casualty faster than you can possibly imagine, and I have no intention of calling in Starlight tonight, okay?"

She really didn't know what he was talking about, but she nodded her head quickly.

About ten paces away, Paco waited beside Clyde. In addition to Alex, Paco, and Clyde, there were four others in the cover party: Clara, Gus, Connor, and Eric. She couldn't remember their last names, nor was she certain they had even given them. In truth, she was just happy she could remember their first names. Her thinking was a little bit addled at the moment. Clara, she knew, was a sergeant and acted as Alex's second in command, but she didn't know what rank the others were. It didn't really matter, if she were being honest. They seemed really, really competent. They each carried a very dangerous-looking rifle with a collapsible stock and all sorts of high-tech doodads attached to it—Special Forces laser scopes and stuff like that, she guessed. She noticed Paco also carried a hunting rifle.

Am I the only one who's unarmed?

"Do I need one of those?" she asked Alex, pointing at his rifle.

His lips tightened as he silently contemplated her request. She had expected him to laugh, to mock her, maybe to make a joke. *Jesus, do I need a weapon?*

"No, you just stick close by me." He gripped her shoulder and squeezed it. "You'll be fine." He turned away, faced Paco. "Let's get this done."

Paco nodded and knelt down beside the dog, who stared into his face expectantly. "Okay, Clyde. Way to find the scent. Now we need to hunt it. *Dehdzat,* Clyde. *Dehdzat.*"

Deh-dzat. Cassie sounded this word out in her head as well as the other, *Kaanetaah.* Look. Hunt.

The dog trotted into the woods, and the cover team followed.

* * *

Hours later, Cassie's lungs were on fire, her thighs literally trembled—not in a good way—and every inch of her was drenched in sweat. Exhausted, she had to stop once more. Leaning over at the waist, she placed her hands against her knees and gasped for air. It was pitch dark, and all she had to light her way was the flashlight strapped to her load-bearing vest.

She had made a lot of mistakes in her life—a *lot* of mistakes—but volunteering to come along with the cover team had been a doozy. She should have stayed with the trucks, with Elizabeth and Duncan. She didn't belong here, hiking through the brush at night with professional soldiers. She was slowing them down. They must hate her guts for this. They had to be swearing at her beneath their breath, wishing she weren't there. Sure enough, she saw Alex coming back for her once again. He dropped down on one knee and peered into her face. He had been a constant presence, always checking on her, making sure she was all right. She must be such a burden to him.

"I'm fine," she mumbled, feeling anything but fine.

He felt her Camelbak, lifting it and squeezing. She had emptied it some time ago. She felt her face heat. She had hoped he wouldn't notice that she had burned through all her water already.

"Take it off," he said.

She slipped the straps off, and he pulled it away. A moment later, he had shrugged off his own Camelbak and was holding it out for her to slip onto her back.

She shook her head, unable to talk coherently. "Yours," she

managed.

"Jesus, Cassie, you're worse than my sister. Take the water."

Feeling like she was going to die from shame, she slipped her arms through the Camelbak and pulled it on. A moment later, Alex put the nozzle in her mouth and stood and watched her as she drank. It tasted so good, so unbelievably good. Water had never tasted this good before.

She was so out of shape.

They had been tracking the hellhounds for more than five hours—five near-nonstop hours of climbing over, under, and through the bush. At first, she had kept up well enough, but all too quickly she had begun to get tired, and once that happened, her balance began to go. She had started to stumble, to fall. Now, her palms were skinned, her knee hurt, and her shoulders ached. When this torture was over, she was never, not ever, hiking again. Nature sucked.

None of the others seemed to have any problems keeping up at all—and they were the ones carrying all the equipment. These guys—and she was definitely including Clara with the guys—were insanely fit.

Not her. She needed a beer. She needed a bath. Neither was likely anytime soon.

Up ahead, Paco squatted down again and used his flashlight to examine the ground. Clyde stood about two feet away, watching him. The dog's eyes reflected the light from the flashlights. Alex and the other four soldiers used their night-vision devices, but Paco had insisted on his flashlight, stating he needed white light. Paco glanced over his shoulder, saw Cassie watching him, and then motioned for her to come closer. Sighing and wheezing, she staggered over before dropping down on her hands and knees beside him, grateful for the rest.

"You gonna make it?"

Not trusting herself to talk, she nodded.

Paco watched her face closely for several more moments then used his flashlight to highlight the ground in front of him, angling the light so that it cast shadows against a large set of prints on the ground, creating a contrast.

"This is our Alpha," Paco said. "We're catching up, so the track is fresh, maybe only one to two hours old. Clyde's still on the scent, but the closer we get, the more restless he gets. He's scared, and no shame on him, 'cause these things scare the shit out of me, too." He paused, watching Cassie's face. "Can you tell me anything?"

She closed her eyes and concentrated, measuring the presence of mana around her. It was becoming easier for her. The more she used her mana-tracking sense, the more accustomed she became to it. "Nothing. They must be far away still."

"Do you feel them far away? Or not at all?"

"It's hard to describe, to put into words, but I think, and this is only a working theory, that I can tell when they draw or use mana."

"Okay, so you can track this mana use, not the actual creatures. All the time, or only when they're using it?"

"I think only when they're using it… but I just don't know for sure."

Paco's face took on a deadly serious look, at odds with his constant smile. "Not so good, then. If they're not using magic, maybe they could sneak up on us."

"It's possible, but why would they do that?"

"We don't know these things at all. We don't know what's normal for them or how they hunt or whether anything from their world hunts them by their use of magic."

"Their world?"

Paco glanced at Alex, who knelt beside Clara not too far away, their heads together in whispered conversation. The other soldiers had each taken up a different position, watching outward. They did this every single time they stopped. Even when they were just walking, each soldier watched a different direction, often stopping to aim down the scope of their weapons.

"These things have to be aliens," Paco whispered. "It's the only possible conclusion."

"How is that possible?"

"I don't know. They must have crash-landed on our planet."

"Giant fire-breathing wolves flew here in a spaceship and then crash-landed?"

Paco's face look pained. "Best I can come up with."

"Wait a minute," she said, closing her eyes again. "There, I just sensed one of them, that way." She pointed to the northeast.

"Close?" Paco asked.

"No. I don't think so."

"Can you tell how far?"

Cassie shook her head again. "No, just not close."

Paco nodded and then began examining the tracks before them. He drew several Popsicle sticks from his shirt pocket, something he had done several times already, and planted one of them in the ground near one of the paw prints.

"Why are you doing that?" she asked.

He scrunched up his features in a noncommittal manner. "Just want to mark the sign, make sure we don't come upon them again and think they're new. Also, if the others follow along, they'll know for sure we came this way."

Cassie glanced over at Alex. "I think he's been calling in our location. I'm pretty sure he has a GPS."

"No doubt, but some habits are hard to break."

Thunder rumbled overhead. The storm clouds Paco had pointed out at sunset had only gathered thicker since nightfall. A patter of raindrops began to fall. *Perfect.*

"What now?" she asked.

"We're okay for a bit… probably. Their scent is hard to mask, but eventually, the rain will wash it away. We'll lose the sign first, though."

"You mean the tracks?"

Paco grunted. "Yeah, but not just the tracks. You have to look at everything. Scuffs on trees, creased leaves, bruised grass stems, even their hairs left stuck against bark. That's why it's so hard to track in the dark. Even with a flashlight, it's easy to miss things."

"What if we lose them?"

"Then we wait until morning and try to find them again with better light. Good thing I got the Popsicle sticks, eh?"

She did not want to spend the night sitting in the rain while those things were out there.

"I think we're good, though. I think I know what they're doing, where they're going."

"Well?"

Paco pulled out his compass. It was one of those fancy kinds with the flip-up mirrored lid. He took a bearing and nodded. "Pretty sure they're headed for water, for the Moberly River."

"I thought you said they wouldn't cross it."

"I'm not saying they're going to, and I didn't say they wouldn't—just that it's unlikely. I'm saying that they're heading toward it. It's fresh water. All animals need fresh water, even alien wolves that breathe fire."

At that moment, Alex came over and knelt beside Paco and Cassie, swinging his rifle out of his way. "What's going on?" He glanced at Paco's compass. "They change direction?"

"No. Toward the water still," Paco answered.

Alex nodded. "Good."

"Can your boys get ahead of them?" Paco asked. "Set up an ambush near the river?"

Alex chewed the inside of his cheek while he considered it. He reached his hand up and wiped rain and sweat from his eyes. "Maybe. Buck can use the helicopter to get ahead of them."

Helicopter? Why are we driving and walking if they have a helicopter?

"Try it," Paco said. "A fire team with NVGs in a hide at the edge of the water could make all the difference."

"I hope there's trees to climb at the river bank," said Alex. "I sure as hell wouldn't want to lie on the ground waiting for these things."

"There's trees," Paco said. "And some high ground. Here, I'll show you on the map."

Alex pulled his map out and laid it out on the ground. Both men bent over it while Paco indicated the best place for the soldiers to lie in wait. Then, sitting back, Alex used his radio to talk to Buck, calling out a series of numbers that must have been coordinates for the ambush spot Paco had indicated.

Feeling her energy returning, Cassie began to get bored with the inactivity. She looked about at the others. The four soldiers had remained on sentry, occasionally raising their rifles to look down their scopes. Had she not known they were there, she never would have seen them. Each was little more than a shadow in the dark, like a ninja. The patter of the rainfall picked up, creating a constant drone. At least it had driven away the mosquitoes.

Alex rose and looked at Paco, who sighed and stood up, putting his hands against the small of his back and stretching. "Let's pick it up, move faster while I can still follow the sign." He paused and watched Cassie's face. "Can you do this?"

Probably not, but she'd be damned if she'd admit it. "I'm fine."

Paco grinned and squeezed her elbow. Then he and Clyde took off, heading north once again.

Alex stood in place, watching her face carefully. "You get tired, you tell me. Otherwise, you stay behind me. Okay?"

"Yeah, I'm fine."

"Okay, then." He turned away, following Paco and Clyde.

With a weary sigh, Cassie followed after him.

* * *

For Cassie, the next two hours were rain-drenched agony. She was so exhausted she couldn't think properly. Her entire world became a matter of putting one foot in front of the other and staggering along behind Alex as they climbed through the underbrush. Several times, she had actually fallen to her knees, certain she wouldn't be able to get back up again, but each time, Alex was there, helping her back to her feet, encouraging her to go just a little bit farther. Once, she heard a helicopter as it swept over them, and she vaguely knew that was important for some reason, but it was just too hard to make sense of anything. The ground began to rise as they climbed a long slope. Each step felt like wading through mud. She was barely aware when they finally stopped moving, and she dropped to her knees in exhaustion, not knowing or caring where they were. In a moment, Alex was beside her.

"I'm... I'm sorry," she gasped, unable to see him in the dark but certain his gaze was full of contempt.

"Don't be," he whispered near her ear. "You did amazing."

He remained beside her, and as the minutes passed, she somehow managed to catch her breath again. Now, for the first time, she noticed the low drone of rushing water to their front and below them. "Where are we?"

"Close to the river. Up on a high feature Paco's used before for hunting. It's a good vantage point for watching."

Watching what?

Alex fumbled with the four-eyed night-vision device that hung from Cassie's neck, lifting it over her face and tightening the straps for her. It was heavy and awkward, and she saw nothing at all— until he flipped a switch on the side of the device. It hummed suddenly and then lit the world up in a flash of green hues. She gasped in surprise. It was literally the difference between night and day... well, almost. Looking about, she noticed for the first time that Alex had already put on his own night-vision device. He looked like an alien, four-eyed insect.

"Your depth perception is going to be off," he whispered. "It takes some getting used to, but we're done now. We don't have any farther to go. The rest of this is Buck's show." He placed his hands on either side of her sweaty, rain-soaked cheeks and stared at her. "You ready?"

She nodded, but her heart still hammered in her chest, and she shivered despite the muggy heat.

"I'm proud of you," he whispered.

He began to crawl, keeping low, to the top of the hill, which she could now see was only about twenty feet away from where she knelt along its reverse slope. Paco and Clyde lay prone at the summit. She began to crawl after Alex, sweaty and exhausted but somehow also exhilarated.

I kept up, she realized with a flush of pride. She crawled between Paco and Alex and lay on her belly at the summit's edge. The others took up their usual defensive positions, watching outward. Cassie could see the Moberly River below them. She guessed it was about a hundred meters or more to the water's edge, but it was hard to judge distance with the night-vision devices.

"You sure they're down there?" Alex whispered to Paco.

Clyde whimpered, and Paco reached out and scratched behind the dog's ear. "They're there," he whispered back.

Cassie's gaze swept back and forth as she looked for the hellhounds. The tree line didn't reach all the way to the water but petered out before the rocky riverbank. But as Paco had promised, there were copses in the open ground in front of the river, and Cassie peered at them, trying to see some sign of the ambush team. She saw nothing.

"Are they there?" she asked.

"The animals or the ambush team?" Paco replied.

"Both."

"The team is there," Alex replied.

"How many?" she asked.

"Buck and two others. But I don't see the animals."

"These things are smart," Paco whispered. "And very careful. They won't approach the water until they're certain it's safe. They're new here. They don't yet know that they have nothing to fear in these woods."

Alex aimed down the scope of his rifle, through the NVGs. "They need to fear us."

Do they? Cassie prayed he was right. She closed her eyes, concentrating on the flow of mana around her, seeking some sign of the creatures. At first, she felt nothing. Then, almost unexpectedly, something drew in power in the forest line below them. *Close now, so very close.*

"They're here," she whispered, feeling her heart pound wildly. "Just below us." She pointed to the trees.

"Come on," whispered Paco. "Go for it."

She didn't even realize she was holding her breath until spots formed in the corner of her eyes. She exhaled, forcing herself to breathe. Then a hellhound stepped out of the trees and stood silently in the open ground before the riverbank. It lifted its monstrous snout and began sniffing the air. In the green glow of her vision, the hellhound's dark fur glistened wetly. She knew, without having to be told, that this was Paco's alpha, the leader of the pack. Three more of the giant wolf creatures cautiously stepped out, clustering around the alpha. The alpha lifted its massive shaggy head to the sky and howled. Immediately, the others joined in.

The howling sent chills down Cassie's back. Nothing on Earth had ever made a sound like that. Where had these things come from?

Clyde whimpered once more, and the alpha turned and stared up in their direction, its eyes looking as though they were glowing in the green light of the night-vision devices. Paco reached out and placed an arm around the terrified shepherd. Long moments passed with the alpha staring up at them. Then it turned away and trotted toward the riverbank. The other hellhounds followed. Cassie could actually hear her own heartbeat vibrating in her skull.

Beside her, Alex looked down the scope of his rifle. If he was frightened, she couldn't tell. His finger moved toward the trigger. Could he even hit something that far way, through the rain, and while wearing night-vision glasses? Glancing over at Paco, she saw he was also now aiming down the scope of his hunting rifle. *This is just too goddamned surreal.*

Menace and expectation hung in the air like a shroud. If something didn't happen soon, she was certain she would pass out.

"Close your eyes," Alex whispered, still looking down his scope.

Without thinking about it, she did as she was told—and a

moment later, everything went crazy. A huge explosion rocked the night. The ground vibrated beneath her.

God, that was loud! Her eyes flashed open again just as another explosion lit up the night, causing her NVGs to flare out for a moment. She heard the hellhounds howling in rage, fear, or pain. Then, she heard the loud booming of gunfire. She yelped in surprise as Alex began to fire his rifle only inches away from her. This close, the shots were unbelievably loud and painful. Spent casings flew through the air as he fired shot after shot. One of the empty casings landed on the back of her hand, burning her. She brushed at it furiously, rising up from where she lay. Paco grabbed her shoulder and shoved her back down.

"Stay down!" he yelled then pulled back the bolt on his hunting rifle, ramming it forward and loading another bullet into the firing chamber.

She lay where she was, covering her ears with her hands. *Please stop, please stop, please stop.* And then it did.

The silence, so unexpected after the thunder of the ambush, seemed unnatural. Then, down by the water, a rifle fired once more, and Cassie jerked in surprise. Two more shots followed, and then there was silence again. Cassie, Alex, and Paco remained in place, lying prone. The stench of gunfire, harsh and discordant, clogged her nostrils.

Alex, still aiming down the scope of his rifle, made a sound of acknowledgment into the mike near his lips. He lowered his weapon, turned to face Cassie and Paco. "They're all down. We got 'em all."

Cassie concentrated on the surrounding mana but felt nothing.

Paco and Alex rose to their feet, as did the four other soldiers.

So, that's what an ambush is like, she mused as she rose to her knees. She hadn't cared for it. In fact, her limbs were still trembling from emotion and fear and the rampant adrenaline coursing through her blood. What she *needed* was a good night's sleep. What she *wanted* was a cold beer, a hot bath, and another cold beer. "What now?"

Paco looked to Alex, who keyed his radio again and began talking as he stood at the edge of the cliff, looking down upon the scene of the carnage below. All four of the hellhounds lay haphazardly in place as if they were only sleeping.

Alex nodded as he spoke and then glanced toward Cassie and Paco. "The helicopter will return to take the carcasses, but it'll have to make a number of trips and can't take us as well. The MRAPs are only about three klicks that way." He pointed behind them, in the direction they had come from. "We can make them in about twenty minutes. You'll be home before you know it."

"Home?"

"Well, back to the Magic Kingdom."

Home away from home. She raised her arms above her head, standing on her toes and stretching. God, she was tired. She wanted to take the damned boots off and massage her aching feet. She had blisters now—she could feel the points of heat on the soles of her feet. Walking was going to be painful for the next few days. Maybe she'd say the hell with the beer and just take a shower and pass out. Maybe she'd pass out in the back of the MRAP. As uncomfortable as those bench seats had been earlier, right now she figured they'd be pretty damned good for lying down on and taking a quick—

A bizarre sensation swept through her like a wave of cold water rushing up her spine. Something was *off*—something was wrong. She couldn't say why, but she turned in place and stared down the hill into the woods at its base. There, less than thirty feet away, next to a large pine tree, stood a figure—a huge figure—far too large to be a man.

What the hell? Her hands fell to her sides. The sensation of coldness she had felt a moment ago turned into an electric tingling that coursed through her body, making her numb all over. This was impossible, but she saw the creature clearly through the NVGs. It was like a gorilla only larger and standing upright like a person. Easily nine feet tall, its body was covered in a thick layer of fur. It did nothing but simply stood in place watching her, staring right at her. Clyde darted forward to stand in front of Cassie. Like her, the dog only stared in wonder at the creature, panting.

And then she felt it channel. Her vision flared into a blinding green light. Gasping, she staggered back, falling onto her ass on the wet ground. Clyde whined, as if in pain. Someone swore; another person cried out that he was blind. Cassie ripped the NVGs from her head but saw nothing more than green dots dancing in the darkness. Now, as if released from a spell, Clyde began to bark furiously. It was several moments before she could make out the light of a flashlight shining in her face. It was Paco. He was asking her something. She couldn't understand his words. Like her, he had removed his NVGs.

"What?" she asked, shaking her head. "What happened?"

"Don't know," Paco said.

"I saw someone... some... *thing*," Cassie blurted.

"Where?" Paco asked.

Alex was there a moment later, his rifle raised into his shoulder, ready to fire. Like her and Paco, he had also removed his NVGs. He glanced over at her. "What did you see?"

"Over there, by that big tree." Cassie pointed down the hill, but whatever that thing had been, it was gone now.

Alex keyed his radio. "Romeo-1, this is cover party. We have a secondary contact. Danger close."

Alex turned and whistled at the other four soldiers and then motioned down the hill. Each had also removed their NVGs and had turned on powerful flashlights attached to the barrels of their rifles. Without hesitation, the four soldiers spread out, moving down the hill with Clara leading them. The beams of their flashlights scanned back and forth. Paco followed the four soldiers and then got down on all fours to examine the ground near the tree where Cassie had seen the creature. Cassie stood at the summit of the hill, watching him, feeling useless. Again, she closed her eyes and tried sensing for channeling but felt nothing.

"Wrap it up, Paco," Alex called out from beside her. "We're moving."

Paco looked back over his shoulder. "There was something here, something big."

"Now!" Alex yelled.

Paco had a look of exasperation on his tired features, but he nodded and trotted back up the hill, followed by Clara and the others.

"New plan," Alex said to Cassie. "The helicopter is on its way here. You're getting on it and heading back."

"I thought there was no room?"

There was a bright flare of fire from down below, along the riverbank, so bright it hurt her eyes. It was followed by another flash of fire, then two more. Within moments, four red fires like miniature suns blazed below. The ambush team had lit the carcasses of the hellhounds on fire, she realized, using something like road flares only much more powerful. The entire riverbank lit up with a surreal bright red glow, chasing away the darkness.

"We just made room," said Alex. "Come on; let's move. This site isn't secure."

"Let's go, little sister," said Paco. "I'll show you the safest way down. Don't trip."

Still shading her eyes, she followed Alex and Paco. Clyde stayed beside her. The four soldiers were close behind: her own personal escort.

Chapter 26

The helicopter landed beside the bank of the river. Within moments of its skids touching the soft ground, Alex propelled Cassie onto it. One of the aircrew helped strap her in. Then, seconds later, the helicopter was in the air again, carrying only her. There had been room for the others, she saw, so why hadn't they boarded as well?

All questions disappeared when the helicopter banked suddenly and deeply, as if it were standing on its side. Her stomach lurched into her throat, and she closed her eyes, remembering why she hated flying.

The trip back was far faster than she would have thought. They must have been closer to the base than she had realized—or the helicopter was just that quick. She saw the lights of the Magic Kingdom below, nestled against the Peace River and the lakelike reservoir. The aircrew must have been insanely skilled because no sooner had she seen the lights of the base than they stood the helicopter on its side again, spun about, and dropped so quickly she thought they were crashing. Her eyes shut tight, and she gripped the nylon webbing of the bench with a death grip, swearing to herself that this would be the very last time she ever flew.

The helicopter set down so softly that she didn't realize they were on the ground until the side door slid back and a soldier motioned for her to get out. She ran bent over, holding onto her bush hat so the gale from the rotors didn't blow it away. The second she was off and safely away, the helicopter took off, spun about, and disappeared once more into the night.

Where's it going now? Back to help look for the creature I saw. Sighing, she looked around. Other than a couple of soldiers who must have been ground crew, she was alone. It was late, and the base was silent. Everyone must have been asleep. No one was there to meet her. Now that she was safe, it seemed no one cared about her anymore. The others, including Duncan and Elizabeth, would still be out there in the MRAPs, probably making their way back. For the moment, she was left to herself.

She stumbled back to the barracks in the dark. In her room, she stripped out of her filthy clothing and made her way down the hall to the women's shower room, where she had a very hot, very long shower. Then she returned to her room and crawled into her bed. When she closed her eyes, she once again saw the giant, hirsute creature that had been watching them.

She knew what it had to be, but it was too ridiculous to even consider. Her life was already too weird. But it had been watching her—she was certain of that. Why? Because she could use magic—why else?

Exhaustion finally overcame her. As she drifted off to sleep, one word swirled through her subconscious: *Sasquatch.*

* * *

Bright sunlight woke Cassie. In her exhaustion the night before, she had left her curtains open. Outside, birds sang. Groaning, she squinted at the digital clock on the nightstand beside her bed, not quite certain where she was or what was going on. The clock read 10:27 a.m. So why was she so tired? She considered going back to sleep, but then she remembered the events of the night before: the hunt, the ambush at the river, the mysterious creature spying on her. *Are Elizabeth and Duncan back yet? Are Alex, Paco, and Clyde safe?*

She swung her legs over the side of her bed and sat there for several moments, trying to find her equilibrium, before finally forcing herself to get up, throw on a T-shirt and some track pants, and stagger out of her room and down the hallway to the communal bathroom. She couldn't recall ever being this sore.

It was Tuesday morning. She had been with the army for two weeks, mostly wasting time in a laboratory, levitating stuff, but last night they had finally done something important, something real. And, she had been part of that team. She took satisfaction in knowing the hellhounds weren't going to hurt anyone else. Where had they come from—space? Paco's UFO theories were possible but just didn't feel right.

She cleaned up, brushed her teeth, went back to her room, and dragged on a hoodie. She made her way over to the base cafeteria... mess hall... whatever, hoping she could still get some breakfast this late in the morning. She was in luck; there were no set dining hours. Conscious of the growling in her stomach, she began scooping scrambled eggs—and way too much bacon—onto her plate. Balancing an overfull cup of coffee on her tray, she sat down by herself. It was only then she noticed Alex sitting with the other members of the cover party. He met her eye, smiled, and motioned her over. She was about to pick up her tray and go join them when Duncan set his tray down across from her. "Morning."

She forced back her momentary pang of annoyance, reminding

herself that Duncan had few friends here. It wouldn't kill her to eat with him. She smiled at him. "Morning. You sleep in as well?"

Duncan mumbled something incoherent and began to eat.

"Where's Elizabeth?"

"I think she's back in the lab, practicing."

Why was that absolutely no surprise?

Duncan sipped his coffee, watching Cassie over the top of his cup. Something was clearly on his mind.

"What?"

He stared at his plate.

"Duncan, *what?*"

He finally looked her in the eye again, his expression determined. "What the hell were you doing last night?"

"What do you mean?"

"Why on earth would you do something so stupid as to go into the woods on foot after those things?"

"Why? Because they needed to be stopped. They were killing people. That's why we're here—to help."

"Bullshit. We're here because the government wants to control us. We're just a new weapon for them. They don't care about us; they only care about what their precious mag-sens can do for them. If something had happened to you last night—if they had lost you—do you think any of them would really care? That's crazy, taking chances like that—especially for you."

Duncan looked away, shaking his head as if he couldn't believe how dumb she was.

She felt a flush of heat. "What do you mean, *especially for me?*"

"Look, I'm as liberal as the next guy, okay? I'm all for women's rights and all that shit, but seriously, you could have been killed last night, and for what? Nothing. You don't see me taking chances like that, do you?"

Cassie sat back in her chair and pushed her plate away from her. "Duncan, those monsters killed all the people on that farm, *all* of them, even the children. They weren't going to stop, and more people would have died. You know that, right?"

"It's not our problem. The army can clean up their own mess." He looked around at the nearly empty cafeteria then lowered his voice to a whisper. "And let's be clear about something, okay? This whole shitty situation is the result of something these people have done. I think we all know that. Those damned things probably escaped from a secret laboratory on this base. The army probably cloned them or something."

"I have absolutely no idea where those things came from, but at least the army is trying to do something. What are you doing?"

Duncan snorted. "Do something? Are you kidding me? What did you really do last night? What can you do? You're just a girl, not a soldier. You, me, Elizabeth, we're nothing, just a trio of freaks who can do little magic tricks. What did you think you could accomplish out there?"

Cassie stood up and snatched at her tray. "At least I was out there. I wasn't hiding in a truck. And by the way, I'm a woman, not a girl." She stormed off, feeling the heat of indignation course through her body. She dropped her tray on the counter near the stack of used dishes and headed for the front door. *Girl? How clueless is he?*

She paused, staring at the glass door leading outside. Was he right? She had been terrified last night, helpless and unarmed. It had been a very unpleasant feeling. She spun in place and stared at Alex and his friends, still sitting at their table, talking and laughing.

No. Duncan wasn't right. She took a deep breath, set her shoulders, then headed straight for Alex's table. They stopped their conversation and watched her. Stopping in front of Alex, she glared at him in challenge, committed to a course of action. "I want you to teach me how to shoot a gun."

He met her gaze. An awkward silence settled over them all. The other soldiers looked from Alex to Cassie.

Clara sipped her coffee, a look of profound amusement on her face. "I thought you were a gentleman, Boss."

Alex frowned at Clara then pushed himself away from the table, his metal chair legs screeching on the floor. "Is now a good time?"

Chapter 27

The M4 carbine—not a rifle, she had learned; rifles had longer barrels—jerked in Cassie's hands when she pulled the trigger. She'd closed her eyes at the last moment, expecting a far worse jolt than had actually happened.

"Keep your eyes open," Alex said from where he knelt beside her. "It won't bite."

Snorting, she placed her cheek back against the carbine's stock once more. Gazing through the scope, she reacquired the paper target, a man-shaped figure holding a rifle and charging at her, and placed the aiming arrow—not a crosshair—over the center of the target's torso.

She lay on her belly—in a position Alex had called "prone"—in one of the ten firing bays in the indoor range. She didn't ask why a power dam had been built with an indoor rifle range. Pointing out the flaws in the army's ever-more-ridiculous cover story would have been rude. She pulled the collapsible stock of the weapon tighter against her shoulder.

"Three breaths," Alex said, speaking loudly enough that she could hear him through the ear defenders she wore. "The barrel will naturally rise and fall with your breathing. On the third breath, as you're letting it out, slowly pause and then squeeze—not *pull*—the trigger. It should almost be a surprise when the weapon fires. And keep your eyes open this time."

She did as he instructed. Not surprisingly, the aiming arrow in her scope did exactly what he had said it would do: rise and fall with her breathing. On her third breath, she paused as the aiming arrow dipped down upon the center of the target. Holding her breath, she very, very slowly squeezed the trigger, concentrating on keeping the target in her sights. When the weapon fired, it did almost surprise her, just as he had described.

That felt right. She looked up at Alex, waiting for him, grinning.

He put down the binoculars he had been looking through and nodded. "Bang on with that last one. Now do it again just like that."

This time, she really pulled the weapon in tightly against her shoulder, resting its weight on the bottom of the plastic thirty-round magazine beneath the weapon. She took her time and concentrated, firing round after round into the target. Her mouth felt dry, and her pulse was racing, but her senses were alive. She had had no idea firing a gun could be this much fun. Growing up, she had never been into hunting, hating the idea of killing animals.

She squeezed the trigger, but this time nothing happened. Lifting her head, she gazed over the top of the weapon. The firing chamber was open, exposed, and the bolt was all the way to the rear, indicating there were no more bullets in the magazine. "I'm out."

"So, what do you do now?" Alex asked.

"Reload?"

"Well?"

She did as he had shown her, only fumbling around for a

moment looking for the magazine release catch. She placed the empty magazine on the ground beside her, loaded a full one, and released the bolt, letting it slide forward, loading another round in the firing chamber.

She waited.

"You're not done until you start firing again."

She grinned and commenced firing once more, loving this. When she had fired all thirty rounds, he told her to clear the weapon and make safe. She removed the magazine, let the chamber go forward, and dry fired it down range. Then she cocked it once more and dry fired it again. Finally, she locked the bolt all the way to the rear. Alex gazed into the empty firing chamber.

"Clear." He patted her shoulder.

She released the bolt's catch, sending it forward again with a metallic click, then dry fired the weapon one last time, releasing the pressure on the trigger—just as he had shown her.

"Lay the weapon down."

She did as he directed then climbed to her feet and pulled the ear protectors off. Alex walked to the wall, where a control box had been installed. He pushed a button on the box, and there was a metallic clanging of chains from down the range and a low droning of gears as the target she had been shooting at began to move toward them, dangling from a chain on the ceiling. When it was a foot or so in front of her, Alex released the button.

Most of her bullets had hit in the center of the target, with only a smattering of wild shots around the edges. Grinning, she pointed to a cluster of holes where his genitalia would have been. "I killed him good."

Alex snorted, shaking his head. "Not too bad, deadeye. You're a natural at this."

"Not a whole lot of things I've ever been a natural at."

"You want to try a pistol?"

She faced him, her hand on her waist, and cocked her hip. "Oh, hell yes."

He walked over to another firing position, one where the target hung much closer. She followed him and stood beside him, putting her ear defenders back on. He pulled his pistol from his hip holster and, keeping it carefully pointed downrange, held it for her to take. She held it in both hands near her waist.

"Pistols are different. All weapons are dangerous, but because pistols have such short barrels, they have a tendency to point wherever you happen to be looking. And that's really dangerous. So, keep the weapon pointed downrange at all times, especially around me."

Her smile vanished when she saw the serious look on his face. "Got it. Downrange only."

"Okay, there's already a round chambered. All you have to do is release the safety catch, here." He showed her where it was.

Using her thumb, she moved the safety catch to the firing position.

"Use both hands," he said, demonstrating how to hold the weapon. "There's not much of a kick, but there's still enough of a recoil that you need to keep reacquiring the target with each shot. You try that quick-firing shit you see in the movies—or God help us, hold it sideways gangsta-style—and you'll miss with everything but the first round."

She nodded, feeling a lightness in her chest and a sense of breathlessness.

"Whenever you're ready."

A moment later, she fired. The weapon jumped in her grip, but it was almost nothing compared to the recoil from the M4. This time, the target was much closer than it had been before, but she still couldn't tell if she was hitting it or not.

"You're a bit high. And to the left."

She compensated, firing once more.

"That's it. Again."

Aware she was smiling like the Cheshire cat, she began to fire faster—but still re-acquiring the target before squeezing the trigger. Her heart beat wildly. All too quickly, the weapon stopped firing, and she saw that the bolt was locked back, indicating it was empty. He showed her how to eject the spent magazine and insert a full one, releasing the bolt catch to chamber a new round and keep going. She started firing again.

They stayed on the range for another hour or so, firing magazine after magazine. He showed her numerous firing positions. Lying down prone was the most accurate position, but he also showed her how to shoot from one knee, from standing, and from a seated position.

"Let's try something different." He used the control box to bring the target right in so that it was only about a foot away from her. "Sometimes, you're gonna get crowded by opponents. They'll come right in against you to smother you. What I want you to do is hold the weapon down so it's pointed at the ground then step back quickly one pace while at the same time bringing the weapon up and, as quickly as you can, put two rounds into the chest and one into the face."

"Shit, Alex!" She stared at him, her eyes wide.

"There's shooting at paper targets, and then there's combat. Are you playing or learning?"

Exhaling, she nodded. Holding the pistol in both hands, she moved forward until she was almost touching the target, the pistol aimed at the ground between her feet.

"Finger off the trigger until I say move, and *do not* shoot yourself in the foot."

She concentrated on her breathing, on her focus.

"You ready?"

She inclined her head, and he moved farther back behind her.

"Go!"

In one fluid motion, she stepped back, swinging the pistol up as she did. Before she even realized what she was doing, she had put two rounds into the target's chest, followed a moment later by a third into the nose of the figure.

"Goddamn, girl. That was all right!"

Her heart raced in excitement. "Let's do it again."

They practiced that maneuver several more times until her magazine was spent once again. "That'll do for today," Alex said as he took his pistol back from her. "Best to let us do the gun fighting, though. You concentrate on the magic."

"I'm not good enough?"

"You're as good as you're going to get after one session. But we do this for a living, *a lot*. Besides, I'm not sure it's something you really want to get good at." His voice had trailed off, and a look of melancholy passed over his features, but only for a second.

"What now?" she asked.

He chuckled. "Best part. Now you learn how to clean my weapons."

She noticed for the first time that other soldiers had arrived. All along the firing range, they were laying out their weapons. One of them nodded approvingly at Cassie. Alex slung his carbine, holstered his pistol, and then led Cassie off the range to a small room with benches and cleaning kits. He showed her how to break both the weapons down, disassembling them into many small parts.

"They heard about last night," Alex said, showing her how to wipe the dirty parts down with gun oil.

In moments, her fingers were filthy, covered with carbon and oil. "What about last night?"

"They heard you did well last night."

"I didn't do anything last night. Other than slow you down."

He frowned. "Bullshit. You kept up with a Special Forces team on a hunt through the woods at night in shitty weather, and you held your own in your first action." He reached over and squeezed her elbow. "You did just fine."

A surge of warmth flushed through her. She regarded him out of the corner of her eye. How old was he—twenty-five? He wasn't much older than her. She didn't really know anything about him. Less than two weeks ago, he had pretty much kidnapped her from the hospital—yes, he had saved her life; she did get that, but still... she barely knew him.

So why did she care what he thought about her?

"I think McKnight expects you in the lab with the other two," he said.

She nodded. Other soldiers had just walked in, watching her with curious gazes.

"We can do this again tomorrow if you want."

She grinned. "Oh, I do want. I want very much."

Chapter 28

The volleyball flew over the top of the net then seemed to hang for a moment. Finally, it began to descend toward Cassie, picking up speed. She darted across the sand, placing herself under the ball. By habit, she started to reach out for it but then stopped herself and instead channeled just enough mana to knock it back across the net. Duncan only just managed to catch the volleyball with his own mana flow this time, sending it back but really setting Cassie up. She grinned as she spiked the ball in front of him. It rebounded, smashing him in the chin. He fell on his butt, and unable to help herself, Cassie laughed. There was an angry glare in his eyes.

He doesn't like losing to women. Sucks to be him.

They had been outside, behind the gym, playing magic volleyball for about twenty minutes. Cassie felt pretty good, but the near-constant mana use was taking its toll on Duncan, and the front of his T-shirt was now drenched in sweat. Their two scientist minders, Amy and Pierce, sat on a wooden picnic table in the shade, taking notes. She couldn't help but notice Amy seemed kind of sweet on Pierce. *Egghead love?*

The two scientists should have been documenting and testing

the three mag-sens, but Cassie knew now that they had no idea how to monitor something they couldn't see or measure. After more than two weeks, all the scientists could do was record the results of their developing mana use. It was like a blind person trying to understand colors: they simply had no basis from which to begin. Cassie, Duncan, and Elizabeth had had to train themselves and learn by doing. Which was pretty much what they were doing right at that moment. While Cassie and Duncan played magic volleyball, Elizabeth stood, not ten paces away, practicing hitting a punching bag with blows of mana.

Cassie ducked under the net and picked up the ball. "Let's take a break."

Duncan nodded and climbed to his feet before stumbling over to the picnic table where the two scientists sat. Amy handed Duncan a water bottle. Cassie considered him as he upended the bottle and drank. He wasn't what anyone would ever describe as a physical guy. Cassie wasn't even breathing hard, but Duncan looked as though he was ready to fall down. Nor could she figure out why he was so physically exhausted. As near as any of them could guess, mana was channeled through the brain and central nervous system. But really, even that was a guess. At any rate, using mana didn't seem to have anything to do with the body's muscular system. If Duncan sucked at athletics—which he clearly did—then shouldn't he excel at the more cerebral use of mana? Maybe, but he didn't. He kind of sucked. Both Cassie and Elizabeth were far better at channeling mana than he was. And unfortunately, the oversensitive Duncan seemed acutely aware of that fact.

Drinking from her own water bottle, Cassie watched Elizabeth channel mana and use air to pummel a man-shaped martial-arts heavy bag that stood on a water-filled base only about a dozen paces away from the volleyball court. She was striking the mannequin so hard it actually rocked back and forth. Even from here, Elizabeth radiated power and mystical energy. She may have been a nut-bar religious bitch, but she was a powerful nut-bar religious bitch. Elizabeth could now use mana as a weapon. Not a terribly Christian thing to do, maybe, but Elizabeth was training for a fight while Cassie was playing volleyball. She stared out past Elizabeth, past the perimeter fence, and into the woods surrounding the base.

Where was the basilisk now? It hadn't been seen since the attack at the hospital two weeks ago. And there were a lot of people looking for it. Hundreds of journalists, hunters, scientists, and others had converged on Fort St. John. The media circus had continued unabated, with most of the experts still claiming it was some type of undiscovered dinosaur.

Bullshit. She didn't know where it came from, but it wasn't a dinosaur. Dinosaurs didn't use magic to turn people to stone with their gaze. Whatever it was, it came from the same place the hellhounds had.

Paco and Clyde were still waiting, as was the rest of Task Force Devil. And, as frightened as Cassie was of it, she wanted to get on with finding the basilisk. She needed payback. Maybe she could even help Paco track it. She was growing increasingly confident of the soldiers here. Once they found the basilisk, she was certain they could kill it. These people were serious about their work. Each one was a specialist. The ambush on the hellhounds had demonstrated that readily enough. They'd be able to kill it. And she desperately wanted to be a part of that.

She plopped down on the bench across from Amy and Pierce. Duncan sat beside her. She wrinkled her nose at his stench but didn't say anything. He didn't need another reason to feel bad about himself.

"The power of the Lord," he said as Elizabeth beat down on the dummy.

She glanced at him. He had a sly smile on his sweaty face.

"Sure it is," she said.

"How do you know it's not?" asked Amy.

Cassie glanced over her shoulder at her. "I thought science and religion weren't compatible."

"Maybe," said Amy. "Some people feel that way."

"Most educated, intelligent people feel that way," Pierce said, not looking up from where he scribbled in his notebook.

"A lot don't," said Amy. "But some people find a way to reconcile faith with science."

"Rubbish." Pierce shook his head, missing the frown on Amy's face.

Careful, Pierce, Cassie thought as she watched them. *You might want to pay more attention to what the lady says.* Guys could be so clueless.

"Well," said Cassie, "I don't think anyone, even her enemies, would accuse Elizabeth of being stupid or uneducated. She believes this... power comes from God. I have no idea what's going on." Cassie paused, glancing at Amy and Pierce, who both looked away. "But I don't think Elizabeth is right. If there really was a God, why would he, she... *it* give this power to someone like me, an atheist? That makes no sense."

Neither scientist would meet her eye.

"I kind of find the whole religious thing a big freaking joke," Duncan said. "I mean, come on, who's got the right religion anyhow? How can Christians, Muslims, and Jews all be right?"

"Well," said Amy, "those religions you just mentioned are all monotheistic. Their believers worship the same God, just with different belief systems, different dogma; that's all."

"Elizabeth would consider that blasphemy," said Cassie.

"So would all the other hard-core Christians, Jews, and Muslims," noted Pierce.

Elizabeth stood motionless in front of the mannequin, staring at it with a look of fierce determination. *What's she doing now?* Cassie picked up her water bottle, whose surface was beaded with moisture, and rolled it across her forehead. "It's hot today, isn't it? Hotter than normal for this time of the year."

"Supposed to be around twenty-six degrees Celsius today," said Duncan.

That was way hotter than it should have been this early in the spring, especially so far north. She felt Elizabeth draw mana into her body, a *lot* of mana. Cassie stared at the other woman, her gaze narrowing. A wave of hot air washed over Cassie's face, actually moving her hair with its rush. It had felt as if she had just opened a furnace door.

The heat had come from Elizabeth.

Cassie jumped up from the bench. "Elizabeth, stop!"

Another intense wave of heat rushed into Cassie, forcing her to turn her head away and shield her face with her forearm. She staggered back against the picnic table just as a fireball a foot wide materialized out of the air in front of Elizabeth's outstretched hands and flew into the dummy, which erupted in flames. The worst of the heat was suddenly gone as quickly as it had begun.

Cassie stared, openmouthed. The martial-arts mannequin was now engulfed in flames. Burning tendrils of sooty black smoke poured into the air as latex and rubber dripped and sizzled onto the ground beneath it. Elizabeth turned and faced them, a euphoric smile on her face. "Praise the Lord. Look at His glory."

"How... how did you do that?" Cassie staggered closer until she was standing beside Elizabeth.

"It just kind of made sense," said Elizabeth.

"Way more impressive than setting paper on fire."

"I'm blessed. Truly blessed."

A soldier inside the gym rushed out with a fire extinguisher, yelling at them to get back. Someone yanked on Cassie's arm, and she noted with annoyance that it was Duncan.

"Get back," he said.

"Why?" Cassie ripped her arm loose just as the soldier sprayed the mannequin with the fire extinguisher, putting the blaze out.

"Try it," said Elizabeth, grabbing her shoulders and turning her to face the now-smoking mannequin. "See if you can do it, too."

"I don't know how to—"

"I'll show you—walk you through it."

"But..."

"Trust me."

Cassie exhaled heavily, squared herself off, and faced the mannequin.

"You might want to get out of the way," Elizabeth said to the soldier.

He stared at her in confusion.

"Now," she repeated.

The young man jumped back, still hugging the fire extinguisher.

"So," Elizabeth said to Cassie, squeezing her shoulders and softly speaking into her ear, "draw in the mana, more than you feel comfortable with. Don't release it right away the way you normally would. Hold on to it. Let it roil and build."

"Isn't that danger—"

"Trust me. Trust God. Picture the mana becoming hotter, and let it burn. When you feel it becoming too hot to safely hold, that's when you release it at the dummy. Throw the heat; throw the fire."

"But—"

"Just try it," Elizabeth said.

Cassie glanced over her shoulder. Elizabeth looked so earnest, so excited.

"I don't think this is a good idea," Duncan muttered.

Turning her head, Cassie saw Duncan standing with Amy, Pierce, and the young soldier with the fire extinguisher.

Amy's face shone with excitement. "This is amazing."

Pierce nodded. "Go ahead; try it."

"This is a really bad idea," Duncan said.

Elizabeth, still gripping Elizabeth's shoulders from behind, turned her to face the smoking dummy once again. "Go on—try it. Remember, let the mana burn. Think *burn*."

"Got it," said Cassie, not really getting it at all but willing to try. She opened herself up and channeled.

"More," said Elizabeth. "You're gonna need a lot more."

"What about too much? I don't want to get hurt."

"You won't get hurt… I think. Anyhow, I'm going to try something new, something we haven't done before. If it works, I don't want you to freak out."

"Okay, now you're scaring me." Cassie turned to look at Elizabeth, but the other woman turned her back toward the dummy once more.

"I think… maybe," said Elizabeth, "maybe, we can share… whatever this is we're drawing upon."

"Share mana?"

"I don't like that term, but fine, let's call it that. I'm going to draw in some… *mana*, try and send it to you, and see if I can't… you know, energize you, help you."

"You've got to be kidding me."

"I'm not. I've been thinking about trying this for a while now.

No time like the present. Let me help you."

"This is a bad idea."

Elizabeth didn't answer, but a moment later, more mana flowed into Cassie, filling her. It happened so suddenly, so unexpectedly, she gasped in surprise. Only Elizabeth's hands on her shoulders held her in place. There was so much power it was exhilarating and terrifying at the same time. She was now holding way more mana than she ever had before, more than she would have thought possible. All her senses became supercharged, and the metallic taste in the back of her throat grew sharper. She began to feel like a balloon, overfilling with air. Strangest of all, though, was the physical connection she felt with Elizabeth. The mana flowing between them linked them somehow.

"Good," said Elizabeth, squeezing her shoulders. "Now, focus on the mana. Let it burn."

Within her, the mana felt as if it were twisting and bubbling. *Something* was happening.

"No, that's not right," said Elizabeth, sensing what Cassie was doing. "You need to heat the mana. I don't know what you're doing."

"I'm trying."

She began to sway. Her heart hammered in her chest. Her vision grew dim. She felt as if she were dreaming, as if this was all happening to someone else. But the more she concentrated on heating the mana, the more the energy seemed to do something else entirely, to twist and knot and slip away. Her knees began to shake, and her legs felt weak.

"I don't think—"

"Don't stop now," said Elizabeth. "Just do it—burn it!"

Her vision tunneled in on the mannequin. She had to do something before she passed out. She couldn't do what Elizabeth was telling her to do; it just didn't feel right. So, she did what did feel right. Extending her arm, she released the mana flows at the target.

The air around it seemed to warp, and then the dummy disappeared. Cassie gasped and fell back against Elizabeth. Entangled, both women fell down. The connection she had felt with Elizabeth disappeared. Then someone was helping her to her feet, holding her upright. She saw it was Amy. Pierce helped Elizabeth. Duncan stood away from them all, a look of stark disbelief on his face.

"What... what just happened?" Cassie asked. "Did I burn it?"

After several uncomfortable seconds, Amy stepped closer to where the dummy had been, raised her hand, and reached out toward the empty space. A moment later, she drew back her hand as if it had been burned, and her mouth opened wide. She turned and stared at Cassie. "It's still there. You made it invisible."

The air in front of Amy warped once more, and then the dummy reappeared. One moment it wasn't there; the next, it was. Amy jumped back, smashing into Elizabeth.

"I did that?" whispered Cassie in disbelief.

"Praise the Lord," said Elizabeth. "It's another miracle. Two in one day." She hugged Cassie so hard it took her breath away.

How did I do that? Cassie wondered. *And can I do it again?*

Chapter 29

Duncan lay on his bed, propped up against the headboard, staring blankly at the wall. It was close to midnight, but he couldn't sleep. Everyone had been so excited about what Elizabeth and Cassie had done that day. Linking their powers, throwing fireballs—and Cassie had actually turned an object invisible.

Invisible! And what have you done, Duncan? Lost at magic volleyball to a girl. Some wizard.

It was so unfair. This should have been the coolest moment in his life. After all, he was a freaking wizard, a real twenty-first-century magic user. So what if they didn't understand how any of this had happened—it *had* happened. Duncan was a mag-sens, one of only three people on the planet who were sensitive to this new power. His life should be awesome right now. The government should be bringing him hookers and blow, not frigging recording him levitating balls in the air. He should be special.

But he wasn't. Of the three mag-sens, he was by far the weakest, barely sensitive at all compared to Elizabeth and Cassie. He was failing at being a magic user, just as he had failed at everything else in his life. Tears filled his eyes. He knew he was only feeling self-pity, but he just couldn't help it. It was so unfair.

Maybe he was the loser his dad had always said he was, no good for anything but working at a fast-food restaurant and jerking off because girls had no time for him.

Even now, nobody thought he was cool because he was a mag-sens, and no one gave a shit that he could levitate small objects. What a joke! How bitterly unfair. Anything he could do, the girls could do better.

Girls! All his life, he had wanted to be special, and now that he was, he wasn't special at all. Everyone treated him like a freak, especially all these a-hole soldiers with all their muscles and guns. Even the scientists just treated him like a curiosity, when they paid any attention to him at all. He had no friends—no one liked him. Even Cassie and Elizabeth weren't really his friends. They treated him more like someone they were stuck with. He could tell they weren't interested in him in the slightest. And why should they be? He was nothing but a skinny, ugly dork who couldn't get laid to save his life. Had he really expected things to change just because he suddenly had really weak magic powers?

What a crock of shit! After all those years of daydreaming about becoming more than he was, the universe had finally answered his prayers and made him special, only to make others way *more* special.

Nothing. He was a big nothing. He'd never be more than a big nothing. Unless...

The genesis of an idea came to him: what if he simply hadn't developed his potential enough? After all, he was a man; he should be way more powerful than the girls. That was how the universe worked. The males were always more powerful, and better. Maybe Cassie and Elizabeth weren't stronger than he was; maybe he simply hadn't tried hard enough.

He felt as though he was having an epiphany. *Fear is my enemy.*

It's stopping me from achieving my true destiny. He had been holding back, afraid that something bad might happen. He had been limiting himself. Opening himself up to mana was both an empowering and a terrifying experience, in many ways like using drugs. A little bit was amazing, but too much...

He never went all the way, never embraced all the mana he could hold. The more he considered the matter, the more certain he became. He just hadn't drawn in enough mana.

But how could he conquer his fear? When the answer came, he realized he had known it all along. *Drugs.* It was so simple. Drugs could help him use more mana, just as drugs had helped him cope with the pain of his life.

Duncan had been thirteen the first time he had gotten drunk, stealing booze from his stepmother. From the very first sip, alcohol had provided the answer to his misery, at least until his father had caught him. Then, his dad had taken a cane to his backside. His father didn't do things in half measures. The bruises had been there for weeks, and everyone at school had laughed at him. After that, the liquor cabinet had been kept locked. Fortunately for Duncan, there were lots of other drugs out there. Ecstasy became his go-to drug, and getting a steady supply of it was way easier than anybody realized. Kids at high school sold it; you just had to know who. And while drugs didn't make him any less lonely, they did take the edge off his misery. Soon, every dollar he made working at the A&W went to feeding his growing drug habit. But the money from flipping burgers wasn't enough, so Duncan started dealing as well. He still didn't make much money, but he did manage to keep himself supplied. That was enough.

But ever since the evening of the lightning storm, he had been too frightened to use. He had passed out at work but had woken up again within a couple of minutes. Someone had called an ambulance, but he had refused to go to the hospital. He knew they wouldn't let him use there. They might search his stuff and take his stash—maybe even report him to the police.

Soon after, he had accidentally levitated a small object. At first he had been terrified, but he quickly realized how cool this all was, and he began showing off at work. Word spread quickly—really quickly. When McKnight had shown up at his home, telling him he could serve his country and be a hero, Duncan couldn't believe his luck. Finally, he was going to be special. And at first, he was. The scientists made a huge deal about him, documenting every little thing he did. But then Elizabeth showed up and immediately outshone him, making him look like a fool. Then Cassie arrived, and even she was stronger than he was. Suddenly, he wasn't special at all.

Stupid bitches! Screw it. I'm doing this. Time to man up.

He jumped up off the bed and began rooting through his duffel bag. He pulled out the small plastic bag stuffed into an old running shoe. The bag only held three tiny pills of Ecstasy, but it was all he had left and would have to do. If the army had bothered searching his stuff, they would have found the drugs easily enough, but why would they? He wasn't a prisoner; he was a volunteer. Duncan opened the bag, his fingers trembling, and pulled out the pills, cupping them in the palm of his hand and staring at them. His tongue darted out, licking his dry lips.

He hesitated. *Should I?* Then, in one quick moment, he brought his palm up to his mouth and swallowed all three pills. He lay back down on his bed and waited for the buzz to start, terrified and excited at the same time. It only took a few minutes. He felt his heart beating faster and faster. A layer of sweat drenched his skin. Then, he felt the first stirrings of the high.

Sighing, he closed his eyes. He loved this part. But now he also wanted a smoke—needed a smoke—to enhance the high.

Jumping up from his bed, he grabbed his cigarettes and stormed out of his room. If he lit up inside, as he had done on his first night on base, he'd set off the smoke detectors again and get everyone pissed at him once more.

Shit—how was I supposed to have known? Should have told me. A-hole soldiers.

In the darkened hallway, he passed one of them, a big dude with bodybuilder shoulders. Duncan nodded eagerly at him. "Wassup?"

The soldier simply walked past without saying a word.

Arrogant motherfucker. I could set your ass on fire. Except he couldn't set anything on fire—he was too weak for that. *For now.*

He descended the stairwell, pushed open the exit door, and stepped out into the cool night air. There was a picnic table with a butt can just beside the door. Duncan sat on top of the picnic table and lit a cigarette. There was no reason he couldn't be great, no reason he couldn't be better than the girls. Then they'd want him. They'd fight over each other for the chance to polish his knob. Maybe he'd let them. He grinned, feeling his erection grow.

All he had to do was seize his destiny. He opened his cigarette package and emptied its contents onto the picnic table, a little pile of cigarettes. *Time to get great.*

He channeled mana. At first, as always, he held back. But then, he forced himself to draw in just a trickle more than he was used to. It felt... wrong, like an overfilled balloon, but he forced himself to keep going. Then, he began to levitate the cigarettes. In moments, he had each of the cigarettes spinning about his head. He exhaled and forced himself to draw in even more energy.

Nothing terrible happened. The cigarettes continued to spin about his head, faster and faster. He felt the heady rush of euphoria as he realized he *had* been holding himself back and could do so much more. He pulled in even more mana, far more than he'd ever held before. Again, nothing terrible happened, and the cigarettes began to spin so fast they blurred together.

"Way too easy," he said.

Throwing all caution to the wind, he filled himself with as much mana as he could possibly hold. His heart pounded against his chest, the sweat poured down his back, but he kept going, taking long deep breaths. He wasn't a man; he was a racehorse, a thoroughbred. He could do this—he could so do this. He could do anything.

The picnic table vibrated, jerked in place.

This is great.

The picnic table lurched into the air—first one foot and then another. All the while, the cigarettes continued their mad spin in front of Duncan's eyes.

"I'm doing it! I'm fucking doing it!" he cackled.

He thought he heard someone yelling, but he just didn't care anymore. Nothing would stop the joy he was feeling at that moment. He was great; he was powerful. He had been holding back. Everybody had been wrong about him, all wrong, especially his dad. Duncan wasn't a loser—he was awesome; he was a wizard.

What had Elizabeth told Cassie? Let the mana heat within you and then channel it out? Okay, he'd try that and light the cigarettes on fire.

He concentrated and soon felt the mana begin to heat. He released just a trickle of mana, instantly setting the spinning cigarettes on fire in a glowing red whirl about him. Sparks flew off into the night. His joy was profound.

"I'm fucking awesome! Suck it, Dad. Fucking suck it, you cock-eating bat hole! I *am* special! I am!"

But then the heated mana began to spill out on its own, suddenly blanketing his skin in torment. He screamed, but when he did, the heat roared down his throat. Unimaginable pain lanced through his body. Terrified, he tried to release the mana, to dissipate it, but instead, it flowed over him, burning him.

He was burning.

The picnic table crashed back to the ground, and Duncan fell onto the grass, spinning and screaming. Someone beat at the flames covering him, trying to roll him over, but he was too far gone to care anymore.

* * *

From the grass outside the barracks, Cassie watched the medical staff move Duncan's covered body onto a gurney and then load it into the back of an ambulance. Elizabeth stood beside her, silently watching. McKnight, Alex, and Buck stood removed, talking silently among themselves. It was still dark out, still early morning. There were no police cars, no police officers—just the base's medical staff, the ambulance, and Duncan's dead body. And soon, when the ambulance drove away, it would be as if Duncan had never been there, had never been alive at all. She stood in place, shivering, wringing her hands in front of her, not sure what she should do.

Duncan was dead. He had been drawing so much mana it had woken her from her sleep. She had run downstairs just in time to see the flames erupt over his body. She had tried to roll him over, to put out the flames, but they had been too intense for her.

Well, now we know what happens when you draw in too much magic: you die. She shivered again, her teeth chattering.

"What was he thinking?" Elizabeth softly said.

"I'm not sure he was," Cassie answered.

"I keep thinking back to yesterday, outside the gym. Was he...?"

"Jealous? Who knows?" Cassie hugged herself. "Maybe."

They were silent for a while. Elizabeth finally spoke. "Yesterday, when you and I were channeling, linked together, we drew in a lot of mana. How close do you think we came to... you know, this?"

Cassie shook her head, feeling sick to her stomach. "There are no answers to this, Elizabeth. Who knows what our limits are, or what Duncan's limits *were*? We're in uncharted territory here."

"Why would God select him for these amazing new abilities and then let... this happen?"

"God didn't do this, Elizabeth. Duncan did this. He made a choice, and it turned out very, very badly."

"I didn't know this could happen, or that this gift was so dangerous."

"Still think it's God's glory?" Cassie asked, knowing she was picking a fight but unable to stop herself.

To her surprise, Elizabeth reached out and hugged her tightly, burying her head against Cassie's shoulder. At first, Cassie just stood there, too surprised to move. Then, she tentatively wrapped her arms around Elizabeth and hugged her back. The medical staff closed the rear doors on the ambulance. In moments, the vehicle moved away, disappearing into the night. McKnight, Buck, and Alex stopped their conversation long enough to watch it go.

How are they going to hide this?

Chapter 30

For days, Maelhrandia had been spying on the manling camp, noting their sentry patterns, watching their wondrous war chariots as they arrived and departed, and estimating their strength. Now, she was balanced atop the branch of a large tree overlooking the metal fence that surrounded the camp. Gazekiller waited in the bush below. The sun had set hours ago, but lights illuminated the camp, revealing all its secrets.

They had built their camp along the shore of the river. To her considerable surprise, she had noted that the manlings had actually dammed the river. Impressive. No longer were they the savages they had once been, living in caves, huddled around fires, hiding from her people. After her mother was done with them, some might make useful slaves.

For the hundredth time, she considered the layout of their camp. From this distance, it appeared utterly indefensible, but her intuition warned her this was not the case. The metal fence ran the entire length of the camp, all the way to the riverbank. They had cleared the ground of trees and bush within the camp but had allowed the forest to approach almost as far as the fence. Had the manlings no enemies? They should have created a kill zone on the other side of the fence and built towers all along its length. For that matter, why a fence? Why not a stone wall? Truly, they were bizarre. Even the buildings within the camp seemed foolishly laid out with each one standing separate from the others so that in an attack, they might fall quickly, one after another. That made no sense. Had the manlings never fought a war before?

They did patrol the perimeter of their camp, sending both foot soldiers and their war chariots. They even varied the timing of the patrols, making it impossible for her to guess when the next one would come by. The last war chariot had roared past only minutes before, belching smoke. She didn't know when the next would come by, but it would be at least a while yet.

Perhaps her mother would be interested in those wondrous constructions. She was nothing if not practical. Such a terrifying machine would help subjugate the slave races. Most of the fae seelie, though, would consider them to be abominations. Her people abhorred mechanical creations. Only a dwarf or gnome could love such a thing.

She ran her fingers over the hilt of her dagger. She had seen enough. It was finally time to act.

Lithely climbing down, she landed silently next to Gazekiller on the forest floor. She ran her fingers over his scaled head. Using the mind-tether, she sent him a single command: *the fence.*

Gazekiller surged forward, ramming his head into the fence. The metal links popped and snapped under the impact. Gazekiller gripped the broken edges of the fence in his jaws and thrashed his head back and forth, ripping entire segments of it from the ground. In moments, Gazekiller had ripped loose an opening large enough to cross through.

Walking beside the basilisk, cloaked in Shadow-Soul, Maelhrandia entered the manling camp.

* * *

When the perimeter alarm went off in the base's Tactical Operations Center, the TOC, the three soldiers on duty stared at it then at each other. The perimeter alarm never activated. The duty officer moved to stand behind the soldier manning the monitors linked to the infrared security cameras.

"Where?" he asked.

"Zulu-7, sir," the soldier answered, pointing to a monitor.

The duty officer leaned over the soldier, his eyes growing wide. The giant lizard, the basilisk, the same creature that had attacked the hospital in Fort St. John and then disappeared, was ripping apart their perimeter fence. "Son of a bitch," he whispered. "Okay. Go to Alert One. Make the announcement and vector in the Rapid Reaction Team. Let's see how tough it is against an armored vehicle."

The soldier reached for the microphone.

* * *

Cassie had been watching television in the common room when the alarm went off. A red light on the ceiling that she hadn't noticed before began to flash. The two female soldiers who had been watching television with her, Clara and Ginger, turned and stared at an intercom on the wall, waiting. Moments later, a clearly excited voice came across the intercom. "Attention, attention. The base is under ground attack. The base is under ground attack. We are now at Alert Level One. All duty personnel are to report to stand-to locations. All nonduty personnel are to remain in their present locations."

The two soldiers jumped to their feet and ran for the door.

"What do I do?" Cassie yelled at their backs.

"It's probably a false alarm," Clara yelled over her shoulder as she went out the door. "Stay here."

Alone, Cassie stared about her. *Under attack by whom?*

Just for a moment, she felt panic well up within her, but she forced it back down. She went to stand beside the doorway, watching the hallway. Within moments, the barracks came to life. Half-asleep soldiers burst from their rooms, pulling on body armor as they ran out. Each also carried a M4 carbine. Cassie was suddenly conscious of the fact that she was unarmed and defenseless. Within minutes, the barracks emptied, leaving Cassie alone. She stood in place, wondering if she should stay or go back to her room, when Elizabeth appeared, dressed in track pants and a T-shirt.

"What should we do?"

Cassie shook her head. "Hang out, I guess. They'll come and get us if they need us."

Elizabeth bit her lip and nodded.

Then, from a distance, Cassie felt flows of mana being manipulated. It was coming from outside. Fear spiked within her. The last time she had felt this mana use was the attack at the hospital.

Elizabeth's eyes widened. "Who?"

"You feel it, too?"

Elizabeth nodded.

Cassie felt her legs tremble. "I think it's the basilisk."

"What? Why?"

Cassie moved to stand beside the window. She looked out into the darkness.

"Us. It's here for us."

* * *

In the ready hangar, Master Corporal Jennifer Stark, the Rapid Reaction Team leader, ran for her MRAP with Groeker and Williams right behind her, their boot steps pounding across the cement floor. Groeker was her gunner, Williams her second in command. She reached the vehicle first and threw herself into the co-driver's seat. Rico, her driver, was already seated with the engine running. He glanced at her as she slammed the door closed, excitement in his eyes.

She pressed the transmit button on her radio. "Zero, this is Harper-1. We're mobile. Over."

Out of her side window, she saw other soldiers running for a second MRAP—Mark and his backup team. They'd be a few minutes yet. They needed to mount their weapon, load ammo, check radios. Whatever was going down, it would be her show. Outside the hangar doors, she saw other soldiers running for their stand-to locations. It was hard to think clearly, but she took a deep breath, forcing herself to calm down, reminding herself she was a professional soldier.

"Gear up," she ordered as she strapped on her helmet and lowered the GPNVGs over her face. She flicked the power switch on, turning her vision green. Beside her, Rico, already wearing his helmet and GPNVGs, was watching her with his four telescopic eyes. Although the TOC, call-sign Zero, had yet to reply to her transmission, she ordered Rico to head out. She knew her job and knew what to do. The defense of the Magic Kingdom was her responsibility that night.

The MRAP was almost at the hangar entrance when the radio activated. "Harper-1, this is Zero. Stop what you're doing and wait for an additional passenger. Acknowledge; over."

Jennifer frowned and glanced at Rico. With the GPNVGs on, she couldn't tell if he was as confused as she was. She activated her

MBITR. "Harper-1, roger; over."

"Zero; out."

Rico threw the transmission into park. "What the hell?"

Jennifer shook her head. "I don't know, but we wait."

She turned and looked over her shoulder at the remainder of her team in the rear of the MRAP. Groeker was already in his gunner's seat, staring intently at his monitor, the control for the machine gun, a joystick, in his hand. Unlike the others, Groeker wasn't wearing his GPNVGs. The night-vision device would only get in the way of his targeting, and his machine-gun monitor targeted through an infrared camera anyway. Williams got out of his seat and moved closer to Jennifer, so she wouldn't need to shout.

"Open the back door," she said. "Someone's coming with us."

Williams nodded then did as she ordered, swinging the heavy metal rear door open.

They didn't have long to wait. No sooner had they opened the back hatch than Porter, one of the American Deltas, ran up to her MRAP, an odd-looking rifle under his arm. In his other hand, he clutched a metallic briefcase. Major Buchanan—Buck—was with him, and while Porter climbed into the back, Buck ran to Jennifer's door and yanked it open again.

His face was flush with excitement. "You take my man with you. This is *the* basilisk. It's come to us."

Jennifer nodded, swallowing nervously.

He leaned in. "He's in charge out there, you got it?"

She hesitated only a moment. "Yes, sir. What do you want me to do?"

"Get him within range of that thing. He's got a tranq gun, so he needs to get close, a hundred meters or less. Better with less."

"A tranq gun? Are you kidding me? This thing is dangerous."

Buck glared at her, the contempt clear in his face. "You're in an armored vehicle, honey. I think you'll be fine."

She felt her anger rise, but she nodded. "Yes, sir. We get close."

Buck stepped back. "Don't fuck this up, split-ass." He slammed the door shut and pointed toward the hangar entrance.

Dickhead, she thought.

Glancing over her shoulder, she saw Porter was ready, his tranquillizer gun held across his lap. Williams was yanking the locking lever on the rear door into place.

"Move," Jennifer ordered Rico.

Rico put the MRAP into gear and stomped on the gas. In moments they were outside. Jennifer pointed toward the perimeter breach, and Rico left the road and started driving cross-country. The MRAP jumped and bounced over the rough ground. They'd be there in less than a minute.

* * *

From where she hid near the ruined fence, Maelhrandia could hear the discordant wailing that could only be an alarm. How had they known she and Gazekiller were there? She was certain no one was close enough to see the basilisk, yet alone her, cloaked as she was in magic. Yet just the same, the manlings were already aware of her attack. *Impressive.*

They'd be there quickly, she knew, in one of their war chariots. Their defenses were better than she had thought. She considered fleeing but only for a moment. She was a princess of the fae-seelie court. She didn't run from manlings. She had a plan, and she needed to follow it. That plan came with risk. She exhaled, steeling herself. No coward, she would do her duty.

* * *

284

Jennifer's MRAP quickly vectored in on the security breach. The TOC reported they still had eyes on the basilisk. It was actually waiting near the ruined fence.

And then she saw it. "Holy shit." She leaned forward in her seat.

The basilisk stood in place, watching the MRAP approach. Behind it, an entire segment of the perimeter fence had been trampled and torn down. Jennifer fought the panic she felt. It was so much bigger than she had realized, easily thirty feet long, with eight articulated, spindly legs. She had heard the stories, seen the news reports, but still hadn't fully understood until that very moment. In the green glow of her night vision, the creature's demonic horned head faced them, its eyes glowing. She could see why others were calling it a dinosaur. It was as big as their MRAP—far longer with its spiked tail!

"Fuck me," muttered Rico beside her, terror in his voice.

She reached over and gripped his forearm. "Slow down, stop. Here, stop here."

Turning around in her seat, she faced Porter. "Close enough?"

Porter, also wearing his GPNVGs, nodded. Then, he stood up and opened the roof hatch before climbing up onto the bench, leaving just his lower torso within the MRAP. Williams handed the tranquilizer gun to him. Jennifer returned her gaze to the basilisk. The creature began to walk toward the vehicle as if it were only curious. *On Rubicon it's an apex predator,* Jennifer realized. It wasn't afraid of them.

But this isn't Rubicon. "Do it," Jennifer whispered.

At about fifty meters away, the basilisk halted and raised itself up onto its back legs, lifting its massive head high above the MRAP, glaring down at it. Its eyes began to glow brighter. She remembered the task-force intelligence officer said that this thing could turn people to stone, that it had some form of death gaze. She was about to yell a warning to Porter when the sudden flaring from the basilisk's eyes washed out her night vision.

* * *

Excitement coursed through Maelhrandia as Gazekiller turned its magic on the occupants of the war chariot. One of the manlings had actually exposed himself by standing up in an opening through the top of the vehicle. She knew what would happen next: Gazekiller would soon be feasting on petrified prey.

But nothing happened. She felt a sudden coldness rush through her being. Gazekiller's magic had failed. Impossible.

The exposed manling was now aiming a long weapon at Gazekiller. The basilisk just stood there. She could feel his confusion through the mind-tether. When the manling weapon fired, it barely made any noise—more like a bolt from a crossbow than the thunder that usually accompanied their fire weapons. Something struck Gazekiller: a dart.

Within moments, she began to feel the effects of the dart, a poison of some type, flow through her mount. Panic swept through her. *They're going to kill Gazekiller!*

Still cloaked, she stepped forward, drawing in magic, sending it into Gazekiller's body, negating the effects of the poison. Though she was a poor healer at best, she could at least do this.

But her plan of attack had failed, and she needed to get Gazekiller away from there. Through the mind-tether, she ordered the basilisk to flee. The noble beast roared in outrage and indignation but did as she commanded, whipping about and bounding away toward the safety of the woods. The war chariot roared in pursuit much faster than she would have thought possible. It would seem the manlings were not as pathetic as she had first believed and could pose a threat after all.

Damn them to the Ether. They will not have him!

She sprinted forward, placing herself between the fleeing basilisk and the war chariot. The evil vehicle sped right at her, unaware she was even there.

Now, in the thick of combat, she felt no fear. She was a true daughter of the fae seelie. She drew in magic, warping it into Drake's-Gift.

Chapter 31

Jennifer's excitement spiked when the basilisk turned and began to flee. "It's making for the woods."

"I'm after it," Rico said.

"Hit it again," she yelled to Porter. "Before it gets into the trees."

"I got it, I got it," he yelled back, his voice barely audible from outside the vehicle.

She squeezed Rico's shoulder. "Slow down; give him the shot."

Rico nodded, taking his foot off the gas. The MRAP decelerated quickly, stabilizing.

Just ahead, the basilisk slowed, glanced back over its spiked back. Jennifer smiled and shook her head. "No way, T. rex. You're not going anywhere."

And then the night lit up in bright flame, completely overwhelming her GPNVGs, searing into her brain. She screamed and swore as she ripped the headgear from her eyes. The windshield of the MRAP was covered in roaring flames. She could literally feel the heat surrounding the vehicle. Porter screamed but only for a moment, and then a jet of fire poured through the open hatch. The flames rushed over the occupants of the MRAP like a fiery waterfall.

I'm burning! She screamed, but then the fire cooked off the ammo within the MRAP, creating a series of explosions that ripped the top of the armored vehicle open, mercifully ending her torment.

* * *

When Cassie and Elizabeth felt the tremendous amount of mana being channeled, they jumped to their feet and ran to the window to see what was going on. A large fire blazed near the edge of the woods. Something really bad had just happened; Cassie was certain of that. They stood there like that for some time, staring out at the fire. Was it still coming?

Some minutes later, they heard pounding boot steps in the hallway. They turned as Alex rushed through the doorway. He wore body armor over his uniform and held his M4 in one hand, his face white.

Something had happened.

He looked from Cassie to Elizabeth. "I need you both dressed in combat clothing and ready to go in five minutes."

"What's going on?" Cassie heard the panic in her own voice. She hated herself for it but couldn't help the reaction.

"The basilisk ran off, but we're going after it."

Cassie stared at his face. There was something in his eyes, something he wasn't telling them. Elizabeth jumped to her feet without a word and ran for her room, leaving Cassie alone with Alex. She glided up to him, putting her hand on his forearm. It was trembling. "What's happened?"

Alex didn't look her in the eye, staring at his hands instead. "There's... there's been... an incident with the reaction team. They were killed. The soldier in charge was a friend."

Cassie's hand rose to her mouth. "I'm sorry. This is my fault, isn't it? That thing has followed me here."

Alex shook his head. "No. It's our..." He paused, pain in his eyes. "It doesn't matter now. Get dressed quickly before it gets away. The trail is fresh right now. Paco and Clyde will track it, but we want you and Elizabeth along just in case. For... well, for whatever it is that you can do."

Cassie nodded, still watching his face. She squeezed his forearm and turned away. "I'll only be a few minutes." Her pulse was racing as she ran for her room. She felt sick and excited at the same time. They were finally going after the monster that had murdered Alice. This was her chance for revenge.

* * *

Twenty minutes later, Cassie was sitting in the rear of an MRAP following another one as it sped across the rough terrain toward the base perimeter. Once again, they were divided into two teams: Elizabeth and Paco accompanied Buck in the first MRAP, and Cassie and Alex followed in the second. Cassie gripped the nylon webbing on the vehicle hull, hanging on as the MRAP jumped in the air. She looked about the interior of the armored vehicle, watching the faces of the other occupants. There was a grim determination in their eyes, but they made no easy banter this time. Their friends had died. The soldier sitting across from Cassie held a long, odd-looking rifle between his knees. She watched him remove a dart the length of his hand from a metal briefcase near his feet and insert it into a loading chamber in the rifle, locking it in place.

A tranquilizer gun? Her heart began to pound wildly. What was he thinking?

She leaned forward, snapping her fingers to get the soldier's attention. "Hey! You need something bigger—a lot bigger. That's not going to work."

The soldier frowned at her and then looked away, ignoring her.

Cassie leaned back in her seat, staring at the rifle. *They're not trying to kill it,* she realized. *They're trying to capture it.*

She released her seatbelt, got out of her chair, and almost tripped as she made her way to the front of the vehicle where Alex sat with the driver. He glanced over his shoulder, annoyance on his features. Before he could say anything, she spoke first. "You're trying to capture that thing? Are you insane? Don't you remember the hospital?"

His eyes narrowed. "Cassie, go sit down before you get hurt."

She was about to say something else when she saw the flames of the burning MRAP through the windshield. The fire shot out the top of the vehicle. Huge clouds of black smoke obscured the stars in the otherwise clear night sky.

"Oh my God," she whispered.

Three other vehicles were already on site, illuminating the scene with their headlights. One of the vehicles was an ambulance, its red-and-blue lights flashing. The second was a fire truck and the third another MRAP. The soldiers already on site stood back from the burning MRAP, spraying it with a water hose. As their MRAPs maneuvered around the scene, Cassie saw what looked like a charred body hanging from the destroyed vehicle. They drove past the carnage, heading for the perimeter fence, which had been mangled and torn loose and now lay across the ground.

"Cassie!" barked Alex.

Her focus darted back to him, and she realized he had been talking to her.

"Get your ass back in your seat!"

At that moment, the MRAP hit a rough spot and jumped into

the air again, almost knocking her down. She grasped at the back of Alex's seat and nodded, before making her way quickly back to her bench. She didn't want to be there anymore. Despite her need for revenge, she knew this was going to end badly. None of the other soldiers looked at her as she sat back down again.

They're all afraid, she realized. *Good.*

* * *

Maelhrandia followed quickly behind Gazekiller, pausing only long enough to make sure the manling war chariot had been destroyed and no further dangers loomed. Then she turned and ran through the night behind her mount, her heart pounding wildly. Her plans had fallen apart so quickly.

* * *

The MRAP rolled to a halt. The soldier sitting in the gunner's chair used his joystick to move the turret gun and infrared camera to sweep around their vehicle. Cassie stared over his shoulder at the television monitor and its green display, but all she saw were trees. Without a word, Alex and the other soldiers rushed out of the MRAP, their weapons held ready. Only Cassie, the gunner, and the driver remained within the vehicle. She peered through her side window, watching the soldiers set up a defensive perimeter. Each soldier had one of the powerful flashlights attached to the barrel of his carbine, and the beams swept across the broken ground.

Clyde began barking, and then Cassie saw the German shepherd and Paco moving back and forth across the ground. The dog's nose was down low, sniffing.

She closed her eyes and concentrated on her surroundings, seeking some sign of ongoing mana use, but felt nothing. She had sensed when the basilisk had used its petrification gaze, recognized it from the hospital attack, but now it seemed it could also breathe fire like the hellhounds... like a dragon. She wondered what else it could do.

Paco was right. They had to be aliens. But how had an alien that large gotten here? From outside the MRAP, she heard Clyde whining. Clearly, he didn't want to be anywhere near this thing. *Smart dog.*

She could no longer see Paco or his dog from where she sat, so she moved to the front of the vehicle and peered through the windshield just in time to see Clyde's rear end going under the chassis of the MRAP in front of them. Paco was on his hands and knees, trying to coax the animal back out.

The hell with this. She climbed out the back of the MRAP, through the still-open rear door. She knew they didn't want her out there, but she didn't really give a damn. One of the soldiers guarding their perimeter turned and glanced at her, frowning. He touched the side of his ear and began talking.

Tattletale, she mused as she approached Paco.

He looked over his shoulder, resignation in his eyes. "He won't come out. The second he caught the scent of this thing, he freaked out."

Cassie dropped down on her knees beside him and peered under the MRAP at Clyde's terrified features only a foot away. The poor dog was actually shivering. "He's the only one around here that gets it."

Paco sighed and looked at the ruined perimeter fence and burning MRAP. "I think you might be right, little sister."

"Maybe Clyde should stay in the MRAP."

"Yeah, maybe." Paco's normally exuberant face was troubled. "As long as the trail doesn't just disappear again like it did at the hospital. This thing is so big, ain't no way I can't track it by myself."

They heard boot steps behind them and turned to see Buck and Alex approaching, followed closely by the soldier carrying the tranquilizer gun.

"What up, Tonto?" Buck asked. "We goin' after this thing or not?"

Paco grimaced and reached under the MRAP, grabbing Clyde by his collar and pulling the whining animal out. Holding the cringing dog, Paco glared at Buck for a moment and then nodded. "I'm gonna secure Clyde inside the vehicle. Then I'll track this thing for you."

Cassie stared out at the dark woods before them. There was no way the vehicles would be able to move through those trees. Alex must have been thinking the same thing because he said as much to Buck, who nodded knowingly.

"Okay, on foot," Buck said. "We'll move in two teams. You take the cover team and go with Tonto."

"His name is Paco," Cassie snapped. "And he's here to help you."

"I don't give a fuck," snarled Buck. "You can go with the Injun as well, Blondie. Try to not be in the way this time." He turned back to Alex and started jabbing him with his finger as he spoke. "Don't get too far ahead. I'll be in the second leg with the other mag-sens." He glanced disdainfully at Cassie. "The one who isn't useless. Take Ramirez with you." Buck indicated the soldier beside him carrying the tranquilizer gun. "You get a shot; you put it to sleep."

"That may not be an option," Alex said, meeting Buck's stare. "This thing might be too big for the drugs."

"Well that's the mission, isn't it? You don't like it, you stay here. We clear?"

Cassie felt the heat between the two men. After several uncomfortable moments, Alex nodded. "We're clear."

Buck grinned. "Well?"

Alex sighed and turned to face Cassie and Paco. "Secure the dog. We're moving out."

Minutes later, they headed out into the woods, Paco leading, Alex and Cassie right behind, and four other soldiers—including the one with the tranquilizer rifle—taking up the rear. They moved with flashlights so Paco could see the basilisk's sign, but they still wore their GPNVGs around their necks. The night was bright, with an almost-full moon, so they moved quickly. No tracker, Cassie saw the passage of the basilisk easily enough: giant paw prints smashed into the ground and snapped branches. That thing didn't care if anyone followed it. So, why had it run away at all?

Alex halted in front of Cassie then turned and grabbed her elbow, pulling her in close to him. "Take this." He handed her his pistol.

She only hesitated for a moment before taking the weapon. "Is there a—"

"Yes. There's a round chambered, but the safety is on. Please be careful."

"You're chasing a giant fire-breathing death-gaze lizard…" She slipped the weapon into the large cargo pocket in her combat pants. The angular features of the weapon dug into her skin through the fabric, but she was just happy to be armed at all even if it was just a pistol. "And you're worried about me shooting myself?"

"It's my ass if you do."

"Don't worry." She slapped him on his butt as she walked past him. "We wouldn't want anything happening to that ass, now, would we?"

She breathed in the cool night air, feeling her senses come alive. She was still terrified—only a moron wouldn't be. But as the adrenaline coursed through her, she also felt energized.

That goddamned thing had killed Alice, and it needed to be stopped. If anyone had any chance of doing that, it was these guys. And they had taken down the hellhounds easily enough. *But it isn't just a fire-breathing dog, is it? It's a freaking giant monster that rips buildings apart and destroys tanks.*

They pushed on through the woods at a fast pace. Her breathing became more strained, and she began to lean into each step, forcing herself to keep up. If nothing else, she was definitely getting her fitness groove back.

* * *

Maelhrandia and Gazekiller didn't go far into the woods before she stopped to assess their situation. Through the mind-tether, she could still feel the effects of the manling poison on Gazekiller's consciousness, clouding his thinking, making him want to lie down and sleep. Once again, she focused a weave of magic into the basilisk's blood, trying to burn away more of the drugs. She had to be so careful, though: too much magic, and she might hurt the basilisk, maybe even kill him. *Damn those evil manlings to the Red Ether!*

They had come so close to capturing Gazekiller. His Death-Gaze had failed, and she didn't understand why. It had never—not ever—failed before. Had it not been for her... she shook her head, feeling a cold spike of fear run through her. That had been a near thing but necessary. Still, she needed to be more careful. It was too soon to reveal her presence. She was the first of her kind to return, and she was alone here, vulnerable. What would happen if she failed? Would her mother send other scouts? *Of course she will. I would.*

This was the Old World. It belonged to the fae seelie. They would not abandon it now that they had found the path back again.

Her eyes narrowed. She had heard something. Ordering the still-groggy basilisk to remain, she leapt into the branches of a tall tree and lithely climbed to its top. From its summit, she saw the lights of the manlings as they moved through the woods behind her. They were tracking Gazekiller.

She wasn't surprised. After all, she had goaded them for just that purpose. Still, this night had not turned out as she had expected, and Gazekiller, it seemed, was vulnerable to their weapons. She needed to be very careful.

From a pouch within her cloak, she removed the Shatkur Orb and stared into its dark depths. She'd create another local Gateway for her mount, just as she had done after trying—and failing—to kill that golden-haired mage. This time, though, she'd send Gazekiller behind the trackers. A sly smile crept across her delicate features. She dropped back to the ground, held the orb before her, and began to draw magic, sending the weaves into the orb, empowering it.

Despite the setbacks, her plan might still work after all.

Chapter 32

Cassie stopped abruptly. Paco and Alex turned to stare at her.

"Something just used mana."

"Where?" Alex asked.

"Ahead of us."

"The basilisk," Paco said. "It must be. That's what you're sensing."

"I don't know," said Cassie. "This felt... different. It's hard to explain."

"Could it be that creature you saw at the riverbank, the ape thing?" Alex asked.

Cassie paused. "Maybe. I don't know. This is all new to me. But something just used mana."

"Well," said Alex, "how far?"

"Just ahead, not far. I think—"

"Wait." Alex raised his hand to his ear. After several seconds, he acknowledged the radio message he had just received. Then he looked up at Cassie. "Elizabeth just felt it as well, but she thinks it was the basilisk."

"How would she know? She's never even seen it."

"Let's go. Everybody be ready." Alex pointed at Ramirez, who had moved closer to listen to their conversation. "We get a chance, use the tranq gun. If not, we're going to put it down with everything we've got."

Ramirez shook his head. "That's not what Buck—"

"I don't give a damn. We have civilians with us, and I'm not risking lives on the chance we might be able to weaponize this thing."

Weaponize this thing? Cassie stared at him. *Is he kidding?*

Ramirez opened his mouth to argue, but Alex had already turned away to address the others. "Okay, kill the white lights. We go with night vision from this point on."

Paco stepped forward. "I'm not sure I can track it with—"

"It's cool, Paco." Alex reached out and gripped Cassie's shoulder. "Our little blond mine canary will let us know if it gets too close."

She shook her head. "I don't think—"

He squeezed her shoulder. "Yes, you can. So just do it, all right?"

Sighing, she nodded.

They strapped their GPNVGs on and turned off their flashlights. Cassie was amazed again at how well she could see with the night-vision device. The hunting party moved forward again, more carefully this time. After a few minutes, she saw a clearing ahead of them. Even she could make out the massive tracks the basilisk had made as it crossed the open ground. Paco dropped down on one knee, examining the ground.

And then Cassie felt something. She looked about herself and then up into the trees on the opposite side of the clearing. Puzzled, she stared into the branches of a tree, near its summit. It was hard to describe, but she felt as if something were watching her. A presence she couldn't explain pulled her attention to the branches of that one particular tree. She opened her mouth to say something to the others but then closed it again. There was nothing there. Her imagination was playing tricks on her. That was all.

Paco stood up, looked over his shoulder, and nodded at Alex. Alex led them into the clearing, and Cassie, still feeling… *something* drawing her attention to that one tree, followed.

* * *

Maelhrandia, cloaked in Shadow-Soul, watched the manlings enter her killing ground. Her plan was simple. The best ones always were. As the manlings reached the center of the clearing, she'd cast Drake's-Gift among them. When they ran about, burning, Gazekiller—now behind them thanks to the Shatkur Orb—would charge into them and feast. The manlings might be able to somehow resist his Death-Gaze, but there was no defense against his claws and fangs.

What a travesty it would be for the manlings, she thought, smiling to herself. *Why, then they'd have to bring in someone important to take charge—a leader or a war chief. They'll bring their leader to me.*

She smiled as the manling hunting party approached. Now, they wore their strange masks again, but she still recognized the hideous golden-haired mage. *Good.*

This time, the mage wouldn't escape. She briefly considered taking her alive but discarded the idea almost instantly. Her mother hadn't sent her here to capture a lowly mage, particularly one as weak as this. The manlings, led by their tracker, came closer, and Maelhrandia drew magic within her, preparing her spell.

* * *

Almost halfway into the clearing, Paco stopped again and stared at the ground before him.

"What is it?" Alex said from behind him.

Cassie paused as well, still staring intently at that damned tree. *There's nothing there, so why—*

"The tracks are gone," Paco said, the confusion clear in his voice.

Cassie tore her eyes from the tree to examine the ground in front of them. It didn't take an expert to see that the giant paw prints that had torn the soft ground up just stopped abruptly as if the basilisk had just vanished in the middle of the clearing.

"This is all wrong," said Alex, looking around. "We're too exposed out here. We'll pull back and—"

Magic flared into being.

"Look out," Cassie screamed. "Someone's channeling!"

* * *

Filled with magic, Maelhrandia prepared to loose her spell. The manlings were less than a hundred paces away, right in the open. Her senses, all charged with the forces of magic, were now hyperaware. She felt a lightness in her chest and a feeling of breathlessness. This was the moment she loved, just before the kill. She'd cast her spell at the female mage, killing the most dangerous opponent first. But before she could release the spell, she felt magic well up from the forest just behind her.

She was the one being ambushed! Only the razor-sharp instincts honed from survival amongst her sisters saved her life. In an instant, she refocused the magic she had been about to cast, turning it into Egis's-Shield instead, sending it behind her. A bolt of brilliant blue Storm-Tongue arced up into the tree, striking her poorly formed shield and shredding it, throwing her from the branches to the ground.

Merciless Mother—no one is that powerful!

She landed on her feet, despite falling a dozen strides, and spun to face her attacker, already weaving another shield.

Once again, a massive bolt of Storm-Tongue cut across the ground, smashing into her new shield and throwing her back through the air again. In the glow of the strike, she had the briefest glimpse of her attacker: a giant bipedal beast with long limbs and a shaggy coat of fur.

An Ancient One, she realized with horror. *They still live!*

She lay on her back, gasping for air, her skin clammy. Pain pulsed through her skull, making it difficult to think. Her spell—though poorly formed—had still managed to blunt the worst of the attack, but she couldn't possibly survive another.

In desperation, she called for help through the mind-tether.

Come to me, mighty one. Save me!

* * *

Pandemonium erupted in the clearing. Cassie fell to the ground as a bright flash of lightning lit up the night. It was so powerful it washed out their GPNVGs. Then—from the woods just behind them—came the snapping of trees, the unmistakable staccato roaring of the basilisk.

She tore away her now-useless night vision glasses, dropping them, and stared about herself wild-eyed, still seeing nothing but spots. At that moment, another bolt of lightning erupted from the trees in front of them, turning night into day again. The basilisk burst from behind them, smashing several trees down, coming straight at them. She dropped to the ground and covered her head with her hands. The stench of ozone burnt in the air, and the ground shook under the pounding of the basilisk's charge. It barreled through them. One of the others flew through the air like a bowling pin. A long burst of automatic fire lit up the night. Alex was screaming orders, trying to control the situation.

Cassie lost it. In terror, she jumped to her feet and ran for the trees, not knowing which direction she was going and not caring.

* * *

Once again, the Ancient One launched Storm-Tongue at Maelhrandia. It was so powerful, so strong. Again, her shield ruptured under its impact. The legends were true. Maelhrandia had never believed them before, but they were true nonetheless. Aeons ago, these monsters had driven her people from this realm. They were still here, still all-powerful.

And this one was going to kill her. In helpless frustration, she launched her own attack, sending a weak fireball at her foe. But her efforts were distracted by the need to keep re-forming her shield. The monster blocked her clumsy spell, sending the fireball crashing into the trees nearby and catching them aflame. She had been so certain the legends had been false, or that none of the Ancient Ones yet lived. It had been so long ago. If only they had known, she would have begged her mother to send more scouts—or an army.

As her foe launched another attack, an uncomfortable thought occurred to Maelhrandia: what if her mother had suspected the Ancient Ones still lived? Perhaps that was why she had sent Maelhrandia alone: she was expendable. Her presence had drawn out the Ancient One, and her failure to return from this realm would confirm her mother's suspicions.

One more Storm-Tongue blast hit her, shattering her shield. Exhausted, Maelhrandia could only raise herself up on hands and knees and glare defiance. *And now, I die.*

The demon stepped closer, and she saw it clearly. She had grown up studying their caricature on the murals of her mother's palace. Truly creatures of nightmare, they were more than twice her height and at least four times her weight. Long limbed and covered in disgusting fur, its giant gaping teeth were bared, ready to devour her. What a cosmic joke. As horrific and bestial as they were, somehow these monsters were masters of magic.

"Damn you to the Red Ether, demon," she said as she clutched her dagger before her, intending to die fighting as befitted a princess of the fae seelie. "You may kill me, but we know where you are now. Others will follow, others will hunt you down, and we will eradicate your kind. We are stronger now than we were before. So much stronger."

It didn't speak. Perhaps it couldn't. Perhaps it didn't understand her words, or perhaps it didn't care. It raised a long arm and pointed it at Maelhrandia, and then she saw it wore a glove with silver chains. She gasped, suddenly understanding what it was: a talisman! Her people's ancient texts spoke of this legendary weapon wielded by the foe. No wonder its attack had been so strong.

Trees crashed behind her. *Gazekiller!*

The Ancient One reacted instantly to this new threat, releasing its bolt of arcane lightning at the basilisk instead of at her. Gazekiller roared in challenge as it leapt over Maelhrandia, crashing into the monster. Basilisk and demon rolled across the forest floor, shattering trees.

In a moment, the forest was silent and dark once again.

Then Gazekiller limped to her. The air stank of charred lizard flesh, and she felt his terrible pain through the mind-tether, but he lived. She leapt onto his back and ordered him to run. He screamed in agony and pawed at the soft ground. Then he took off, leaving smashed trees in his wake. She clung to his neck, too terrified to look behind her, expecting a bolt of magical fire at any moment. But the attack never came.

She had survived a confrontation with an Ancient One, the first of the fae seelie to have done so in living memory. If she survived this night, she'd be a hero, a legend among her people. And she'd have much to tell her mother, the woman who had sent her to her death. Much indeed.

Chapter 33

Lost and becoming increasingly frantic, Cassie stumbled through the dark woods. She knew she had to still be close to the others; there hadn't been enough time for her to go far. Her night-vision glasses were gone, and she had only the moonlight by which to see. She did have a small flashlight, but she was afraid the basilisk might detect it.

She no longer heard the monster's roars, but that didn't mean it wasn't still out there, silently stalking them. She needed a radio. The others all had a radio. She was out there risking her life just like them. Being left out was bullshit. She should have the same gear as the rest of the task force. If she got out of these woods alive, she was going to tear a strip off somebody.

Cassie suddenly remembered the pistol Alex had given her. She drew it from her pocket, being careful not to snag its hammer on the fabric. The last thing she needed was to shoot herself in the foot. Holding the weapon in both hands, she began to move in the direction she thought she had come from, hoping she was heading back toward the others and not straight at the basilisk.

The cool night air brushed against her sweaty skin. Fortunately, this part of the woods was open with little underbrush; otherwise, moving at all in the dark would have been much harder. Alone, she realized the forest was a lot noisier than she'd thought, and every time she heard the rustling of leaves or a branch creaking in the wind, she almost jumped out of her skin.

How did it get behind us? The basilisk had had them cold and could have killed them all before they even had a chance to fight back. But instead, it had simply charged through them as if they were in its way. And someone had been channeling mana; she was sure of it—an enormous amount of mana. There was no way it had been the basilisk this time. There was someone else out here who could use magic. They had all seen and heard the flashes of lightning in the trees ahead of them. She could still smell the ozone in the air.

Where were Alex and the others? Were they even still alive? She considered calling out for them but immediately discarded that idea. Maybe she'd wait for them to find her. If she kept moving in the dark, she might get even more lost. But she just couldn't stay put; she was too frightened.

Then, she felt someone channeling. It was just a trickle of mana but coming from close by just ahead of her. It wasn't the basilisk. When the basilisk and the hellhounds used mana, it felt more… natural. This felt arcane, artificial. She stood silently, gripped by indecision.

What are you doing, dummy? You can't just stand here. Do something!

Taking several deep breaths, she stepped off toward the source of the channeling—and immediately tripped and fell, smashing her knee and dropping the pistol. *Goddamn it!*

Sighing, she pulled out her flashlight and turned it on. If she kept stumbling about in the dark, she was going to shoot herself. If the basilisk were still looking for her, it would have found her by now. Probably.

Alex's pistol lay just in front of her, and she picked it up before dragging herself back to her feet. Using the flashlight's weak beam, she began to make her way toward the source of the mana use. The sensation grew in potency as she got closer. The smell of ozone was much stronger than before, as was the stench of burning wood. Just ahead, the trunk of a tree smoldered and burned. She tentatively touched its singed bark, amazed that the entire tree wasn't engulfed in flames. *This must be where the lightning flashes were coming from.* That meant she wasn't far from the clearing, which meant the others must also be nearby. *What happened here?*

She jumped back, almost falling, when she heard a groan of agony only paces away, a sound that did not come from human lips. Pointing both the flashlight and the pistol in front of her, she scanned the ground. The basilisk must have been there, because entire trees had been smashed down and lay in scattered fragments across the area. Among the wreckage, a large form moved—too large for a human but too small for the basilisk.

She stood frozen, staring at it, her pulse pounding in her ears. The form moved slightly, and a cry of agony hissed through what had to be a broken body. Without realizing what she was doing, Cassie stepped closer.

Gasping, she almost dropped the light. It was the same creature she had seen watching them after the ambush of the hellhounds. Simian in form, its fur was now glistening with its own blood. It resembled a nightmarish cross between an ape and a man and could only be one thing: this was the legendary Bigfoot, a Sasquatch. It looked exactly as described in the tales. Impossible though it seemed, it fit right in with giant lizards that could turn people to stone and fire-breathing wolves—and wizards. These days, impossible was normal.

The creature was dying. She could tell that right away. Its long legs were bent at an obscene, impossible angle, and its entire left rib cage was caved in. It watched her with strangely intelligent eyes, focusing on her face. It tried to raise its head but cried out in agony instead. She dropped to her knees beside it, all the while aware that only an idiot would approach a wounded animal. She laid Alex's pistol down beside her, reached out, and ran her fingers across the beast's bloody forehead, smoothing its glistening fur. She had her Camelbak and, for a moment, considered giving it something to drink. But with its extensive internal injuries, drinking would only bring it more pain. Judging by its caved-in chest, she was amazed it still lived at all.

And then, somehow, it managed to raise its massive, elongated arm—an arm that was twice the length of hers. It dropped an object into Cassie's lap. She stared down in confusion at what looked to be a glove of some type, made of dark leather and silver chains. The creature reached forward again—impossibly fast—and grabbed the nape of her neck with a hand so large it could almost wrap its fingers all the way around her head. Terror suddenly gripped her as she realized it could crush her skull in a moment.

Its huge yellow eyes stared into Cassie's, and its fangs glistened. *The Brace*, an alien voice whispered within her head. *Focus*, it whispered again.

She heard human voices calling out her name. The others were looking for her. They'd be here any moment.

Please, the creature thought to her. *Help me.*

"What do you want me to do?"

For a moment, she felt its pain lance through her, unimaginable currents of torment. Gasping, she gripped its enormous hand, still holding her head, with both of hers. Her eyes filled with tears.

Please. Please.

Suddenly understanding, she glanced down at the pistol that lay beside her and shook her head. "I can't."

Please. Release... free me.

She heard Alex and the others calling for her. They were closer now. They must have discovered the smoking ruins that lay about them. They'd be here in moments. What would happen when the army discovered this creature?

They'd keep it alive as long as they could, even if they prolonged its misery. After all, it might be valuable to them.

Please.

Tears running down her cheeks, she gripped the pistol in both hands and placed the barrel against the creature's skull.

"I'm sorry." She pulled the trigger.

Part 3
Hunting Monsters

Chapter 34

Cassie knelt by the dead creature, her shoulders trembling. In a daze, she placed Alex's smoking pistol on the ground—right next to the glove-like object, the *Brace,* that the creature had given her. She sat there, staring blankly at the creature's body.

What have I done?

She heard the others approach and saw their lights through the trees. They must have heard the gunshot. She glanced down at the glove bound in silver chains. Without understanding why, she carefully folded it and slipped it within the cargo pocket of her combat pants, hiding it. Paco found her first, calling out to the others. She shielded her eyes from his flashlight, wiping the tears from her face.

"You all right, little sister?" When he saw the corpse of the creature on the ground in front of her, his body stiffened and his eyes went wide.

"I'm not hurt."

Alex joined them. Wordlessly, he reached down, took his pistol from the ground, and stared at the dead creature, his gaze flicking to Cassie. "You all right? Did it hurt you?"

She shook her head, looking away, unable to look him in the

eye. Heat rushed through her body, and her cheeks burned. "I... I had to. It was dying. It was in agony."

Paco knelt beside her. He reached out a trembling hand toward the carcass then stopped as if afraid to touch it. "This is no alien. I think this might be *Chiye-tanka*, the Great Elder Brother." He looked up at Alex, his face white. "This is bad. This is really, really bad. What the hell is going on here? What have you people done?"

"I think it was trying to help us," said Cassie in a small voice. She pointed to the devastation around them—to the smashed trees, now lying like tinder. "I think it fought the basilisk."

"Is this the same creature you saw spying on us the other night?" Alex asked.

Cassie inclined her head. "Yes."

More lights moved through the trees. They heard the diesel whine of the MRAPs and saw the powerful headlights as Buck and the rest of the team arrived, slowly maneuvering the two vehicles through the trees.

Alex spoke into his radio. "Roger, acknowledge your last." He paused for a moment, staring at the carcass of the creature. "We need to get the boss here. We have a... situation." He paused again for a few moments as he listened to the transmission in his earpiece then sighed. "You need to see this for yourself. It defies explanation. Out."

Paco climbed to his feet, distress in his eyes. He wiped a hand across his forehead. "Alex, listen to me. Buck is too stupid to understand how important this creature is. If this is *Chiye-tanka*— and I think it is—it's important, really important. Not something you can disrespect. You can't drag his corpse back to some lab to be dissected."

Dissected? Adrenaline spiked through Cassie. She jumped to her feet and spun on Alex. "Is this a joke? You're not really going to do that, are you? This isn't... wasn't an animal. It spoke to me."

Alex's head jerked back. "It *spoke* to you?"

Cassie paused. "Well, not exactly. I... I heard it in my head."

"In your head?"

"Listen to her," said Paco. "This is a supernatural being, one that lives between this world and the spiritual. *Chiye-tanka* always shows up during times of trouble to help the people. He has powerful psychic abilities and could easily communicate telepathically."

Alex sighed. "So what did it say?"

Cassie opened her mouth to answer but then considered the object that was hidden in her pocket. "Well... it didn't exactly talk to me... but it could."

Alex stared at her for several seconds then shook his head. "You're killing me."

The headlights of an MRAP lit up the trees as Buck and the remainder of the team arrived. Soldiers poured out from the rear of the vehicles and began to move about, securing the area. Buck, his GPNVGs sitting on top of his helmet and his M4 held nonchalantly across his chest, approached. Elizabeth, looking small next to him, followed behind like his shadow. When Buck saw the dead creature, he stopped in his tracks, staring at it. He snorted then nudged its large hairy head with his combat boot. A spasm of heat flashed through Cassie.

"Boss," said Paco, his voice trembling with rage, "listen. This isn't one of your aliens. This is something sacred."

Buck held his palm out toward Paco's face, cutting him off. He turned to Alex. "Report."

Alex sighed. "We were tracking the basilisk, crossing a clearing when... we saw what looked like lightning strikes in the trees ahead of us."

Buck frowned then glanced up at a starless sky.

Alex continued. "Next thing we knew, the basilisk came on us from behind."

"It got behind you?" Buck asked, glaring at Paco.

Paco, his lips tight, nodded, but Alex answered. "Yes, but it didn't attack us—just barreled through us like we weren't important. I think maybe we were in its way. Grandi's hurt, though. He's going to need medevac."

Buck nodded, as if such a thing were unimportant, and waited for Alex to continue.

"In the confusion, Cassie got separated."

"Separated or wandered off?"

"Separated," said Cassie. *But screw you.*

"She was the one who found the creature," continued Alex. "As near as I can tell, the basilisk did this."

Buck's lips twisted into a macabre smile. "The basilisk put a round into its head?"

Alex paused, glanced at Cassie. "No. I—"

"*I* shot it," she blurted out. "It was dying, in agony."

Buck stared at her in surprise and was smiling cruelly. "Goddamn! Hey everybody, keep Blondie away from Grandi."

An uncomfortable silence followed.

"Screw you people," Buck muttered.

Paco stepped forward. "Somehow, the basilisk knew we were tracking it and got around us. I don't know how. But then it must have sensed the Great Elder Brother and came back to fight it." Paco squared his shoulders and stared at Buck. "*Chiye-tanka* saved our lives and died saving us. He deserves our gratitude and respect. We should leave him here in case he has brothers or sisters. They might want to honor him."

Buck barked out a laugh. "Right—like *that's* going to happen."

"At any rate," said Alex, "this is the creature from the other night. Maybe it's been following us."

"You didn't know that, Tonto?" asked Buck.

"There isn't a tracker on this planet that would be able to tell if *Chiye-tanka* was following them. He's a spiritual creature who can move between dimensions."

Buck glared suspiciously at Paco. Alex was also watching Paco's face carefully.

Hit a nerve, did we, Paco? Cassie stepped forward between them. "Something else was going on, as well. Something was channeling mana—a great deal of mana."

"I felt it too," said Elizabeth, speaking for the first time and nodding at Cassie. "More than any of us have ever used. Even now, the air around here reeks of it."

"What do you mean?" asked Buck.

Elizabeth looked to Cassie. "There's something still here, radiating mana. Don't you feel it?"

She did. It was the object hidden in her pocket, the glove the creature had called the Brace.

"It's coming from Cassie," said Elizabeth.

They were all watching her, waiting. She bit her lower lip, trying to decide what to do. "Okay, here's the thing," she finally said. "I found this... well, the creature gave this to me. It wanted me to have it." With that, she pulled the Brace from her pocket and held it up for the others to see.

"Son of a bitch," whispered Paco. "That's a talisman."

"A what?" asked Alex.

"An object of great spiritual power."

Buck snorted. "You know a lot about magical objects, do you, Tonto?"

"I know a talisman when I see one," Paco said.

Elizabeth moved closer, letting her fingers drift toward the glove, wonder in her eyes. When Elizabeth's fingers brushed it, she snatched them back as if it had given her a shock. "That's it," Elizabeth said, wonder in her voice. "That's the source." She nodded at Paco. "I think you're right. It must be a talisman or a focus of some kind."

"Try it," said Buck to Elizabeth.

"*I'll* do it," said Cassie, snapping back the Brace. "I found it."

"I'm not sure that's such a great idea," said Alex.

Paco nodded. "This is not something to play with."

Buck stepped forward, putting himself in front of Cassie. "Well, go ahead then, Blondie. Try it out." When Cassie hesitated, Buck added, "Grow a pair."

"I'll try it," insisted Elizabeth.

"No! I'll do it," said Cassie, turning away and pulling the glove onto her hand quickly, before she changed her mind. Despite the fact that the creature had been wearing it, the leather seemed to meld perfectly to her much smaller hand as if it had been designed just for her. The glove covered her entire forearm, stopping just past her elbow. "Jesus Christ," she muttered as she felt the arcane energy coursing up her arm. It wasn't painful, just unexpected. Her entire arm was tingling.

"Language," said Elizabeth.

Cassie, ignoring her, turned away. She had no idea how to use the talisman, but she extended her glove-clad arm and pointed toward a Douglas fir tree about ten paces away. Elizabeth stood just behind her, with her hand on Cassie's shoulder, almost breathing down her neck.

"I don't know what to do," Cassie whispered.

"Trust in the Lord," Elizabeth said. "Channel, and try and direct the energy outward."

"Are you sure?"

Elizabeth paused and sighed. "No."

Cassie closed her eyes and drew in mana. Normally, using mana invigorated her, filling her with power. Now, vastly more mana than she had ever held before rushed into her body, filling it to capacity with arcane energy. The rush was indescribable, and her eyes opened wide in abject surprise as she released the pent-up mana in one burst, by instinct more than anything else. A brilliant bolt of white lightning lit up the night as it arced from her gloved hand, striking the Douglas fir. The trunk of the tree shattered, cutting it in half and sending it crashing to the forest floor. Startled curses and exclamations erupted from behind her.

Cassie's hand fell to her side, and her mouth dropped open. At first, she couldn't see anything but spots of bright light, but then her eyesight returned. In front of her, the base of the fir tree crackled and burned. "Oh my God," said Cassie, yanking the Brace off her hand.

"Exactly," said Elizabeth.

"Okay," said Buck, a look of shock on his angular features. "Here's what we're going to do. You put that thing down on the ground, right goddamn now, and you don't touch it again."

Still trembling, Cassie laid it carefully on the ground.

Buck turned to Alex. "I'm calling in McKnight. No one touches that thing or Bigfoot. McKnight will want to see this."

"Roger that," said Alex, wonder in his voice.

* * *

Alex stood beside Buck in the same clearing where the basilisk had scattered them earlier, waiting for McKnight. They had moved one of the MRAPs to the edge of the clearing and used its headlights to illuminate the ground. They were still close to the Magic

Kingdom, so it was only minutes before they heard the sound of rotors. Moments later, the aircraft darted over the trees, spun about, and dropped down, its skids touching the ground. The side door slid open, and McKnight, dressed in combat gear, jumped out and strode over to meet them. Helena Simmons, looking out of place in blue jeans and a sweater, followed him. As they left the helicopter, two of the other soldiers carried the injured Grandi onto it. McKnight paused and grabbed Grandi's arm, leaning in to speak to him. McKnight nodded, and the two soldiers secured Grandi in the helicopter. McKnight and Helena walked over to meet Alex and Buck.

"Report," ordered McKnight, moving past the two men and heading for the lights of the other MRAP still within the trees.

"We've recovered the carcass of a simian beast, more than eight feet tall and likely weighing about five hundred pounds," said Buck. "As well as an object of some type that might be a weapon. At least, it seems to amplify the abilities of the mag-sens."

Helena stared at him in shock, but McKnight's face betrayed no emotion.

How many other commanders would just take news like this in stride? Alex wondered. *Both governments, American and Canadian, chose well when they had assigned this man to command Task Force Devil.*

"Where's the basilisk?" McKnight asked.

"Don't know, sir," answered Buck, glancing at Alex.

"We were tracking it when it somehow circled behind us," said Alex. "But instead of attacking us, it just ran through us and attacked the Big Foot creature instead."

McKnight stopped, spun on Alex. "Big Foot?"

Alex met his gaze and nodded. "Yes sir, Big Foot. The same creature that was observing us when we took out the hellhounds."

McKnight sighed then swatted at a mosquito buzzing near his face. "There's no way I'm talking to the White House or the Privy Council Office about Big Foot," he said, more to himself than the other two men. He shook his head and started walking again. "How did it die?"

"We think the basilisk and the creature fought," said Alex. "It was near death when Cassie found it."

"Blondie capped it," said Buck. "Put a 9mm into its brainpan."

McKnight stopped again, his eyes narrowing. "She did what?"

"It was a mercy killing, sir," said Alex. "You'll see once you look at the carcass. It was a miracle it survived as long as it did."

"How'd she get a weapon, Captain?"

"I gave her my pistol, sir, for protection."

McKnight sighed and started walking again. "So, where's this weapon you mentioned?"

"Secured on site," said Buck. "It's like a... glove of some type. The Big Foot creature had it."

"Cassie found it," said Alex. "She said the creature gave it to her, told her it was a gift."

"She *spoke* to it?"

"Not exactly, sir," said Alex. "She said it was capable of telepathy."

"Really?" said Helena. "Now that's interesting."

"Sir," said Buck. "Captain Benoit lost control of the civilian, and she got away from him and his team. No great surprise there— she doesn't follow orders worth shit. Not like the other one, the religious freak. *Her* I can control."

"As I recall, it was your command, your team, and your responsibility, Major," said McKnight. "Anyone else hurt?"

"Just Sergeant Grandi, sir," said Alex. "And I take responsibility for Cassie. As I said, the basilisk scattered us, and she became separated in the dark. She says she was drawn to the creature." He paused then continued. "In fact, if not for her, we might not have found it at all." He glanced out the corner of his eye at Buck. "Or the weapon."

They arrived at the site of the battle, still secured by sentries. Cassie, Elizabeth, and Paco stood waiting beside the MRAP. Someone—Paco probably, given his earlier concern—had draped a poncho over the carcass. McKnight nodded briefly at the three of them before approaching the creature. He pulled back the poncho and knelt beside it for several minutes, shining the beam of his flashlight over its body. Helena knelt down on the opposite side of the beast, staring at it in wonder. Buck and Alex stood back, waiting. McKnight finally stood up again and looked to Buck, raising his eyebrows inquisitively.

Buck shook his head. "I've never seen anything like this before."

"So, maybe it's terrestrial, from Earth. But if so, why is it here now? What's the connection with the basilisk and Rubicon?"

"I don't know, sir," said Buck.

"Paco says it's a supernatural being," said Alex. "Says that it can move between dimensions."

At this, Helena's eyes darted to Alex and then to McKnight.

"Oh, please." Buck cast Alex a disdainful look. "Like he would know anything about anything. He's talking out of his ass. That fucking Indian's bullshit mumbo jumbo—"

McKnight raised his hand. "We don't know what's going on, Major. Let's not be so quick to discard theories, no matter how outlandish they may seem. Some of the things we've observed on Rubicon are easily identifiable in humanity's legends. How is that possible? We didn't make up the name basilisk, did we? It just fit. Describe a giant lizard that turns people to stone with its gaze, and any ten-year-old would name it in about two seconds. And creatures that move between dimensions are not that impossible, are they?"

Buck looked as if he had been kicked in the balls. "No, sir."

"Show me the weapon," McKnight said.

Buck approached the spot where Cassie had placed the object—the talisman, according to Paco. McKnight joined Buck, staring at it, then his gaze took in the smoldering remains of the pine tree.

"It seems to amplify mana," said Buck. "Blondie fried that tree with a bolt of lightning."

"Lightning?" repeated Helena in surprise.

"They haven't done *that* yet," said McKnight.

"No sir," said Buck with a lopsided grin. "It was actually pretty impressive."

"I bet."

Alex stepped closer, hesitant to say what was on his mind but determined to say it anyway even if it pissed off Buck. "Sir." He waited as the older man turned to face him, choosing his words carefully.

"Captain?"

"We should bring it with us when we go after the basilisk." Alex's pulse was racing, and he could feel Buck glaring at him. *Screw you and your feelings of insecurity,* he thought. "Sir, we're going to need everything we have to take this creature down."

"I don't want you to take it down, Captain. I want it alive. We need something positive to show the politicians, something to make them believe we're getting results after they've spent all this money."

"Sir, we may not be able to bring it in alive. We don't even know if the drugs will have any effect. Its central nervous system could be completely alien to our understanding."

"That's not what the science dorks say," snapped Buck, his

glare ready to burn holes through Alex.

Alex rounded on Buck. "The scientists are just guessing, and you know it. They've never faced this thing, and neither have you. It's way more dangerous than anyone is giving it credit for."

Buck's posture went rigid, and Alex was certain he was moments from violence.

McKnight stepped between them, his face granite. "Enough! I hear what you're saying, Captain, and believe me, I do understand how dangerous it is, but you have your orders." He spun on Buck. "And Major, I want your team ready to go again in fifteen minutes. We've got it on the run now, so keep after it. Mr. Nelson should have no problems following it." He jabbed a finger into Buck's chest, forcing the larger man back a pace. "And don't ever refer to him as a 'fucking Indian' again. He's out here risking his life helping us clean up our mess. I won't tolerate racism. Got it?"

Instantly, the fight disappeared from Buck, and he seemed to shrink in on himself. "Yes, sir."

McKnight turned to Alex. "Captain. Point taken about the weapon. Major, go ahead and bring it with you, but keep it secure unless you absolutely need it. We don't know anything about it, or the creature that was carrying it."

"You want *me* to carry it?" asked Buck. "But what if—"

"I'll carry it," said Alex. "Keep it in my small pack."

"No," said Buck. "*I'll* carry it. I'm in charge."

"Whatever you feel is best, Major," said McKnight. "But make sure it comes back to base with you when this is done. If it does augment the mag-sens' talents, we'll need to examine it and see if we can duplicate it."

"If we do need it—and I'll make that determination, sir—the Jesus freak gets it. She's way more dependable, less... flighty."

"*Elizabeth Chambers*, Major. Learn their names."

"Yes sir."

Alex kept his mouth shut and looked toward where the others waited beside the MRAP. Cassie would be pissed, he knew. She had insisted the creature had given it to her. *She'll have to live with it.*

"Okay, Major," said McKnight. "Have the carcass loaded onto the helicopter and brought back to base. Then, get going while the trail is still hot. Hopefully, it won't go cold again. Let's bag this damned thing before it kills someone else."

Chapter 35

The basilisk's trail led south. Cassie and the team, in two MRAPs, followed. This time, Elizabeth accompanied Paco and Alex on foot while Cassie followed along with the vehicles, being shaken violently as they navigated the rough ground.

Cassie fumed silently, her anger building. The creature, Paco's Great Elder Brother, had given the Brace to her. It certainly hadn't given it to Buck, who couldn't even channel. Yet just the same, the jerk had taken it from her without a word as if her opinion meant nothing. She hadn't even been given the opportunity to better examine it. Her one test with it had been over all too soon. The excitement she had experienced channeling mana through the Brace had left goose bumps on her skin and the desire to use it again. Channeling had already become a rush, but with the Brace, that thrill had been magnified tenfold.

The driver of the MRAP gunned the motor and barreled over a particularly rough patch of ground. Cassie flew from her bench seat, hitting her ass on the metal floor. She glared at the back of the driver's head as she dragged herself back up onto the bench and fumbled to attach her seat belt this time. The driver paid her no heed; he was too focused on keeping up with the other vehicle. The only other occupant in the MRAP was the soldier manning the turret gun, and he sat hunched over his monitor, strapped into his seat, constantly scanning the MRAP's surroundings.

The two MRAPs had been very slowly following behind the tracking party for about three hours, moving for a bit and then sitting and waiting with the engine running while the tracking party moved forward again on foot. It was almost two in the morning, and Cassie started nodding off in the back of the MRAP. Despite getting jostled about—and her anger at losing the Brace— the constant vibration of the diesel engine was putting her to sleep.

She watched the two soldiers. The vehicles drove without headlights with both men wearing their GPNVGs. Clearly, they saw exactly where they were going, but in the dark, Cassie saw nothing—other than the occasional glimpse of the northern lights above the tree line.

They were moving in the direction of the Pine River, she knew, north of the area where they had tracked the hellhounds. It was mostly hilly ground and pine forests, with the occasional trail that was just wide enough for the armored vehicles.

This cycle of nodding off and being jostled awake again continued for some time, and she began to wish she were on foot with Paco. She wondered how Elizabeth was doing.

Probably awesome. No doubt, the others have to hurry to keep up with her.

The driver, Gus—the same baby-faced young man who had been with her on the hellhound hunt—started speaking into his radio, acknowledging something. Then, he turned in his seat to face her. "The basilisk has crossed the Pine River. We can't follow in the MRAPs."

She nodded, trying to remember where they could cross. There were only two bridges that she knew of. The closest was behind them, near Fort St. John; the other was… where? Pretty far south, east of Chetwynd in the East Pine Provincial Park, where the John Hart Highway crossed the river. She undid her seat belt, moved forward, crouching behind the driver's seat, and looked over Gus's shoulder.

The other soldier, Marcus Beorn, lifted up his GPNVGs so she could see his face. Marcus was a tall, very blond, very Nordic young man with prominent cheekbones and amazing gray eyes. He held up a folded map, indicating their location with his finger. She glanced at his face as she leaned in closer. He reminded her of a Viking hero—he was so good-looking.

"We're going to move back. Hit the road and cross near Fort St. John on the Alaskan Highway. Then we'll move south along this secondary road." He pointed to a road on the map that seemed to head west, back toward the Pine River. "While we're doing this, Captain Benoit and your buddies are going to be getting wet."

"Really?" Concern for the others spiked through her, driving away her lethargy.

He showed her the location on the map where they thought the basilisk had crossed the river. When she saw it, and understood the tracking party was going to have to swim a river in the dark of night, she felt relieved she wasn't with them—and then guilty for feeling relieved.

"I'm kidding," Marcus said, flashing his perfect teeth at her. "We're going to hook up with them here." He pointed to the map again, showing her a spot not too far from the bank of the Pine River. "We have an inflatable raft on each of the MRAPs. They'll use them to cross over while we provide overwatch with the co-ax."

"What's a co-ax?"

"The big machine gun on top. Once they're across, we'll move back to Fort St. John, cross the bridge, and rendezvous with them on the other side."

Cassie found her way back to her seat just as the MRAP began to move forward again. This was going to be a very long night, she knew, but at least she was warm and dry. Elizabeth must be miserable. That thought kind of comforted her.

* * *

The tracking party's river crossing took place with both MRAPs sitting on a high point north of the Pine River, providing security. Cassie had tried to watch the small rafts cross the river on the monitor from behind the gunner's shoulder, but instead of focusing on the rafts, the gunner kept panning the camera back and forth along the opposite bank.

The basilisk seemed to be long gone, and the crossing was uneventful. Once both rafts were safely across, the MRAPs pulled back, leaving the tracking party on their own on the other side of the river. Within an hour, they'd made their way back to a real road and were headed toward the bridge south of Fort St. John. Cassie kept falling asleep and remembered little of the drive. It wasn't until they were south of the Pine River and once again moving cross-country that she woke up again—or rather, was bounced awake by the rough terrain.

It seemed to take forever to move across country and reach the point where the tracking party was waiting for them, and it was almost five in the morning before they did—which was, unfortunately, plenty of time for the basilisk to move even farther away. A creature that large had to be capable of moving very quickly over the forested terrain, much faster than they could follow it on foot. Would it sleep? Could they make up the time then?

As the two MRAPs approached the southern bank of the Pine

River, the sun was rising in the east, creating a brilliant canvas of reds. The vehicles rolled to a stop and, grateful to get out, Cassie walked about, stretching her legs. She helped the soldiers secure the inflatable rafts back on the MRAPs, making small talk with Elizabeth as they worked. The other woman looked exhausted but smiled when she told Cassie about the river crossing.

Alex and a couple of the soldiers accompanied Paco as he looked for sign. Another of the soldiers broke out a camping stove and began boiling water to make instant coffee and breakfast. Desperately needing something with caffeine in it, she made herself a cup of coffee, pouring in two packets of sugar and coffee cream powder—what the soldiers of Task Force Devil called "NATO standard," whatever that was. When she took a sip, she was delighted to find that coffee had rarely ever tasted this good.

She joined Elizabeth, leaning against the side of one of the MRAPs, drinking coffee and chatting while they waited for Paco and the others to return. Smelling food, she saw that several of the soldiers were eating from silver packets the size of a DVD case. When her stomach rumbled, she realized just how hungry she was. One of the soldiers handed her and Elizabeth each a hot package and a plastic spoon. "Sausage and Eggs" was printed on the side of Cassie's package. She tore it open and was surprised to find how good it smelled. It wasn't the most delicious thing she had ever eaten, but it was hot and it filled her belly. Washing it down with a second cup of coffee, she quietly enjoyed the beautiful sunrise.

Several of the soldiers came back to the camp, having been replaced on sentry by other men so they would have a chance to eat. They made small talk with Cassie and Elizabeth while they ate. At some indeterminate point, the Task Force Devil soldiers had become used to the two young women, accepting their presence. Wordlessly, they had become part of the team.

Cassie wondered whether Duncan would have been accepted as well. Poor Duncan. What had he been thinking? He'd taken a huge risk, filling himself with so much mana, too much mana. One day he had been there; the next he was gone. No funeral, no ceremony, simply one less mag-sens on the team. The same thing could happen to her or Elizabeth if they pushed themselves too hard. They'd just... disappear.

Paco and Clyde reappeared through the trees, accompanied by Alex. Cassie dropped down on one knee and held her arms out, calling for the dog to come to her, which it happily did. The German shepherd still wouldn't track the basilisk, but if it decided the creature wasn't close by, as it obviously did now, it would at least accompany Paco as he searched for signs. She gave Clyde a big hug, and he gave her doggy kisses, licking the side of her face. As Paco joined them, Elizabeth handed him a cup of coffee and one of the breakfast packages. Alex nodded at Cassie before he went off to talk to Buck, who was eating his own breakfast near the open door of the lead MRAP.

"So?" asked Cassie, standing up and leaning against the side of the MRAP as she watched Paco eat.

Paco indicated the pine trees from which he had just come. "It's moving south, maybe a bit southwest, following the Pine River—at least for now."

"Could it cross over again?" Elizabeth asked.

Paco shrugged. "This is a big animal, but I don't imagine it likes crossing water. Still, there are no lizard experts among my people. If it wanted to, it can cross again easily enough."

"I overheard Buck saying that we're going to have the helicopter soon," said Elizabeth, "to help us track it."

"That'll work for me and the cover party," said Paco, "but not the vehicles."

"Do you think it knows it's being tracked?" Cassie asked. "Could it have crossed the river just to make it more difficult for us?"

Paco sipped his coffee and stared out into the trees. "I'm sure it knows we're tracking it. It knew earlier. But I don't think that's why it crossed."

"Why not?" asked Elizabeth.

"'Cause I don't think it sweats us. I think it crossed the river because it *wanted* to cross the river. We may be nothing more than an irritant to it."

"That's not a comforting thought," Cassie said.

"Not trying to be comforting; trying to be realistic."

"I'm praying for us," said Elizabeth. "God will keep us safe."

Paco dipped his spoon into his breakfast and chewed as he talked. "I hope you're right, honey, 'cause I'm not so sure these soldier boys can handle anything that can kill one of the Great Elder Brothers."

There was pain in his voice. She felt it herself. They had lost something important last night, she knew, something that could never be replaced.

"My uncle said he saw one once decades ago," Paco said, speaking softly, almost to himself. "Wildfires were burning close to our village. My people recognized this sighting as a sign, a warning from the *Chiye-tanka*. So, that very day, they moved away from their homes, carrying everything they could, even though the government weather people said there was nothing to worry about. They headed downriver—men, women, children, elders..." He grinned, winking. "A little boy named Yancy that everyone calls Paco now. It was a crazy thing to do—insane. But then the winds just... changed direction, grew stronger, like they were angry, and the wildfires swept over the village, burning everything. Had they still been there, they'd have all died, and I wouldn't be here talking to you now." Paco sighed, looking very tired. "We should have left his body where it fell. There's no honor in prodding him, cutting him apart."

"What does that mean, *Chiye-tanka*?" Elizabeth asked.

"Big man," Paco said. "Or, Great Elder Brother if you prefer."

"It was trying to protect us," Cassie said. "I'm sure of it."

"I think you're right," Paco said.

"What else can you tell us about it?" Elizabeth asked.

At first, Cassie thought that Paco was ignoring her and that perhaps the other woman had insulted him by asking, but after several moments of quiet contemplation, Paco started talking again, choosing his words carefully. "There are different beliefs among different tribes. My people, the *Dane-zaa*, believe that the Great Elder Brother comes from the Great Spirit, the Earth Father, to look after us."

"I believe that, too," said Elizabeth, a look of profound innocence in her big brown eyes.

Paco smiled, but out of sight, Cassie rolled her eyes.

"The Great Elder Brother is a special type of being, a supernatural spirit and a messenger during times of trouble. This is why he appeared to my uncle to warn us that the fires would change direction. But not all First Nations people think that way. Others, like the Métis, don't see him as a benevolent spirit at all. To them, he's the *Rugaru*, a beast."

"*Rugaru*?" repeated Cassie, sounding the word out.

"It's a bastardization of the French words *Loup Garou*."

"Werewolf?" asked Elizabeth, making the sign of the cross.

Paco nodded. "The Ojibway see him in much the same way, but they believe he's a form of the *Windago*, the beast that eats the flesh of men."

A shudder ran through Cassie. Anyone who grew up in the North had heard tales of the *Windago*, the cannibal monster.

"It isn't true," said Paco. "Maybe there's such a creature in the south, but up north, the Great Elder Brother is a friend. You'll never find agreement between all of the native peoples on this matter. We're too diverse, with too many different stories. But I believe we lost a great friend last night. One we're going to need."

Cassie nodded vigorously. "It *was* a friend. That's why it gave me the gift, the Brace."

"Us," insisted Elizabeth, "he gave *us* the Brace."

Cassie felt her face heat, but she ignored the other woman. The creature had given it to *her*, and Buck had stolen it. Even now, he had it stowed away somewhere in his vehicle. She downed the dregs of her coffee, feeling her bitterness rise. "So, what now?"

"Now we go after it," said Paco. "This time, hopefully, it doesn't ambush us again."

At that moment, they heard the low roar of an aircraft then the distinctive stuttering of a helicopter's rotor blades. Within moments, a dark-green helicopter flew over them, skimming the treetops and heading south in the direction the basilisk had gone. Paco smiled, indicating the passage of the helicopter with his coffee cup. "*That* should help."

Buck stepped away from his MRAP and faced the two women and native tracker. "Finish eating," he called out. "We're moving again in five."

Where's my Brace, you arrogant son of a bitch?

* * *

Just as Paco had said, the basilisk's trail moved southwest, following the shore of the Pine River. Elizabeth had moved out on foot again with Paco and the tracking party, while Cassie remained a passenger in the MRAP. Later that day, around one in the afternoon, the MRAPs met up with the tracking party once more at a bend in the Pine River. At that point, the mag-sens changed places, and Cassie went out on foot. This time, it was much easier keeping up with the others. She was still scared, but it was also a relief to finally get out of the MRAP and into the fresh air.

A light breeze caressed her skin, carrying with it the scent of pine needles. They followed the river south and every now and again saw small pleasure boats out on the water, probably carrying fishing or hunting parties. Sometimes, the people on board would see them and stare at the soldiers. After all, there was no army base this far north, no reason for them to be here. Cassie waved to one boatload of hunters, but Alex met her gaze and shook his head disapprovingly, and she didn't do it again.

A large blackfly buzzed her face, and she swatted it away in annoyance. The flies would only get worse as the weather got warmer—so would the constantly annoying mosquitoes. This was the North, after all. Just then, she heard rotors overhead and looked up to see their helicopter flash by over the treetops. No doubt, the noise was scaring the hell out of the local wildlife and pissing off the hunters, but with the basilisk running loose, that was probably a good thing. Hunters shouldn't be anywhere near these woods right now. Everyone needed to stay clear out of the area.

Except for us dummies actually looking for the monster.

As the sound of the helicopter receded, Cassie pushed on again, catching up to the rest of the tracking party. How long would it take to find this thing—days or weeks? And for that matter, why hadn't the helicopter found it already? How hard could it be to locate a creature the size of a truck? The hunt for the hellhounds had only taken one night, but they had been tracking the basilisk for much longer than that.

Paco must be exhausted by now. She sighed, pushed her field cap back a bit, and wiped the sweat from her forehead before redoubling her efforts to catch up.

Chapter 36

It was early evening as the Bell CH-146 Griffon utility helicopter banked sharply, making a one-hundred-eighty-degree turn. Its pilot, Captain Paul Linders, scanned the pine trees below, as did his copilot, Lieutenant Jean-Phillipe Bastien, and the two door gunners, each crewing a C-6 general-purpose machine gun. His flight engineer, Second Lieutenant Karen Higgins, was too busy monitoring her instruments to help search for giant man-eating lizards. The only passenger was one of the American Delta Force operators, who had boarded carrying a high-powered air gun. Paul's job, which he privately thought of as a complete waste of his considerable flying skills, was to find the basilisk and put the Delta soldier into a firing position with the air gun.

They were a flying hunting party, and so far, the mission was a bust. Had Paul not seen the evidence of the basilisk's attack on the Magic Kingdom the night before, as well as the burning wreckage of the MRAP it had destroyed, he would have called bullshit. Even after seeing firsthand the black-and-white video feed of the creature ripping through the perimeter fence, he still struggled to accept that he was really out here, flying around looking for a mythical beast.

Paul flew the helicopter over the tree line at close to 220 kilometers an hour, crisscrossing the terrain ahead of the tracking party on the ground. They had been up for almost an hour and a half. At best, they could only stay airborne another thirty minutes before he began pushing his fuel reserves.

How is it possible we haven't seen this thing yet? It's freaking huge.

In mounting frustration, he pushed the transmit button on his microphone, activating his crew communications. "Guys?" This was the sixth time he had asked in the last twenty minutes, so there was a noticeable pause before the two door gunners answered.

"Nothing yet," said Master Corporal Keith Howard on his starboard.

"Nada," replied Corporal Ken Otachi on the port side.

Paul sighed and shook his head. Why was he even bothering? If anyone had seen a giant lizard, they sure as hell weren't going to wait for him to ask before sounding off. He activated his communications link to the ground team and advised them he was going to swing farther south for several more passes. If they still hadn't seen anything after that, he was going to have to return to base for refueling before coming back again. There was a second Griffon at the Magic Kingdom, with another crew ready to go. They'd fly in shifts until they found this damned thing.

He banked the aircraft, putting the setting sun on his right. Long shadows stretched across the ground. By the time he returned to base to refuel and come back, it'd be dark, and they'd have to fly with night vision. And while he and his crew were really, really goddamned good at flying with night vision, daylight was always better for visibility. *Honestly*, he wondered for the hundredth time, *how the hell is it we can't find it?*

And then they did.

Jean-Phillipe swore excitedly in French, pointing to the forest in front of them. "You see that?"

Less than a half kilometer away, a giant lizard rose up on its hind legs, staring at the approaching helicopter. It actually stood there watching them for several seconds before turning and darting back into the tree line, disappearing from sight.

"Cheeky bastard," said Paul as he adjusted the aircraft's course, heading directly for the basilisk. "Get ready," he said over the intercom. "We've found it." Then he transmitted the same message to Buck with the ground team.

Behind him, the US Special Forces operator prepped his air gun for firing and made sure his harness was secured. Paul didn't pay any more attention because he knew Karen would help him. Paul's concern was driving the Griffon and putting it in the best position for the soldier to take his shot. And if by some chance the drugs didn't work, Paul was going to let the door gunners light it up with the C-6s. There was no way he was letting this thing go—the hell with orders. It had killed people, including fellow soldiers.

Within seconds, they cut over the copse of trees in which the basilisk had disappeared. All eyes scanned the forest, which was a mixture of thick pines and trembling asp trees interspersed with bushes and other sight-obscuring foliage. It didn't matter how dense the foliage was, though; now that they had found it, the basilisk wasn't going any farther. Paul would fly the Griffon on fumes if he had to.

"There! There it is." Jean-Phillipe pointed.

Paul had expected the basilisk to run as all other animals did when chased by a helicopter. But instead, it sat within the copse, glaring up at them. Paul slowed the aircraft to a crawl and then turned it, positioning the starboard side toward the basilisk so his passenger could take a shot.

After several moments, Karen came forward, sticking her head between him and Jean-Phillipe. "He says he needs you to get closer," she yelled, excitement in her eyes.

"Closer? Are you shitting me?" Paul asked. "How close?"

"Says he needs to be within fifty meters to be sure."

Jesus, that close? Aren't these guys supposed to be expert shots? Paul shook his head. "I'll do what I can, but I'm not getting *that* close. We don't know how its death-gaze thingie works, and I'm not risking the aircraft."

Karen nodded. "I'll tell him."

"Tell him to just make the goddamned shot and quit whining."

Karen darted back, and Paul returned his attention to the basilisk, now less than a hundred meters away and still watching them. He edged the aircraft closer, keeping a wary eye on the tops of the trees. The last thing he needed was to go down anywhere near this thing.

"I'm going to paint a dragon silhouette on the fuselage," Jean-Phillipe muttered. "It's going to be so awesome."

Paul grinned, bobbing his head. And then the cabin filled with flames.

Paul inhaled, sending fire down his throat, scorching his lungs. There wasn't even time to scream.

* * *

"Something's channeling," Cassie yelled to Alex and the others in the tracking party.

In the forest about a kilometer away, there was an impossibly loud explosion, followed almost immediately by a thick cloud of oily black smoke.

"Oh, crap," Cassie whispered.

More people had just died.

Chapter 37

Although the MRAPs arrived at the crash scene within minutes, the basilisk was already gone. Alex saw right away that there was no one left alive to save. The helicopter fuselage was a blazing wreck, its heat so intense he and Buck could only circle it in helpless rage. On the other side of the inferno, Paco moved through the trees with two soldiers, looking for signs of the beast. Cassie and Elizabeth waited inside one of the MRAPs, where they might be safer if it came to a sudden fight.

Wherever it was, it had to still be close, Alex knew.

Buck removed his bush cap and ran his hands back over his crew cut, pulling the skin on his already gaunt face even tighter. "I'm so goddamned tired of this shit."

"That's two of the tranq guns gone now," Alex said.

Buck said nothing.

"Two down, and we still don't know if the drugs will even work."

"You just fucking know everything, don't you?"

"This isn't going to work, you know," Alex said, turning his face away from the heat of the fire. They still had one tranquilizer gun, but now—without the helicopter—how were they even going to get close enough to use it without risking losing the shooter, or the rest of the team?

The burning helicopter had set fire to a number of the surrounding pine trees, which now cracked and roared. The province would need to get a water bomber out there right away. If not, the fire might spread and maybe even threaten a community. At any other time, they'd stay and help fight it, but Alex knew they were going to just keep going—they had to. They were too close to stop now.

"We have to take it alive," Buck said, perspiration making his face shine. "McKnight said—"

"McKnight isn't here. And if he were, I don't think he'd want us to lose the entire team trying."

Buck grimaced, shook his head. "Well, Newf, we're gonna."

Paco approached them, his hunting rifle held across his chest.

"Well?" Buck asked.

"The sign is fresh and pretty clear. This thing isn't exactly hard to track." Paco pulled out a cigarette and lit it with a smoldering branch. "It's moving south, but it's only about ten to fifteen minutes ahead of us."

"The second helicopter?" Alex asked Buck.

Buck shook his head. "McKnight doesn't want to risk it, not without knowing what happened to this one. We're on our own."

"The basilisk happened to this helicopter," Paco said, staring at the fire.

"Can you get a shooter close enough to it without being seen?" Alex asked Paco.

Paco took a drag of his cigarette and paused, considering the question. "Maybe. But this thing is smart, not like the hellhounds. It knows when it's being tracked and understands what's a danger and what isn't. That's why it took out the chopper. And last night, had it not been for the Great Elder Brother…"

"You're pulling this out of your ass. You don't know; you're guessing," said Buck. "Someone needs to go in there after it on foot."

An ominous silence settled over them, broken only by the crackling of the burning pines. Alex watched Buck's face as the other man considered his options. McKnight wanted it alive, and Alex could see why. If they could somehow replicate the creature's gaze, it would make a powerful weapon. But now, the shooter was going to be at risk.

"*I'll* go," Alex said.

Buck frowned. Paco looked frightened.

"I'm not sure McKnight wants the senior Canadian officer on Task Force Devil—"

"Don't worry about McKnight. He'll understand. All I need is for Paco to get me close enough to take a shot."

Buck chewed his lip as he considered Alex's offer. "All right. Let's try that. You two go ahead alone. Less chance it'll see you. We'll follow behind on foot without the MRAPs."

"You sure?" Alex asked. "We may need the firepower."

"Buck's right," said Paco. "This thing will hear the vehicles. I'm sure of it. There's no way you'll get close enough to use the co-ax."

"We'll get by without the vehicles," Buck said. "We'll finish this on foot. Today."

"And if the drugs don't work?" Alex asked.

"Then we use the anti-armor weapons. An assault team with the M-72s. McKnight won't like it, but if you fail, then we're all out of other options."

"M-72s are short-range. You sure they'll work?" Alex asked.

"If we can hit it, we can kill it," Buck said.

"And if we don't?"

Buck sighed and nodded to himself. "Okay. I'm giving the magic glove thingy to the girl, just in case."

"Cassie?" Alex asked.

"No, the other one, the good one."

He understood Buck's reasoning. Elizabeth had consistently demonstrated more skill and potential than Cassie. They knew nothing about the glove, so the smart money was on arming Elizabeth.

Buck turned away from both of them. "You two get moving. We'll follow behind as soon as we can."

Alex grabbed his arm. "Wait. I want to bring Cassie with me, just in case."

Paco stepped forward. "I don't—"

"Not your call, Chief," said Buck. "Go ahead. Bring Blondie with you. I don't need her. But for your sake, I sure hope she can move quietly."

"So do I," Alex said.

* * *

Heat flushed through Cassie's body as she watched Buck give the Brace—her Brace—to Elizabeth. Elizabeth, with a self-satisfied look on her face, took the talisman, folded it up, and slipped it into the pocket of her combat pants. Then she actually looked over at Cassie and smiled. Cassie breathed deeply, trying to remain calm. The rest of the soldiers bustled about the two MRAPs, unloading weapons and ammunition. This time, she knew, no one would remain behind, not even a driver. The vehicles would be locked up and left hidden in the trees. The soldiers prepared themselves for battle, stuffing grenades and magazines of ammunition into their load-bearing vests. Several of them slung metal tubes the length of their arms over their backs. They were rocket launchers; Cassie was certain of that.

When they were done and as ready as they were going to be, Alex drew everyone together for another impromptu orders group, or O Group. She was starting to understand their lingo. Everyone gathered around the side of one of the MRAPs, where Buck was waiting for them.

He began his O Group, issuing complex instructions quickly without a care for the civilians among them, but she still understood most of it. There were to be two teams: the hunting party—consisting of Alex and Paco—and the assault team, consisting of everyone else. The hunting party would remain in radio contact with the assault team, who would be following behind but not too closely. Paco's job was to get Alex close enough to the basilisk undetected to use the tranquilizer gun. Cassie raised her hand, interrupting Buck, and he frowned at her but nodded.

"What if the drugs don't work? What then?" she asked.

Buck snorted. "Then, Blondie, the rest of us get to earn our pay. The assault team will move in and engage with everything we have—heavy weapons, anti-armor weapons." He glanced at Elizabeth. "And anything else we can throw at it."

There were a few other questions, with a lot of military words like *enfilade* and *defilade* that Cassie didn't understand, but the brunt of the plan was this: let Alex and Paco go after it alone, and if that failed, attack it with everything they had. Sadly, Cassie knew she wouldn't be much help—not without the Brace. At that moment, Alex approached her, a look of trepidation on his features. *He might die out there. He's risking his life going after this monster, and I'm feeling sorry for myself.*

She forced herself to smile if only for him. "Hey, how are you?"

He paused, his face white. "Cassie..."

Her eyes narrowed, and she stepped closer, putting her hand on his forearm. "What's wrong?"

"Here's the thing, Cassie. I need you with me."

"What are you talking about? I am with you."

"I mean *now*. Paco, me, and… you."

Her hands went clammy, and she stepped back as if he had shoved her. "Are you drunk? I'm not going with you while you try to sneak up on this thing."

Clearly surprised, Alex frowned. "Cassie, this is what you're here for." He glanced over his shoulder, and she followed his gaze. Not twenty feet away, Buck was talking with another soldier but at the same time watching her and Alex, a smug smile on his lips.

The asshole knew what Alex was over here asking her to do, she realized, but there was no goddamned way she was sneaking around the woods to try and shoot a dart at that monster. She had no interest in taking it alive. Her heart hammered within her chest, and her legs felt weak. She shook her head. "You can tell that jerk to go fuck himself."

"*I'm* asking you, not Buck."

"Okay, fine, and I'm saying no!"

"Cassie, this thing killed your sister."

"Really? Have you forgotten I was there when it happened?"

"So, what's the problem then? I thought you wanted this."

"No. I want to kill it; you want to capture it."

"We have our orders," Alex said. "You have to trust us."

She snorted, shaking her head. "You're so full of shit, you know that? What are you keeping from us? There's no good reason to capture this thing—none. And you're going to get yourselves killed trying it. You want to get *me* killed, too."

"Cassie," he said, lowering his voice, "this isn't like you. What's really going on?"

"You want to know what's really going on?" she asked, glaring at him. "Fine, I'll spell it out for you. I'm scared, all right? This thing scares the living shit out of me. It scares me because it's a goddamned monster, something that shouldn't exist. It scares me because it's dangerous, because it just destroyed a helicopter and killed everyone on board, and it scares me because the last time we got close to it, it knew we were coming and almost killed all of us. But most of all, I'm scared *and angry*. I'm angry because I want my glove back. The Brace is mine, not Elizabeth's. *Mine*. The Great Elder Brother gave it to me. It didn't give it to Buck to decide who gets it."

"That isn't going to happen. Buck's in charge. It's his decision, and he's already made it. Besides, we need to capture the basilisk alive, not fry it with magic."

"No, we don't. We really don't. What we need to do is to kill it. Everything else is just you playing games with people's lives."

"Okay, I get it. You're pissed about the glove. Fine, be angry, but you're acting like an immature little kid. Sometimes you don't get what you want. I don't particularly want to try to take this thing alive, either. Believe me; I'd rather just shoot anti-tank missiles at it from as far away as I can get. But I've got my orders. We all have our orders."

"I'm not one of your soldiers," she snapped. "I don't have to follow your stupid orders."

"Goddamn it, Cassie, come here." He reached out, grabbed her elbow, and yanked her along with him, farther into the trees, away from the others. She resisted at first but then came with him, still glaring at him. When they had a little more privacy, he rounded on her. "You're wrong! You may not be a soldier, but you made a promise. You said you'd help us and follow our instructions. Now, you just don't want to anymore."

"Just give me back the Brace, then I'll go with you. It's not yours to keep from me."

"Too bad. You're not getting it back. Elizabeth gets it."

"The Great Elder Brother gave it to me."

"Only because you were the one who found it. Had Elizabeth been the first one on the scene, it probably would have given it to her instead."

She shook her head. "No. I can't explain, but it's me. I was chosen."

"Chosen? By a dying animal?"

"It wasn't an animal. It was intelligent—maybe even smarter than us. Alex. I... I shot it in the head. I killed it. I murdered it."

He rubbed his face. "Cassie, I don't know if you were *meant* to have this thing or not, but Buck is in charge. You may not like this, but his decision is a good one."

"He's a racist asshole."

Alex smiled despite the fact that she was arguing with him. "Agreed, but he's still in charge, and asshole or not, he knows what he's doing. Elizabeth is stronger than you. From a tactical perspective, giving it to her makes the most sense."

"How the hell would you know? You can't channel."

"I'm calling bullshit on you on this one, Cassie. We have a job to do, and it's a dangerous one. You knew that before you said you'd help us. I support Buck's decision. I know you don't, but your choices now are limited to helping Paco and me or sitting on your ass back here with the vehicles. If you're going to act like an eight-year-old, pissed at the world for taking her toys, then you're going to be a danger to the rest of us, and I can't allow that."

"Just ask him," she pleaded. "He'll listen to you. Tell him I need it. Please."

Alex shook his head. "He's not the kind of guy who makes deals with subordinates. We both know that. He'll just have the confirmation he wants that you can't be trusted."

Is he right? Am I acting like a child?

He reached over and gripped her arms, but she kept staring at the ground, unable to meet his eyes. Finally, she spoke in a small voice. "I'm afraid of it."

"So am I, but Paco and I need your help. This thing has a disturbing habit of disappearing and then reappearing somewhere else."

When she spoke again, it was almost a whisper. "But everything I do goes bad."

"Cassie, please?"

She didn't answer for a while. Finally, she nodded.

Chapter 38

Cassie, Alex, and Paco stripped themselves down to the bare essentials, carrying only what they would need. This time, Cassie was unarmed. Remaining undetected would be her only defense. Even Paco left behind his hunting rifle. Alex removed the sling on his tranquilizer gun, worried that it might snag on a branch and get in the way. He also removed his body armor, carrying only water and spare darts. All too soon, they were ready, despite her not feeling ready at all. She wiped her sweaty palms on her pants, wishing she were somewhere else.

Elizabeth came over and hugged her. "Be careful."

"I will."

"God will watch over you."

"I hope someone does."

Alex and Paco were waiting. She faked a smile and nodded. Then Paco turned and entered the trees. Alex followed him, and Cassie took up the rear, her heart racing, her legs weak. She closed her eyes and let the tiniest trickle of mana flow through her, drawing comfort from the arcane energy. Then, feeling just a little bit more reassured, she released the mana and hurried to catch up to Paco and Alex.

* * *

Maelhrandia ordered Gazekiller to stop. She sat atop his back, concentrating. The forest was still and silent, but she had sensed someone using magic. She closed her eyes and focused, trying to recapture the sensation. There was nothing now, but that small sensation had been enough warning.

They were coming for her. Even after she had destroyed their wondrous flying machine, they were coming. She could still smell the smoke from its fire. Bringing the machine down had been surprisingly easy. The manlings had been focused on Gazekiller, unaware of the true threat. Despite its frightening appearance and thunderous noise, the flying machine had been fragile.

Dismounting lithely, she dropped to the forest floor. She considered using the Shatkur Orb to once again send Gazekiller behind the manlings but discarded the idea. A Shatkur Orb had two main uses: one use was to create local Rift-Rings for instantaneous travel within a single realm, and the second was to create a single interdimensional Rift-Ring that would allow travel across the cosmos. There were limitations, however. Using the orb to create local Rift-Rings required casting a significant amount of magic, which weakened the user. The last time, the demon had ambushed her shortly after she had used it.

Then a new idea began to coalesce within her mind, a way to get her mission back on track after the last two disastrous attempts. They were trying to capture Gazekiller. She had no idea why, but perhaps she could take advantage of that. After all, her mother had sent her here with a goal.

Go, she ordered. The mighty beast charged farther into the forest, disappearing into the foliage. Maelhrandia cast Shadow-Soul, warping the light around her and once again disappearing from sight. Then she began to move silently back through the woods, toward the manlings. She'd trail them this time and wait for her moment.

* * *

Cassie followed Alex and Paco through the forest. As before, the basilisk made no attempt to hide its trail. At one point, they even passed a pile of lizard waste at least two feet high, the air around it alive with flies. The stench was gag inducing. Cassie breathed through her mouth and hurried past, not wanting to see what the basilisk had been eating.

This close to the beast, the woods seemed unnaturally quiet: there were no birds and no other animals. She had never really noticed the presence of the animals before, but their silence was thunderous. In this vacuum, whenever she made the slightest noise, the sound seemed magnified. Her eyes drifted to Alex and Paco. Both men moved with grace and skill. They didn't walk through the woods—they drifted like spirits. They had both tried to teach her how to move, how to walk on the outside of her foot and roll each step rather than clumping along. She did the best she could, but next to them, she knew she moved with the grace of a pregnant water buffalo. A cold sweat drenched her skin. She didn't belong here. Her ineptness was going to get somebody killed.

Ahead, Paco paused midstep, raised his hand for the others to halt as well, and then dropped down onto one knee. Immediately, both Alex and Cassie did the same. Cassie's heart lurched into her throat, and her eyes darted about, looking for whatever had spooked Paco. She heard nothing, saw nothing. A light breeze gently brushed through the pines, rustling needles. She was certain that at any moment, though, the basilisk would burst through the trees and tear them to pieces.

Something felt… *wrong*, as if she was being watched. She turned her head, seeking the source of her unease, certain someone was right behind her. There was no one there. Just trees.

Goose bumps pebbled the skin on her arms. Her unease grew, and she closed her eyes and concentrated. Just for a moment, she felt… an absence of… something, as if there was a void just before her, but a moment later, the sensation vanished. Her eyes narrowed as she stared at the area where she had felt something, but there was clearly nothing there.

Then Paco slowly raised himself to his feet, paused for several moments, and motioned for the others to follow him once again. Whatever it was she had felt—or didn't feel—it must have been just a trick of her overactive mind.

* * *

Surrounded by Shadow-Soul, Maelhrandia watched the backs of the three manlings as they moved on, hunting Gazekiller. For several heart-stopping moments, the golden-haired mage had turned and stared directly at Maelhrandia. But luckily, the mage had turned away again. Maelhrandia exhaled, realizing she had been holding her breath. That was the second time that particular mage had stared right at her when she wore Shadow-Soul.

Was it chance, or something else? No. It had to be chance.

Maelhrandia was the greatest mage-scout of her people. Few among the fae seelie could detect her when she cast that spell. It was absurd to suspect a manling could. After all, they were nothing more than clumsy children, playing with forces beyond their understanding. No doubt, in time, they'd push themselves too far and burn themselves out.

That is the nature of things: lesser beings have no business playing with magic.

She ran her slender fingers through her long hair, smoothing the strands as she watched the manlings disappear through the trees. She'd had no sense of the Ancient One since escaping its ambush. Perhaps it was dead, crushed by Gazekiller. But it could still be out there, waiting for Maelhrandia to expose herself again.

She turned and looked behind her, scrutinizing the trees, feeling hidden eyes upon her. The demons were masters at magic; one could be sneaking up on her at that very moment, waiting for her to move forward with her plan and leave herself open to attack. Dread began to gnaw at her and eat away at her resolve. Her plan, which had seemed so clever before, now seemed crazy—certain to fail and to get her killed.

No! She yanked a handful of her hair from her head. Pain, refreshing and vital, rushed through her skull, chasing away her cowardice. She might have been a minor daughter, but she was still a princess of the fae seelie. She wouldn't let fear stop her. She'd succeed or die.

* * *

With the tranquilizer gun held across his chest, Alex followed Paco through the woods. The forest was mostly pine trees and brush, more boreal hinterland than the southern BC rain forests that the province was famous for. But the sparse terrain was both a blessing and a curse: it was easier to move through but provided less cover—for both the basilisk and its hunters. And although the terrain was sparse, it was in the foothills of the Rockies and consisted of hills, ravines, and gullies, all of which needed to be traversed. Alex was superbly fit, but even he was tiring. It had to be much worse for Cassie, who wasn't used to this. Still, she somehow managed to keep up. She was far tougher than she looked.

Alex paused at the top of a gully, waiting for Cassie. Holding the rifle with one hand, he held out his other to her. Cassie's face, bright red from exertion, reflected her exhaustion as she took his hand, and he pulled her up. She tried to smile but failed. He squeezed her shoulder and pushed on again, catching back up to Paco.

His tranquilizer rifle was a Pneu Dart X-Caliber, a top-of-the-line weapon, and weighed almost nine pounds, roughly as much as a fully loaded assault rifle. He was checked out in its use, having spent several hours on the firing range back at the Magic Kingdom, shooting its .50 caliber darts—essentially ballistic syringes stabilized by a tailpiece. He was hardly an expert—tranquilizer rifles weren't standard gear for Special Forces. He was, however, reasonably certain that if he could get within one hundred meters of the basilisk, he could hit it. After all, the thing was huge.

In the cargo pocket of his combat pants, he carried a small leather case containing the preloaded barbed darts for the weapon. Each dart contained one cc of M-99 Etorphine, a Schedule 1 drug used to bring down elephants. The penalty for possession of this drug in Canada without a permit—which he didn't have—was a de facto life sentence: a single drop of M-99 was more than enough to kill a human being; in a creature the size of the basilisk, roughly twice as large as an African elephant—some thirty thousand pounds—the sedative should cause torpor and prostration. At least, that was what Helena and her staff thought. The sad truth was that no one had ever used the drug on an animal as large as this one—there were no terrestrial animals this big.

Alex really, really hoped the drug worked fast. But if the dosage was too high, it might kill the monster outright, which, personally, Alex didn't have that much trouble with. He understood why the colonel wanted it alive but wasn't sure he agreed. Some things were just too dangerous to screw around with—especially when he was the one hunting it. The most likely scenario, Alex surmised, was that the drug would take some time to work, maybe even as long as thirty minutes. And really, he could only afford to shoot it once; a double dosage could be lethal. Then there was the matter of the basilisk's armored hide, which was tough enough to stop pistol fire. To get past the natural armor, he'd have to ramp up the velocity on the weapon. So, one of two things was going to happen: the dart was going to bounce off, possibly alerting the creature, or it was going to penetrate the hide—and there was no way it wasn't going to feel that. Then the creature was going to come looking for whoever had just shot it before the drug could take effect. And it was going to be pissed.

He sighed, wiping his forearm across his sweaty forehead. This was a shit mission. Why had he volunteered? *Because I'm an idiot*, he answered himself.

The smart money was on taking this thing down with a high-powered sniper rifle from far, far away, maybe a .50 caliber Barrett anti-vehicle rifle. Now, that was a shot Alex would prefer to be making. This little jaunt was, without a doubt, the dumbest thing he had ever done, and he had done some pretty dumb things. To make matters worse, he was now dragging along civilians, risking Cassie and Paco's lives as well as his own. The two of them had no part in this; they weren't responsible for the basilisk's presence, and they shouldn't be out here risking their lives. Alex adjusted his orange-tinted ballistic glasses. Orders were orders, and he needed Paco and Cassie: Alex wasn't a tracker; he certainly didn't know the ground the way Paco did. Only Paco had any chance of giving him a shot at this thing. And Cassie's sensitivity for magic might save their lives. *Please, God, don't let me get them killed.*

They pushed on through the trees as stealthily as they could. Cassie, bless her heart, did her best, but every now and then she'd make noise, and Alex would cringe, certain the basilisk would hear and come crashing through the trees after them. At irregular intervals, Paco would pause, drop down on his belly, and examine the ground, lowering his head to gain a different perspective on some sign he had found. Alex was no tracker, but he knew hunters needed shadow and contrast to see signs—they needed to see the light striking the ground at a low angle. That was why trackers preferred to work in the early morning—or later in the day, as they were doing now. Paco silently pointed out the creature's trail, which even Alex could see: three-toed lizard-paw prints in the soft ground, scuffed trees the monster had scraped against, even crushed vegetation. This thing didn't seem at all concerned about covering its passage; perhaps it had decided there was nothing on this world that could harm it.

Alex squatted down beside Paco and watched the other man. Paco's face was cold and serious, and Alex could see the strain in his eyes. "Well?" Alex whispered.

Paco bit his lower lip and pointed to a giant paw print the size of a man's head. "We're close. It's no more than ten to fifteen minutes ahead of us," he whispered back, "and maybe not even that."

"I need to be close."

Paco nodded. At that moment, a high-pitched, alien shriek cut across the tree line ahead of them, and both men's gaze snapped toward it. Alex saw nothing, but a moment later, he heard a loud crack as a branch broke.

"Less than ten minutes," Paco whispered, still staring in the direction of the shriek.

"Whether we live or die now is up to you, my friend. You've got to put me in a good spot."

Paco wet his index finger and held it up, measuring the wind's direction and speed. He closed his eyes and remained like that for some time. Alex heard Cassie drop down just behind them. He turned and regarded her. Her face was pale, and she was clearly terrified. So was he, but he forced himself to smile reassuringly anyway. She wasn't that much younger than him, really, but she was still way too young to be out here doing this. Once again, he reflected on just how fucking stupid this mission was. *Duty is a mountain,* he told himself, *and you have to climb it every day.*

Paco reached over and gripped Alex's knee in a calloused hand while motioning with his head to the left, toward a bush-filled gully that seemed to snake around in the direction from which they had just heard the basilisk. Alex inclined his head, showing he understood: Paco was going to try to bring them around the basilisk and approach it from downwind.

Paco set off again, keeping hunched over and low. The man was quiet when he wanted to be, Alex noted. Unfortunately, as good a woodsman as Alex was, he wasn't *that* good, and Cassie, bless her heart, kind of sucked. While Paco might be quiet enough to sneak up on the basilisk, Alex and Cassie were almost certain to give away their presence. But they had no other choice. Heading back to the others wasn't an option; Buck would just send someone else out, maybe one of Alex's men. He wasn't going to let that happen. The basilisk was his responsibility.

Alex pulled his tranquilizer rifle in close against his chest then followed the other man. A moment later, he heard Cassie behind him, doing a reasonable job of moving silently for a change. Fear was a wonderful motivator, it seemed, but would it be enough?

* * *

Cloaked in magic, Maelhrandia silently followed the manlings. Only one of them exhibited any skill at all, but even he would have been easily heard and seen by the smallest fae-seelie child. Still, as clumsy as they were, Gazekiller had yet to detect them. If he did, he might kill them all before she could stop him. The noble beast would not tolerate being hunted.

And then the manling mage turned and stared directly at Maelhrandia again. A chill ran through her, and her body went rigid with panic. Even now, the mage was staring right at her. How was that possible? Three times, she had looked right at Maelhrandia when she had been cloaked in Shadow-Soul.

Once, maybe; twice, doubtful, but three times?

The damned hideous mage turned away again, and—her mouth dry, her heart racing—Maelhrandia forced herself to slowly breathe. She hadn't been detected. That would have been impossible. It was just really bad luck.

Of course, she hadn't been detected. It was absurd to think any of these manlings could see through her spell. Her prey began to slowly creep forward again, now trying to use a gully to stalk Gazekiller from downwind. They couldn't detect Maelhrandia, but she'd let them get farther away, keep some distance. Just in case.

* * *

Alex lay on his stomach, waiting, watching the world, which was tinted orange through the lens of his ballistic glasses—clearer, sharper. Paco lay prone at the lip of the gully, peering over it, his hand held out to Alex, motioning him to stay still. From his position, Alex couldn't see anything, but he was close enough to hear the basilisk moving about in the trees on the other side of the gully. Cassie lay beside Alex. In her terror, she was almost hyperventilating. Alex slowly reached over and placed his hand on top of hers. Her breathing slowed. They stayed like that, unmoving and silent, for several minutes. Finally, Paco motioned for Alex to move up beside him. His tranquilizer gun held in front of him, Alex very slowly crawled forward. Mosquitoes buzzed madly about his head, free to torment him. Alex peered over the edge of the gully.

And there it was, less than fifty meters away: the basilisk.

His breath caught in his throat. Even at the hospital, he hadn't been this close. And then, he had been focused on escape with no chance to examine this... this monster. It was, by far, the largest living thing Alex had ever seen. It faced away from them, rubbing its hide against a tree trunk, causing the upper branches to sway and creak and shower the beast in pine needles. Thick, scaly hide covered most of its upper body, but the skin underneath the creature and on its legs looked less tough—the backs of its legs had no scales. While its upper body was huge and powerful, its eight legs seemed spindly, too weak to support such a weight. Clearly, though, the legs were far more powerful than they appeared. A long ridge of spiked barbs ran down its spine, commencing at the triangular head and extending all the way to the tip of the long tail.

Just then, the basilisk ceased rubbing itself and raised its massive horned head to the sky, exposing its long, scaled neck. It shrieked a stuttering, alien challenge that reverberated through the trees, freezing Alex's blood. Getting this close to the creature had been a mistake. McKnight was wrong. They needed to kill it, take it out from a distance. *Duty is a mountain.*

Paco slowly gripped Alex's forearm. Although his face reflected the same terror Alex felt, Paco motioned to himself and then to the trees on the far side of the beast. Alex stared at him, puzzled, and then he understood: Paco wanted to move around in front of the basilisk to distract it so that Alex would have a clear shot at its unarmored hind quarters.

Too dangerous. Alex shook his head. Paco just squeezed his

forearm again and then held his hand up, displaying five fingers: five minutes. He was going to do it whether Alex wanted him to or not. Alex nodded.

Paco crawled back down the gully. Then he began to make his way to the left so that he could come out on the other side of the basilisk. Soon, he was out of sight.

There was a slight rustling as Cassie crawled up to take the spot where Paco had been. She gasped when she saw the monster. Alex met her eye and tried to give her a reassuring smile and to hide his own terror. The basilisk began grooming itself again, rubbing its bulk against the tree trunk.

Reaching down, Alex undid the flap on his pants pocket and withdrew the leather case containing the M-99 darts. He opened the case in front of him, exposing the ten darts within. Using his thumb, he depressed the rifle's safety button and, as quietly as he could, rotated it to the safety position, exposing the opening for the CO_2 tank, which he very carefully and very quietly threaded onto the O-ring valve in front of the trigger assembly. There was only the slightest hiss of air when the tank's pin was engaged, charging the weapon. Alex glanced up, but the basilisk hadn't noticed; it continued rubbing itself. The creaking of the tree covered any noise Alex may have made. He prayed it would do the same for Paco. He then opened the rear-stock section of the rifle, exposing the ammunition chamber. Removing one of the darts from the open case, Alex carefully slipped off the plastic tip covering its barbed point and inserted the dart inside the chamber then rotated the stock section back into place. He breathed deeply but quietly, wishing once again he could have just put a 50-caliber sniper bullet through the damned thing's skull. *Goddamn you and your stupid ideas, McKnight!*

Once again, the basilisk raised its horned head, exposing the row of spikes beneath its snout; it cocked its head to the side and remained like that, silent and unmoving, for long moments. Finally, it lowered its head and returned to rubbing itself against the trunk. Exhaling, Alex reached forward with his left hand and adjusted the weapon's muzzle velocity, setting it to maximum power.

The weapon was loaded, charged, and ready for firing, but the basilisk was still moving too much to risk a shot. He had to hit the unarmored underbelly, or his dart would just bounce off. He needed to be ready to shoot quickly once Paco made his move and did whatever it was he was going to do. *We really should have talked this through beforehand*, he mused.

And then they heard a bird calling from the woods opposite the basilisk, from the direction that Paco had been heading for. That was Paco; Alex was certain of it. A very small moan escaped Cassie's lips when the basilisk suddenly swung its massive head toward the sound of the bird. The back of the animal's body swung toward Alex, exposing the unarmored rear legs.

Now. He aimed down the weapon's three-by-nine adjustable scope, instantly acquiring his target. Alex had many flaws, but he never had a problem shooting under pressure. He set the crosshairs on the back of one of the basilisk's rear legs, right on the muscle, exhaled half of his breath, and then paused, holding the remainder of the air within his lungs. With his thumb, he flicked the safety to fire and, with a single crisp movement, squeezed the trigger.

The shot was good. Alex knew it would be even before he pulled the trigger. The basilisk must have felt the impact of the dart, because it suddenly and violently reared up on its hind legs, smashing into the pine tree beside it, snapping the tree trunk in half. The monster bellowed in rage and whipped about far faster than a creature that big should have been able to move. Its horned head swung directly toward Cassie and Alex, its bulbous blue eyes looking right at them.

Oh, crap! In a flash of insight, Alex suddenly realized he didn't give a shit if he overdosed this monster and killed it. He rushed to load another dart. The basilisk thundered toward them. *Move, move, move,* he screamed in his mind.

With another dart loaded, Alex snapped the rear-stock section closed again. Too slow; he was way too slow. Had the first dart even penetrated its hide? If so, how long before the drug took effect? The basilisk was almost on them. Alex raised the weapon to fire but knew it was already too late.

"Run!" he yelled to Cassie.

She didn't. Instead, in her panic, she hugged him, knocking the barrel of his weapon down, losing him any shot he might have had. *Oh Christ,* he thought, *we're dead.*

And then he gasped in surprise as a wave of energy swept over him. Less than twenty meters away, the basilisk just… stopped. The creature's horned head swung back and forth. Its nostrils flared in an explosion of air. It was no longer looking at them, as though it had suddenly lost them. It rushed forward again, stopping less than five feet away, swinging its body around and trampling the brush but somehow missing the two of them. Its tail whipped through the air right over their heads, smashing a small tree down and cascading Alex and Cassie with leaves. Alex had no idea what was going on, but the beast was so close it might still crush them at any moment.

Then Paco began screaming, yelling obscenities at the basilisk. Alex's gaze darted toward him. Paco—the crazy fool—was standing out in the open, waving his arms and yelling. The basilisk roared in fury and spun, charging at Paco, who now turned and fled back into the trees. Alex raised his weapon again, reacquired his target, and took the shot. The basilisk smashed through the trees where Paco had been standing, splintering them into tinder. Then, without any warning, it just collapsed as if it had been smashed down by the hand of God.

Cassie jumped to her feet, and the feeling of warmth abruptly disappeared. What had she done? "Paco!" She bolted toward the unmoving beast.

Breathless, Alex stared at her. "Cassie, no!" He dropped the tranquilizer rifle, jumped up, and chased after her, terrified the basilisk would get back up and crush her.

It didn't, and she ran right past it into the trees. Alex followed her, skirting the basilisk. It shifted abruptly, one of its three-toed legs almost hitting him. But its bulbous blue eyes now seemed dull, clouded over. Its head twitched and rubbed against the ground then lay still. He could still hear it breathing and see its nostrils flaring, but the drugs had worked; it was out cold. Excitement coursed through him. *Goddamn—it worked after all!*

When Cassie cried out in anguish, he turned and chased after her, forgetting the basilisk. He found her beside a pile of smashed pine trees, kneeling next to Paco, cradling his head against her chest. Paco's eyes were glassing over, and blood poured down his shattered nose and out of his open mouth. Alex dropped next to him and felt for a pulse on the side of his neck while running his eyes over his body, making a combat assessment. It wasn't good. Paco was dying. His torso had been smashed against a tree, crushing his ribs into his chest. If they got him to a hospital right away, he might make it... maybe.

Alex keyed his MBITR. "Buck. We need Starlight and a medevac flight. We've got a man down."

Buck's voice came back in his earpiece. "What's the status of the target?"

Paco coughed up blood, moaning in agony.

"Do something," Cassie cried, her blue eyes wide with fear.

"The creature's down, but so is Paco. We need medevac, now!"

"Ack," Buck said. "Be there in twenty mikes. Out."

Alex pulled out his combat knife and cut away Paco's shirt. When he saw the extent of Paco's injuries, he knew the other man would be long dead in twenty minutes. Even if they put him on a helicopter that very moment, he wouldn't survive the flight. The entire left side of his body looked as if a sledgehammer had smashed it. Several ribs must have punctured his lungs, which even now had to be filling with blood.

Cassie stared at him, tears in her eyes. "How bad is it?"

"It's bad," he whispered. "I… I don't think—"

"Do something," she pleaded.

He bit his lip and shook his head. Paco's breathing was wet. "I can give him some morphine and make him comfortable, but… I think his lungs have collapsed."

Her lip quivered, and she stared at her bloody hands. Then determination filled her eyes. "Stand back."

"What are you—"

"Just do it!"

She laid Paco's head against the ground then put her palms against his crushed left side. She closed her eyes, and the air around her hands blurred and became distorted. A wave of heat, emanating from her, rushed against Alex's face. He felt the hairs on the back of his neck stand up. Paco's crushed left side rose on its own as if pushed back into place from the inside. The injured man abruptly inhaled deeply, his head and shoulders rising off the ground. His breathing became less raspy, less watery.

Cassie sat back again, looking exhausted. The heat was gone. Whatever she had done, it was over. Paco's skin was less pale than before, and he was definitely breathing better. Alex reached out his hand and ran his fingers lightly over the man's previously shattered chest. He stared in wonder at Cassie. "What did you do?"

Her eyes closed, she shook her head. "Don't know, but it... felt like the right thing to do."

"I didn't know you could do that."

"Neither did I," she said, opening her eyes. She tried to smile but failed, clearly too worn out.

He grinned for her, feeling a rush of euphoria. "You're a regular Starlight, aren't you? Full of surprises."

"A what?"

"Starlight. It's a radio call sign for medical services."

She tried to smile again, succeeding this time. "Starlight, huh? I like that."

By the time Buck and the others arrived, Paco was doing even better, and Alex was sure he'd survive the flight to a hospital. A score of paces away, the basilisk slept soundly.

If duty was a mountain, they had climbed it that day.

Chapter 39

As Buck and the assault team secured the scene and prepared for the medevac helicopter, Cassie sat with the sleeping Paco. She was still wiped from having healed him. Never before had she used so much mana. Now that it was all over, she felt... thin, as if she had been stretched too far. She hadn't known what she was doing when she'd woven the mana through Paco's shattered body, but it had felt right establishing a connection with him and feeling his damaged flesh and bones knot together again. It was the same thing with the invisibility shield she had put up around her and Alex, protecting them from the basilisk's charge. If Elizabeth's natural skills lay with fire and destruction, Cassie's were with healing and invisibility. She smiled. There were things she was good at after all.

The soldiers carefully carried Paco on an improvised stretcher to a small clearing nearby. When they heard the medevac helicopter, Alex threw a yellow smoke grenade to draw the attention of its crew. The helicopter appeared over the trees, hovering in place. Then it set down quickly, blowing away the smoke and throwing leaves about. Cassie remained with Paco while the medic with the helicopter's crew prepped him for the flight.

The medic was very professional, and minutes later, Paco was secured on board with an IV running into his arm. The helicopter took off again, and the team turned their attention back to the sleeping basilisk.

Cassie stayed out of their way, sitting slumped against a tree trunk, watching them prep the monster for travel, securing it in a heavy-duty cargo net. The soldiers moved quickly—with Buck stalking about, ready to rip into anyone who didn't move quickly enough. After all, nobody really knew how long the drugs would last. The scientists, she was told by Alex, were reasonably certain the beast would be out for hours yet. But the last thing anybody wanted was to be anywhere near an enraged mythical beast when it woke up, pissed off and with a hangover. Only Elizabeth seemed to have no fear of the monster. She stood beside the sleeping beast, trailing her fingers over its armored hide, a look of awe on her face.

Cassie sniffed to herself. The basilisk wasn't so awesome when it was trying to kill you. This monster had killed Alice, and here it was, still alive, being prepped for transport to a secret military base. If she had had the Brace, Cassie would have killed it right at that moment, and the hell with McKnight. Did he really believe they could somehow duplicate its petrification gaze? The beast used mana, just as she and Elizabeth did. And so far, the scientists couldn't even detect mana let alone channel it. So, if they couldn't even duplicate what the mag-sens could do, what made them think they could do so with the basilisk? *Insanity.*

Elizabeth stepped away from the slumbering beast, looked over at Cassie, as if noticing her for the first time, and walked over. Cassie's gaze drifted to the bulge in the cargo pocket of Elizabeth's combat pants: *her* Brace. Elizabeth dropped down beside Cassie, sitting back against the tree trunk. "You all right?"

"Exhausted. I used a lot of mana, like a crazy lot of mana. You should have been there."

"I heard. Alex says you saved everyone—that you can heal and turn yourself invisible. How'd you do that?"

"Which one?"

"Either."

"Don't know. Both felt... right, especially healing Paco. But I'm just kind of like a child playing with fire."

"Some of us are more like that than others." Elizabeth held her palm up and then channeled a small ball of fire the size of a marble, like a miniature sun, spinning in place. "We're all playing with fire now."

"Show off," muttered Cassie, but she smiled anyway. She closed her eyes, letting her head drop back against the tree trunk. "God, I'm so tired. I could sleep for days."

"You'll get your chance soon enough. You've done the Lord's work today. God has blessed you, helped you defeat your foes."

Cassie snorted. "He wasn't much help with Paco."

"Not true. He gave you the strength to heal him."

"I think I could do it again, too... heal people. Well... maybe after some sleep."

"I'd like to see that," said Elizabeth. "Maybe I could copy you."

"Maybe." Cassie let her head hang back and stared up at the canopy of trees above them.

One of the soldiers approached—Marcus, the good-looking Viking. "Hey ladies. I'm gonna need both of you to move on over to the MRAPs." He turned and pointed to the clearing where the helicopter had landed earlier. Cassie saw the first of the armored vehicles arriving.

"You should lie down inside one of them," said Elizabeth. "Take a nap."

"Great idea," said Marcus. "But you can't stay here. We're

going to use demolitions on these trees, clear an opening for the Osprey."

"Why?" asked Cassie, not really sure she cared.

"'Cause, honey, we can't carry that big lizard over to the clearing. Next time you hunt monsters, you need to put 'em to sleep somewhere more convenient."

"Oh."

"Now, unless you want to be around when these trees come down, please move it along, ladies."

Elizabeth insisted on holding her arm and leading her toward the MRAPs. But then Cassie paused, feeling as though she was being watched again. *What the hell is going on?* She turned around, scanning the trees about her.

"What is it?" asked Elizabeth.

Cassie bit her lower lip. It was the same sense of emptiness. It had come on each time she got near the basilisk last night and today. She stared at Elizabeth, trying to put her thoughts into words, but the other woman didn't seem to sense anything unusual, and she was so much more gifted than Cassie was. "Nothing. It's nothing. I need coffee."

"I'll put the Coleman stove on and boil some water," Elizabeth said, dragging her toward the MRAPs.

As she did, Cassie looked over her shoulder once more at the area where the basilisk was now prepped for flight. She saw nothing there but the unconscious monster.

* * *

Cassie held the hot cup of coffee in both of her hands, letting its warmth flow through her palms. She leaned against the side of the MRAP and watched the Osprey V-22 lift the basilisk into the air. The Osprey was a large aircraft, much bigger than a helicopter, but she was still surprised to see it lift a creature that big. As it rose, the basilisk, wrapped in cargo netting, swayed slightly as if it had brushed against something. But then the basilisk cleared the last of the trees, and the Osprey began to slowly move forward, hauling the creature beneath it. The rotors on the aircraft began to tilt forward, turning it back into an airplane. Its turbines roared as the aircraft picked up speed and altitude, and within moments, it was gone from sight.

Silence settled over the forest once more. The soldiers congregated at the two MRAPs, and Elizabeth began handing out white Styrofoam cups filled with hot water. Buck took one of the cups, filled it with instant coffee, and lit a cigarette. For the first time since this had started, he looked happy, or maybe just less pissed.

"All right," said Buck. "We're done here. Let's get some chow downrange and then go home."

Home? The Magic Kingdom was hardly home. Still, she was so tired, it would do very nicely right now. At least the basilisk wasn't going to hurt anyone else. But now what? McKnight had asked her to help them hunt it. Now that it was captured, what would become of her? It wasn't as if she could just go back to Hudson's Hope.

Clyde moved next to her and rubbed himself against her leg. The animal had been secured inside an MRAP while Paco had been hurt, but clearly, he knew something was wrong. Reaching down, she scratched his back. "That's all right, Clyde; you hang with me for now."

She sipped her coffee. She'd sleep first and then decide what to do. She was relieved to note that the feeling of being watched, of emptiness, was gone. It had disappeared as quickly as it had come on.

Clearly, she had been imagining things.

Chapter 40

It took several hours for the MRAPs to drive back to the Magic Kingdom. When they arrived at the large vehicle hangar, the sun had already set, and Cassie saw McKnight waiting for them, a smile on his normally stoic features. Buck was first out, and McKnight hurried over to greet him, hand held out. "Well done, Major, well done indeed."

"Thank you, sir."

Cassie climbed out the back of the second MRAP, frowning. *Alex was the one who did all the work, not that jerk. Buck didn't even show up until the basilisk was down.* Cassie walked between the two men, interrupting them. "How's Paco?" she asked, secretly pleased with the look of annoyance that both men gave her.

"Mr. Nelson is still in emergency care," McKnight said. "When I know more, I will see that the information gets passed down to everyone."

Cassie snorted, but then she saw Alex standing just behind McKnight and Buck. He caught her eye and shook his head.

Whatever.

Elizabeth joined the men as Cassie stepped back. She felt a momentary spasm of anger as Elizabeth pulled the Brace from her pocket and handed it to McKnight, but there obviously wasn't anything she could do about it. Clyde jumped out of the back of the MRAP, ran up to her, and nuzzled her hand. She stroked the dog's head and then turned and walked away from McKnight and Buck without saying another word. Clyde trotted along beside her.

The hangar doors were still open, and as she stepped out into the cool evening air, she felt a strange burst of energy. She knew she was overtired, and despite this false feeling of energy, when she finally put her head down on her pillow, she was going to sleep the sleep of the dead. Clyde pushed against her thigh and whined.

She had done it. Her. Cassie Rogan. The world's greatest screwup had helped capture a mythical monster. And this time, unlike the hunt for the hellhounds, she had really contributed—had been essential, in fact. And she had definitely saved Paco's life. Perhaps, now that this was all coming to an end, there was a future for her in medicine.

Once that idea was in her head, it began to take root and solidify. Why not? Elizabeth may have been the stronger mag-sens, but she had yet to demonstrate either of the skills Cassie had used: healing and invisibility. Cassie's strengths apparently lay in a different direction than Elizabeth's. And Duncan, poor sad Duncan who had been so weak in everything—maybe he just hadn't discovered where his strengths lay.

Now, he never would. *Use too much mana, and you burn yourself out.* It was a brave new world with the sudden emergence of magic, but it was also a dangerous one. *So, where do I belong in it?*

She jumped when she heard the stuttering cry of the basilisk shattering the quiet night. Her skin instantly turned clammy, and Clyde whined and hid behind her legs as a large tractor-trailer with flashing blue lights approached, pulling a cargo container into the hangar. The container was like a shipping crate except heavily reinforced with steel bands and thick metal plating. She stared as it slowly went by. Once more, the basilisk cried out from within, its scream distorted by the metal. Four soldiers, each carrying a shotgun, walked along beside it. At that moment, the container rocked violently in place as the monster smashed itself against its prison.

They should just kill it. Nothing good was going to come from studying it. The first time it turned a scientist to stone, they'd realize they had made a mistake. No matter how careful they were, that thing was going to kill someone—maybe a lot of someones. Clyde whined once more, and Cassie reached down and patted the top of his head. "Let's get out of here."

She took a few steps and then paused, feeling that strange sensation of emptiness once more. She turned and stared behind her. The container was now within the vehicle hangar, and the huge metal doors were slowly closing. Two of the shotgun-toting soldiers stood sentry outside the hangar. She exhaled, shaking her head. How many times had she had this feeling? Almost every single time she came near the basilisk. Maybe it was coming from it somehow.

Should she say something? *Say what, Cassie? You're going to tell people that you have a bad feeling?* She could see Buck making fun of her.

Clyde pushed his head against her hand, and she turned away from the hanger. "No," she finally said to herself. "I'm just tired and spooked. I need sleep. Come on, Clyde. You can hang out in my room."

When she approached the barracks, two soldiers were sitting on the picnic table, smoking and chatting: Gus and Connor. When they saw Cassie and Clyde, they waved. "Hey, Starlight," said baby-faced Gus. "How you doin', girl?"

Her new nickname had preceded her. She smiled, feeling pleased with herself. "Doing good, but I need some down time."

"You earned it," Connor said. "See you around."

She held the door open for Clyde, not knowing or caring if dogs were allowed inside, and then followed the animal in.

Starlight. That rocked.

* * *

Maelhrandia held her Shadow-Soul spell in place for hours as she moved undetected among the manlings, waiting until late in the night to make her move. The flight here, hanging onto the netting they had wrapped around Gazekiller, had been both terrifying and exhilarating—like flying a wyvern but so much louder. The manlings' constructs truly were amazing, far superior to anything a dwarf could build. Pity. She knew what her mother had in store for them, for their life energy. The Fae Seelie Empire had more than enough slaves, and she had seen enough of their excesses since arriving to understand that these creatures had caused plenty of damage to this realm already.

Their machines, though wondrous, were also filthy, spewing noxious fumes all about them. This land needed the return of the fae seelie. It was, perhaps, the only thing that would save it from these parasites. And if their deaths could empower select fae seelie, say the royal family, then they would finally be giving back to the natural order of things. And that was most fitting.

She walked, unseen, past several of their soldiers. They didn't seem to have any magical wards in place. She wasn't that surprised. While it seemed inconceivable not to have wards to safeguard against the very thing she was doing—slipping amongst them—she had to remind herself that the manlings knew little more than animals, especially in their sad attempts to wield magic. They had no idea what they were doing. Such amazing toys but such weak mages. In truth, the Old World would be so much better off without them.

She glided through the night, approaching the huge metal building where they had secured Gazekiller. The gigantic sliding doors at the front were mostly closed, but the manlings had left them open several feet, more than enough for her to slip through. Two of their soldiers stood sentry. But she could tell by their slack posture they paid no real attention. They were secure in the knowledge that there was no danger here.

She stood in front of them, watching their ugly faces. Even after having moved unseen among them for weeks, she was amazed at their arrogance. These blind fools had dared to invade the Fae Seelie Empire? *Does the field mouse spy upon the Great Dragon?* They must have forgotten the fae seelie, forgotten their masters. In the long centuries since the Ancient Ones had tricked Maelhrandia's ancestors and brought about the Banishment, the manlings had somehow believed themselves their own masters. Now, simply because they could build machines, they thought they could spy upon their betters.

No one spies upon the fae seelie. It is time to learn the price of such arrogance. It is time to remember why they used to cower in caves, hiding from the darkness.

She slipped behind them, drawing her fighting knife. Manlings were tall, so she had to stand on tiptoes to reach the first sentry from behind, but—with one smooth slash—she opened his throat. His body went suddenly erect, and his blood sprayed out before him. Staggering forward, he reached up to his cut throat and then fell to his knees, dying before he even realized he was under attack. His companion stared in shock, not understanding what had just happened. He stepped forward, reaching toward his friend.

Maelhrandia sighed. She didn't enjoy this butchery; it was like killing babes, but it was necessary. She set the second manling on fire with Drake's-Gift. He ran screaming, spinning like a Gerlite. *And so it begins.*

She slipped through the open doors of the building. Inside, two other manlings ran for the entrance, their faces expressing their shock. Nestled within the spacious open interior, which also held two of their war chariots, was the huge metal cage containing Gazekiller. The basilisk, sensing her presence through the mind-tether, howled in greeting. She cast Storm-Tongue at one of the manlings. Her bolt was a pale, weak shadow of that used by the Ancient One and augmented through its magical talisman, but it was still powerful enough to throw the manling warrior back at least twenty paces. His body smashed into the side of one of their war chariots with a wet crunch. The second manling staggered to a stunned stop and stared uncomprehending at his colleague.

Babes. Maelhrandia slipped behind him and opened his throat with her knife. He fell forward, making a wet, gurgling sound much like a Sher-cat kitten. She approached the metal cage containing her mount. Behind her, the manling's booted feet pounded against the hard floor as his life bled out. Once again, Gazekiller cried out, his staccato roar fueling Maelhrandia's anticipation. A moment later, one of the manlings' hideous alarms sounded, its shrill piping giving warning that something was wrong.

Maelhrandia cocked her head and smiled. Something was very wrong indeed.

A metal chain with a large lock secured the doors of the cage. She frowned as she examined it. Drake's-Gift might burn through it, but it might not. And if she were to cast Storm-Tongue at it, the shock might hurt Gazekiller. She turned away and approached the still-smoking corpse of the guard she had struck with lightning, immediately finding the key on a large metal ring attached to his belt. This was far too easy.

Grinning, she returned to the lock just as three more manlings, weapons in hand, rushed through the open doors. She cast Drake's-Gift into them, scattering them, setting them ablaze.

Inserting the key into the lock, she opened it, pulling it and the thick chain free. The handles on the door, however, were stiff and resisted her efforts to remove the locking pin. She strained and pulled, but the locking pin was stuck fast. Her frustration grew as she grunted and strained against it with both hands. It was inconceivable that she could come this far just to be defeated by a stiff bolt. She jumped in place as she yanked on the pin, but it still didn't budge.

She was about to give up and cast Drake's-Gift at it when it slipped free. Satisfaction took her as she yanked one of the heavy metal double doors open. No fool, she jumped out of the way as Gazekiller rushed forward, smashing his way through the opening and toward freedom.

The basilisk rushed out into the chamber, paused, and raised his horned head up toward the rafters, stuttering out his primal challenge. Then he turned and ambled toward the sliding doors that led out into the night. Maelhrandia, her small fingers brushing against his scales, walked beside him, still cloaked in magic.

There was no room for Gazekiller to slip through the doors, but before the basilisk could begin smashing itself against them, Maelhrandia pushed a bright-red button mounted on the doors that she had seen one of the manlings use hours earlier after they had moved Gazekiller inside. Instantly, there was a machine roar and a grinding of chains. The doors slid open, and the cool night air brushed her skin.

A manling machine sped toward her with red-and-blue lights flashing. It wasn't one of their mighty war chariots; this one was made of glass and thin metal. She braced herself, extending both hands in front of her, drawing in as much magic as she could safely hold. Then she cast double bolts of Storm-Tongue into the oncoming chariot, right through the glass where she knew its occupants sat. The vehicle swerved and flipped over with an ear-splitting roar. Just for fun, she put Drake's-Gift into its interior, setting it ablaze. Perspiration ran down her skin. As gifted a mage as she was, casting this much magic while still maintaining her Shadow-Soul was beginning to tire her.

Turning away from the blazing chariot, she sent a mental command to Gazekiller: *Kill*.

The basilisk cried out and stormed forward. Maelhrandia turned away. Now that she had caused enough mayhem, her mount would continue the massacre. It was time for her to accomplish her true mission.

* * *

McKnight bolted upright, yanked from sleep by the two-toned shrieking of the base's alarm. *What the hell! That's the stand-to alarm.* He picked up the digital clock beside his bed and stared at it in confusion with eyes still blurry from sleep. It was 2:17 a.m. *Why is the stand-to alarm sounding?*

The basilisk! Fear and adrenaline rocketed through him, and in a moment, he was out of bed, hopping on one foot as he pulled on his pants. Somehow, the basilisk had gotten free. *But how?*

He stumbled about in the dark before switching on his bedside lamp. There was a standing quick-response team, he knew—four soldiers in a patrol car. It was their responsibility to be first on the scene. By now, they must already be reacting to the alarm. As he yanked on his boots, shame and responsibility flushed through him. The response team was in a soft-skinned vehicle. Normally, they would have been in an MRAP, but there had only been four MRAPs with the task force. One had been destroyed during the basilisk's attack, a second was unserviceable, and the other two had gone out with Major Buchanan. Right now, both MRAPs—with their turret-mounted heavy-caliber machine guns—were parked in the same hangar as the basilisk's cage.

Useless to anyone. That was his fault. He should have insisted that at least one of the vehicles be prepped for use the moment the team had pulled in last night. Instead, he had cut his people some slack, trying to give them a well-deserved break.

If the creature had somehow gotten free of a steel-reinforced crate, nothing they could do was ever going to hold it. He had needed something positive to show Ottawa and Washington, especially after all the deaths, but now Operation Rubicon and Task Force Devil were going to be taken from him—if not outright shut down.

He had been in command when the recon team had been ambushed, when Rubicon's creatures had somehow breached the Earth and crossed over on their own. Everything was on him.

He inhaled deeply, gripping the sides of his head, forcing himself to concentrate. When he felt in control of his emotions, he reached for his pistol, still in its shoulder holster hanging over the back of his desk chair, and slipped his arms through the harness. He drew the pistol and rushed out of his quarters, down the stairwell, and into the night.

He'd feel sorry for himself later. For the moment, his people needed him. He was still in charge—for now.

* * *

Maelhrandia let more of the manling soldiers rush past her. They were of no importance. *Where is the dark-skinned one, the warlord?*

* * *

As soon as he was outside, McKnight heard the basilisk's cry echoing across the base. He had been right—no great surprise there. Somehow, the monster had gotten loose. McKnight had gotten enough people killed; this time he was going to see it put down for good. Screw Ottawa; screw Washington. Screw his career. Louise would be happy about that—she'd have him home.

Two armed soldiers rushed past him, sprinting toward the hangar. Even from here, he could see that a fire burned out of control next to the large building, illuminating its walls in orange flame. The patrol car.

His heart sinking, McKnight broke into a run behind the two soldiers. This time, that goddamned thing was going to die; this time he'd—

Night turned to day. A blue-white bolt of lightning arced between the two soldiers ahead of him with the force of an explosion. The blast picked McKnight up and tossed him like a doll. He landed with a bone-jarring thud, stunned and blind, a burning stench in the air. *What?*

It was impossible to concentrate, to make sense of what was happening, but at some point, the spots of light in his vision began to clear. He had to be hallucinating, he knew, because he saw a woman just... *appear* in front of him. He stared at her in confusion. She wasn't right: diminutive and thin, she was more like a child than a woman, yet he was certain she was no child. Her skin was dark, not black like his, but... *purple*. Her eyes, almond-shaped and yellow, were far too large—impossibly large. She wore a dark cloak with a hood pulled up, but he could make out her long white hair beneath it—hair the color of crushed ice. She squatted down in front of him, examining him, tilting her head to the side and regarding him with those alien eyes. Up close, he saw she wore finely crafted black leather: armor of some type. Intricate silver threads had been woven throughout the armor, creating a magnificent patchwork of bizarre-looking geometric markings.

And in that moment, he realized where she came from—and began to understand how wrong they had all been.

He tried to rise, to push himself up, but the shock of the electrical blast had paralyzed him. His muscles wouldn't respond. She leaned in closer, a look of profound sadness on her features. She spoke, but McKnight didn't understand her. Then he saw she held something that wriggled and thrashed in her hand. Heart-shuddering fear washed over him when he saw it more clearly: a huge alien insect, at least six inches long, like a dark, furry caterpillar with quivering long antennae and horns. It twisted and writhed in her grip, but she held it by the back of its head so it couldn't turn and bite her hand—although it tried. He stared at it in horror and revulsion as she brought it closer to his face.

"Please, no," he whispered.

She flipped him over onto his side, exposing his back. He felt something soft and furry brushing the back of his neck.

"No, please don't!" He was too terrified to feel shame as warm urine spread out from his crotch.

The pain when it bit into the back of his skull was almost beyond description, like a white-hot bolt of fire driven right between his eyes—only far, far worse.

* * *

The manling warlord writhed and moaned on the ground before Maelhrandia as the Ashtori grimworm buried itself into the back of his neck. She looked about, making sure they remained alone while the grimworm took control of his body. He thrashed about for some time—as they all did—but then began to slow, to quietly whimper and pound his heels against the ground. When she was certain the grimworm had fully attached itself, she established a mind-tether with it. *Rise,* she ordered.

The grimworm-controlled manling slowly climbed to his feet, his eyes reflecting his horror. He was no longer in control of his body—the grimworm was and, through it, Maelhrandia. He could see and hear and feel pain but could do nothing without her expressed command.

She considered her options. Exhausted from near-constant magic use, she knew she would not be able to maintain another Shadow-Soul spell. But with the manling prisoner, she had just accomplished her mission and could now use the Shatkur Orb to return home, which was its true purpose. All she need do was find Gazekiller again, and then she could activate the orb.

But she wasn't going to. Not yet. She faced the manling. *Where is the talisman you took from the Ancient One?* she asked him through the grimworm.

He stared at her in confusion. *What?* His mind flashed back to her.

Annoyed, she sent pain flashing through the grimworm, and he screamed and fell to the ground, curling into a ball. Then, she saw a mental image of it in his unshielded thoughts, saw him locking it within a steel box.

The Ancient One's talisman, the most powerful weapon she had ever seen.

Take me to it, she ordered, now smiling, thinking of her sisters.

Chapter 41

Cassie had been so deeply asleep that it took the base's alarm some minutes to finally wake her up. She tried pulling the blankets up over her head, but it didn't do any good, and the discordant screeching reverberated within her skull, driving her to an unthinking rage. Confused and angry, she gave up, reached over, and switched on the lamp beside her bed. She sat there, staring about herself, so tired she wanted to cry... or smash something.

"What the hell is it now?" Vaguely, she became aware that Clyde was whining in terror from beneath her bed.

Then she heard the gunfire, followed a moment later by the stuttering roar of the basilisk. Her heart hammered in her chest, and a cold sweat drenched her skin. She needed to be awake—now!

Tossing the covers off, she jumped from the bed and stumbled to her window. Flames poured from a burning vehicle near the hangar, casting an orange glow. The alarm, so loud within the barracks that it hurt her ears, was screeching nonstop. Shadows moved in the darkness outside—soldiers, with rifles, sprinting for the hangar. And then she saw the basilisk, outlined in the glow of the vehicle fire, its horned head raised to the sky in challenge.

It's free? Of course it's free!

At that moment, a giant ball of fire erupted on the other side of the base, and Cassie immediately felt the presence of someone channeling mana. *What the hell—*

She almost jumped out of her skin when someone began pounding on her door. For a moment, she stared in terror at it, unable to think clearly. *Idiot*, she finally told herself. *No enemy is going to knock.* She opened the door to find Elizabeth standing there in pajamas, her hand raised to pound on the door again, her eyes wide, her hair disheveled.

"Do you feel it?" Elizabeth asked.

"Someone's channeling."

"Whoever it is, they're so strong."

A long burst of rifle fire cut across the night. A moment later, Cassie felt the distinctive channeling of the basilisk using its petrification gaze. The gunfire ceased.

Elizabeth's face went white. "Was that…?"

Cassie swayed in place, feeling overwhelmed. "It just killed someone." She saw Clyde's tail sticking out from beneath her bed, vibrating in terror. Clyde understood. Clyde got it. Her senses screamed at her to run away, to go hide somewhere until it was all over. Instead, she surprised herself with her own stupidity. "We should go help."

Elizabeth swallowed nervously and then nodded. "God help us."

"Someone has to," Cassie said as she ran past the other woman and out into the hallway.

Elizabeth was right behind her, and moments later, they were outside, still in their pajamas, running toward the sounds of combat. Cassie was pretty sure they should have been running away.

* * *

The manling warlord led Maelhrandia to a two-story structure with glass windows. A sentry stood in front of its entrance, confusion on his features as the manling approached, followed by Maelhrandia, her cloak thrown over her head. His confusion lasted only a second before Maelhrandia set him on fire, his shrieks adding to the discord rampant within the manling camp.

The manling warlord's face reflected his horror, his pain. *Please,* his mind begged.

Bring me to the talisman, now!

The manling entered the building, and she followed. It was deserted, almost dark. He led her up a flight of stairs, down a corridor, to a spacious, comfortable chamber, obviously his private work quarters. He paused before a metal box that sat beside a wooden desk.

Open it now! she ordered him through the mind-link.

He knelt down before it and turned a dial first one way, then another, and finally a third way. He cranked a lever, and the door clicked open. She pushed him aside, knocking him to the carpeted floor in her haste.

Yes! There it is. The Ancient One's talisman.

The moment her fingers touched the glove-like object, she felt a current of magic throb through her like nothing she had ever experienced before.

Such power! Far more than she had thought possible.

She pulled it over her hand. It was far too large and kept sliding down, and she had to keep pulling it back up, but her entire body throbbed with arcane energy.

Smiling, she turned away. *Time to test it.*

* * *

Alex, wearing only combat pants, running shoes, and his GPNVGs, sprinted for the vehicle hangar, his M4 held across his chest. On his way out of his room, he'd had the foresight to pause and grab his night-vision glasses, so at least he could now see how everything had gone completely to shit.

The basilisk charged about in front of the hangar, crushing anyone unfortunate or foolish enough to get near it—just like he was trying to do. All was chaos—soldiers ran to fight the basilisk; technicians ran to get away. Bodies and parts of bodies lay strewn about. The flash of gunfire lit up the night as someone opened fire.

What a disaster. How had it gotten free? And how many of his friends were dead?

He threw himself down in the grass, going prone and acquiring the basilisk through his rifle's scope. Just in front of the monster, several other soldiers were also firing at it. The basilisk roared in fury and spun in place toward them. Its eyes flared with light, and the soldiers froze. The basilisk charged forward, shattering their bodies.

Goddamn it! Alex fired shot after shot, certain he was hitting it, but it was moving so fast he had to aim for its center of mass, not the more vulnerable head or unprotected underbelly. Still, wherever he was hitting it, the rounds were getting past the scales, because the beast raised its head and howled in agony.

Good, you ugly bastard. I hope it hurts. Then, the basilisk turned to face him. Surprisingly, he was calm as he realized he was about to be turned to stone. *Will it hurt?*

But then a ball of fire the size of a basketball smashed into its horned head, sending flames cascading over it. Shrieking in pain, it turned away from Alex, seeking the source of this new threat.

"Run!" Cassie screamed, standing twenty feet away, near the corner of a building, her hands on Elizabeth's shoulders. Elizabeth was already channeling another ball of fire.

Alex jumped to his feet and sprinted for the women. As he ran, Elizabeth let loose again, and the fireball flashed past Alex. He felt the heat of its passing but couldn't tell if it hit the monster or not. Moments later, he reached the women, spun in place, and fired several half-assed wild shots.

Cassie had a look of intense concentration on her face. That concentration was mirrored on Elizabeth's face, as well, as she channeled another ball of fire. The monster scuttled backward as flames burned across its torso. Seeing his chance, Alex dropped to one knee and aimed for its head. *Let's see you shrug off a 5.56mm round through the brainpan, lizard.* He exhaled, letting his aiming point drop down onto the target—right between the basilisk's bulbous eyes—then held his breath as he slowly squeezed the trigger.

The night lit up in a flash, completely washing out his vision. Pain lanced his body as he flew through the air, convulsing. He hit the ground hard. His GPNVGs were gone; he tried to rise but couldn't move. Had he just been electrocuted? How?

The basilisk screamed. He knew he had to move, had to react—but he couldn't. Even breathing was agony. All his muscles twitched violently. As he lay on his side, his vision began to return although everything was still blurry. Cassie and Elizabeth lay nearby, and his heart rose in his throat. Were they still alive? All around him, the air reeked of a foul burnt-egg smell.

Get up! Do something. But he couldn't. His limbs wouldn't obey his commands. Any moment now, the basilisk was going to rush forward and finish them.

But it didn't. Instead, it turned and ambled away, with its weird eight-legged gait, to join a small figure walking toward it. Alex shook his head, trying to understand what he was seeing. It appeared to be a small woman with dark skin, dressed all in black. Glowing arcs of electricity danced along her arm. The basilisk stopped beside her, lowering itself so she could climb up onto its back.

And Colonel McKnight was with her.

* * *

Wracked with pain, Cassie lay on her side, watching the basilisk turn away from them and approach the strange woman who had just channeled the lightning bolt that had missed them and hit the wall just beside them instead. Her body still vibrated from the impact, though, and her teeth chattered against one another. The small woman was next to Colonel McKnight—who stood like a statue. She threw back her hood, revealing skin so purple it blended into the night. Her hair was long and pure white, reaching the small of her back. The basilisk lowered itself to the ground for her, and with one smooth motion, she leapt up onto its back and sat astride it, perfectly at ease. She pointed behind her, and McKnight clumsily climbed onto the beast's back as well, gripping the woman around her waist.

The basilisk turned away from them and began walking away with its ungainly eight-legged gait, its long tail whipping back and forth behind it. The woman, still astride the beast, lifted both arms up into the air, holding aloft an object—a glowing globe just larger than her hand.

Cassie managed to rise up into a kneeling position although she felt as though she was going to pass out at any moment. The white-haired woman was channeling now, and the sensation of mana was indescribable. Bolts of red lightning arced down, smashing into the pavement on either side of the basilisk. Clouds roiled in the dark sky above, and winds and pellets of heavy rain began lashing Cassie in the face as thunder boomed.

Just like the night of the electrical storm, when all this insanity started.

A glowing ring of bright light appeared in front of the basilisk. The ring began to spin, growing larger and brighter, so bright it hurt Cassie's eyes, and she raised her hand to shield them, peeking through her fingers. The circle of light grew in size, widening to allow the basilisk room to pass through. Through the glowing ring, Cassie saw a vibrant green jungle, the likes of which she had never seen before, so beautiful it made her gasp in wonder.

And then her gaze snapped to the woman's arm, to the glove she wore. *My Brace.* She was wearing Cassie's Brace.

Outrage energized Cassie, driving her to act. She extended her hand, channeling telekinesis. The Brace, clearly too large for the woman, slipped off her arm and flew back through the air toward Cassie, landing on the ground just paces in front of her. The woman's head spun about, her gaze instantly locking on Cassie, her alien eyes reflecting her rage.

"Mine, bitch!" Cassie said through clenched teeth.

She felt the other woman channeling and realized she was going to attack her, kill her for interfering... and Cassie knew there was nothing she could do to stop her. But then a whooshing sound filled the air, and fire flashed past Cassie, blinding her.

What followed happened so fast that Cassie wasn't sure what she saw, but the diminutive woman released the mana she had been channeling, redirecting it to create some kind of shield. The shield erupted in flames and smoke, the explosion flattening Cassie again. She lay on her side, watching Buck, who knelt on one knee, holding a huge metal tube on his shoulder.

A bazooka—he has a bazooka!

Another soldier stood behind Buck, rushing to reload the

weapon for him so he could take another shot. More soldiers darted about, and Cassie heard loud cracking noises in the air over her head and realized it was the sound of bullets.

The white-haired woman glared at Cassie. Then her eyes flicked to the Brace lying on the ground. Cassie extended her arm and channeled telekinesis again: the Brace flew to her hand, and she pulled it tight against her chest as her world began to go dim. The woman's face contorted in rage—and the basilisk leaped forward through the glowing ring, the magical portal—just as Buck fired another missile. A moment later, the portal simply winked out of existence, and the missile flew past, exploding against another building.

Cassie rolled onto her back. In the dark sky above them, clouds still roiled and churned, exposing bright stars, other worlds.

The basilisk, the white-haired woman, and Colonel McKnight were gone.

Part 4
Gateway

Chapter 42

Cassie watched as the base staff laid the dead in neat rows along the cold stone floor of the vehicle hangar, the same building that had held the basilisk for such a brief time. Together, the basilisk and the mysterious white-haired woman—*elf, Cassie; that's what she was, like something right out of a fantasy story, a dark elf*—had killed more than a dozen people. Some had been petrified and then crushed by the basilisk, creating obscene fragments of stone on the outside with still-bleeding flesh on the inside. The basilisk's gaze, it seemed, only turned the exterior of people to stone, which kind of made sense—in a grisly way. After all, it had to feed; it was a predator. The sight of the broken, bleeding body parts was both absurd and shocking—no, revolting. Other bodies had been burned to charred husks. The stench was unimaginable, yet somehow, Elizabeth stood right beside them, her rosary in hand, praying for the dead. Cassie knew she should do something to help, as well, but a sense of profound ennui gripped her.

Helping was pointless. Everything was pointless. This was a secret army base, staffed by Special Forces, supposedly the best on the planet, and they had just had their asses handed to them by one woman.

How was any of this possible? The basilisk was a creature from humanity's legends. So were elves. If those creatures came from another world—and it had certainly looked like an alien jungle that she had seen through the magical portal the elf woman had opened—then how was it possible that they resembled creatures she knew so well from stories?

There was so much going on that she didn't understand. Everyone had been lying to her, she now knew: McKnight, Buck, even Alex. All these people were liars, and they were responsible for everything that had gone wrong—for the basilisk, for all the deaths, for the sudden presence of magic in the world. She was done helping them. It had all been a waste of time anyway. They should have killed that damned monster when they had the chance.

And who was that damned dark-elf woman? Cassie was certain now that it had been her that she had sensed out in the woods and later on the base. The woman had made herself invisible, but somehow Cassie—perhaps because she could duplicate that particular ability—could still sense her. But where Cassie had only been able to hold the spell in place for seconds, the woman had somehow been able to maintain it for hours. Her strength was remarkable, far beyond anything she or Elizabeth could do even when linked. She must have been out there in the woods the whole time, secretly controlling the basilisk, directing it.

As she began to understand, Cassie felt sick to her stomach. *It was that dark-elf woman who sent the basilisk to attack the hospital, to murder all those people, to murder Alice.*

Even worse, Cassie had felt her presence earlier that evening but had done nothing, warned no one. There was blood on her hands, too. She swayed in place, shame threatening to overwhelm her, tears spilling out of her eyes.

Once again, Cassie had let everyone down. She had failed her family; she had failed at school; she had failed here. Nothing but failure.

Why had she thought this would be any different? She needed to stop making choices entirely. No matter what she did or didn't do, people died. It was far safer to do nothing.

Because when you take chances, Cassie Rogan, people die.

Her eyes closed, she swayed in place, once again seeing the cold slurry of mud roaring down the mountainside, striking their car...

She jumped in place when Elizabeth touched her elbow. She hadn't seen the other woman approach. "What?"

"They're having a meeting. I heard Buck tell Alex."

Cassie stared at her, not really comprehending. Her eyes narrowed. "And?"

"And we're not invited. They're going to decide what to do now, how to handle this."

"Handle what? It's over."

"I think they're going to shut everything down and pull out of here," Elizabeth said, a hint of panic in her voice.

Cassie sighed and forced herself to remain calm. "Elizabeth, what do you want?"

"Don't you get it? They're going to abandon us, send us back home, while they pull out of here and pretend none of this ever happened. They're just going to cover it all up."

Cassie glanced at the long line of corpses, the still-smoking wreckage. "Maybe that's for the best. Look what happened here."

"Cassie, we're a part of this. God has a plan for us, whether you believe in Him or not, He has a plan for you. They can't just give up and go away. What about McKnight?"

"I..." What about McKnight? Why had the dark-elf woman taken him? What was happening to him? He had given her a

397

chance, offered her a role to play, and now she had no idea what to do about him.

She saw the fear in Elizabeth's eyes, and then she realized something: *there is no such thing as going home again, not for a modern-day wizard.* She felt her anger spike within her, burning away her self-pity. She couldn't go home; McKnight couldn't go home; why the hell should the others, Buck and Alex, get that option?

"All right," Cassie said. "Let's go make them talk to us."

Elizabeth stalked out of the hangar with Cassie right behind. She didn't know what role she and Elizabeth would be allowed to play but was determined to find out. Elizabeth led her to the dam's two-story building, which the soldiers used as a headquarters. McKnight had kept his office in that building, Cassie knew, but neither she nor Elizabeth had ever been in there before; they had never been invited to the colonel's staff meetings. And there had always been an armed guard out front. *Screw Buck, and screw Alex.* Both Elizabeth and Cassie were a part of this now. They had a right to be involved in any decision that was going to be made.

This time, there was no sentry at the entrance, no one to stop them. Everyone was too busy cleaning up after the attack. Inside, they entered a reception area that looked pretty much like every other office that Cassie had ever seen. There was a counter in front of them, behind which were workstations, telephones, and office supplies. They filed past the deserted reception area and past empty offices filled with cubicles. The first floor was deserted, so they found a stairwell and climbed to the second floor. As they walked down a hallway, they heard voices raised in argument. The women glanced at each other nervously then began to make their way toward the noise.

As they got closer, they heard Alex's voice coming through an open door. Cassie peered around the doorway. Alex and Buck were confronting one another, their faces flushed with anger. They were standing in a large conference room with a wooden table that could have comfortably seated a dozen people. The only other person in the room was Dr. Simmons, who looked miserable. A large plasma screen was mounted on the wall, the footage split to show two conference rooms—one with a Canadian flag hanging in the background, the other with an American flag. Both rooms were empty, but it was two in the morning. What time was it in Washington or in Ottawa? Midnight? Earlier? She steeled herself then stormed into the room.

Both men stopped abruptly and stared at her in surprise. "What are you doing here?" Buck said, glaring at her. "You're not allowed in here. This is private."

"Bullshit," Cassie said, meeting his gaze. "We're way past the time for secrets now."

"We're a part of this," said Elizabeth, moving to stand beside her. "And we demand to be involved."

Rage filled Buck's face, and he stormed toward them, his hands reaching out. Cassie felt Elizabeth channel, then Buck flew backwards, stumbling into an office chair before falling hard on his ass, shock on his face.

Elizabeth stepped forward. "You will not put your hands on us. Do you understand?"

Cassie saw hatred in Buck's eyes but also a trace of fear. He climbed to his feet, watching Elizabeth warily.

Dr. Simmons looked from Buck to the women and then to Alex. "We might as well tell them. Why keep it a secret now? They almost died last night, too."

"Do you want to go to jail, Doctor?" Buck demanded. "Because that's exactly what's going to happen to you if you open your stupid mouth again." Buck rubbed the small of his back.

Alex sighed, looking exhausted. "Enough. Just let it go. We're way past the Security of Information Act now." He pulled out a chair and sat down, placing both booted feet up on the table and crossing his arms. "Besides, as soon as the project managers in Ottawa and Washington get in, they're going to shut us down. We're done here. Operation Rubicon is done. Task Force Devil is done." Alex extended his arm to the empty chairs across from him, looking at Cassie and Elizabeth, waiting for them.

Cassie glanced at Buck, who shook his head. She pulled out a chair and sat down. "So, what's really going on here?"

Buck examined his fingernails. "Hope you like prison, Newf."

Alex glanced at him with utter contempt. "Whatever."

Elizabeth sat down beside Cassie and leaned forward. "They're aliens, right?"

"Not exactly," Alex said.

"Well?" Cassie prodded him.

"They're from another world," said Dr. Simmons, "sort of. They're actually from another dimension. We're not sure where. We discovered it by accident."

"You discovered another dimension by accident?" Cassie said. "What does that even mean?"

"It means we were trying to do something else, develop a cloaking field that could evade radar and visual observation. It would have been a huge leap forward in stealth technology—true invisibility from all sensors. Instead, one of the tests had... unexpected results. We somehow opened a wormhole."

"A wormhole?" asked Elizabeth.

"To another dimension in time, space... perhaps even reality. We really don't know which. There's so much we don't know." Dr. Simmons looked decidedly unhappy. She leaned forward, resting her forearms on the table. "Two years ago, at a US Air Force testing site in Nevada, we inadvertently managed to create a localized wormhole, or *gateway,* if you prefer. It was only opened for a few moments, but it clearly showed an alien landscape."

"Oh my God," said Elizabeth.

"So why are you here? Why Canada?" Cassie asked.

"We needed more power to keep the gateway stable long enough to send someone through," Dr. Simmons answered. "A *lot* more power."

"Site C," Elizabeth said. "You're siphoning off power from the dam, aren't you?"

"No, we're using *all* the power from the dam," Dr. Simmons said. "What we send to Fort St. John is almost nothing, a fraction of the power generated here."

"This dam is supposed to be supplying energy to northern British Columbia, to all of Fort St. John," Cassie said. "That was the entire point behind building it and behind all the damage done to the environment. Fort St. John needed more power."

Buck laughed unkindly then shook his head. "Honey, the United States government paid for this dam. Hell, we *built* this dam. We're funding just about everything up here, and we're sure as hell not doing it to provide you hicks with electricity. And let's be honest: I don't know anybody who gives a shit about your environment."

"Here's the thing, Cassie," said Alex. "The truth is that Fort St. John doesn't need more power and never has. It's just not that large. The power this dam generates goes into Operation Rubicon, into powering the Gateway Machine."

"Operation Rubicon?" Cassie asked.

"As in *crossing the Rubicon*?" asked Elizabeth.

"I don't get it," Cassie said.

"It's from ancient Rome," Elizabeth said. "The Rubicon was a river close to the city. Rome's generals were prohibited from bringing their armies across it for fear of them mounting a coup. So, when Julius Caesar chose to bring his legions across the river, crossing the Rubicon, it was a momentous decision, one that he couldn't ever go back on. He was committed to treason."

"In this case," Dr. Simmons said, "we committed to secretly visiting an alien world we've named Rubicon. The first true interstellar visit was amazing, wondrous. The creatures we saw…"

"Wait a minute," said Cassie. "You just started visiting an alien world? How?"

"The Gateway Machine," Alex answered. "It's underground, beneath the dam infrastructure. It powers something we call a Jump Tunnel, a tube that when activated leads through a localized, stable wormhole—a gateway."

"There's a machine that lets you travel to another world?" Cassie asked.

Alex nodded, and Dr. Simmons grinned like an excited child. Buck stared at the wall, shaking his head and muttering beneath his breath.

"So, you've been visiting this other world, this Rubicon?" Cassie asked.

Dr. Simmons's eyes practically shone as she nodded.

"So, what happened? Did you bring these creatures back—the basilisk, the hellhounds?"

"No, of course we didn't bring specimens back," Dr. Simmons snapped. "That would have been irresponsible!"

Irresponsible? Did she really just use that word? Cassie stared at her but let it go. "Go on."

"There was… an incident," Dr. Simmons said.

Buck snorted.

The scientist glanced at Buck and then lowered her eyes and her voice. "There were some… complications."

"The aliens apparently don't like being spied on," Alex said. "They attacked us. There were some deaths."

"Try all of my team," said Buck. "I only just managed to get away."

"Within a day of that attack," said Dr. Simmons, "we had our first intrusion."

"Intrusion?" said Elizabeth. "What do you mean?"

"Hellhounds," said Alex. "Somehow, they crossed over into our world. That's the pack we hunted down."

"They came through your Gateway Machine?" asked Cassie.

Dr. Simmons and Alex shook their heads.

"The breach," Dr. Simmons said softly.

"You used that term on the Osprey," Elizabeth said, "when we were looking for—"

Cassie gasped. "The night of the bizarre electrical storm. The night mana flowed into our world."

Dr. Simmons inclined her head. "Somehow, the inhabitants of Rubicon, those elf creatures, are able to duplicate the effects of the Gateway Machine. They've breached our world."

"That's where the mana, the magic, comes from," Cassie said.

They nodded, and Buck glared.

"How is any of this possible?" Cassie asked.

Alex raised his hands.

A coldness seeped through Cassie. "You brought this on us."

Alex and Dr. Simmons looked down. Buck snorted again.

"The basilisk?" Elizabeth asked.

Dr. Simmons sighed. "At first, we thought the breach was an accident, an unintentional rift between the two worlds caused by the Gateway Machine, a side-effect of interdimensional string theory. So, we stopped all missions to Rubicon, at least until we could deal with the intrusion of the creatures. We thought perhaps that the presence of the hellhounds and the basilisk was a mistake, that somehow the animals had wandered through an unexpected wormhole. That… that hypothesis doesn't look very likely now."

"Doesn't look likely?" Cassie repeated. "Do you want to know what looks likely? That this dark-elf woman opened a portal between our world and hers. I saw her do it, all right? She channeled mana and opened a portal by herself, *after* she kidnapped Colonel McKnight." Cassie glared at the middle-aged woman, then at Buck, then at Alex. "You idiots opened our world up to them. The basilisk wasn't here accidentally. That damned dark-elf woman was controlling it."

Alex sighed and rubbed his eyes. "I think you're right."

"Oh, come on," said Buck. "What are you getting at?"

"That we've been played," said Alex. "The intrusions, even the basilisk, were just a distraction. The dark-elf woman was spying on us. She was a scout, just like the teams we sent to Rubicon."

"And now she's taken our leader," said Cassie. "What does McKnight know?"

"Everything," said Alex.

Cassie looked from face to face. An uncomfortable silence settled over the room. *Don't they get it? Why won't any of them say what's needed to be said?* "What the hell is wrong with you people?" Cassie finally asked in disbelief. "We need to go after McKnight. Right goddamned now!"

"Cassie," Alex said then paused as he considered what to say. "We can't just—"

"Bullshit! You *can*. You have to. You just don't want to. McKnight is your leader. You can't just throw him away and say *Oh well*."

"What will they do to him?" Elizabeth asked. "Why take him?"

"Because, honey," said Buck, "he knows things. First, you scout out an enemy. Then you capture a prisoner, interrogate him. That way—"

"That way you know everything about your enemy," finished Cassie. "Even more reason to go get him back."

"Blondie, we just had our asses kicked by one woman and her pet lizard." Buck jabbed a finger at the wall-mounted screen. "We've already reported the attack. This train is off the rails. Right now, a bunch of very senior government officials are waking up some of the most powerful people in North America, including the President. Once they're sitting across from us in a video teleconference, they're going to want to know what just happened. For Christ's sake, aliens have attacked us. They're not going to want to hear some bullshit rescue plan that's only going to make things worse."

"Can't get much worse," said Alex.

Buck's face looked as if he'd been kicked in the balls.

"Cassie's right," said Alex, taking his boots off the table and leaning forward. "Why can't we go after him? We still have most of Task Force Devil, over a dozen tier-one assaulters. We have some serious firepower, heavy machine guns, anti-armor weapons, explosives. They wouldn't be expecting us. Who would?"

"Don't be an idiot," said Buck. "We'd go to jail."

"Maybe, but I'd go to jail for McKnight. From what I've heard, you owe him as well."

"That's not your—"

"We could bring the Gateway Machine on line rather quickly, actually," Dr. Simmons said. "It's been on standby for some time, but it would be easy." She looked up at the plasma screen. "How long do we have?"

"Not long," said Alex. "Maybe forty minutes, maybe less. Right now, the Prime Minister and the President are probably getting rushed to National Defense Headquarters and the Pentagon. But if we're still sitting here when they arrive, it'll all be over."

"Jesus Christ," said Buck. "Can you hear yourselves? Nobody's going anywhere. This is over. I'm in charge, not you. This isn't a debate."

"They're going to torture him," Alex said. "That's what interrogation really means."

"Look, I love the colonel like a father. You have no goddamned idea!" Spit flew from Buck's mouth. Cassie could hear the emotion in his voice. "But they can't even speak to him. They don't know our language. They're savages. We have time. We can mount a real rescue mission once—"

Alex shook his head. "There won't be a rescue mission. Come on, you know that. This is it. The grown-ups are going to shut us down while they *reassess* the operation and assign all new people. There've been too many deaths. If we don't go after him, McKnight *will be* tortured and killed."

"I…"

"You told me once that the colonel saved your life in El Salvador."

"Yes, but…"

"You're not going to get another shot," said Alex. "This is it. I'm done; you're done. There's no coming back from this kind of failure. Hell, you've lost your commanding officer. Under your watch and under my watch. Whatever else happens, your time in uniform is over. You're about to become retired."

Buck went pale as a ghost. "But… how would we even…? We can't find him, not now."

"Clyde can," Cassie said.

They stared at her in silence for several seconds. Elizabeth reached over and squeezed her hand. She prayed she was right.

"If you're going to go," Dr. Simmons said, "it needs to be now." Her eyes flicked to the plasma screen once more.

"Even if we find him and bring him back..." Buck stared at his hands. "Even then, they won't..."

"No, even then it's all over for you and me. But *he'd* do it—he'd come after us." Alex stared at Buck. "You're in charge now. It's your call."

All eyes were on Buck. Cassie watched him, knowing he wouldn't do it—not Buck, that mean bastard. McKnight was screwed.

Buck made a fist, squeezed it tightly, then closed his eyes and nodded. "Okay," he finally said, almost in a whisper. "We go. All hands on deck, with everything we've got. Let's go get the boss."

Chapter 43

The decision to go after McKnight made, time sped up for Cassie, becoming a blur of activity. She ran back to the barracks and dressed quickly in one of the combat uniforms they had given her. Clyde had finally come out from under the bed. She hugged him briefly, reassuring him. As she yanked the laces tight on her combat boots, she mentally wrestled with the existence of a device that could transport people across the void of space. It was amazing—impossible—but then again, everything these days was impossible.

Ready as she was going to be, she dashed out of her room, Clyde at her heels. Without him and his sense of smell, his hunting ability, they had no way to find McKnight again. It was bring the dog or abandon the man.

She hoped Paco would forgive her. She hoped Clyde wouldn't just hide under a bush.

In the hallway, she almost ran right into Elizabeth, also wearing combat clothing. The two women stared at each other, breathless, then together rushed down the stairwell and back out into the night. Buck, who she was secretly afraid might change his mind again at any moment and cancel the rescue attempt, had ordered them to get ready ASAP—before they were ordered to stand down by Ottawa and Washington.

Minutes later, they ran up to the rendezvous point near the dam's infrastructure. A military van was parked in front of a huge concrete bunker. On the side of the bunker was a round tunnel opening, at least twelve feet high, looking like the entrance to a bank vault. Several soldiers, already wearing full combat loads with body armor, stood watching as Cassie, Elizabeth, and Clyde approached. The troops had stuffed the pockets of their load-bearing vests with ammunition and grenades, giving them a surreal appearance that was totally out of place in the quiet northern forests of British Columbia. Cassie only recognized one of them: Marcus.

As they approached, Marcus, clearly waiting for them, pushed himself off the bumper of the van and motioned them over. "Alex wants me to kit you up." He walked around to the open doors at the rear of the van. Cassie and Elizabeth followed. The back of the van was stuffed with weapons and equipment, some of it thrown in haphazardly.

"Is that safe?" she asked, pointing at what looked like a small missile lying beside crates of ammunition.

Marcus flashed her a smile. "Probably not." He grabbed a bulky armored vest and held it out for Cassie to slip her arms through. "Try this one on. There's only a few women on the team, so we don't have a lot of choice. This is about the smallest we have."

She wriggled into the vest, instantly feeling its hefty weight pushing down on her shoulders. Covering her chest and back, it was secured around the waist with Velcro straps. Marcus helped her tighten the straps then stepped back and punched her in the chest, hitting something hard and unyielding, knocking her back a pace.

"That's a ceramic plate. It covers your vitals and will stop most rifle rounds… unless the shooter is real close. The rest of the vest will only stop fragmentation—little pieces of jagged metal." Marcus turned back to the van and pulled out another vest.

As Elizabeth pulled it on, she glanced at Marcus. "How does it do against lightning bolts?"

Marcus snorted. "Probably fuse the plate right to your body."

"That's about what we thought," Cassie said.

"So, don't stand in front of dark elves casting magic." Marcus handed helmets to her and Elizabeth.

"Is this bulletproof, too?" Cassie asked.

"Not even a little bit." Marcus flashed another of his perfect smiles. "It's a Pro-Tek bike helmet painted black and weighs a lot less than a Kevlar helmet but looks totally bad-ass, don't you think? Better than Oakleys."

She frowned at him, puzzled, but let it go. These people lived in their own special world.

Next, he handed each of them GPNVGs then helped attach them to a swinging frame bolted to the top of the bike helmets. When he was done, they could just flip the four-eyed night-vision devices up or down as they needed them. When they were done adjusting the chinstraps, he had them jump in place and shake their heads. With the GPNVGs sitting on top, the helmets were heavy and unwieldy, putting weight on Cassie's neck. Maybe in time she'd get used to them, but at the moment they were awkward, and the body armor was heavy and restrictive.

"Is this really necessary?" Cassie asked.

"You know how many people we lost last night?" Marcus asked.

She looked down, staring at her feet. Beside her, Clyde sat on his bum, watching the three of them, his tongue hanging out.

At that moment, Alex appeared, walking out of the tunnel entrance. He frowned as he examined Cassie and Elizabeth. "Give them MBITRs, too."

Marcus nodded. "Just about to set them up, Cap." He turned back to the van and began to root among the equipment. With Marcus's back to him, Alex glanced to make sure no one else was watching before sliding up next to Cassie. He undid the cargo pocket of her pants, held up a silenced 9mm pistol for her to see, then slipped it into her pocket, meeting her eye as he refastened the flap and winked. He leaned in close to her ear. "Buck said he'd shoot me himself if I armed you again. Don't get me in any more trouble, okay?"

Cassie put on a fake smile and nodded quickly.

Elizabeth looked from Alex to Cassie. "What about me?" she whispered, glancing at Marcus's back.

Alex snorted. He gripped her bicep and squeezed it. "Elizabeth, you *are* a weapon."

Cassie reached into her pocket and withdrew the Brace. "Here," she said, handing it to Elizabeth.

Elizabeth raised her hand and then stopped, her fingers only inches from the talisman. "Are... are you sure? The Great Elder Brother gave it to you."

"Maybe. But maybe he just wanted someone other than that elf bitch to have it. Look. You're way better than I am with the offensive stuff, and this thing is a weapon. If we're going to war, then you need to be packing the heat, not me."

Elizabeth gingerly took the Brace from Cassie's somewhat reluctant grip.

Am I making a mistake or finally acting like a grown-up? She didn't know, but maybe she did want the Brace back after all, because as Elizabeth slipped it into her pocket, she felt a sudden pang of regret as if she had just made a horrible mistake.

Cassie bit her lower lip and looked away.

Marcus returned with small radios, each with a one-eared headset and mouthpiece on a wire. He kitted up both women, attaching the radios for them to their vests, then quickly showed them how they worked. Cassie wasn't at all sure she'd remember, but at least now she had a radio if she became separated again. Next, he gave them each a first-aid kit, three of the ready-to-eat meals in a bag, a pair of orange-tinted ballistic glasses that they hung around their necks, and a wicked-looking fighting knife that clipped to their vests. Finally, he helped them strap on a full Camelbak canteen. When he was done, Marcus stepped back, admiring his work. "Consider yourselves in full *battle rattle,* ladies. Absolutely bad-ass."

"I feel like a turtle," Cassie said.

"If it keeps you alive, it's worth the discomfort. Besides, this is all your idea anyway." He slapped her on the back, and she staggered forward before catching herself.

"Let's get going before I change my mind," she said.

Alex led the way into the tunnel, which was lit by overhead florescent tubing and sloped downward. The lights hummed above them, flickering. She must have seen this bunker a dozen times before from the outside but had never wondered about it and certainly hadn't known that it led deep below ground. What else had she been oblivious to?

As they went deeper, the air became noticeably cooler. "Well, that's a bit of a blessing, isn't it?" she said. "It's hot in all this gear."

"Enjoy it," said Alex. "It won't last."

The tunnel continued downward, angling back and forth at set intervals like a mountain pass. How deep did it go? Then, just ahead, it led to a large open area, a cavern of some type. As she stepped out of the tunnel, her breath caught in her throat. A giant hole, at least a hundred feet across and supported by concrete walls, had been drilled into the earth. A large platform with an oversize open-aired cargo lift awaited them at the edge of the hole. She was acutely aware of the presence of millions of tons of rock and earth overhead, held up only by the science of modern engineering. There was a wet, muddy smell in the air, reminding her of worms after a fresh rain. The lift, she noted as she stepped closer, was completely open with only guardrails running around it. It was attached to rails on the inside wall of the giant bore hole—much like train tracks—that circled its interior. The lift didn't go straight up and down, she realized, but rotated along the rails, spiraling. She wondered how far down it went. Several other soldiers, also geared for battle, waited for them before the lift.

Clara stepped forward, her face painted green. She held up a small tube. "Time for some makeup, ladies."

Cassie and Elizabeth held their chins up as Clara judiciously applied the wet paint, smearing it across their exposed skin. While she did this, Alex and Marcus also applied their own camouflage paint, making them look even more warlike and aggressive. They were almost unrecognizable.

Alex motioned them over to the waiting lift. "You all set?"

"As much as I'm going to be." Cassie's fingers went up to touch her face, which felt sticky.

"*We're* going to be," Elizabeth said.

Cassie hoped she didn't look as silly in war paint as Elizabeth did. Clara, on the other hand, looked right at home, as if she were born to do this.

Alex extended a hand toward the lift. "We're running out of time."

The lift easily held all of them and, in fact, could have held more without being crowded. Alex stood near a control panel and pushed a button. The platform shuddered momentarily and then began to slide along the rails, slowly circling the inside of the hole as it descended, humming and grinding along. Cassie approached the guardrails and braved a glance over the side. All she saw below was darkness. "How far does it go?"

"The Bore Hole goes down about two hundred meters," answered Alex. "The Gateway Machine needs to be beneath the dam's reservoir, nestled into the bedrock."

"Why?" asked Elizabeth.

"It creates tremors—sometimes a lot of them. In bedrock, the machine is less likely to shake itself apart."

Cassie stared at him, her eyes widening. "Oh, this is just getting better and better."

Alex put his hand on her shoulder and smiled. "It's safe."

"When was the last time you used it?"

"Just before the breach."

At that moment, the lift shuddered—far too violently—and Cassie grabbed at Alex's shoulder.

"It's okay," he said. "Sometimes it does that. It's just a rough patch along the way down. Don't worry about it."

"Don't worry about it, he says." Cassie let go of his shoulder but transferred her grip to the lift's railing. She stood there quietly, concentrating on her breathing. They descended for several more minutes. Looking up, Cassie could still see the lights from the platform near the top, but they were far away. How many revolutions around the inside of the hole had they made so far— four? More?

"We'll be at the bottom soon," Alex said, shuffling in place.

Cassie, feeling a touch of vertigo, took his word for it. She looked over at him. "So, these dark-elf creatures can control monsters, channel way more mana than us, and are intelligent enough to figure out a way to follow you guys back to our world?"

Alex, not meeting her gaze, shrugged. "Seems so."

"And you had no idea?"

"We knew there had to be a dominant species on Rubicon, but no one knew what they were or what they could do. I mean, come on, magic? Dark elves?"

"But you had to know they wouldn't like being spied on, right? I mean, who would?"

"Damage is done, Cassie. Time to move on."

"We're here," Marcus called out.

The platform slowed to a shuddering halt, and Cassie risked a glance over the railing. The bottom of the tunnel was only about twenty feet below. Across from the lift, the platform had stopped in front of another tunnel. Alex stepped off the lift and approached the tunnel. A very solid-looking glass door, probably hermetically sealed, blocked it. Alex keyed a code into a wall-mounted keypad, and the glass door slid open, releasing a gust of air. Cassie felt two sensations. The first was air that had suddenly become a *lot* warmer; the second was the invigorating, breathtaking sensation of mana that suddenly flowed around her—so much mana. "Oh my God," she whispered.

Elizabeth gripped her arm tightly, turning her to look into her face. "You feel it, too?"

Cassie nodded. "I've never felt this much mana before."

"I have," said Elizabeth. "On the hilltop, where the breach was."

Alex stared at them, his face puzzled. "There's mana down here?"

"Like you wouldn't believe," Cassie answered him. "What the hell have you people been doing down here?"

"Come on," he said. "I'll show you."

Alex led them down the tunnel. The air became even warmer,

at least ten to fifteen degrees hotter than it should have been. Sweat rolled down her face. "What's up with the heat?"

"It's the depth we're at," Alex answered. "It's only cold when you're a little ways underground. Go deeper, and it starts getting uncomfortably warm. It has something to do with the pressure. Trust me, it'd get worse if we went any farther."

"The fires of hell?" Cassie said.

"Don't even," Elizabeth said from behind.

The passageway led into a large open cavern filled with rows of tall machines that emitted a constant and somewhat disturbing hum. Bright overhead lamps lit up the room. "What is that?" Cassie stopped in place, shaking her head.

"You're feeling the electricity, the current," Alex answered. "It makes everyone uncomfortable. Stay here too long, and you'll get toothaches, maybe go sterile. This room is one of several power nodes. The Gateway Machine is a pig. It eats way more power than you could possibly imagine."

"My father worked in a dam," Cassie said. "I wonder what he'd say about all this."

"I don't know, but if you think this is impressive, wait until you see what's next." Alex stopped in front of another hermetically sealed sliding doorway and stepped aside as the door slid open with a hiss.

Cassie walked past him, through the doorway, and then staggered to a stop. A giant cavern stood before her, far too large to have been cut out of the rock. As far as she could see, the cave was filled with banks upon banks of tall machines, rows of monitors, and seemingly endless electrical tubing that ran everywhere. Clouds of vapor spilled from pipes on the floor, creating mist that further obscured her vision. She could literally feel the current in the air thrumming in her very bones—and the mana, so much mana. She felt as though she could do anything with power like that. The hairs on the back of her neck stood straight up, and her skin tingled as if constantly caressed by the flows of unseen energy.

"Wow," she whispered.

In the very center of the cavern, on a raised platform, was a massive glass-and-wire tube at least thirty feet long and large enough for a person to comfortably walk through. The tube was matte black with glowing silver rings along its length that warped and distorted the air around them. Metal stairs led up to its opening. *That could only be the Jump Tube Alex described.* A control center had been built around the Jump Tube. Even now, a small army of technicians, commanded by Dr. Simmons, manned each of the positions, their faces reflecting their excitement. Everything they had told her was true, she realized, only now accepting it for the first time: there really was a Gateway Machine, a portal to an alien world.

And she was going to go through it. "Holy Goddamn," she muttered.

For once, Elizabeth didn't correct her.

"Don't stare at the glowing rings too long. They'll give you a headache. Come on, they're waiting for us." Alex gripped her elbow and pulled her along with him.

At the foot of the metal stairs stood two ranks of soldiers, each fully armed and clearly ready for battle, their faces painted green. Buck was among them, looking even more frightening than normal in war paint. This was, Cassie realized, the very first time she had ever seen all of Task Force Devil gathered together in one location. There were at least a dozen soldiers, each carrying enough armament to take on an army.

Which was fitting because, this time, Task Force Devil was going to war.

Chapter 44

Maelhrandia cast Spider-Mother's-Blessing, sending healing energy coursing into her wounded mount. Gazekiller cried in pain, his blood still coating his flank. At her best, she had always been a poor healer, and this time was no exception. Still, the worst of his wounds scabbed over and ceased bleeding. That was all the healing she was going to manage that day. She'd try again later, after she was rested. Basilisk scales were notoriously tough but were no defense, it seemed, against the larger manling fire-weapons. She'd need to remember that during the war that would follow. As primitive as they were, manlings could still prove dangerous.

She climbed back on Gazekiller and led him through the thick brush of her own lands. Above, the double moons of faerum—one red, one blue—smiled down upon their daughter. She could tell by the stars that it was still early evening. Her prisoner, the manling warlord, sat just behind her, controlled by the grimworm. Insects the size of her hand darted about, but she was too angry to pay attention.

She had lost the Ancient One's talisman. She'd had it, had used it in battle—and it had been just as glorious as she had imagined it would be, with *such power*—but it was lost in a single unbelievable moment, stolen from her by that execrable golden-haired manling mage who so vexed her. Going back for it had not been possible, not after having already used the Shatkur Orb to open a portal back to faerum. A Shatkur Orb could be used many times to open local portals, but only once for travel between worlds. To stay would have meant her own death.

At least, Maelhrandia now knew who had the talisman. And she would return for it—with her mother's armies. She was the only member of the seelie court who knew of its existence, and she would make sure it remained that way. Not a word of it would she say to her mother. It would be hers again. And she'd finally kill that damnable golden-haired mage.

Gazekiller traveled quickly, oblivious to the dangers in the jungle around him. Nothing that lived in this jungle would challenge his passage anyhow. Here, he was master. Soon, they were approaching the Red Moon Rynde. She saw the river through the trees then the bridge leading across it. She smelled the mud of the riverbanks. A torch burned beside the dockside quay. And there, rising up on the opposite bank, was her home.

Finally home after such a long mission.

As Gazekiller trotted across the wooden bridge, her boggart guardsmen rushed to open the gate doors for her. Then they prostrated themselves on the ground before her, grateful for her return. She smiled with satisfaction, relishing the homecoming. It had been so long since she had been among creatures that knew their place.

Her prisoner, unable to move, sat stiffly behind her. The manling was aware of all that was happening—she could see the terror in his eyes. Just for a moment, knowing what her mother had planned for him, she felt pity. But his fate was his own fault: he had dared to send his scouts here to spy upon the fae seelie.

Such hubris could only end one way. Her mother would strip all the manling's secrets from him and all of his defenses. And when she was done with him, he'd be a shattered husk.

That was how the fae seelie went to war and how they defeated theirs foes.

* * *

Breathless with anticipation, her pulse racing, Cassie stood with the others in two tightly packed lines facing the entrance to the Jump Tube. Clyde stood next to her, rubbing himself against her leg, shivering and whining in fear. Paco never used a leash, so only Cassie's reassuring presence kept the dog in place. If he bolted, this mission was going to be over before it began. Reaching down, she stroked his head, telling him everything was going to be all right—telling herself the same.

All of the remaining members of Task Force Devil were with her, a total of twelve soldiers led by Buck and Alex. Cassie stood just behind Elizabeth, so close she was breathing down her neck, as was Clara behind Cassie. She felt like a sardine—or, dressed in battle armor, like a turtle-sardine. Every time she moved, the bottom of the armor caught the skin of her abdomen and pinched it against her belt. Wearing all this kit sucked; being hot and uncomfortable sucked; having to pee sucked. But it was almost time to move. Their GPNVGs lenses were flipped up, but Dr. Simmons had warned them it would be dark when they arrived. No one knew what to expect on the other side, but the Jump Tube always opened in the exact same spot, and no one, including Dr. Simmons, could say why.

Am I really about to travel to another world? Cassie exhaled heavily and rolled her shoulders. *It couldn't possibly be worse than flying.*

From her position, she strained to see what was going on. She could just see over Elizabeth's shoulder, but she was too short to see past the soldier standing in front of Elizabeth. Something was going on. She could hear it, feel it. Energy arced and crackled in front of them as the technicians activated the Gateway Machine. Ahead of her, the Jump Tube now crackled with bolts of electricity, literally snapping in the air. She could smell the ozone burning. *God, it's hot here.*

"Get ready," Buck yelled from up front. "The field is almost strong enough."

Clyde whined louder, agitated, rubbing so hard against Cassie she thought he might knock her out of line. Clara put her hands on the back of Cassie's shoulders and told her to do the same to Elizabeth. All down the line, each soldier reached up and grabbed the shoulders of the person in front of them. When Elizabeth touched the shoulders of the soldier in front of her, Cassie saw she held her rosary beads in one hand. She had been praying.

At that moment, the tube flared up, illuminating the cavern in a rapturous blue glow. Just for a second, Cassie saw past the soldiers in front of her. The end of the tube showed the briefest glimmer of a dark jungle with stars shining down from a night sky—and two moons!

This is real. This is happening.

"Move, move, move!" yelled Buck as he ran forward into the Jump Tube. At the same time, all of the soldiers, like a single entity, surged forward. Alex, in the rear, made sure everyone was moving. Elizabeth, not hesitating at all, rushed forward with the others. Surprising herself, Cassie followed right along, glued to Elizabeth's back. Clyde ran right beside her.

Oh shit, oh shit! This is way worse than flying.

Moments later, she was within the Jump Tube, feeling both

exhilarated and terrified. The air throbbed with electrical current and mana—so much mana. Then she realized Elizabeth and the other soldiers in front of her were gone, and she was at the edge of the tube, an alien world opening up before her. Clyde leaped forward, jumping into the darkness, but Cassie hesitated, suddenly frozen with terror, unable to go through with it. Clara, her hands on Cassie's shoulders, shoved her. Cassie tumbled forward.

Into another world.

Chapter 45

In the top level of her tower in a chamber that was forbidden to all, Maelhrandia stood in front of a Seeing Stone, awaiting her mother. The stone, a slab of darkest obsidian, was taller than Maelhrandia and twice as wide. Each of Maelhrandia's sisters possessed an identical stone, crafted by the master dwarven stonemasons of Deep Terlholm—before they were put to the sword so no one would learn their secrets.

Maelhrandia steeled herself before placing a palm against the cold stone and casting the spell that activated its magic. A moment later, a deep sensation of vertigo flushed through her, and she fell to her knees, instantly finding herself in her mother's throne room—or rather, finding her astral projection in her mother's throne room; her flesh-and-bone body still remained in her own tower. The throne room was devoid of all light except the dim glow that surrounded her mother atop the Bane Throne.

Her mother's ageless face looked down upon her without the slightest hint of emotion. *Report, my daughter.* Her mother's lips didn't move, but her voice resonated throughout Maelhrandia's skull.

Maelhrandia took a deep breath and then began. "Mother, I

have succeeded."

You have a prisoner?

"I do—a manling warlord. One who knows all their secrets."

The barest hint of a smile touched her mother's cruel lips. *You have succeeded, daughter. Your sisters all promised you would fail, but I always had faith in you. And what of the manlings, what of their strength?*

"They have wondrous machines, Mother, but little power. And almost no magic."

And nothing changes. The ancient texts speak of their weakness, their lack of magical affinity. They are little more than animals— further evidence that the Ancient Ones were secretly herding them for their own use, not protecting them as they claimed. Such foul liars.

"In truth, Mother, I don't think the manlings had any magic at all, not until you opened the ley lines connecting us to the Old World. Now, our magic has flowed through the portal. It is localized still, but growing, I think, and spreading. *Something* is happening. Perhaps magic is reawakening in the Old World."

Interesting. Why, I wonder, would the ancient foe orchestrate this stagnation? What benefit to them if magic dies out? It limits their powers, as well.

"You think it was their doing, Mother? Why would they do such a thing? They are masters of magic."

The demons are behind everything, child. Everything. Nothing happens that is not a part of their foul plan.

The thought of a world without magic was terrifying to Maelhrandia. Magic was the true blood of the fae seelie. Without it, they were helpless. Without it, their long lives would be cut short and they would become little more than animals. This could never be.

"There's more, Mother. In the centuries since the Banishment, the manlings have multiplied and spread. I saw an entire city of them, thousands and thousands. So many. The life energy for the Culling. Perhaps… perhaps *others*… could also… benefit?"

A silence settled between the two women, as heavy as death. Her mother's expression never changed, but Maelhrandia knew she had just made a horrible mistake. *Is this what you wish, daughter? Is this the secret desire that festers in your heart? To become as me? TO SUPPLANT ME?*

"No, loving Mother, of course not. I misspoke. I—"

Pain lanced Maelhrandia. She cried out in agony and dropped to the cold stone floor, curling up into a fetal position and screaming. The pain seemed to go on and on for an eternity, but finally, it lifted like a heavy curtain, and she could breathe again. She lay on her side, gasping for air, spit running down her chin.

Because you are my daughter and I love you, I will forgive you this one time. But we shall never speak of this again. Such hateful things you force on me.

"Yes… yes, Mother. I am… sorry. I—"

What of the Ancient Foe? What of the engineers behind the Banishment—the manlings' supposed protectors?

"I… I fought one and defeated it."

You defeated one of the Enemy? You?

"Yes, Mother. My mount crushed it."

Perhaps there is more to you than just skulking about in the shadows. Who knew about this? Were there others?

"I saw no others, Mother. Just the one. Perhaps they are all dead now."

Perhaps. But if not, they will not stop us this time. We are returning. The fae seelie are returning to take back what was stolen from us. You have done well. I will send one of your sisters to take delivery of the prisoner. Once we have pried all of their secrets from him, we shall be ready.

Instantly, the magical connection was gone, and Maelhrandia found herself back in her tower. Now, the tall Seeing Stone stood dark and cold before her. She pulled her hand back.

To give voice to her desires, openly speaking of her own wish for longer life… that had almost been a fatal mistake. The fae seelie lived at the top of a pyramid of life, consuming the life essence of lesser species in order to prolong their existence and maintain their dominance. But only the Queen, only her mother, was permitted to consume enough lives to live countless cycles. She would not share that gift any more than she would share the Bane Throne. No matter how many manlings existed, there would never be enough for all.

But if Maelhrandia once again possessed the Ancient One's talisman? She smiled, thinking of how things could be.

Chapter 46

Cassie landed hard, off balance and stumbling forward, almost falling on her face. Someone caught her, and she staggered to a stop, trying to sort out her surroundings.

It was night, pitch black. Only the stars and moons above provided any light at all. *And the mana!* So much mana all around her, everywhere.

She flipped her GPNVGs down, adjusted them over her face, then turned on the power. Instantly, she saw the world around her clearly, like green-tinted daylight. Clyde stood not three feet away, watching her, clearly able to see just fine—that, or his other senses compensated for the lack of sight. Thick jungle foliage surrounded them. She thought it was how the thickest, darkest part of the Amazon must look. She turned in place, her mouth open. There were trees everywhere, massive and misshapen, their limbs reaching out, twisting, and falling to the ground. A thick, almost furry, blanket of moss covered the branches. The air throbbed with a sweet, sickly stench, hot and humid. Almost instantly, Cassie was drenched in sweat.

She jumped back as a giant insect buzzed madly past her face, its wings a translucent blur of motion. Clyde barked and snapped his jaws at it. The back of Cassie's knees hit something hard, and she almost fell down. Spinning, she saw she had backed into stone ruins crumbling with age. She was standing in a clearing with broken pieces of strange statues of elf-like beings interspersed among broken marble columns. The resemblance to the dark-elf woman was unmistakable. Dark elves had built this clearing; they really were in their world—an alien world. *Rubicon.*

At first, she thought the jungle had been cut down, cleared from the ruins, but then she realized the open space was natural, not artificial. There were no tree stumps, no bushes. For some reason, nothing grew within this space, which was a perfect circle dozens of paces wide.

She turned, staring in wonder at the Gateway through which she had just come. All of the soldiers were through now; the jump had only taken moments. The end of the tube now simply hung in the air, floating a foot off the ground. Stepping around it, to the side, she saw that it simply disappeared, existing only when faced head-on. What would happen if she were to stand directly behind it and move forward through where the opening must exist— would she be in two worlds at once?

"This is unbelievable," she said in wonder, reaching out her hand to touch the end of the Jump Tube.

Someone grabbed her wrist and pulled her away. "Don't."

It took her a moment to recognize Alex, who was also wearing his GPNVGs over his face.

"Why not? How do we go back?"

"It's not that the Jump Tube itself is dangerous. It's just that—"

The opening collapsed in on itself, winking out of existence in a moment. It happened so quickly that Cassie fell back into Alex.

Alex sighed, helping her upright. "It's just that it's only there long enough for us to come through. The power to keep it open is… well, you just wouldn't believe me."

She turned to stare at him, feeling overwhelmed. "But how do we—"

"We have a keying device." Alex pointed to a flat-black cylindrical piece of equipment with carrying handles sitting between two of the soldiers.

She had seen them carrying it in line but hadn't had the opportunity to ask about it. It looked, she thought, like one of those atomic bombs you see in the movies, with a sophisticated keypad and monitor. "What does it do?"

"The Gateway isn't truly closed… well, it is and it isn't. Don't ask me to explain the string-theory physics; ask Helena—Dr. Simmons. She'd love to go on and on about it. But the keying device will open the Gateway again or at least shift it back into this dimension at a time when it was still open, linking both worlds."

"I have no idea what you just said."

"It opens the Gateway on command for us, so we can go home when we want to."

"Oh, okay then."

Clyde began barking furiously. She had never heard him do that before.

"What is it?" she asked him. He jumped in place, growling and barking.

One of the soldiers swore in disgust. Cassie turned to see what was wrong. Two soldiers stood near the forest edge, staring at something hanging from the trees, something that didn't quite reach the ground. She squinted, not understanding what she was looking at. At first, she thought it was moving, then she realized it was covered in a living carpet of insects. Despite her revulsion, she edged closer to see better. There was something…

"Cassie, don't," said Alex.

Clyde went crazy, barking like mad. He smashed against her leg, almost knocking her down, as he rushed in front of her.

And then she understood what she was looking at. In a moment of perfect clarity, she saw a human face, or at least what was left of the face, now frozen in a rictus of terror and pain. She recognized the shreds of torn green clothing—a uniform. This was a member of Task Force Devil.

"Oh, Goddamn," she whispered, feeling sick.

Someone moved past her, bumping into her. Buck, she thought, from his size.

"Cut him down," Buck ordered, staring up at the body. Clyde was hopping in place, still barking furiously. "Somebody shut that damned dog up before I shoot him myself."

"He's onto something," said Cassie. "It can't just be the body, can it?" She reached out and grabbed Clyde's collar, holding him in place with both hands.

One of the soldiers stepped forward, pulling a knife from his webbing.

"Wait," said Alex. "The LZ is compromised. We need to—"

Alien screams of rage erupted as the jungle came alive around them. Cassie spun about. From everywhere, monstrous figures, vaguely man-shaped but wrong somehow—with too many arms—burst out of the jungle from where they had been hiding, charging at them with spears and swords. Their faces were bestial with huge all-black eyes. Projectiles whistled through the air; one brushed past her ear. *They're trying to kill us.*

The soldier who had been about to cut down the body staggered back and fell to the ground, a shaft—an arrow—protruding from his throat. Cassie stared, dumbfounded, her limbs locked in place as the man grasped feebly at the arrow. Someone grabbed her and threw her roughly to the ground. She landed atop

Clyde, still holding onto his collar for dear life, but the dog pulled free and leaped forward at the attacking creatures.

"Clyde, no!" she yelled.

A moment later, her vision was washed out by the muzzle flash of gunfire. The sound of the silenced weapons was not what she had expected—they were far louder than movies would have had her believe. Moments later, more soldiers began firing. She lay on her stomach, terrified. The optics of her GPNVGs adjusted to the gunfire around her, and she saw the attackers cut down, shredded by the withering impact of subsonic fire. Clyde leapt for the throat of one of the creatures, latched onto it, and dragged it to the ground. Another of the attackers danced back, one of its long arms spinning through the air, severed by a bullet.

All around her, the fighting intensified as the members of Task Force Devil each dropped down onto one knee and began firing in short, controlled bursts. She knew she should do something, help somehow, but all she could do was stare in horror. It was so violent, so quick, so overwhelming.

The trees and bushes behind the attackers disintegrated under the impact of the bullets. The sweet smell of jungle rot was gone now, instantly overpowered by the stench of burning cordite. Empty brass casings flew through the air.

She started to climb to her knees to help.

"Get your ass down!" Alex yelled from behind her.

Bullets whipped over her head, and she dropped down again, trying to bury herself into the earth.

The attackers never stood a chance. Those closest went down first, cut apart by a wall of gunfire. Their odd, four-armed bodies just... came apart under the onslaught. The ones in the rear staggered into the dying front ranks, no doubt stunned by the carnage of modern firearms. But then a massive form burst through the stumbling attackers, knocking several down as it rushed at the soldiers. Cassie gasped, unable to believe her eyes. It was a creature out of a nightmare, more than twice the height of a man and wearing pieces of dangling metal and chain mail over its giant bloated body. Piglike tusks extended from its huge, tooth-filled mouth as it howled in rage. She recognized it from a lifetime of children's books and movies. *It's a troll.*

Rifle fire hit it, staggering the troll and slowing it down, but it kept coming, wounded perhaps but still dangerous. It was going to reach them. The bullets weren't stopping it.

Lightning arced across the clearing, washing out her GPNVGs again as a bolt of white-hot electricity struck the troll in its armored chest, picking it up and throwing it back to smash into the trees as though it had been hit by a truck. When her optics readjusted, Cassie saw Elizabeth standing her ground, the Brace on her hand crackling with electricity.

The troll didn't get back up. The other creatures, those that still lived, stood in stunned silence then tried to flee. Gunfire cut them down. "Pour it on, pour it on," Buck yelled. "Take 'em down. No survivors." He stepped forward after them, firing short bursts into the backs of the fleeing creatures.

The soldiers kept up their withering fire, now rising to move forward after Buck and putting down the attackers with aimed shots. Elizabeth stood in place, staring at the smoking corpse of the troll. Cassie climbed to her feet, her senses and emotions wild, dumbfounded at the carnage around her. What had started as an ambush had become a massacre for the attackers. None of the creatures had even gotten close enough to use their weapons.

No, that wasn't true. Cassie's eyes darted to the soldier who had been struck in the throat by the arrow. He was alive, still thrashing, and had dislodged his GPNVGs; it was Marcus, she saw with horror. His bloody fingers grasped feebly at the arrow in his throat. His eyes were wide with pain and fear. She ran to his side and fell to her knees next to him. Putting her hands over his body, she drew in mana and prepared to channel. *So much mana*, she thought and then felt immediately guilty. She needed to concentrate, needed to heal Marcus. *How is he even still alive?*

She channeled, sending healing energy into him. He reached up, grasping her, pulling her closer, trying to say something. She ignored him, concentrating on saving his life. She could feel his flesh reknitting, but the tissue damage was so severe—and that damned arrow! Every time she healed him, it cut him again.

She needed to get it out, and then she could heal him properly. This was pointless!

"What can I do?" asked Elizabeth from behind her.

"It's the arrow. I can't heal him."

Elizabeth grabbed her shoulders. In an instant, she felt the other woman sending mana into her, linking with her and augmenting her powers. Marcus gripped her hand. His eyes reflected his pain, his terror. His lips kept moving, but now he was only making unintelligible, wet grunts.

Someone knelt beside her. "Cassie, what do you need?" Alex asked.

"Get that fucking arrow out."

Alex grasped the arrow shaft, holding it tightly in both hands. Marcus stopped trying to talk and removed his hand from Cassie's, placing it on top of Alex's instead. Alex and Marcus stared at one another. Marcus nodded. Alex yanked the shaft, and Marcus went spastic with pain, but the arrow remained lodged in place, unwilling to come free. Someone else dropped down in front of Marcus's helmeted head and gripped it tightly between his knees, holding him in place. Cassie looked up, feeling helpless.

"Again," said Buck, the man holding Marcus's head. "Try again. Wiggle it this time."

"He'll die," said Alex.

"He's already dying. Do it."

Alex leaned over Marcus and pulled again. This time, as he pulled on the shaft, he rocked it back and forth. Marcus thrashed, but Buck leaned in, holding him down.

The arrow still wouldn't come free.

"I think it's barbed," said Alex.

"Again, Newf—do it!" yelled Buck.

Marcus had stopped screaming. Now, he was only making a pathetic mewling noise.

"Goddamn it," cried Cassie. "Please."

Alex swore and yanked again. This time, the arrowhead ripped free. Blood sprayed in Cassie's face, running down the lenses of her GPNVGs, obscuring her sight. Alex threw the wicked-looking barbed arrowhead aside with disgust. Now, Cassie channeled with everything she had and every little bit that Elizabeth lent her. She could feel the magic working, feel Marcus's flesh pulling back together.

Then, the healing just... stopped. The mana was no longer having any effect. Everyone stared at her.

Alex put his hand on her forearm. "Cassie. It's—"

She screamed in rage and tried again, redoubling her efforts. Nothing.

Elizabeth let go of her shoulders and stopped channeling. *She's given up. They've all given up.* Marcus stared at her with unmoving eyes.

Cassie stopped channeling, sat back, and pulled her knees up against her chest, wrapping her arms around them as she finally accepted what the others already had: she couldn't heal the dead.

Chapter 47

Cassie watched the soldiers wrap Marcus's corpse in a poncho and tie it closed. They cut down the desiccated corpse their attackers had left hanging—perhaps as some kind of macabre warning, perhaps only as a distraction—then wrapped it in another poncho, laying him, whoever he had been, beside Marcus. They left the bodies of the creatures—the four-armed, fish-faced monsters— where they had fallen. Up close, they looked even more frightening even in death. Their giant, saucerlike black eyes reminded Cassie of sharks as did their double rows of jagged teeth. Their skin was blue and covered in thick bristles. Two of their four arms were shriveled, weak little things that jutted out from just beneath their pectoral muscles. The other two arms, though, were long and strong with thick cords of muscle. Their necks were almost nonexistent, with bulbous, fishlike heads sitting on the shoulders. Even their legs were angled wrong—backwards—and they had cloven hoofs. They were clearly intelligent because they wore chain mail and iron helmets. They were armed with crude-looking but dangerous two-handed swords and axes. Several had also been armed with crossbows; a crossbow quarrel, not an arrow, had killed Marcus. Up close, their stench was gag inducing. No wonder

Clyde had been losing his mind.

Alex stood staring down at the two poncho-wrapped corpses.

"Did you know him?" Cassie asked.

He nodded, looking strange under his four-eyed optics. "His name was Eric. Eric MacDonald. He went through selection with me. He was a friend. So was Marcus, although Marcus was one of the US Deltas. Too many dead friends these days."

The men and women of Task Force Devil were more like a family, she realized, than an ad-hoc grouping of Americans and Canadians. *Is it because of shared dangers, the crucible of combat? Or maybe that's just how soldiers are.*

Lee would fit right in, she knew. Lee knew where he belonged in the world. Cassie wondered what that felt like.

Elizabeth shuffled beside Cassie, holding her rosary beads. She had been noticeably quiet since using the Brace to stop the troll. "You're not going to just leave them there, are you? Not like that on the ground?"

Her voice was strained, Cassie realized, and filled with pain as though she were crying beneath her GPNVGs. Clyde, standing next to Elizabeth for some reason, rubbed himself against her leg. She dropped down on one knee and hugged his large head tightly.

"For now, yes," Alex said. "Later, when we come back with McKnight, we'll take them home with us."

"But—"

"We have a job to do, Elizabeth. We've only got about eighteen hours to find the colonel and activate the keying device. There are limitations to how long the keying device can work. After that... well... we don't want to find out."

And with that, he turned away and approached Buck, who even now knelt by himself, studying a map he had placed on the ground. Alex dropped down on his knee beside the other man and moved his rifle, hanging from its sling, out of the way.

Cassie moved closer and looked over their shoulders, leaving Elizabeth to her solitude. *If she wants to talk, she'll talk.*

The map looked hand drawn, reflecting only the local surroundings, incomplete. "That's the best you got?" she asked.

"Yes, and it'll have to do." Buck traced what looked like a river with his finger.

"And where are we going?" she asked.

"Here." Buck let his finger rest on a bend in the river.

Alex looked up. "There's a settlement of some kind along the river. That might be where the dark-elf woman came from."

"How do you know that?" Cassie asked.

"Well… we don't," said Alex. "But that's all we have."

"No, we have Clyde," she said, glancing back to where the dog still sat next to Elizabeth.

Buck paused, watching her. "I let you bring that mutt, but what now? 'Cause I don't have a clue."

"I brought this." Alex pulled a green sock out of his pocket. "It's McKnight's. Maybe the dog will take the scent and just… you know, work on autopilot."

"That's a big maybe," said Buck. "And what the hell are you doin' with the colonel's dirty laundry?"

"I took it from his quarters."

Buck snorted. "Well… good then, good for you, Newf." This time Buck actually smiled, a big, gap-toothed grin. "How we doin' for ammo, 2-IC?"

It only took a moment for Cassie to figure it out. *2-IC: Second in command.* She was starting to speak army now.

"We're in reasonably good shape," Alex said. "Went through a mag or two each. They weren't expecting our firepower."

"Maybe," said Buck. "But now they know we're coming.

Advantage gone."

"Not necessarily." Alex leaned over the map and ran his finger from their LZ to the river. "The river makes a lot of noise, and we're at least three klicks away. That's a lot of distance in a jungle. With silenced weapons? I don't think anyone near the river could have heard the fight. And I'm pretty sure we got them all. We may still be good."

Buck sat upright, put his hands against the small of his back, and arched his spine, grunting. "Unless there's other patrols out there that are closer."

"This wasn't a patrol. They were here for us in case we came back. They've figured out this is where we show up. This was an ambush, but how long have they been waiting for us? It's been weeks since the last mission. If these things had known we were coming for sure, or what kind of heat we were packing, there would have been a whole lot more of them."

"Maybe," Buck said. "But for all we know, McKnight is already dead and in some monster's stew pot. We lost men back at the base, a lot of men. We just lost Marcus. How many more? And for what? This is all on me now, and it's starting to feel like a really bad idea. I'm thinking of calling it."

"The colonel's not dead. If that elf woman was going to just kill him, why go to all the trouble of bringing him here? The basilisk, the hellhounds? They were just cover so she could get onto the base and identify McKnight. He's still alive."

Buck shook his head. "I don't know. If they were waiting for us here, then…"

"We kicked their asses here," Alex said.

"Did you not see that fucking troll thing? Bullets didn't even slow it down. Had it reached us—"

"Elizabeth handled the troll," said Cassie. "She's tough. And I can heal anyone who gets hurt."

"You couldn't heal Marcus," Buck snapped.

She stood, speechless.

Alex gripped Buck's forearm. "Boss, we've got two sections of tier-one assaulters. We're armed with enough ammo and explosives to bring down a battalion. And we've got two mag-sens, one of whom can throw lightning bolts while the other can heal injuries. We're good. We're *real* good. We can still do this thing, especially if we move before the elves discover we're here. We've got the momentum now, and the surprise. Let's take advantage of it."

Buck stared long and hard at Alex and exhaled deeply. "I don't like you, Newf. I never did. I think you're weak, too concerned about what the troops think of you. But you're right about one thing. *El Salvador.* I do owe Colonel McKnight. He was there when I needed him, and I don't want to leave him, not if there's still a chance. Besides, maybe, just maybe, if we come back with the colonel, we can still turn this all around and keep our jobs. So, here's what we're gonna do: we'll give it a try. See if the dog-thing idea works. But when the time comes, I make the call. And if I say no, it's over. Got it?"

"Got it. You're in charge."

"No shit, I'm in charge. Okay then, two teams. You take wolfy boy there and Blondie—"

"My name is Cassie."

"She's not good for shit, but maybe she can be some kind of magic detector, give us an edge for a change."

Cassie sighed. "Thank you. You're too kind."

"Follow the dog, but stay away from the riverbank. If the natives have boats, I don't want to be seen. I'd rather not be hunted again."

Alex nodded. "Got it."

"Let's be clear. The locals see you, we're going home—got it? I've lost enough men on this shit-hole world."

"Got it," Alex said. "We'll be ghosts."

"See that you are." Buck folded up his map, stuck it in a pocket.

Alex climbed to his feet, grabbed Cassie's sleeve, and led her away. "Get ready. Can you really control the dog?"

She snorted. "I don't have a clue."

Elizabeth approached them, tugging on the sleeve of the Brace. "What about me?"

"You're going with the main group, the assault team," Alex said. "It'll be me and Cassie and three others. And Clyde."

"When?" Cassie asked.

"In about two minutes. Get some water into you. We'll be moving quickly, and it's easy to become dehydrated here."

Elizabeth gripped her hand. "Be safe."

Cassie nodded then dropped down on one knee and whispered into Clyde's ear. "You, my shaggy friend—I'm counting on you. We're all counting on you."

Clyde licked her face.

Chapter 48

Alex quickly picked the other three members of his recon team: Clara Anderson and Michael Toombs, fellow Canadians who had come over with Alex from Joint Task Force 2; and Paul Winters, an American Delta Force operator. He had served in Afghanistan with Clara and Michael and trusted both of them with his life, and so far, Paul had shown himself to be a solid soldier. But most importantly, all three were experienced jungle fighters who could move quietly through the thick brush, not an easy feat even for Special Forces.

Alex patted himself down one final time, satisfied that everything was where it needed to be. Cassie approached him, Clyde trotting along beside her. "You all set?" he asked.

She nodded, looking unrecognizable with her GPNVGs covering her face.

He didn't say it, but Alex thought they were going to look pretty stupid if the dog sniffed McKnight's sock then sat on his butt. Alex pulled the wool sock from his pocket.

"He doesn't like the basilisk," Cassie said, kneeling down beside the dog and stroking his head. "He may not want to follow it."

Alex snorted. "Neither do I."

Bending over, he held the sock out to Clyde. Clyde cocked his head, staring suspiciously at Alex and the sock. He sniffed it once, then looked away, clearly uninterested.

"Go on, Clyde," urged Cassie. "Go find McKnight. Hunt."

Clyde sat down on his bum and yawned.

"Come on, buddy," said Alex, aware that the others were watching them. "Go."

Clyde looked up at Alex, his canine eyes looking as though they were glowing green in the glare of Alex's GPNVGs. A sick feeling began to spread through Alex. "This isn't going to work, is it?"

Cassie slapped Clyde's flank, then pointed to the jungle around them. "Go, Clyde, go. Find McKnight."

"Come on, boy," said Alex. "Hunt. Track."

Clyde dropped down onto his belly.

Alex sighed, crossed his arms, and considered the dog. "I don't get it. The scent should still be strong, right?"

"There's something we're missing," said Cassie, stroking the dog.

Buck approached. "Something I need to know, Newf?"

"We'll figure it out," Alex answered. "Just give us a minute."

"This is stupid. I should never have—"

Cassie's head jerked up. "*Kaanetaah*," she said, excitement in her voice.

Clyde jumped to his feet, wagged his tail, and then began to pace back and forth across the clearing, his nose to the ground, sniffing in quick, short inhalations.

"What'd you do?" Alex asked.

"I paid attention. Clyde only works in Dane-Zaa, Athapaskan."

"You speak Dane-Zaa?"

"No. But I watched Paco back when we hunted the hellhounds."

At that moment, Clyde ceased his back-and-forth pacing and began to move more slowly, taking longer sniffs, focusing on one area of the clearing. Then he stopped. His body became erect, standing very tall. The German shepherd turned, stared at Cassie, and barked once, loudly.

"He's onto something," Alex said.

Cassie stepped closer. "He's got it. Good boy."

"What now?"

Cassie shook her head. "I'm thinking."

"Is there another—"

"Shh." She stood in place, watching Clyde, who stared back at her, waiting.

"Cassie."

"Shh."

Buck took a step closer, but without turning, Cassie raised her hand, palm pointing toward Buck, forestalling any attempt on his part to speak. Alex smiled. Even from here, he could feel the other man's anger.

"Aha!" Cassie suddenly seemed to stand taller. "*Dehdzat*," she exclaimed, pointing in the direction the dog had been facing.

Clyde turned and trotted into the jungle, following one of the many large game trails. Alex, smiling, pulled his carbine into his shoulder. "Let's go," he said to the others. "Cassie, you're with me. Danger close, everyone."

* * *

Alex followed Clyde through the thick jungle with Cassie and the others just behind him. They had been following the dog for over an hour. Alex had expected a tough go through thick vegetation, but the dog stuck to the animal trail. Had the basilisk and the dark-elf woman also taken this trail? Was it even wide enough for a creature that big? Certainly, a giant lizard would be at home in the jungle. Alex was no tracker. For all he knew, there could be spoor all around him, and he just wasn't seeing it. Or maybe the brush just grew back so quickly it had already covered the evidence of the basilisk's trail.

Maybe I just don't know what the hell I'm doing. Once again, Alex wished Paco were with them. He didn't say anything to Cassie, but the truth was that they really knew almost nothing of Rubicon. The first trip Alex had ever made had been the last one. And then, he hadn't made it off the LZ. Obviously, the dark elves had managed to train the hellhounds and the basilisk, but what other predators lived in this jungle that they had yet to run into?

Just ahead, Clyde had stopped and now stood silent, staring at the trail. Alex saw nothing but still felt very uneasy. Something was wrong, he knew, but he couldn't put his finger on what. Clyde growled a low, menacing rumble.

Alex slowly panned left and right, looking over the top of his M4. He saw nothing but jungle. Holding the weapon by the pistol grip, he raised his other hand and motioned for the others to stop. Then he slowly dropped down on one knee, lowering his silhouette. Clyde remained like a statue, still growling, his large bat-like ears standing straight up. Glancing over his shoulder, Alex looked at Cassie, wondering if she had detected any magic. She stared back, unrecognizable in her helmet and GPNVGs. She said nothing about mana.

They stayed like that, unmoving, for several minutes. Beads of sweat trickled down Alex's face, around and under his GPNVGs. The lenses were beginning to fog, always a problem in the jungle. Still, he saw nothing. Clyde had yet to move. The dog was far better equipped to detect threats, Alex knew, especially in an environment like this. But unlike Alex, who was constantly scanning back and forth, Clyde was staring directly ahead at the trail in front of them.

What am I missing?

The trail was empty. Other than a small pile of leaves rotting just ahead of them, there was nothing. He considered passing the dog, letting Clyde follow. Immediately, he changed his mind. *What's the point in bringing a dog if you're not going to trust its senses?*

With his left hand, he let go of the forestock of his rifle and pulled an M-84 flashbang free from his webbing. He brought the cylindrical grenade next to the hand holding the pistol grip of his rifle, taking his finger off the trigger just long enough to pull the pin. He still held the arming lever in place with his left hand, so the grenade wouldn't arm until he threw it, which would then release the lever.

Still watching his front, he held the flashbang up high for the others to see until he heard three distinct clicks through his MBITR—three individual acknowledgments that the others understood what was coming.

He let go of his pistol grip once again, letting the weapon hang from its sling, then tossed the flashbang at the trail ahead of them. He turned his head away quickly, closing his eyes as tightly as he could and sticking his fingers in his ears.

Sorry, Cassie. Sorry, Clyde. He didn't know how much Cassie would know about flashbangs, and there was no way to prepare the dog. Flashbangs produced a blinding flash of light, followed by a hundred-and-seventy-decibel bang, activating all of the human eye's photoreceptor cells while at the same time forcing all the fluid from the inner ear, resulting in a complete loss of balance. Those within the blast radius—especially if they were unprepared—would be blinded for seconds, their vision literally frozen to the image of whatever they had been looking at when the grenade detonated.

There was a popping sound as the arming pin spun free. Then the flashbang hit the path with a clunk. A moment later, it went off, the blinding flash still visible through Alex's tightly closed eyelids. The flash was accompanied by a senses-shattering bang that shocked him even though he knew it was coming.

It took a moment for the optics to readjust, but when they did, his heart pounded wildly. Not fifteen feet away, a massive spider thing, at least ten feet from pincerlike leg to pincerlike leg, with a torso as large as Clyde's, burst out of a trap hole in the center of the trail that had been covered by the rotting pile of leaves. The spider chittered angrily as it spun about, its legs thrashing madly. Clyde lay on his side, stunned by the flashbang.

To his credit, Alex's revulsion only made him pause for a moment, and then he opened fire, making sure he shot over the stunned German shepherd. He hit the spider with a quick burst of auto-fire that pinned it to the ground. It tried to rise again, but Alex switched his fire selector to semiautomatic and put multiple aimed shots of 5.56mm subsonic ammunition into it, shredding it. Pieces of spider splattered the jungle. Two of its legs, each at least the width of a tent pole, were cut loose from its body, as it stuttered to a jittery, bloody halt. Despite the effects of the flashbang, despite its wounds, the spider had still been trying to reach the helpless Clyde.

Alex shuddered.

"Enemy left, enemy left," someone called out from behind him.

A moment later came a long burst of suppressed fire. He glanced over his shoulder just in time to see another spider rushing them from the left side of the trail and then coming to a halt under the impact of bullets.

"Enemy right, enemy right," Clara called out, followed a moment later by more shots.

Jesus, I've led us right into a trap.

He snapped his attention back to his front. In an all-around defense, each of them needed to watch their own interlacing arcs of fire. His responsibility was to the front. He'd have to trust the others to do their own jobs. Another spider, seemingly coming from nowhere, was rushing at him. He opened fire again—perhaps a tad wildly this time, but he still hit it, dancing it back down the trail. Then he forced himself to slow down and put aimed shot after aimed shot into it. When he pulled the trigger and nothing happened, it came as a surprise. He canted the weapon to the side and saw the firing chamber was locked all the way back. He was out of ammo.

Focus, Alex. Focus. Stop acting like an amateur, and start counting rounds.

He ignored the dying spider as his fingers ran over his webbing, seeking a new magazine. As he did, he looked for new threats. Left to right, he saw nothing. Behind him, at least two of the others were still firing short bursts and aimed shots.

How many of these things are there?

Now Clyde began moving again, the effect of the flashbang wearing off. The dog shook his head then climbed to his feet, fell over again, and finally stood back up. He began to bark furiously, spinning in place. Alex ejected his empty magazine, let it fall to the jungle floor, and began to insert another.

"Above you," Cassie yelled out.

Alex's gaze darted up—just in time to see the spider on the tree branch above the trail, not six feet away. He rushed to finish loading and hit the holding-open device. It slammed forward, loading another round into the firing chamber, but it was taking too long, way too long. Any moment now, the spider would launch itself at Alex.

Can my armor stop its teeth?

But then, a small ball of fire, no larger than a baseball, struck the spider in its multi-eyed face, knocking it backwards off the tree branch. The spider shrieked as it struck the ground, landing on its back, its legs thrashing in the air. The stench of burning hair was foul. He raised his weapon to fire, but before he could, Clyde, a flash of green-hued fur and fangs, ripped into the spider, snarling and biting. Alex moved around them, trying to find a firing angle where he wouldn't hit Clyde, but he couldn't tell where the spider ended and the dog began.

So be it. Clyde is on his own.

He risked a glance behind him, doing a three-hundred-and-sixty-degree scan of his team. He counted three soldiers, all on one knee, all still alive and watching their surroundings. Three other monstrous spiders lay dead on the ground; the closest had come within several paces of their left flank before it had been stopped. Cassie, still standing, held her hands out in front of her as though she were about to throw a volleyball. She rushed forward, trying to get around Alex, to come to the aid of Clyde.

"No!" He grabbed her arm and pulled her back.

She couldn't do anything to help—she'd only get in the way or get hurt. With relief, he saw that Clyde didn't need any help anyway. The shepherd snarled and yanked his head back and forth, ripping free a massive chunk of the spider's body, including several of its legs. The rest of the body went flinging off into the jungle.

Clyde tensed, preparing to go after it.

"Clyde, stop!" Cassie yelled.

Impossibly, the dog came over to stand next to her, panting, spider blood dripping from his teeth, looking guilty. Alex looked around them again, now watching the trees above as well. He saw nothing.

"Call it," he said to the others.

"Nothing left," Michael reported.

"Clear right," Clara reported.

"Clear rear," Paul reported.

Alex sighed in relief. *Thank you, God.* That was more luck than he deserved.

"Reload and get ready to move again," he said. "Clara, call the contact in to Buck's team, and warn them to watch out for spider holes along the trails."

"Ack," Clara said as she loaded a new magazine into her weapon and began to communicate through her MBITR to the assault team.

Beside him, Cassie dropped down on one knee and hugged Clyde against her chest. Then she began to pat down the animal, searching for wounds.

"He okay?" Alex asked.

It took her a few moments, but she nodded. "I think so. Good boy. Good, good boy."

Alex snorted, prodding the carcass of the first spider with his carbine's silenced barrel. "No, that's a *great* boy. He saved our lives. If those things had hit us as we were walking over them…" He shuddered then faced Cassie. "And you. I didn't know you had it in you. Fireballs?"

She grinned, her teeth flashing beneath her GPNVGs. "Neither did I. The mana is crazy powerful here. Elizabeth would have burned it to a crisp, though."

"Don't sell yourself short. That was amazing."

"You're lucky I didn't set *you* on fire." She stood back up, confronting him, her hands on her hips. "I was still seeing two of everything. A little warning next time."

He slapped her on the butt as he walked past to check on the others. "Next time I hold up a flashbang, that *is* your little warning."

Chapter 49

Clyde led them down the trail for another forty minutes or so. On their left, Alex could now hear the river. There was a settlement nearby, he knew. Buck and his team had reported it while on an earlier mission—although, at the time, they had kept their distance. Luckily, it was still dark; there shouldn't be anyone awake—unless the locals were nocturnal. In truth, they didn't have a clue about the habits of the locals.

On occasion, the trail they followed ran into other trails, some leading to the river, others moving deeper into the jungle. At other times, they ran across what looked to be more spider holes, but fortunately they turned out to be nothing. Each time, though, stopping to check them out slowed the party down, and Alex warily watched the lightening sky. Rubicon's day-night cycle was similar to Earth's. And like Earth, it circled a star at just the right distance for life. All too soon, that star would begin to rise, greatly increasing the chances they would be seen.

A fog had settled in, blanketing the lowest furrows of the jungle in mist. Did it also presage the coming dawn? The jungle foliage began to thin, and the terrain opened up. The roaring of the river became much more pronounced, and Alex was sure the trail led to the water. Ahead, Clyde stopped again, turned back to look at Alex, and waited.

Alex crept up next to the animal and understood why he had waited. Just ahead, the trail met a pathway cleared through the jungle—a road. Wide enough for a cart or wagon, the road was churned and muddy with deep wheel ruts. *Well used, and recently, too.* A shiver of excitement ran through him. In the jungle, you only build roads to important places. He looked down at Clyde, who even now stared down the road—north, toward the river.

"That way?" he whispered to the dog.

Clyde panted.

"Go on, boy. *Dehdzat.*"

Clyde moved onto the road, his nose inches from the mud, sniffing. Alex and the others followed. The sound of flowing water intensified, and not long after, he saw the river for the first time, glowing green through the thinning trees and the light of his GPNVGs.

At the edge of the tree line, Alex crouched down beside Clyde. It was a large river, quickly moving, probably eighty meters wide at least. Where the road met the river, someone had gone to the trouble to clear away the trees, burning an open area—a primitive yet effective form of clear-cutting. Where the ground had been cleared was a sturdy wooden bridge, supported by massive twisting ropes and large enough for a wide wagon to pass over—or a basilisk. This was the only way across the river, and someone had gone to a great deal of trouble to build it, making sure it was high enough for small boats to pass beneath. On the other side of the bridge stood a wooden dock with small river barges tied up next to it. The land beyond the dock rose into a great dark hill that climbed out of the trees, dominating the surrounding jungle. He stared at the hill. Something wasn't...

It isn't a hill! It was too cylindrical, too natural. Nature hated perfect lines. It was a building—a stone fort with gently curving walls rising up like an upside-down bowl. He had almost completely missed it.

That's some serious camouflage. He pulled out his binoculars and examined the fort more closely. It was built entirely of dark stone and at least twenty meters high. Almost every inch of the walls was blanketed by a thick skin of grasping vines and brush, natural cover that further obscured the fort and hid it from prying eyes. Even staring right at it, the structure was easy to miss.

But the road led to the bridge, the bridge crossed the river, and the fort ruled the river. This was the center of power around here, Alex knew for a certainty. Because whoever sat within that fort dominated the main line of communication within the jungle: the river.

McKnight is in there. He has to be.

There was a tunnel entrance in the side of the fort. He could just make out the two large wooden doors, banded with iron bars, set within the tunnel. Guards stood before the entrance: at least six of those same four-armed humanoid creatures that had ambushed them earlier. They wore the same chain mail and carried large round shields and long spears. Over their backs, they wore the same curved two-handed great swords the others had carried. He didn't see any crossbows, but that didn't mean they weren't there. He scanned the curved walls of the fort but saw no fighting positions.

Alex lowered his binoculars. There was a soft rustling of leaves as Cassie dropped down beside him. He handed her the binoculars and waited. It took her some seconds to recognize what she was looking at, but when she did, her body stiffened, and she gasped.

"We're going in there?" she whispered.

"McKnight will be there. Can you sense anything?"

She closed her eyes for several moments as she concentrated then opened them again and nodded. "Someone's channeling, very close, very powerful. I think it's *her,* that dark elf. It feels like her."

Alex keyed his MBITR and reported what they had found to Buck. Buck acknowledged, noting that the assault team had also made good progress and was only about twenty minutes away. Alex cut the communications and glanced over at Cassie. "Sun's coming up. We need to move away from the road, get farther back into the jungle."

Alex left Toombs in place to watch the road, the bridge, and the fort—especially the fort. Being this close was dangerous, but they needed to keep eyes on the objective. Then he led Cassie back into the thick jungle, moving at least fifty meters away—far enough so that there'd be no way anyone could possibly see them. The rest of the team remained with Cassie and Alex, lying on their bellies and facing outward in a circle, watching the jungle as they waited for the assault team. Alex drank deeply from his Camelbak and had Cassie drink as well. Then he made sure they all ate. Even cold rations would give them calories for energy.

The sun began to rise, turning the eastern sky bright red. Here, just like Earth, the sun rose in the east. *What else is the same?* With the sun coming up, they lost their night-vision advantage. Alex sighed but flipped up his optics.

Less than a half hour later, the first members of the assault team appeared, moving silently through the bush. Alex sent Paul out to meet them, to guide them in to his position. When they were all in, Buck knelt down next to him, the lenses of his GPNVGs now also raised.

"Well?" Buck whispered.

"Come on," Alex said, climbing to his feet and leading the

other man to the edge of the river, where Toombs lay watching the fort. Both men lay down beside him, bringing out their binoculars to watch the enemy position.

Buck sighed heavily. "That's a strong position." He lowered his binoculars and looked at Alex's eye. "Too strong. That's a fortress."

"McKnight is in there."

"You don't know that." Buck looked through his binoculars again.

"The dog led us here. It makes sense."

Buck stiffened. "Fuck me…"

Alex lifted his binoculars just in time to see a giant flying creature the size of a minivan circling in the predawn sky above the fort. It looked like a cross between a lizard and a bat. Abruptly, the creature began to beat its massive wings to slow down and descended. It disappeared from sight, probably having landed on the domed top of the fort.

There had been a figure sitting atop the beast, riding it. Controlling it.

Buck lowered his binoculars. "We're done here."

"But—"

"This isn't going to happen—too much security."

"What are you talking about? McKnight's in there."

"No. This is insane. There's no way we're assaulting a castle. We don't have the firepower. We'll come back in force."

Alex stared at him. "What are you talking about? We need to—"

"Nothing!" Buck climbed to his feet, turned, and still hunched over, moved back to join the others within the bush.

Alex, feeling his anger building, went after him. Buck moved into the center of the soldiers, who each now lay prone, awaiting orders. He dropped down on one knee, pulled his map back out, and pondered it, his back to Alex. The message was clear: *we're done.*

We're not fucking done. Alex knelt beside him. "Sir, we can't just leave. We need to—"

"We don't need to do nothing." Buck glared at him, spit flying from his mouth. "There is no *we*. I'm in charge, and we're done here. I've made my call. We've got intel now. We know where they are. We head back and report what we've discovered. Someone much more senior can decide what to do next. At any rate, it's pretty obvious to anyone with half a brain that our governments won't want us starting an intergalactic war, not over one man."

"These dark-elf creatures have already started this, not us. They attacked us." Alex fought to remain in control of his emotions, but it was becoming increasingly difficult, and he knew it. *This is just like the last time, just like when I let him bully me into doing the wrong thing, into leaving men behind.* He exhaled and tried to choose his words carefully. "Sir, please listen to me. By the time we come back, *if* we come back, McKnight will be dead or gone. He's in there right now, and he's alive. I'm sure of it. This is the only chance we're ever going to get. You and I both know our governments will never, not ever, authorize a direct action against an alien race. They'll rationalize what these elves have done and explain how it was all our fault to begin with."

"Maybe it was our fault. You ever think about that?"

Alex sat back, suddenly understanding what was happening.

"Jesus Christ. You're afraid. Coming here, the rescue mission. It's all been an act, hasn't it? You're completely full of shit."

"The fuck you say?" Buck's face turned bright red.

Alex stood up as did Buck. The two men confronted one another, the threat of violence rolling from them in waves. Alex, too angry to think clearly, raised his voice. "This was all a show for the troops, maybe even for yourself. You never really meant it when you talked shit about going after the colonel, about owing him a debt. You just wanted people to see you as the warrior you think you are. You were never going to go through with this. You were only looking for an excuse to say, *Well, fuck it; we tried.* It's all bullshit, an act."

Buck's hatred and rage was palpable, a living thing. But behind the anger in the other man's eyes, Alex saw the briefest hint of indecision.

"We're done here, you immature little shit," Buck snarled. "You Canucks never should have been brought on board this op. You're not professional enough. We're going home. Now!"

Alex exhaled, briefly noting his surroundings and making sure he had room to move.

So, he thought, surprisingly calm. *This is really going to happen.* "No," he said quietly, simply… with finality.

Buck's chin rose as he looked down at Alex. "What's that, Captain? I didn't catch that."

"You caught it. We're not going without McKnight. We're not leaving anybody behind—not this time, not again."

Alex could feel the eyes of the others on them. Buck must have, as well, because his gaze darted to them. Once again, there was a flash of indecision in his eyes. Then Buck snorted, ignoring Alex. "Captain Benoit is under arrest. Take him into custody."

No one moved.

"We're going after the colonel," Alex said. "Leave if you want."

"No, we're not," said Buck.

"Balls yes, we are," said Clara. "You can go fuck yourself, you chickenshit prick."

Some of the others murmured their assent, but still others seemed uncertain, their gaze going from Buck to Alex. The tension built. *Mutiny,* Alex thought, aware of what he was doing but unable to stop it. *I'm advocating mutiny.* In centuries of warfare, soldiers had been killed for far less. But he couldn't help it, and he couldn't go back now.

I'm not leaving anyone behind again.

Masters, one of the Americans, came up behind Buck. "Major. You saw what they did to MacDonald. We can't leave the colonel to that. We can't—"

Buck rounded on the other man and rammed a heavy finger into his chest, knocking him back. "You shut your goddamned insubordinate mouth, or you're under arrest, too."

Masters flinched. "Sir... we can't leave—"

"We're going," Buck snarled, scanning the assembled soldiers, staring them down.

"Let's talk about MacDonald," Alex said. "Didn't you say he was dead?"

Buck's gaze snapped back to Alex, his eyes filled with desperation like a cornered animal.

"MacDonald is dead. They hung his—"

"He died *after* you bailed on him. His body was mutilated while he was still alive. You'd told me he was already dead. You ordered us to exfil while he was still alive, while he was being tortured. We don't leave our people behind."

"Fuck no, we don't," Clara said. Others mumbled angrily.

"We're moving," Buck said, his hand reaching down to the M4 hanging from his combat sling in front of him.

"After we get the colonel. Then, we're out of here." Alex's own hand rested on the butt of his M4, also hanging off his own sling. How fast was Buck?

Fast.

The world around Alex became crystal clear as the adrenaline rushed through his blood system, enhancing his fight-or-flight responses. Everything became fine-tuned—every leaf on the trees, every vine. He heard the gurgling rush of the river and the droning of insects around them; he saw the bead of sweat running down Buck's green-painted face.

Am I really going to shoot my superior officer? he asked himself, knowing the answer almost instantly, his heartbeat pounding a cadence in his ears: *no.*

I can't do that. So where does that leave me? About to die.

From somewhere nearby, Clyde growled.

Buck moved first, grasping for his M4, raising it to shoot from the hip. Rather than go for his own rifle, Alex threw himself to the side, hitting the ground, knowing all the while that it was pointless; at this range, Buck couldn't miss. But then Buck's M4 flew from his hand, the weapon's sling yanking him off balance before it snapped free. The carbine soared through the air, smashing into a tree trunk ten paces away.

Elizabeth stepped in front of Buck, her hands raised to stop him. "Wait."

Buck punched her solidly in the face. Alex heard the cartilage crunch as the young woman flew back, her nose a bloody ruin. Clyde leapt for Buck. Buck—insanely fast—twisted out of the way and hammered his fist into the top of the dog's head—dropping the animal in a heart-stopping moment. Alex, ignoring his own M4, which still hung from his sling, launched himself off the ground, tackling Buck around the knees. Both men went down, a tangled flurry of arms and legs. Buck hammered at Alex's jaw with his elbow, ramming into the bone as he tried his best to break it. Pain flared through Alex, but before the other man could hit him again, he head-butted Buck, smashing his helmet into the other man's chin. Blood flowed from Buck's face as his head snapped back. But he came on again, a wild insanity in his eyes, like a wild animal, driven thoughtless by the need to rend and kill.

They rolled atop one another, each fighting for leverage, each trying to control the other's limbs to get an advantage, an opening. Alex was no amateur in ground fighting—he had studied martial arts and jujitsu for most of his adult life—but Buck was crazy good, and so strong. At any moment, Alex expected the others to rush forward and hold him down while Buck finished him. After all, he was a traitor now.

But no one interfered. This fight, it seemed, was just between the two of them. Alex saw a flash of steel. A knife! Buck had somehow freed his fighting knife in the struggle. Knife fighting was always bad, always bloody—even when you won. Alex was only vaguely aware as his body went through an instant adrenaline dump: his mouth went dry, his heartbeat surged, and his vision focused, tunnellike, on the other man. Pain disappeared; fear disappeared—only muscle memory and training remained. Alex assumed full-guard position, locking his legs around Buck's torso to control him. Unable to get in the position of leverage he needed, Buck still tried to ram the knife into Alex, but only managed to catch it against the edge of Alex's ceramic plate. In desperation, Alex gripped Buck's knife hand with both of his and yanked, rolling to the side. Buck elbowed Alex in the face, connecting solidly with his jaw. Alex saw bright lights but rammed his knee into Buck, aiming for the groin. Buck twisted his leg away, and Alex missed, but struck again, this time hitting the mass of nerves along the outside of Buck's thigh. He connected, and Buck gasped in pain, creating space between them. Before Alex could take advantage of his opening, though, Buck was back on top, trying to shove the knifepoint into Alex's throat with both hands. Alex caught Buck's forearms, but the other man was larger, heavier, and stronger. The knifepoint descended.

Then the blade shattered, pieces flying away. Buck stared in confusion at the broken knife. The blade had somehow snapped off, leaving only an inch protruding from the hilt. Alex's eyes darted to the side, where Cassie stood only paces away, the pistol he had given her held in both hands. Tendrils of smoke drifted from the end of the silencer.

"Get off him right goddamned now, you—"

Buck threw the broken knife, hitting her in the face, and she fell back.

Reaching up, Alex gripped the sides of Buck's helmet and wrenched it, twisting it—and Buck's neck. Buck, feeling the pressure on his neck, panicked and rose up on his knees, trying to pry Alex's hands free. But Alex didn't fight his grip; instead, he used the other man's distraction to flip him over onto his side. Then he slipped out from beneath him, coming up over top of the prostrate man, who now lay on his belly in the dirt. Realizing too late his mistake, the larger man thrashed and bucked his hips, desperate to get away, to get Alex off. Alex slammed his knee into Buck, right over the T-12-L1 thoracic vertebra. He grabbed the sides of Buck's helmet again, and—knowing he had to move quickly or risk letting the other man escape—twisted it savagely up and to the side.

Buck's neck snapped—a sickening, grinding crack. He yelped once and stopped fighting.

Alex fell onto his side, panting, gasping huge breaths of air, and still seeing spots in front of his eyes. *What did I just do?*

He got to his knees. Buck stared at him, surprise and terror in his eyes. His lips moved slowly. Spit bubbles popped at the corner of his mouth. Almost instantly, there was the smell of feces in the air. Alex looked up and saw Cassie watching him, her hand held against her cheek, blood tricking through her fingers. Their eyes locked. "Please. Do something," he said.

She ran to Buck's side, the gash in her cheek still dripping. Dropping down on her knees, she placed both hands on Buck's head, closed her eyes, and concentrated.

Alex was sick, certain he was going to vomit. *Traitor. I'm a traitor.*

Cassie looked up at Alex, shook her head quickly. "I'm sorry."

No, he realized, looking at Buck's dead eyes, now glassing over. *Not a traitor. I'm a murderer.* He climbed to shaky feet, meeting the accusing, unbelieving eyes of the other soldiers. He nodded, accepting his fate. "Okay, I give up. Arrest me."

Clara stepped forward, looking from Buck's corpse to Alex, and finally around her at the other soldiers. "You can surrender to the colonel... once this shit is done."

"But..."

Masters stood beside Clara. "We're not leaving the colonel. We told him that. We told him."

"You're in charge now, Captain," said Clara. "Until you're not in charge. Just deal, all right?"

The rest of the task force, or what was left of it—Canadians and Americans—nodded, each looking Alex in the eye.

Then he understood: they had come all this way to bring back Colonel McKnight. And they were *going* to bring him back.

Chapter 50

Cassie couldn't bring Buck back from the dead, but she could heal Elizabeth's broken nose—well, mostly. Even after fusing the cartilage together again, Elizabeth's former pert nose now had a pronounced bump, making her look like a boxer. Cassie had also somehow managed to heal Clyde. Buck's attack had hurt the dog badly, fracturing his canine skull. But even after fusing the bones back together, the dog was still so badly hurt they had decided to sedate him, giving him an injection of painkillers as well as something that put him into a deep slumber. Alex had said it was similar to an induced coma. There had been no other choice: there were no vets here.

Cassie removed her palms from Elizabeth's face. "I'm sorry. I can try again later. It's been a hell of a night."

Elizabeth tentatively reached up and ran her fingers over her nose. "No. It's fine. Thank you." She looked at Cassie's face, at the sutures in her cheek. The gash still throbbed. "I'm sorry I can't heal, or I'd do the same for you."

"It's okay," said Cassie. "Dudes dig scars, right?"

Elizabeth's smile was real, not forced. "Thank you for this, for helping Alex. Thank you."

"Sh… sure." Cassie's voice cracked as her eyes darted to the poncho-wrapped corpse of Buck, not ten feet away, another life she couldn't save.

Elizabeth surged forward and hugged Cassie, too tightly. It was a weird sensation, being hugged while wearing body armor and combat webbing, but Cassie returned the embrace just the same. "God's will, Cassie, not yours. We'll save the colonel—you'll see."

Elizabeth then sat back and handed Cassie her helmet. The jungle around them was still shrouded in shadows, but soon, the sun would be over the trees. Even now, birds and other wildlife were waking, greeting the alien dawn with song. Whatever Alex was planning, he needed to make his move soon. She glanced at where he knelt, apart from the others, scribbling away on a notepad, planning his attack. *How can he concentrate after killing Buck? He must know he's going to jail as soon as we get back.*

If we get back. The basilisk was within that fort. And the dark-elf woman and her strange four-armed soldiers.

Alex leaned back. Then he asked Clara to gather the others, leaving only Toombs still watching the fort. They formed a circle around him, kneeling on the ground close enough so they could hear him. Alex motioned Cassie and Elizabeth over, and the soldiers cleared a space for them. He tore a page out of his notepad and placed it on the ground in front of them. Cassie saw that he had sketched the river, the bridge, and the hill fort. It was actually a pretty good drawing with rough distances drawn in.

He looked up, letting his gaze sweep their faces. "Okay, here's the thing. We've lost the night, and we're running out of time. We know of only two ways into that fort: the dragon-landing pad on the roof, and the entrance across the bridge."

The soldiers jostled each other to see more clearly. Clara leaned in and gazed at the drawing then looked up at Alex. "We haven't scouted out the rear. There may be another way in."

"Maybe. But there's no time to check," Alex said. "This place is isolated, and I think they want it that way. There have to be other settlements—villages, towns—along the river, and this road must lead to the one we do know of. But I think for most of the locals, water is life, even on an alien world. The river is probably the main line of communication. I don't think people hike through this jungle; it's just too dangerous."

"Other than us," someone said. Quiet laughter spread through them, and even Alex smiled.

"Exactly right," said Alex. "So they won't be expecting us to come from the jungle. They haven't even cleared the brush around their fort. These things—these elf creatures and their weird fish-faced, four-armed soldiers—they're not expecting anyone to take them on. I think maybe they're the big dogs around here. They're secure in their fort, not worried about attack."

"But they're living in a stone fortress with only two entrances, one of which we can't get to. The other one is guarded by a small army."

"Not an army, just a section," said Alex.

"Okay, a section, then. How do you expect to get past them? Fight your way in?"

"Maybe. But I don't want to. There's too much we don't know about these things. The last thing I want is that elf woman throwing fireballs down at us as we bunch near the entrance taking on her soldiers. Besides, they might use that flying-dragon thing we saw earlier to move the colonel."

"How do you know that?" Elizabeth asked.

"Because it's what I'd do. Once you capture a significant prisoner, you move him somewhere safe for interrogation."

"A stone fortress in the middle of a jungle isn't safe?" Cassie asked.

Alex sounded tired as he met her eyes. "I don't know, Cassie. We've barely even seen these creatures, these dark elves. We have no real intelligence on them—we don't know how they're organized, how they live. All we've seen is this jungle and the river. I can only guess based on what I would do if I were them."

"So, what do you suggest?" Clara asked.

Alex paused. "We need to put someone inside *before* we hit them. We'll plant C4 on the gate to make sure the entrance stays open. Once that's done, that same team can move deeper within the fort and find and secure McKnight before they can move him or kill him."

Clara leaned in. "You gonna just walk right past the guards?"

Alex stared into Cassie's eyes. "Yes. That's exactly what we're going to do."

Cassie sat back, realization gripping her. "You've got to be kidding me?"

Alex pointed through the trees, in the direction of the river. "Sun's coming up, Cassie. Alien world or not, people have things they have to do. That dock is going to get active. So is the road. Those creatures will open that door. Once they do, we'll slip inside, invisible."

"You don't know that," she said. "What if it stays closed? What if I can't do this? Hell, I almost certainly can't do this. You have no idea how hard it is to channel that much mana for that long."

"The elf woman did it for hours," said Alex.

Elizabeth reached over and gripped Cassie's hand. "You can do this, Cassie. You're good at it."

Cassie pulled back. "You're better. You have the Brace."

"I'm better at fighting, not at turning invisible. I can't do that at all, or heal. It has to be you."

"I don't think I can. You don't understand." Her eyes darted about. She felt trapped by their gazes, by their expectations. They didn't get it, didn't understand what happened whenever she took chances. Once again, she saw the slurry of mud as it poured through the shattered rear window of her parents' car, saving her but killing them. She had taken a chance, taken action—and killed her parents because of it. Then, at the hospital, it had been her channeling—her screwing around with forces she didn't understand—that had attracted the dark elf and her basilisk.

Her parents were dead because of her. Her sister was dead because of her. Whenever she took chances, people died.

"Cassie," said Alex. "We have to try. You have to try."

"You can do this," said Elizabeth. "I know you can. We trust you."

"You can do this, Cassie," said Clara.

The others all murmured in agreement, nodding their heads.

She closed her eyes, heard her mother's last words: *we love you, baby*. Her parents would have wanted her to try, to take a chance and commit to something… even if she failed.

She nodded.

Chapter 51

Cassie stood in place while Alex inspected her, making sure she was ready. Clara stood just to the side, also scrutinizing her—although they both called it "helping." Cassie, under Clara's supervision, had removed most of her kit and was now wearing only what she would need inside the fort: body armor, helmet with GPNVGs, small first-aid kit, and ballistic glasses with orange-tinted lenses. Clara had applied a fresh coat of camouflage paint to Cassie's face, neck, and hands, covering every inch of exposed skin. She still had her pistol, but now she carried it openly in a shoulder holster that had belonged to Buck, which kind of felt ghoulish, but Alex had insisted.

"Jump," Alex ordered.

"What?"

"Jump up and down. We need to make sure you don't jingle."

She gave him her best scornful gaze. "You think I'm stupid enough to come here with change in my pocket?"

I don't have change in my pocket, do I?

"Just jump, Cassie," Alex said, exasperation in his voice.

Frowning, she did as he asked, secretly grateful that she didn't, in fact, jingle.

"Happy?"

He mumbled something incoherent, rubbing his chin.

"What now?"

"I'm wondering if we need the armor at all."

Clara stepped forward, her lips a hard straight line. "Captain, she's gonna need protection once the shooting starts. So will you."

Alex bit his lower lip, a look of concentration on his face.

"There's *going* to be violence," Clara said.

Finally, Alex nodded. "Okay. Fine. We'll go in heavy."

Like Cassie, he had stripped away most of his nonessential gear, and was now only wearing what he'd need. Unlike her, though, he had kept all of his ammunition and weapons. He also carried the plastic explosives for the gate in a small backpack.

"Don't I need some of those?" Cassie asked, pointing to one of the grenades stuffed into his load-bearing vest.

"Not a chance."

"Well, why can't I have a real gun, then?" She glanced at his M4.

He shook his head. "Carbine, and just concentrate on the magic."

"You taught me to shoot for a reason, remember?"

He paused, his mouth partially open, then sighed. Like her, he wore orange-tinted ballistic glasses over skin covered with camouflage paint.

"We've spares now, Captain," Clara said.

He mumbled something incoherent again.

"Someone's gonna have to watch your back in there." Clara said. "You kind of suck at that."

He frowned at Clara then looked back at Cassie. "You put it on safety, and you leave your finger off the trigger unless you intend to kill someone, and then you don't hesitate."

Cassie nodded quickly, repeatedly. "No problem."

He shook his head then faced Clara. "Do it fast. We're moving in five."

"On it, Boss."

He walked away, leaving Cassie alone with Clara. "Not Buck's," he called over his shoulder. "Elizabeth threw it against a tree."

"Marcus's," she said with a nod, darting away. Seconds later she returned with an M4 in one hand and two extra magazines in the other. Stuffing the magazines into a pocket on Cassie's vest, she inspected the rifle, ejecting the magazine and holding it with one hand while she worked the action with the other. Finally, she reinserted the mag and handed the weapon to Cassie. "You've got twenty-nine rounds in the mag with one already in the chamber." She met Cassie's eyes, now looking very serious. "You understand what that means?"

Cassie exhaled, focused on remaining calm. "It means the weapon is ready for firing."

"Once you take the safety off. Do you know how to do that?"

"I... yes, I remember."

"Show me," Clara said.

Cassie did, flicking the fire selector just above where her thumb would be when she held the pistol grip, moving it from safety to repetition.

"Good. Now put it back on safety, and try not to shoot the Captain in the back of the head, okay?"

"Got it."

Alex came back. "We ready?"

Cassie nodded. "As ready as I'm going to be."

"Sun's up. Let's do this."

He led her and Clara back to the water's edge, staying within the tree line. They went prone at the edge of the trees at a spot where they could watch the bridge, the dock, and the fort. In daylight, the river glowed green, just as it did at night with the GPNVGs. What had she been expecting? They remained like that for some minutes, waiting. They were banking a lot on Alex's guess that the inhabitants weren't nocturnal.

Sure enough, as the sun's rays spread across the jungle, the fort came to life. Figures approached the dock, appearing as if from nowhere. They were small—much smaller than the four-armed guards—and slender, with sun-bronzed skin and bright-red hair. They moved about the dock with grace and skill, going about their day. Even from a distance, she could hear their voices, their laughter. Alex was right; there must be a village nearby. But these creatures looked nothing like the dark elf or her guards. They reminded her, she realized, of little people, dwarves or ... gnomes. Yes, gnomes; they reminded her of garden gnomes. Although they didn't have long white beards or pointed shoes.

"Where did they come from?" she whispered.

Alex shook his head.

She peered at the gnomes on the dock, who moved about the barges. They wore little clothing, mostly loincloths, reminding her of pygmies in the rain forests of South America she had read about in National Geographic. Pygmy-gnomes?

Then she heard the creaking of wagon wheels on the road. A wagon appeared, pulled by a six-legged lizard the size of a cow. Seated on the cart was another of the redheaded pygmy-gnomes.

"There *is* a settlement nearby," said Alex. "That's where the road must lead, to a village."

The wagon crossed the wooden bridge, which creaked under its weight. On the other side of the bridge, two of the four-armed guards walked over to meet it. They spoke to the driver, and then one of them climbed onto the back of the wagon, looking through the wooden boxes and barrels stuffed on its bed.

"Come on," whispered Alex, watching through his binoculars. "You know what I need you to do."

The guard on the back of the wagon jumped down again, and the redheaded driver picked up his reins. The wagon began to move forward again toward the still-shut gate doors.

"Do it," said Alex.

The other guards opened the doors wide, exposing a dark tunnel and a raised metal portcullis. The wagon drove through the gate, which remained open. Alex looked over at Cassie. "Ready?"

She didn't feel ready, but if they were going to do this, it had to be now. Closing her eyes, she concentrated, drawing mana into her body and pooling it within her, twisting the energy about her and Alex. The last time she had channeled invisibility, the basilisk had been charging them. She had reacted out of pure instinct and had gotten lucky. This time, though, the casting was much easier than she had expected it to be. The flows of mana did exactly what she wanted, wrapping around her and Alex, forming a light-altering shield. Either she was getting far better at channeling mana and becoming a world-class mag-sens, or magic was just much easier on Rubicon. Maybe both. She suddenly had a new idea: *what if I tie the spell off in place and just leave the energy wrapped around us, like a shield, so it moves with us?* Somehow, that felt right. She gave it a shot, surprising herself when it worked. The invisibility shield held. This way, she realized, it would travel with them, requiring only a trickle of mana to stay in place. She beamed with pleasure, never having realized she even knew how to do this. That must have been what the dark-elf woman had done. *Well, how about that?*

Still smiling, she opened her eyes and flashed a smile at Alex. "Done."

"Are we...?" He paused, staring down at himself. "But I can

still see you."

"There's an invisibility weave... or shield if you prefer, tied around both of us. But we need to stay close, super intimate." She winked. "Still, no one else outside the shield should be able to see us."

Alex glanced at Clara, who stared at them open-mouthed.

"Cap, she's right," said Clara. "I can hear you but you're just... gone."

"Feel better?" Cassie asked Alex.

"I..." The uncertainty was still on his face as he stared at his hands, then Cassie, and then Clara. "This is so weird."

"Tell me about it," Cassie said as she climbed to her feet. "Keep close to me. The shield travels with me, not you. Don't go darting off on your own."

"Good luck, Cap," Clara said.

Alex put his arm around Cassie's shoulder, and they began to make their way down to the road and the bridge. None of the guards reacted. None of the gnomes reacted.

Cassie flashed Alex a smile then led him to the bridge. She knew her spell was still in place, but she still half expected the guards to start yelling and rush at them with their weapons. They did nothing.

"Son of a bitch," whispered Alex. "I think this is working."

"Shh," whispered Cassie.

They crossed the bridge and walked past the dock, right by several of the redheaded gnomes. Their ears were pointy, their skin bronzed and freckled. They worked barefoot and bare chested, laughing and chattering amongst themselves as they jumped about the barges. She didn't understand a word, but their language seemed to have a lyrical quality. If she hadn't been so frightened, she'd have smiled. Instead, she turned her gaze to the approaching guards and the gate.

Standing slightly taller than men, these four-eyed fish things smelled like cold vomit on a hotdog bun. She breathed through her mouth. One of the creatures was staring right at her with its dead black eyes. It sniffed the air like a dog, and Cassie's fear spiked. But then it looked away again. Cassie and Alex drifted past. She was drenched in sweat, but her spell was working.

Seconds later, they were past all six of the guards and at the tunnel entrance. The interior of the tunnel was black, completely dark. She almost bolted in fear when she suddenly heard cloven hooves clumping quickly toward her and Alex from the recesses of the tunnel. Had they been detected?

Alex wrapped his arms around her waist and pulled her back against the wall—just as six more guards marched past, heading out. One of them even brushed against Cassie.

She reminded herself to breathe.

The new guards spoke in a language that sounded to her like a series of guttural grunts and hawking noises, as if they were about to spit out boogers. Then, the first six guards turned and entered the tunnel, again walking right past Cassie and Alex.

Sentry change.

"Wait," Alex whispered into her ear.

He let go of her waist, removed his small pack, and pulled out the block of C4 plastic explosives. Kneeling down beside one of the thick wooden doors, he attached a small device the size of a key fob to the explosives. The block of C4 was much smaller than she would have thought—the size of a paperback novel. *Will that be enough?*

She looked up at the metal portcullis above them, at the half-foot-thick black wooden door. Using adhesive, Alex attached the C4 to the bottom of the door between it and the wall. He then covered it with weeds and dirt from the floor while keeping a wary eye on the guards only paces away.

This is taking too long. She could still see the C4 even though it was covered with dirt. On the other hand, she already knew it was there. *If no one thinks to look down, how long will it go unnoticed?*

He activated his MBITR, made sure the guards were too far away to hear him, and then whispered into his mike. "Clara, we're in. The charge is set. Ten minutes."

Cassie heard the single click in her earpiece, acknowledging Clara had heard Alex.

"Be advised, you're going to need to go in with night vision. The tunnel and interior of the fort is dark."

Once again, there was a single click.

Alex lowered his GPNVGs into place, waiting while Cassie did the same. When she activated them, she saw clearly down the previously dark tunnel. Alex, looking bizarre with the GPVNGs over his face, raised his M4 back into his shoulder and motioned with his head for her to follow him. She stayed so close she was breathing down his neck.

They had ten minutes to find McKnight.

Chapter 52

Maelhrandia lay on cushions, feeling at ease with herself despite the presence of her guest—her sister Horlastia, who had only just arrived on her wyvern with the dawn. Her mage-warden sister also languished on a pile of cushions, nibbling at her plate of spiced Rosena ants. Horlastia had removed her armor and weapons and now wore only a simple green-silk robe cinched tight around her waist. Maelhrandia had provided the robe, but her sister was obviously too large for it in the shoulders. Neither would mention anything, however; that would be rude.

Horlastia picked up a small, engraved silver cup filled with Maelhrandia's finest Talahari ghost-wine and sipped from it, feigning relaxation. Maelhrandia knew that Horlastia, like her, would never truly let down her guard in the presence of another member of the royal family. Everything was an act, an unspoken game of pretend. They'd pretend to love one another; they'd pretend to trust one another—they'd pretend they didn't plot to kill one another. The ghost of a smile pulled at the corners of Maelhrandia's lips as she watched her sister. *How wonderful it would be to have you, dear sister, as a secret prisoner within my dungeon.*

Maelhrandia sighed and reached for a crisped ant. Her teeth crunched through the carapace, letting the bitter juices run across her tongue. There had been no decent food in the Old World, nothing like in faerum.

"Mother is pleased, dear sister," Horlastia said, smiling her fake smile. "The seelie court speaks of nothing but you. Truly, you are the hero of legend we always knew you to be."

Maelhrandia inclined her head. "You are far too kind, sister."

You are a lying sack of stinking dwarf placenta, dear sister.

On at least three occasions, Maelhrandia's spies had brought proof of Horlastia plotting against her. Once, her sister had even tried to kill her.

Horlastia's dark eyes shone in the flickering candlelight. "Our mother would move quickly."

"Really? Our mother moves in haste?"

Horlastia waved her hand. "Oh, she pretends that the Old World is unimportant, but those of us who know her best know better. She is excited."

"I don't think our mother has ever been excited."

Horlastia sipped her wine. "You forget House Tlathlandis. She was excited then."

Maelhrandia inclined her head. When their mother had finally brought down House Tlathlandis, she had ordered their ancient matriarch skinned alive by the royal torturers, along with all thirty-seven of the matriarch's daughters and sons. A magnificent, if chilling, lesson for others who would dare to rise above their station.

"Our mother has no need to move quickly, dear sister," Maelhrandia said in a chastising voice. "One must be patient, careful."

"Until it's time to be bold."

"Indeed."

Maelhrandia wanted to kill Horlastia, but she didn't truly hate her. Horlastia was an older sister, ahead of Maelhrandia in the line of secession. But their mother lived a remarkably long life—thanks to the Culling. The only sure way to gain power was to *remove* those ahead of you and, when necessary, those coming up too quickly behind you as well. Sisters were expected to murder one another. Maelhrandia herself had killed three of her siblings.

"Has Mother dispatched the Blood Lance to the other houses yet?" Maelhrandia asked.

"No. But soon, I think. Much will depend on your prisoner."

"Our mother's prisoner, you mean. I am but a loyal servant of the court. I do everything for her glory." Maelhrandia raised one delicate hand and examined her nails closely, as if this conversation bored her.

"Of course, dear sister." Horlastia wasn't smiling anymore.

"The prisoner will know—"

Someone channeled within her keep, activating one of the wards placed near the main entrance. *There's a mage in my keep. An assassin!*

Maelhrandia's gaze darted to her sister. Her fingers brushed against the blade she had concealed in the small of her back. Was this her sister's treachery? Horlastia gave no indication anything was wrong. It had only been a trickle of magic, just enough to activate the ward, and Horlastia would not be attuned to Maelhrandia's personal ward.

Horlastia, perhaps noting something in Maelhrandia's face, watched her with suspicious eyes. "What is it? Is something wrong?"

Maelhrandia sat up, pulled her knees against her chest, and wrapped her arms around them, considering her sister. She had just successfully completed a glorious mission—she'd been the first of the fae seelie to return to the Old World since the Banishment. At the moment, her honor was unmatched. But she had also made herself a target. Would one of her sisters dare strike her now, before their mother could reward her? Was Horlastia that bold, entering her keep at the same time as her assassin? If the assassin failed, she must know she'd be vulnerable. Horlastia was arrogant, though, and always had been. If she was behind this, she'd die here, in chains, deep beneath the keep. Her mother would let Maelhrandia have her—especially if she had proof of Horlastia's betrayal. But she needed that proof, and she'd get it. The intruding mage was clumsy, inept. She'd capture the mage and obtain a confession.

Then it would be Horlastia's turn in chains.

Maelhrandia watched her sister. "When will you return to the court?"

"This evening, I think. Once the sun sets. A shame to fly all this way and not spend time with my beloved sister, the hero who shall bring us glory, who defeated one of the ancient demons."

"You flatter me, sister. I only did my duty as you would have." Slowly, as if she had not a care in the world, Maelhrandia set her wineglass down and climbed to her feet. She stretched like a burr-cat, both arms above her head, groaning with pretend fatigue. "Oh, my dear sister," she purred. "I would dearly love to spend more time with you. I love you so much, but my mission has tired me so, and I must sleep."

Her sister's eyes narrowed. "Of course, my love. I am the rude one, keeping you awake after all you have done for us—having just returned from the field of battle."

Maelhrandia cocked her hip to the side, placed a hand on it, and arched an eyebrow. "Hardly battle, sister. The manlings are little better than dwarves, ripe for the Culling."

"To the Culling," said her sister, saluting her with her wineglass. "Sleep soundly, hero of the seelie court. I shall bring our mother your love as well as your prisoner."

Maelhrandia forced herself to move slowly, as if turning her back to her sister was of no concern at all. She sauntered to the door, half expecting a knife in her back. But Horlastia did nothing, and Maelhrandia slipped out and onto the landing. Softly closing the door behind her, she turned and faced the spiraling stairs of her tower.

Time to hunt an assassin.

Chapter 53

Cassie followed Alex through the darkened corridors of the stone fort, a feeling of dread hovering over her. This couldn't possibly work, but… so far, it kind of had. She heard the odd language of the four-armed guard creatures ahead. Sure enough, the tunnel led past a large chamber on their right that looked like a guard barracks, filled with tables and beds. At least a dozen of the guards sat around, talking amongst themselves or sleeping or playing some sort of dice game—and there was another of those huge trolls. It sat alone in a corner, staring at nothing, spit running down its chin.

Alex pulled her quickly past the chamber and then farther on into the fort. The corridors were wide, large enough for the basilisk. After only a few minutes, she realized the fort was actually much bigger than it appeared from the outside. Guttering candles burned in wall sconces, creating pools of light in the darkness, but the light didn't travel far; the walls, built entirely from black stone, seemed to leach the glow of the flames. Letting her fingers trace the walls, she considered their construction. They were smooth as glass but without a hint of a reflection and cut so perfectly they left barely a trace of a seam; moving past them was like walking down a dark dream. There were no windows, no ambient light, not even an arrow slit. And other than the guards and the troll they had seen in the barracks, they had yet to see another living creature.

The corridors led on, mazelike. Alex paused, stopping at an intersection. He keyed his MBITR and whispered into it. She heard his radio communication, but there was no other response. He tried again several more times then shook his head. "The walls must be blocking the radio waves." He stared way down the intersecting tunnels. "Which way?"

"I have no idea," Cassie whispered, perhaps a tad sharply.

"You all right?"

"Getting tired. I'm been holding this shield for too long. It's starting to get to me even with it tied off."

"So, let it go."

"Are you crazy? We'll be seen."

"We're already in. If we see someone, we hide."

"And what if that doesn't work?"

"I'll kill them."

She stared at him for a moment, realizing he wasn't joking. She exhaled then let go of the spell. Instantly, a feeling of vertigo swept through her, and she stumbled back into him. He grabbed her shoulders, holding her while the vertigo passed.

"Better?"

She nodded and leaned into his shoulder. "You actually do this for a living?"

He chuckled and shook his head. "Nobody does *this* for a living." He indicated the corridor on their right. "Let's try this way. Keep your eyes open for stairs leading down."

"Why down?"

"Down is where dungeons are. That's where you keep prisoners in a castle, right?"

"I guess."

Minutes later, they came to another intersection. Once again, Alex led them to the right. But this time, no sooner had they started moving down the corridor than they heard movement ahead of them. Someone was coming.

He grabbed her arm, dragging her back the way they had come and into a nearby storeroom filled with stacks of wooden crates and barrels and smelling of mold. They ducked behind several large crates just before a small gaggle of the four-armed fish creatures hurried past, chattering to themselves. Unlike the previous group, these were unarmed and wore only tunics and short pants, making Cassie wonder if they were servants rather than guards.

The two of them remained hidden within the storeroom for another minute. Then Alex moved to the doorway and peered around it in the direction the creatures had gone. After only a moment, he motioned for her to follow, and they continued on. Soon, they came to yet another intersection, and once again, Alex led her to the right. They passed more rooms, most with thick black doors, but saw no other servants and heard no one else.

She wasn't sure how long they had been wandering about, but they had to be running out of time. They came to an elaborate stone entranceway, an arch, that led into a dark open area—a courtyard of some type, filled with bizarre plants and glowing mushrooms that shone brightly through the night-vision devices. Alex peered around the stone archway. "There's a tower in there in the center. It looks like it rises up all the way to the covered ceiling and goes right through it. Maybe it's important."

She peered around his shoulder. "Someone in that tower just channeled," she whispered.

A moment later, her heart almost stopped when she saw the basilisk step out from behind the thick vegetation, spin about, and then plop down, lying on its belly on the stones of the courtyard.

Moving very, very slowly, Alex drew back around the archway, pulling her with him away from the covered courtyard, the tower, and the basilisk. Some moments passed before she realized she was holding her breath. She started breathing normally again.

"Let's keep looking for stairs down," he whispered. "If McKnight is in that tower, we'll never get past the basilisk."

"I can try to cast another invisibility shield."

He shook his head. "We don't know how well it smells or hears or any other senses it may have. If we don't find McKnight in time, we'll let the assault team take it on."

She sighed and followed him as he led her on. They had been incredibly lucky so far, but how long could they push their luck? Then, just when she thought she was going to start screaming, they came to yet another intersection. This time, when they peered around it, they saw a curved archway with stone steps leading down. Was Alex's dungeon that way?

Two of the four-armed guards stood on either side of the archway. Each held a massive two-handed sword, the curved and barbed blades resting against their shoulders. There was no way they could slip past them.

"What now?" she whispered. "The shield?"

Alex looked at his watch and shook his head. "We're out of time." Holding his M4 under his arm, he reached within a pocket of his load-bearing vest, removed something, and held it up for her to see: a grenade!

Oh, shit. She turned away and covered her ears.

* * *

Maelhrandia stalked through the corridors of her keep. Four of her best boggart guardsmen accompanied her. She probably didn't need them, but she didn't like to take chances, not when her own life was at risk. This assassin was here to kill her. Boggarts weren't clever, but they were capable fighters—and hers would die for her. Unfortunately, thus far, the assassin had eluded her. Whoever it was, she or he had stopped using magic, forcing Maelhrandia to search throughout her keep. And that was taking time. She didn't want to sound an alarm and risk alerting the assassin.

She needed a confession, needed to know who was trying to kill her. She was certain the trail would lead back to the Royal Family. Perhaps even to her darling sister Horlastia.

Need drove her on, gave purpose to her stride. She rounded a corner, her guards on her heels. Ahead, two of her boggart guards stood watch on the stairs leading to the dungeon. Her prisoner was down there, awaiting transportation to her mother.

Stopping in midstep, she stared at the two boggart guards. Something felt... wrong. Without knowing why, she stepped back around the corner. Cold fingers of fear brushed her spine—intuition. She hadn't survived this long without trusting her instincts. Yes. Something was very wrong here.

"Go," she whispered to her boggarts.

They slipped past her, wordlessly approaching the stairs and the other guards, who turned, clearly puzzled by their sudden presence. At that moment, something metal clinked as it bounced along the stone floor, skidding to a stop near the cloven hooves of her guards. They stood in place, staring at it. One of them actually bent over to pick it up. Not one of them bothered to look in the direction it had come from, where Maelhrandia saw a furtive movement of someone darting back around the wall.

"No!" she screamed, but it was too late.

A thunderclap rocked the closed confines of the corridor, knocking her down with the force of its concussion. She lay on the stones, her ears ringing, spots of light dancing before her eyes.

What was that—Drake's-Gift? But it was so loud—impossibly loud.

She gritted her teeth and shook her head. If she didn't move now—right now—she'd die here on the floor of her own keep. She forced herself up; on hands and knees, she peered around the corner again. Impossibly, all six of her boggart guards were down. Some lay unmoving, dead, while others—much like her—tried to get up but failed.

If I had been any closer...

Then, she heard the muffled but clearly recognizable sound of one of the manlings' fire-weapons. She saw bursts of flame lighting up the darkened corridor as a manling warrior, face covered by a bug mask, calmly approached her boggarts, his weapon against his shoulder. Unable to stand and fight, her elite boggart guards died where they were, slaughtered by that damned manling as if they were nothing more than Coldari gutter rats.

No! The shame was overwhelming. *This will not stand. Not in my own keep!*

She would cast Drake's-Gift and burn him for this unprovoked attack. But then she felt someone drawing in magic. One of the manling mages was with him, she realized. Then she saw the mage coming up behind the warrior, and even though this manling was also masked, she knew it was that damned golden-haired mage who had caused her so much grief. The mage, too, held a fire-weapon.

Does she have the talisman?

Self-preservation stayed Maelhrandia's attack. She scrambled back, out of sight—desperately praying to the Spider Mother that they hadn't seen her. Climbing to her feet, she stumbled away then began running as she considered her next move. She needed to sound the alarm. She needed more warriors. She needed to—

Thunder rocked her keep, sending her reeling for the second time that day. She smashed her nose into a stone wall, sending blood dripping into her mouth. All around her, dust and dirt fell from above.

What is happening? This isn't an assassination; it's an attack!

Chapter 54

Elizabeth lay on her belly at the edge of the woods with the rest of the assault team, watching the fort across the river, waiting to move. Not far away, Clyde slept beneath bushes, hidden. Elizabeth prayed he would be safe. The Lord only knew the noble animal had earned his rest. But now, it was time for her to do her part.

Clara, right beside her, looked at her watch. "Get ready."

Elizabeth held her breath. Then the tunnel entrance to the fortress exploded, sending a shock wave reverberating all the way across the river. Black smoke poured out, obscuring the gate. Despite knowing it was coming, Elizabeth had still flinched. She couldn't help herself; it was so loud, so violent. As the smoke cleared, she saw the devastation. Both of the heavy wooden doors had been destroyed, turned into so much kindling. Black smoke continued to pour from the tunnel entrance. The guards were down. Cries of horror rose from the diminutive redheaded creatures who had been working on the dock. They broke and ran, clearly terrified.

"Let's move," Clara yelled as she rose to her feet and ran for the bridge, not looking to see if anyone followed.

They did. The remaining members of Task Force Devil were

charging after Clara. Elizabeth, not wanting to get left behind, rose and joined them, her heart going wild.

Nine soldiers. Not much of an army, but it was all they had. God willing, it would be enough—it had to be.

Running in body armor was hard, like running in water, but she had it easy compared to the others, who also carried weapons and ammunition. She was still the last one across the bridge. Ahead of her, Clara and the others fanned out, firing their rifles—the silencers now removed—at the bodies of the guards lying on the ground, making sure they were all dead.

Vaguely, she wondered why she wasn't shocked or outraged. *Because,* she realized, *this is what battle looks like.*

As she ran, she tugged on the end of the Brace, pulling it back up her forearm. Howls of rage echoed from inside the smoking tunnel. A moment later, at least a score of the four-armed beast guards poured out, great swords and axes held high. The one leading the charge, a huge brute, charged straight at Clara, a spear in its grip. Elizabeth swerved to a stop, her mouth open to call out a warning.

She needn't have bothered. Clara dropped to one knee and opened fire on the creature at point-blank range. The automatic fire—so loud, so heart stopping—shredded its chest and sent it falling backward to the ground in a macabre dance. Elizabeth stared openmouthed.

The rest of the soldiers opened fire in a cacophony of gunshots, a symphony of death. The smell of gunfire mingled with the smoke from the explosion and the stench of blood. Empty brass casings flew through the morning air. The attacking guards came to a sudden, shattering halt as they ran into a wall of gunfire.

Then another of the giant troll creatures—this one wearing plate armor over its bloated body—rushed through the ranks of the stunned and dying guards. Easily eight feet tall and weighing hundreds of pounds, it was larger than a Kodiak bear and carried a giant two-handed ax with a gleaming head at least a foot wide. Someone shot it, but the bullets ricocheted off the armor without even slowing it. Frozen in terror, Elizabeth watched as the creature brought its ax down on one of the soldiers, Connor, smashing him into the ground, almost cleaving him in two. The troll raised its bloody ax into the air and roared in victory, exposing huge, tusklike fangs. A missile sped past it, hitting the side of the fort behind it and sending shrapnel winging through the air.

Elizabeth stepped forward, raised the Brace, and channeled a bolt of lightning into the troll, momentarily blinding herself. When her vision came back, she saw the troll, now lying on its back against the stone wall of the fort, about twenty feet from where it had been standing, its body smoking, the armor melted into the gaping cavity where its barrel-shaped chest had been. This time, killing had been easier.

The soldiers moved past her, firing single shots to kill the wounded.

"Jesus Christ, Elizabeth," said Clara, rushing back to her.

Elizabeth's body trembled, and she was nearly breathless, but not with horror, not with revulsion—with excitement. *Thou shalt not kill; thou shalt not kill.* She stepped past Clara, ignoring her, coming closer to the dead troll.

"No time for that shit now, soldier." Clara grabbed Elizabeth and dragged her over to the entrance to the fort where the remaining six soldiers were bunching up—*stacking*, they called it—preparing to go inside.

Clara shoved Elizabeth against the wall behind the soldiers. The ones closest to the tunnel opening tossed grenades inside then ducked back. Elizabeth turned away, covering her ears, but the explosions that followed were far less intense than the main charge had been, sounding more like gunfire. The stacked soldiers rushed into the tunnel, carbines firing.

Elizabeth moved to follow, but Clara held her back. "Wait." She lowered Elizabeth's GPNVGs over her face, switching them on. Elizabeth saw that Clara had already lowered her own optics. Clara gripped the sides of Elizabeth's helmet in both hands and made sure Elizabeth was looking directly at her. "Before you go all Gandalf on us again, you sound off first. Okay?"

Elizabeth nodded—terrified, breathless, and exhilarated.

What's wrong with me? Am I really excited by this... this obscenity?

"Good girl." Clara dragged Elizabeth inside the tunnel. "And thanks for saving our lives."

Inside, the smoke and stench almost made her gag. A long corridor with smooth black walls lay ahead of her. Ahead, gunfire flashed, hurting her ears. The soldiers were engaging more enemies. She couldn't see them, but she could hear their bestial screams as they died.

So much death.

"Move! Move! Move!" Clara screamed as she fired a burst from her weapon down the long corridor.

* * *

Maelhrandia ran through the corridors of her keep and out into the covered inner garden. Her tower stood in the center of the garden, surrounded by the massive vine-laden Vextoral trees and the giant luminescent Shae mushrooms that provided more than enough ambient light for the fae seelie and her boggarts to see. More than two hundred paces wide, it provided living space for Gazekiller to roam freely.

The basilisk would save her. Nothing could stand against him, not even an Ancient One. What chance would manlings have?

They were inside her keep, fighting her boggart guards—and, based on the growing intensity of the noise from their fire-weapons, winning. How had this happened? Hadn't she and Gazekiller reaped enough ruin on them, destroying their camp, stealing their warlord? How dare they attack her? It amazed her that they would even attempt such a thing. Unless... unless she had been betrayed. Perhaps by one of those foul Redcap gnomes. Always fawning on her, always pretending obedience. She wouldn't put it past them.

The sounds of combat were so much closer now. They were coming so fast. Her boggart guardsmen were no match for the manlings' weapons; she knew that now. They'd be coming for her next.

Then she remembered her guest, her dear sister, the mage-warden—the warrior. Hope flared within Maelhrandia. Together, they'd crush these manlings. And Gazekiller would help. He'd feast on them, sucking the juicy bits out of their shells, discarding their petrified skins. Even now, the basilisk appeared through the trees of her garden. Rising up on his hind legs, he sniffed the air, anxious for blood. Panting, she ran to his side and leaned against his scaly flank, catching her breath. Everything would be fine now.

She sent a mind message to her sister: *Horlastia, come. Fight with me. I need your aid.*

There was no answer.

Sister. Where are you? We are under attack, but it is only manlings.

And then she heard the cry of the wyvern from high above, where her tower pierced the roof of the garden.

Another time, dear sister, Horlastia answered. *If you're still alive.*

Maelhrandia heard the beating of the wyvern's wings as it took flight. Even if she couldn't see it, she knew it was flying away with her sister on its back.

Her sister had abandoned her. She exhaled, glaring at the entrance to her garden. The sounds of combat were growing in intensity.

I'm alone.

Gazekiller howled his stuttering challenge.

No, not alone.

She'd deal with these manlings herself as she had before. Later, her sister would pay for her cowardice. Maelhrandia cast Shadow-Soul, turning invisible once more. She'd do what she always did: use Gazekiller to distract while she struck from hiding. It had worked every single time before, and it would work again.

The manlings would die for attacking her.

Chapter 55

Cassie gingerly stepped past the creatures Alex had killed. Somehow, four more had blundered upon the first two just as Alex was throwing his grenade. It made no difference; Alex had killed them easily. She had followed him out into the corridor, thinking she would help and even preparing to channel mana, but then she hadn't—she'd been too stunned. Alex had killed them all quickly, with frightening efficiency, firing burst after burst of well-aimed auto-fire. Not even the wall-shaking detonation of the C4 charge had given him pause. After they were all down, he had calmly walked among the wounded, finishing them off with single shots.

She'd had no idea he could be that cold-blooded. The violence was shocking.

The stairs leading down were unguarded now, but dark. Without the GPNVGs, they'd be blind. He went first, and Cassie followed. Almost immediately, the temperature dropped, and the air stank of rot, damp earth, worms. She almost jumped when vines, hanging from the ceiling, brushed the top of her helmet. At the bottom of the stairs, a long corridor extended. Unlike the upper level of the fort, which had been built from black stones, the underground was simply hacked out of the earth, supported by wooden beams. Small chambers, each only large enough to hold a prisoner and blocked by iron bars, were interspersed evenly on both sides of the corridor. Alex had been right: this was a dungeon. It practically vibrated with misery, depression, and hopelessness. She shivered.

Alex had been about to walk down the corridor when Cassie saw something odd among the vines hanging out of the earth above their heads. She grabbed at his shoulder. "Wait."

He paused and turned his head slightly. "What?"

She pointed up at the ceiling. There, crawling among the vines, were scores of spiders. The fat, bloated bodies of some were as large as her thumb.

"Jesus!" Alex stepped back, almost knocking her down.

"Hang on," she said, channeling fire.

She threw what was by far the largest fireball she had ever created, only slightly smaller than a basketball. It hit the vines and exploded, igniting them in a flash. In moments, the flames spread across the ceiling like a wave, burning everything before them. Blackened husks of spiders fell upon the earthen floor like rain.

Turning, she grinned at Alex. *Even Elizabeth would have been impressed by that.* There was so much more mana here on Rubicon. Everything was so much easier. "All right, then. Let's go."

Alex pointed the way with his barrel. "Ladies first."

"Funny." She shoved him ahead of her.

He sighed and shook his head. "Don't even know why I'm here."

The stench of burnt spiders was nauseating but far preferable to the risk of them falling down the back of her collar. She shuddered.

The cells were empty although some held the remains of bones. Unlike the corridors, the cells had been lined with stone, probably to stop the prisoners from digging their way out through the soft earth. *So why not line the whole tunnel with stone? Why just the cells?*

The answer came to her in a flash of insight. *Because spiders prefer soft earth.*

The dark elves wanted the spiders down here... with their prisoners.

Again, she shivered. *We need to find McKnight and get the hell out of here.*

At the end of the corridor, another set of stairs led farther down. Alex took them slowly, this time watching the ceiling for more vines and spiders.

Below, the stairs opened into a large chamber filled with wooden tables and racks of metal tools—she didn't want to think about what kind of tools—and what looked like a forge. Alex cautiously moved out, his weapon at his shoulder, ready to fire. She followed him closely. Something seemed off. At first, she couldn't put her finger on it, and then she realized this chamber was a lighter shade of green. She flipped her GPNVGs back up on top of her helmet. Immediately, she noticed a candle burning on one of the wooden tables, lighting the room.

"Alex, there's a candle. Someone's—"

The rush of cloven hooves interrupted her. Figures, previously hidden behind the boxes and racks of equipment, rushed out at them, emitting eerie, and clearly nonhuman, shrieks. Cassie spun about. Alex's carbine sent out a long burst of automatic fire that was accompanied by screams of pain. Something smashed into Cassie, and she fell back, dropping her carbine and landing hard on her backside on the stairs. A figure, one of those four-armed creatures, loomed before her, shrieking. She froze, terrified, and in that moment, her attacker brought something down hard, smashing against her helmet, striking the GPNVGs. Her head snapped back as pain shot down her neck. The creature lifted its arms up again, and this time she saw the ax it held. She channeled air, sending the creature flying back hard enough to hit one of the tables and fall down.

She staggered to her feet. "Alex!" she screamed, looking about.

He was fighting hand to hand with another attacker. Two more lay on the stone floor. The creature she had hit with air was now back on its feet, rushing at her again with the ax, crowding her. She snatched at her pistol, yanking it free of her shoulder holster. When she moved, it was entirely by muscle memory. Stepping back a pace, she swung the pistol up and put two rounds into its chest, followed by another into its face. Just the way Alex had taught her.

The creature fell back with a thump. She stared at its body in stunned silence, vaguely thinking this had to be just a nightmare.

But it was real. She had just taken another life. Revulsion gripped her, threatening to bring her to her knees.

A moment later, Alex was beside her, pushing the pistol barrel down. She didn't resist.

"You okay?" he asked, panting heavily. Blood dripped from his chin. His GPNVGs were also gone.

"I... I thought... I... I didn't mean..."

He grabbed the sides of her cheeks and turned her to face him. "Cassie. Listen to me. You haven't done anything wrong."

"Oh, God," she said, feeling as though her world was falling apart. "I... I can't do this. This... killing, this slaughter. I feel so... so filthy. This is so wrong." She stared at the smoking pistol in her hands, wanting nothing more than to throw it from her. "How do I—"

From the rear of the chamber, someone cried out for help—in English.

McKnight!

She breathed deeply as Alex turned and ran to the back of the chamber, where a single cell awaited. *Later. I'll deal with this later, once we're safe. I need to cope... but it's so hard.*

"Please. Help me," a weak voice called out again.

It was McKnight. She recognized his voice. She holstered the pistol, picked up her M4, and followed Alex. Someone needed help—she could do that.

Within the cell, McKnight lay curled up in a fetal position, his eyes pleading. The cell had been left open; it must have been guarded by those creatures. McKnight was unbound and simply lying on the floor. It was strange to see such a powerful man helpless.

And what the hell is on the back of his neck?

Alex dropped to his knees beside him. "You all right, Colonel? Can you move?"

"Alex, wait," Cassie said, fear gripping her. She dropped down beside him and grabbed his hand before he could touch the colonel. "Look at his back, on his neck." She pointed at the monstrosity: an insect the length of her hand—an obscene hybrid centipede-spider *thing*—that had burrowed its head into McKnight's neck. Its many legs were also buried into McKnight's back, puncturing the skin down his spine. His back was covered in dried blood.

"What the fuck is that?" Alex almost fell back, panic in his voice.

Cassie shook her head. "Whatever it is, it's using mana."

"Please... help," McKnight whispered through clenched teeth.

"Can you... can you get it off?" Alex asked.

"Me? How?"

"Please... please," McKnight begged.

She stared in horror at the insect. Its multiple legs tightened where they punctured McKnight's skin, sending fresh blood running down his spine. *Does it somehow understand that we want to remove it? What can I do? Fire? Air? What if I just make it angry and make things worse?* They heard gunfire in the fortress above, followed by the explosions of hand grenades. The assault team was inside.

"Cassie, if you're going to do something, you'd better do it quickly."

"Shit!" She thrust her hands forward and grabbed the furry, disgusting sides of the giant centipede thing with both hands. Immediately, it wriggled violently. McKnight screamed in agony, his back arching as if it were going to snap in two. Cassie channeled electricity, something she had never done before without the Brace. She generated just a fraction—hardly any lightning—but sent it right into the insect, cooking the thing's internal organs in an instant. She yanked, grateful when its disgusting bloody head came free. She had been half-afraid she'd tear its head off inside the man, like a tick. Revulsion gripping her, she threw it as far away from her as she could.

McKnight was still screaming, still thrashing. Alex leaned on top of him, holding him down. Cassie channeled again, this time healing him, trying to repair the damage. Mercifully, McKnight's screams petered out, and he began panting heavily instead.

Alex sat back, letting go of the older man. "You all right, soldier?"

McKnight gasped but nodded. "Thank... thank you."

Alex helped him to a seated position, and McKnight looked at Cassie. "Who?" He stared at her, obviously not recognizing her in camouflage paint and body armor. "Cassie?"

"We'll explain later." Alex helped McKnight up. "Can you walk?"

"I'll damn well walk out of here."

With Alex supporting McKnight, they retraced their steps out of the dungeon and up into the fort. This time, Cassie led the way. She still held her M4, but she wasn't sure she could use it, not anymore. She did, however, turn on its powerful flashlight, using it to light their way. They had to get to the others and get the hell out of here, back to the LZ, and activate the keying device.

Chapter 56

Elizabeth followed Clara and the assault force past what looked like a barracks, now destroyed and smoking. Beds and tables lay haphazardly strewn about, disheveled by the force of numerous hand grenades. Several bodies of alien guards lay in pools of blood. She ignored the horror, focusing on staying behind Clara. Later, once it was safe, she'd pray for what she had seen, what she had done.

The soldiers paused. Over their shoulders, she saw what she thought was an intersection.

Clara reached back and held her hand out against Elizabeth's chest. "Wait," she said curtly, staring ahead of her. "Gus," Clara called loudly to the soldiers who were bunching ahead of her, preparing to rush the intersection. "Use the flashbangs before you—"

Figures darted out from where they had been hiding around the corners of the intersection, with crossbows in their hands. Elizabeth heard something whiz past her head and felt the air of its passage. Two of the soldiers who had been preparing to rush forward fell down. Someone opened fire, lighting the tunnel up with gunfire. More of the four-armed defenders rushed around the corner from only feet away, screaming and swinging axes and swords.

Somehow, one of the creatures had gotten past the others and was rushing right at Elizabeth. Only paces away, its face was a bestial mask of rage and hate. It raised a massive two-handed sword above its head, clearly intent on cutting her down. Elizabeth lifted her brace-enclosed hand but then froze.

In the enclosed space, the lightning bolt might hurt the others.

Clara, kneeling just to her side, fired a short burst into the attacking creature from point-blank range, spinning it about and putting it down. Then, without pausing, she rushed forward down the corridor, where the soldiers were now fighting hand to hand with the attackers. Clara moved among them, like the angel of death, calmly shooting several in the face from only inches away. The last one went down, and the tunnel was silent again except for the moans of the wounded.

Elizabeth stared about herself, wide-eyed, her heart hammering against her ribcage, unable to catch her breath. At least a half dozen of the four-armed defenders were down—and so were some of the task-force members. Elizabeth reached for her first-aid kit in her load-bearing vest, but Clara came back and gripped her arm. Shaking her head, she pulled Elizabeth along with her down the corridor.

"Keep going. Move, move, move," Clara yelled to the other soldiers. "Win the firefight!"

The wounded, Elizabeth noted sadly, were going to have to fend for themselves.

Forcing herself to breathe, she concentrated on keeping up. Now, the assault force began to pick up speed. Every room and every corridor they came to, they led the way with grenades and gunfire. The smell of blood and cordite was soon overpowering.

Twice more, they fought their way past defenders, carving them up with grenades before moving forward.

They moved out of the narrow, confining tunnels, through an archway, and out into a massive covered courtyard, which could only be the heart of the fort. Giant alien trees grew wild, and huge mushrooms glowed with brilliant incandescence under the optics of the GPNVG. Had the jungle somehow burst through the walls of the fortress?

But when Elizabeth looked closer, she saw that there was order to the vegetation. Each plant and tree must have been individually groomed and cared for. It was a garden, a covered garden. And in the very center of the garden stood a dark stone tower. Standing at least twenty feet high, it reached all the way to the covered roof and then passed right through it.

Is that where the flying beast landed, up there?

Now, only five soldiers remained, including Clara. Baby-faced Gus and three others had gone down in the ambush at the intersection.

Cassie can probably heal them. If we can find her.

She stepped over the bodies of guards killed at the stone archway to the garden where they had tried to hold back the assault force. The five remaining soldiers spread out in front of Elizabeth, seeking new targets, new threats.

"Enemy front, enemy front!" Clara yelled.

At the base of the tower, at least a score of defenders had formed ranks, perhaps intending to make a last stand. All they accomplished was to present a massed target for the soldiers, who opened up on them. There was a whooshing sound, and a fiery comet flew through the air as one of the soldiers fired a missile. A moment later, the missile detonated in a brilliant fireball, scattering the defenders. The flare of the explosion washed out her GPNVGs, so she flipped them up, relieved to see that there was more than enough light from the glowing mushrooms. Those guards not killed outright by the explosion were cut down by the advancing soldiers, most at nearly point-blank range. Their four-armed bodies flew back under the impact of 5.56mm rounds.

And through it all, Clara kept giving orders, calling targets, and keeping the assault moving.

She keeps winning the firefight.

"Push through, push through," Clara yelled as she changed magazines, letting the empty one clatter to the ground.

This is going to work, Elizabeth realized. *We're unstoppable. We can—*

The basilisk burst out of the trees on their left, charging right at them from only paces away.

It waited till we were distracted by the guards. Clever.

Several of the soldiers tried to turn and fire, but it was right on them, and their fire was erratic. The basilisk smashed through them, crushing some. In horror, Elizabeth watched its tail sweep right past her face, whistling through the air as it hit two soldiers, sending them flying like bowling pins. The basilisk stood between Elizabeth and the others. She saw a brief glimpse of Clara, on the other side of the monster, standing her ground with the two remaining soldiers, firing up at the basilisk. It reared up, and even from behind, Elizabeth saw the blue flash of its glowing eyes and felt it using its petrification gaze.

She needed to act now! Raising the Brace, she drew in mana. She'd hit with the biggest lightning bolt she had ever cast. Mana rushed through her central nervous system, supercharging her senses. But before she could release the bolt, something struck her—literally picking her up and throwing her back through the air. She smashed hard against something—a tree—and collapsed.

As intense pain flared through her back, she knew she had broken something. But even through her pain, she realized that someone else had just channeled mana.

The dark-elf woman!

She shook her head, trying to focus. She had to act, had to move. To lie still was to die. As her vision cleared, she saw one of the soldiers, Clara, judging by her diminutive size, throw herself out of the basilisk's path as it charged into the remaining soldiers, smashing their petrified bodies into bloody shards. Scrambling back on hands and knees, Clara pulled a pistol from her shoulder holster and started firing point-blank at the basilisk.

Why wasn't Clara turned to stone?

And then Elizabeth understood: Clara had been the only one still wearing her GPNVGs. The other two soldiers—just like Elizabeth—had flipped them up to see better after the missile exploded.

Somehow, the optics of the GPNVGs negate the basilisk's gaze.

Elizabeth staggered to her feet, her back a torrent of agony, and lowered her GPNVGs back over her face. The basilisk was about to leap upon Clara and crush her, but Elizabeth let loose with a bolt of lightning—a tad wildly perhaps, but she still hit its rear legs. The monster roared in pain, jumping into the air, and spun about, enraged.

What if I'm wrong about the GPNVGs?

The basilisk's eyes pulsed with blue light, washing out her optics

Chapter 57

Still hidden within Shadow-Soul, Maelhrandia's fear was replaced by excitement as the battle turned in her favor. There were only two manlings left on their feet. But what truly excited her was that the dark-haired manling mage had brought the Ancient One's talisman, was even now wearing it as she battled Gazekiller. Its power would do the fool no good, however; this battle was almost over.

The manlings' attack had failed. Maelhrandia had survived. She hadn't even been engaged. When she had first seen the dark-haired mage amongst the attacking manling warriors, she had been about to burn her with Drake's-Gift, but she had stopped herself—just in time recognizing the talisman. Instead, she had cast air at her, knocking her back. A talisman as powerful as the Ancient One's weapon would probably have been impervious to fire, but she couldn't take that chance. It was far too valuable.

Besides, victory was almost hers. That victory had come at a cost, though. Incredibly, her boggart guardsmen were all dead, and Gazekiller was badly injured and in need of healing once again.

Those damned fire-weapons! They were far more powerful than Maelhrandia had realized. When the Old World belonged to the fae seelie once more, Maelhrandia would acquire some of their weapons and arm her guards with them. Warfare, it seemed, was changing, even here.

Gazekiller reared up before the dark-haired mage; his eyes glowed with an occult fire as he prepared to use his death gaze once more and finish that sad creature. Maelhrandia would take the talisman from her petrified flesh—breaking the arm off at the elbow if she had to, but it would be hers. After that, she'd deal with her traitorous sister.

But then the impossible happened: the manling mage didn't turn to stone. Instead, from only paces away, she raised the talisman and cast a massive bolt of lightning, striking Gazekiller between his glowing blue eyes.

"No!" Maelhrandia screamed, shielding her eyes from the intensity of the attack and rushing forward.

But it was too late. Gazekiller fell back, his head a bloody, smoking ruin. The ground shook under the impact as the basilisk's carcass landed.

Despair flashed through Maelhrandia. *This isn't possible!* Gazekiller lay upon his back, dead.

* * *

Cassie stumbled along with Alex and McKnight toward the sounds of battle, out into the bizarre courtyard. The corpses of the four-armed guards lay strewn about, and the air stank of gun smoke. Near the tower, two soldiers remained fighting, one on his knees, another standing, confronting the basilisk.

It was Elizabeth. Lightning flared from the Brace on her arm, chasing away the darkness. The basilisk, struck in the head from only paces away, fell back and smashed into the ground, its head a charred ruin. The monster that had killed Alice was dead.

* * *

Cold rage swept through Maelhrandia. Gazekiller, her only true friend, was dead—slaughtered by that foul manling monster. Hate twisted her features, and she stepped forward, still concealed by Shadow-Soul. This time, she'd burn her—even if the spell did destroy the talisman. She filled herself with magical energy.

* * *

Cassie staggered to a stop as Alex and McKnight rushed to help Elizabeth. Even from a distance, Cassie could see she was staggering and holding her back, clearly hurt.

The basilisk was dead, but someone was still channeling.

Someone is about to cast magic. Once again, she felt that strange sense of emptiness, that feeling that she now recognized had to be the dark-elf mage, cloaked in an invisibility shield.

But where? There! Near the dark tower at the center of the garden, something felt... off.

Trusting her feelings, she raised her M4 and emptied it in one long, wild burst that lit up the garden. Spent casings flew everywhere, and Cassie heard bullets ricocheting off the stones of the tower wall, vaguely aware that she might accidentally hit herself or one of her companions with her erratic fire. Then the dark-elf woman appeared suddenly, out of nothing, clutching her side and glaring in fear. Cassie dropped her sight onto the woman and pulled the trigger.

Nothing. Canting the weapon, she saw the bolt was only partially forward, an empty brass casing stuck half-out between the moving parts. As she cocked the weapon to clear the obstruction, the dark elf turned and released her spell at Elizabeth: a huge fireball that grew in size and intensity as it rushed forward. Cassie threw the M4 down and desperately channeled air, trying to knock the fireball aside.

The fireball erupted, sending heat and flames cascading over Elizabeth.

The dark elf turned and bolted for the entrance to the tower. Cassie pulled her pistol from her shoulder holster. But the dark elf disappeared through her tower doorway. Cassie, her heart sinking, turned away.

Elizabeth was screaming.

Chapter 58

Maelhrandia ran up the curving stairs of her tower. She was hurt, bleeding. Pain throbbed in her side where she had been struck by the fire-weapon. They were going to come for her, she knew, and hunt her down like a wounded Meredaal. The humiliation was enough to make her scream.

A princess of the fae seelie has just run from manlings!

She dashed into the chamber at the top of the circling stairwell, her private sanctum—the chamber that held the Seeing Stone. Trembling before the stone, her skin drenched in sweat, she fell to her knees before it, reaching out to place a bloody hand against its cold surface, activating its magic. "Mother, save me."

A moment later, she found herself before the Bane Throne, her mother seated on it, watching her with unbridled contempt. *What is this, daughter? Why do you disturb me?*

"They come for me, Mother. They come to kill me. Please help."

Her mother's cruel eyes narrowed in suspicion, and she leaned forward, her crown gleaming in the glow around her. Behind the Bane Throne, Maelhrandia saw something large, cloaked in darkness. She couldn't make it out but saw one of its massive pincerlike legs, small hairs bristling on it. *Rizleoghin*, her mother's infamous pet.

Maelhrandia shivered.

What have you done, daughter?

"The manlings have attacked me."

Her mother's head rose, her face now unreadable. She then tilted her head to the side, considering Maelhrandia as if she were some sort of interesting... thing, and not her own child. *And your sister Horlastia? Does she bring me the manling warlord?*

"No. She failed you, Mother. She ran away."

Her mother looked away, shaking her head. *How could such as you come from my womb? The Spider Mother must laugh at my suffering, my shame. Now, we'll have to find another prisoner. And after all that effort. How tiresome.*

"Mother, please!"

Sighing, her mother raised her hand, and the throne room went dark. Maelhrandia found herself back in her tower, the Seeing Stone now cold to her touch. She was abandoned. The humiliation was almost worse than her fear.

There was no escape. Maelhrandia kept no wyverns herself. Gazekiller had hated them too much to tolerate them. Soon, the manlings would come for her. Almost certainly, they'd be led by that foul golden-haired manling mage—armed with the talisman.

What could Maelhrandia do? *Hide. Use my strength. I am the knife in the shadows.*

* * *

Cassie rushed to help Elizabeth, as did Alex. The other woman spun about on fire, flames trailing. Alex tackled her, knocking her down and beating at the flames with his bare hands. Elizabeth kept screaming, loud inhuman cries that tore at Cassie's soul. Cassie couldn't think, couldn't concentrate. Everything was happening so fast. She dropped to her knees beside Alex, who had managed to put out the flames. Elizabeth struggled, senseless, mad with pain.

How is she even still alive? Her air spell must have moved the fireball just enough. Cassie tried to examine Elizabeth, but she was thrashing about too much. "Hold her still," she pleaded.

Alex leaned into the other woman, pushing her down, holding her in place. But when Cassie saw the extent of Elizabeth's injuries, a wave of sickness swept through her: Elizabeth's face was charred black and raw. Her eyes had been melted and were now only wet holes. Her screams were wet with fluid. She thrashed about so hard even Alex could barely hold on to her.

So much pain. She's dying. Just like Duncan.

Cassie became aware someone else was kneeling across from her. She looked up and met McKnight's sorrowful eyes. He reached across Elizabeth and gripped Cassie's arm. "Cassie, I'm sorry. But—"

"No!" Cassie wrenched his hand away and channeled, sending every bit of mana she still could into the other woman. But, as with Marcus, the damage was just too extensive. It was like trying to sop up an amputated hand with a Band-Aid.

Elizabeth had finally stopped screaming. Cassie felt dizzy, and she sat back, lifting her eyes to the domed roof, moaning in abject misery. Then she felt Elizabeth's fingers grasp at her, desperate for a human touch before she died, someone to hold her hand at the end.

Cassie gripped her friend's hand—the hand wearing the Brace. Undamaged by the flames, even the silver chains were still cool to the touch. *Focus,* the Great Elder Brother had described it—not a weapon, *a focus.*

She yanked the Brace free of Elizabeth's hand, quickly pulling it over her own. As before, it fit perfectly.

Alex stared at her. "Cassie, what are you—"

"What I'm supposed to do?" She placed her Brace-enclosed palm over Elizabeth's chest. "Heal!"

She channeled, this time focusing on healing energy, not lightning. Elizabeth's body arched off the ground, throwing Alex away. Healing mana, magnified tenfold by the Brace, surged through Cassie into Elizabeth. Elizabeth gasped for air. Cassie redoubled her efforts, ramming even more mana into the other woman, weaving her burnt flesh whole again, willing it to regrow. *And it did!*

She couldn't tell how long it took, but when she finally sat back, withdrawing the Brace from Elizabeth's chest, Cassie was utterly exhausted, ready to fall over.

"Oh my God," Clara said from behind her, wonder in her voice.

"No kidding," said Alex.

Elizabeth watched Cassie with her own eyes, now completely regrown. Her skin was still black, but only with soot. Where before it had been charred and raw, now it was dirty but unblemished—mostly. There was still a discolored patch near her cheekbone, shining like plastic.

"What did you do?" Elizabeth whispered.

"Healed you, stupid. I don't have that many friends. You think I'm gonna let you go?"

Elizabeth tried to sit up, but failed. "Who... how?"

Cassie looked over her shoulder, glaring at the tower.

McKnight knelt beside her, now holding a carbine. Clara stood next to him, blood running down the side of her head, looking very unsteady. "Sir. We need to motor, now! It's going to take us some time to make our way back to the LZ with the wounded...

with the dead."

McKnight looked from Clara to Alex. "Call it, Captain."

Alex turned to face the tower. "We can't leave her behind us—she's too dangerous. But we also need to get everyone ready, to gather the wounded and prepare to move."

Cassie stood, gritting her teeth. She ran her fingers over the silver chains dangling from the Brace. "Let's finish this, then."

Alex turned to Clara. "Get who you can ready to move. If we're not back in five, get the hell out of here. Warn somebody. Warn everybody."

Alex and Cassie walked toward the tower.

Chapter 59

Cassie followed Alex as he climbed up the tower's steps, almost breathing down his neck. Her thoughts were a turmoil of emotions. The basilisk had killed Alice, but this dark-elf woman had been controlling it. *She* had murdered Alice, intending to kill Cassie but slaughtering her sister instead. A part of Cassie screamed for vengeance, but another part of her was still sickened by the blood she had already spilled, the lives she had already taken. The Brace throbbed with power, with potential. *To kill or to heal?*

They climbed the stairs as silently as they could, watching the shadows. The dark-elf woman was a master at hiding herself. She could be anywhere. But now, Cassie was becoming adept at sensing her invisible presence. At each level on the twisting stairs, Alex paused and glanced at Cassie. Each time, she shook her head and pointed up. She could feel her up there—and invisible once more.

At the very top, the last level before coming out on the roof of the tower, a closed black door awaited them. Alex moved to the side of the door, paused, then whispered, "Is she—"

"She's in there," Cassie whispered. "Invisible, but channeling, filled with mana. She'll attack the second we go through the door."

Alex bit his lip, his eyes narrowing.

"I'll go first," Cassie said. "I might be able to do something with the Brace."

She tensed, preparing to throw open the door and dash inside, but Alex stopped her, shaking his head. "She's invisible, right?"

Cassie nodded.

"But not invulnerable?"

Cassie's eyes narrowed. "No. I don't think so."

"Let's say hello first."

Alex pulled a flashbang from his webbing and held it up for her to see. "Little warning."

Cassie turned away, closing her eyes and covering her ears.

* * *

Beads of sweat rolled down Maelhrandia's face, stinging her eyes, but she didn't dare move to wipe them. She needed to be ready, needed to release her spell the moment the manlings entered. She would survive this attack—she would! Then, armed with the Ancient One's talisman, she'd take her revenge—against the other manlings, against her sister... against her cursed mother. Pain still throbbed in her side, and blood soaked the inside of her clothing. She could have tried to heal herself—even poor healing would be better than nothing—but there was no time, and she needed to conserve everything she had for one final fight.

Her eyes narrowed as she heard the sound of metal scraping metal.

They're here, just outside the door, here to kill me. Be brave. She tensed, readying to release her spell.

Just as the door began to open, a thought occurred to her: *I still have the Shatkur Orb.* Its transdimensional charge had been used when she came back from the Old World with her prisoner, but it could still create local Rift-Rings. She could have used it to escape, but in her excitement she had forgotten it, and now there was no time. Her eyes darted to the doorway, which had only opened a crack.

What are they—

An object the size of a rock fell into the room. It clattered onto the stone floor and rolled to a stop near her feet. Cylindrical, with open holes along its length, it hissed in warning.

A weapon!

She cast Egis's-Shield just as the device detonated, but the shield spell was designed to block fire and destruction spells, not sound and light, and she flew back, smashing her head against the wall, instantly dropping her spells. On all fours, she shook her head, trying to make sense of the chaos. A constant ringing throbbed in her ears. *Everything is wrong!* Despite how she moved, she only saw the same frozen scene: the partially open door, the manling weapon, the Seeing Stone.

Get up! Get up and fight, you fool!

Her body wouldn't react.

* * *

Alex had been ready to move first, but when the flashbang detonated, Cassie pushed past him through the doorway. "Cassie, no!" he yelled, grabbing at her but missing.

He charged after her, his fear spiking, but she had paused on the other side of the doorway, staring at a massive black stone in the center of the room—and the dark-elf woman on her knees just behind it, shaking her head back and forth, her long white hair hanging over her face.

Cassie stared at her, her mouth open, letting the arm wearing the Brace fall to the side of her leg. The dark-elf woman was defenseless and would remain that way for seconds yet.

It was a hard thing to do, Alex knew. *To take another's life. It changes you—and not in a good way. Cassie Rogan is a good person, a decent human being, not a cold-blooded killer. Not like me.*

Alex stepped in front of Cassie and opened fire from point-blank range. The woman's body was shredded by the withering burst of 5.56mm ammunition and fell against the stone wall. A black stone orb the size of his fist rolled away from her, stopping near his booted feet. He reached down and picked it up, shoving it into a pocket of his load-bearing vest. It had been important to the elf; maybe Helena Simmons would want to examine it.

Cassie turned and stared at Alex, her mouth open, horror in her eyes. He hated himself for the look she gave him, but he was what he was.

Grabbing her arm, he dragged her back out of the chamber, leaving their enemy's corpse behind. "Time to go home, Cassie."

"But…"

"We're Oscar Mike."

"What?"

"On the move, Cassie. We have to leave."

* * *

Hours later, back at the clearing, Cassie watched as the soldiers activated the keying device. Moments later, the Gateway Machine opened a portal once more, and a glowing circle of light appeared—behind which awaited the Jump Tube and home. Relief surged through Cassie. They had just made it in time.

She had used the Brace to heal the wounded—at least, as well as she could in her exhausted state. Three of the soldiers had died assaulting the fort, but she had somehow managed to find the strength to heal five others, almost certainly saving their lives. Several had remained badly injured, despite Cassie's best efforts, and had to be carried back through the jungle in makeshift stretchers—a monumental undertaking and one that had slowed them down so much that she had been afraid they'd miss their window for opening the Gateway. But this time, Alex insisted, no one was staying behind.

Alex bent over and, with a grunt, picked up the sleeping Clyde. Cradling the dog in his arms, he stepped forward and led the survivors through the Gateway. Looking over her shoulder one last time at the jungle, Cassie said farewell to Rubicon before following Alex. In a vertigo-inducing moment, she was back on Earth within the Jump Tube. The air smelled different—sharp and bitter.

At the foot of the metal stairs, a medical team met them. Dr. Simmons waved wildly, ecstatic to see them—until she saw the extent of their injuries and their dead. Elizabeth, whose burns had been the most severe—despite Cassie's healing—was placed on a gurney and wheeled away, her fingers reaching out for Cassie's.

Cassie stood at the base of the stairs, watching the others, feeling separate from them somehow. The basilisk was dead, as was the dark-elf woman who had been controlling it, and they had rescued the colonel. But now, Cassie felt… empty. She lifted her hand and stared at the Brace. It felt so natural, like a second skin. Its silver chains glittered. She traced her fingers over the soft material.

What now? What do I do now?

A medic screamed for plasma. One of the soldiers she had only been able to partially heal was getting worse. Other medics rushed to help. Alex came up behind her and placed a hand on her shoulder. "Are you all right?"

"Are you?"

"What do you mean?" he asked her.

"What are they going to do to you now? About Buck?"

He opened his mouth, sighed, then shook his head. "I guess we'll find out."

The wounded soldier thrashed, moaning in agony. Cassie was so tired, so utterly exhausted. She wanted to help but just couldn't. Instead, she leaned back against Alex, putting the back of her head on his shoulder. He wrapped his arms around her waist, holding her up. "This is just the beginning, isn't it?" she said so softly she might have been only talking to herself.

"I think so. I think maybe the worst is yet to come. But it's over for you. You did your part—more than your part."

"Did I?" Her gaze locked onto the medics and the wounded soldier.

"Yes, you did. You were amazing, Cassie Rogan. I'm so proud of you."

She stepped away from him, moving to help the wounded soldier. "Call me Starlight."

END OF BOOK ONE OF THE DARK ELF WAR.

Acknowledgment

I'd like to thank my friend and teacher, Kyoshi Maqtewe'k Matto'law Collins of Canada Shindao Goju Karate for his invaluable assistance with a pivotal fight-scene in this novel. He is not only one of the most skilled, knowledgeable, and dangerous men in Canada, but also one of the noblest. Thank you for your help, your training, and most importantly, your patience.

My friend, there is no one else I'd rather swap army stories with.

Previous Works

Novels

Black Monastery

An outlaw Viking. A suspected witch. A demon that wears the skins of its victims.

Asgrim has one chance for redemption, but his quest for a princely blood debt will put him face-to-face with an unearthly evil. He'll team with a suspected Frankish witch to stop a demonic force before it's unleashed upon the world.

Amazon voted *Black Monastery* a 2014 Breakout Novel Award Quarter-Finalist. If you like explosive action that mixes the paranormal and historical, then you'll love this dark fantasy horror novel!

Short Fiction

Earning Valhalla

Sergeant "Wolf" Ostlund is a member of an elite 23rd century commando unit. He is one half of a futuristic fire team, piloting a lethal armored battle walker: a Titan. But Wolf is also spear-marked, a follower of the ancient Nordic gods, a futuristic Viking. All his life, Wolf has sought to win a place in Valhalla amongst Odin's fallen warriors. Now, when Wolf and his shield brother Khan are sent on a suicide mission against an intractable alien foe, he's going to get the chance to prove himself. Wolf will face death and the afterlife. But eternity comes at a price.

Fairy Tale

On her seventh birthday, Cassie finds a wounded fairy in her backyard. The brave little girl intends to help the magical creature no matter the cost. Finn, one of the forest people, is being hunted by the Changeling, a monstrous beast that will stop at nothing to consume her. Together, Cassie and Finn will journey into the forest at night seeking the safety of Finn's people. But the Changeling is still out there, and it doesn't care who it has to kill to get at the fairy. In nature, anything can be hunted.

A Promise of Fire

Following the betrayal and murder of his beloved lord, lowly court jester Humphrey seeks bloody vengeance. And Humphrey might just get it, because he alone now knows of the existence of the secret prisoner deep beneath the castle. But bargains can be perilous.

About the Author

William Stacey is a former Canadian army intelligence officer who served his country for more than thirty years with operational tours in Bosnia and Afghanistan. He is a husband, father, and avid reader, with a love for the macabre. Black Monastery, an Amazon 2014 Breakthrough Novel Award Quarter-Finalist, is his first novel.

For those who want their dark fantasy laced with heroic adventure.

Visit him at **http://williamstaceyauthor.com**

Worlds of Dark Adventure

Printed in Great Britain
by Amazon